NEVER SURRENDER

Book One: The Empire's Corps
Book Two: No Worse Enemy
Book Three: When The Bough Breaks
Book Four: Semper Fi
Book Five: The Outcast
Book Six: To The Shores
Book Seven: Reality Check
Book Eight: Retreat Hell
Book Nine: The Thin Blue Line
Book Ten: Never Surrender
Book Eleven: First To Fight
Book Twelve: They Shall Not Pass
Book Thirteen: Culture Shock

NEVER SURRENDER

CHRISTOPHER G. NUTTALL

The characters and events portrayed in this book are fictitious. Any similarity to real persons, living or dead, is coincidental and not intended by the author.

Text copyright © 2018 Christopher G. Nuttall
All rights reserved.
No part of this book may be reproduced, or stored in a retrieval system, or transmitted in any form or by any means, electronic, mechanical, photocopying, recording, or otherwise, without express written permission of the publisher.

ISBN-13: 9781983510052
ISBN-10: 198351005X

http://www.chrishanger.net
http://chrishanger.wordpress.com/
http://www.facebook.com/ChristopherGNuttall

All Comments Welcome!

A NOTE FROM THE AUTHOR

Never Surrender is the direct sequel to *Retreat Hell*, but features several characters from *Reality Check*. Their backgrounds are detailed there.

As always, I would be grateful for any spelling corrections, grammar suggestions, nitpicking and suchlike. Please send reports directly to my email address or through Amazon.

Thanks for reading! If you liked the book, please write a review.

CGN

PROLOGUE

From: *The Day After: The Post-Empire Universe and its Wars*. Professor Leo Caesius. Avalon University Press. 46PE.

When the Empire fell, it fell into war. Planets that had been held under the crushing grip of the Empire fought to free themselves, military officers and planetary governors sought to claim power for themselves and old grudges, held in check by the Empire's overpowering military might, returned to haunt the human race. It is impossible to even guess at the sheer number of human lives snuffed out by war, or condemned to a horrific existence in the middle of a war zone, located in what was once a peaceful sector. Indeed, there was so much devastation in the former Core Worlds that putting together a viable picture of what actually happened when seems impossible.

However, of all these wars, the most important was, perhaps, the Commonwealth-Wolfbane War. It is also the one where we are able to access records held by both sides in the conflict.

They made an odd pair. The Commonwealth, based on Avalon, was an attempt to escape the mistakes that eventually, inevitably, doomed the Empire. It was a capitalist society, based around maximum personal liberty; indeed, unlike so many other successor states, the Commonwealth never had to force a member world to join. And it flourished. Five years after Avalon was abandoned by the Empire, and the Fall of Earth, it was perhaps one of the most advanced successor states in existence. Personal freedom and technological innovation went hand in hand. By sheer number of ships, the Commonwealth was puny; by technology, the Commonwealth was far stronger than it seemed.

Wolfbane, by contrast, was a corporate plutocracy. Governor Brown of Wolfbane successfully secured control of the sector's military, once he heard the news from Earth, and worked hard to put the sector on a self-sustaining footing. His skill at convincing corporate systems to work together, and his eye for talented manpower, allowed him to save Wolfbane from the chaos sweeping out of the Core Worlds. Indeed, two years after the Fall of Earth, Wolfbane was already expanding and snapping up worlds that would otherwise have remained independent, after cutting ties with the Empire.

It was natural that Wolfbane and the Commonwealth would come into conflict. In the marketplace of ideas, the Commonwealth held a natural advantage that Governor Brown could never hope to match, not without dismantling his own power base. Like other autocratic states, Wolfbane chose to launch an invasion rather than wait for their system to decay, or face violent rebellion when its population started to ask questions. The operation was carefully planned.

The Commonwealth had an Achilles Heel - a world called Thule. Thule was unusual in that it had a sizable minority of people who resisted the idea of joining the Commonwealth, mainly for local reasons. However, it was also an economic powerhouse that could not be disregarded. And so, when the local government, faced with an insurgency that was clearly receiving support from off-world, requested Commonwealth help and support, the Commonwealth reluctantly dispatched the first Commonwealth Expeditionary Force (CEF), under the command of Brigadier Jasmine Yamane, to uphold the planet's legitimate authority.

Those who held misgivings were proved right, however, when the long-dreaded war finally began. Wolfbane's forces surged across the border at several places, targeting - in particular - Thule and its industrial base. The Commonwealth Navy struggled to evacuate as much of the CEF as possible before it was too late, but a number of soldiers - including the CO - remained on the planet when the enemy ships entered orbit. They were forced to surrender.

But while Wolfbane seemed to be winning the war, cracks were already appearing in the enemy's defences ...

CHAPTER ONE

It will come as no surprise that the Empire was disinclined to coddle prisoners of war. As far as the Empire was concerned, it was the sole human power and all other states were in rebellion against it.
- Professor Leo Caesius. *The Empire and its Prisoners of War.*

Meridian, Year 5 (PE)
Jasmine was not used to being alone.

In truth, she had never really been alone, save for her short stint as Admiral Singh's prisoner on Corinthian. Her family had been large, large enough for her to always be with her siblings or cousins, while no one was ever alone in the Terran Marine Corps. She had lived in barracks ever since joining the Marines, like her friends and comrades. But now, even though she was surrounded by hundreds of people, she felt truly alone.

The prison camp wasn't bad, not compared to Admiral Singh's dungeons or the cells used for the dreaded Conduct After Capture course. She had been primed to expect interrogation, perhaps drugs or torture; the Empire had shown no mercy to its prisoners and there was no reason to assume its enemies would do any better. But instead, the remains of the CEF had been transported to Meridian and dumped in a POW camp, some distance from whatever passed for civilisation on a stage-one colony world. It was a mercy part of her would have happily foregone.

She blamed herself. Each and every one of her decisions had been the best one at the time, she was sure, taking into account her limited options and incomplete knowledge. And yet, it had ended with her and her subordinates in a POW camp, while the Commonwealth was under attack. She had failed. She had failed the Commonwealth, the CEF and her fellow Marines. Guilt warred within her soul, demanding retribution for her failures. She was a prisoner, isolated from the war by countless light years, yet she wanted - needed - to get back to the Commonwealth. But how?

The POW camp wasn't quite standard, she'd noted when they'd been unceremoniously dumped off the shuttles and prodded through the gates. Instead of the standard prefabricated buildings, they'd been given barracks made of wood, suggesting the locals had built the POW camp for Wolfbane. They probably hadn't been given much of a choice, Jasmine was sure; a stage-one colony world couldn't hope to defend itself against a single orbiting destroyer, let alone the battle fleet that had hammered Thule into submission. But, non-standard or not, it was secure. There was no way for the prisoners to escape.

They don't care about us, she thought. On one hand, it was something of a relief; she'd expected interrogation precisely because she'd been in command of the CEF. But on the other, it suggested the enemy were very sure they would remain prisoners. *And they think we're irrelevant to the war.*

She closed her eyes, then opened them and looked around the barracks. The guards hadn't bothered to try to separate senior officers from their subordinates, let alone segregate the sexes. Jasmine wasn't bothered - she'd slept in the same barracks with men from the day she'd enlisted - but some of the other prisoners had taken it hard. Wolfbane had set up the POW camp long before the war had begun, she suspected, judging by some of the prisoners held behind barbed wire. *She'd* been in the camp for four days; *they'd* been in the camp for five *years*.

Cursing under her breath, she rose to her feet and walked towards the open door. Outside, rain was pouring from the sky, splashing down around the various buildings and collecting in great puddles under her feet. It would have been fun, the child in her acknowledged, if she hadn't been far too certain that it was wearing away at the wooden buildings. How long would it be, she asked herself, before the roofs started to collapse, or simply leaked water onto the bunk beds? And what would the guards do then?

She sighed, then walked into the rain and made her way slowly towards the edge of the camp, where the barbed wire held the prisoners firmly secure. It wasn't a bad design, the officer in her noted, even if she *was* on the wrong side of the wire. The POWs were all confined in one place, allowing the guards to keep them all under control - or simply hose them down with machine guns, if necessary. A prison riot might be left to burn itself out, or the guards would intervene with overwhelming force. Jasmine would have preferred somewhere more secure, she knew, but even if the prisoners overcame the guards they would still be stuck on Meridian. The only hope was to find a way to get off the planet.

The rain ran down her face and soaked her clothing as she walked away from the wire and around the side of one of the barracks, where two of her former subordinates were waiting for her. Riflemen Carl Watson and Thomas Stewart nodded politely to her - they'd agreed that salutes would only draw more attention to Jasmine - then glanced around, making sure they were alone. Jasmine looked behind her, then leaned against the wall, trying to look nonchalant. There was no one in view, but it was far too easy to imagine microscopic bugs being used to track their movements and monitor their conversation. The guards might have good reason to assume the camp was inescapable.

But if we assume we're doomed, we are doomed, she thought, morbidly. It was their duty to try to escape, no matter the risk. *And if the guards catch and kill us trying to escape, at least we will have tried.*

She knew better than to remain in the camp, if it could be avoided. The war would be won or lost - and if it were lost, Wolfbane would have a free hand to do whatever it liked to prisoners of war. The Empire had normally dumped POWs it considered to be beyond redemption on penal worlds, where they would either fight to subdue a world that could be later settled by the Empire or die, countless light years from home. Wolfbane might treat them better, but nothing Jasmine had heard from any of the other POWs suggested that Governor Brown was interested in anything other than efficiency. He might leave them on Meridian indefinitely - a stage-one colony world would welcome an influx of trained manpower - or he might just transfer them to a penal world. There were several candidates within the Wolfbane Sector alone.

"Brigadier," Watson said.

Jasmine sighed, inwardly. There had been a time when she'd been a Rifleman too …and she looked back to that time with a certain degree of nostalgia. She had been a Marine, one of many, and she hadn't had to worry about making more than tactical judgements in the heat of battle. Captain Stalker had been in command of the company and she'd just been one of his Marines. But the company had been scattered around the Commonwealth after they'd been abandoned by the Empire, leaving only a handful to continue serving as Marines. She envied Watson and Stewart more than she cared to admit.

"Let us hope they are not watching us," Jasmine said, curtly. "Have you met anyone interesting?"

"A handful," Stewart said. "It looks as though Meridian was used as a dumping point for quite a few people from Wolfbane."

Jasmine frowned. It wasn't common to put civilian and military prisoners together, but Governor Brown's people seemed to have ignored that stipulation. Maybe they only had one major POW camp …she shook her head, dismissing the absurd thought. It would have taken less effort, *much* less effort, to set up a POW camp on an isolated island on Wolfbane, well away from any hope of rescue. Anyone sent to Meridian had to be someone the Governor might want to keep alive, but didn't anticipate freeing for years, if at all.

"And a couple from Meridian itself," Watson added. "I think you might be able to talk to one of them, Brigadier. She won't talk to any of us."

"Understood," Jasmine said. She rubbed her scalp, where her short hair was itching under the downpour. "Anyone particularly important?"

"We seem to be sharing a POW camp with a former Imperial Army officer," Stewart said, with the air of a man making a dramatic announcement. "He claims to have been the former CO at Wolfbane, before the Governor took power for himself."

Jasmine felt her eyes narrow. "And he's still alive?"

"He was ranting and raving about how his clients wouldn't let him be killed," Stewart said, dryly. "I don't know how much of it to take seriously …"

"None of it," Watson said. "If he had enough clients to make himself a serious concern, he'd be dead, not mouldering away in a shithole on the edge of settled space."

Jasmine was inclined to agree. Patrons and clients had been the curse of the Empire's military, before the Fall of Earth; senior officers had promoted their own clients into important positions, rather than using competence as a yardstick for promotion. Each senior officer had enjoyed a network of clients, which had allowed them to bolster their positions ... and probably set themselves up as warlords, once the Empire had collapsed into chaos. If this former CO had been outsmarted by Governor Brown, it was a wonder he was still alive. He wouldn't be dangerous once he was buried in a shallow grave.

And if he had enough of a power base to make himself a threat, he wouldn't have been removed so easily, she thought, darkly.

"Talk to him anyway, see what you can learn," she said. "What's his name?"

"Stubbins," Watson said. "General James Stubbins."

Jasmine shrugged. The name wasn't familiar, unsurprisingly. There had been literally hundreds of thousands of generals in the Imperial Army, ranging from competent officers who had been promoted through merit to idiots who had been given the title as a reward from their patrons. The latter had been incredibly common in the dying days of the Empire, if only because everyone knew a competent officer was also a *dangerous* officer. She told herself, firmly, not to let prejudice blind her to the possibility that Stubbins had merely been unlucky ...

But if he had a power base, she thought again, *he shouldn't have been so easy to remove.*

"He has his aide with him," Watson added. "Paula Bartholomew. Very pretty woman - and smart too, I fancy."

"Then talk to her, see what she says too," Jasmine ordered. There was something about the whole affair that puzzled her, but there was no point in worrying about it. If Stubbins was a plant, someone charged with watching for trouble from the prisoners, they would just have to deal with him when he showed his true colours. "And see if you can separate her from him long enough to have a proper conversation."

Watson grinned. "Are you ordering me to seduce her?"

"Of course not," Jasmine said, dryly. "I would never *dream* of issuing an impossible order."

Stewart laughed as Watson glowered at both of them. "I don't think she was hired because she has a pretty face, my dear Watson," he said, mischievously. "And she certainly wouldn't have been sent out here if she hadn't been regarded as dangerous by *someone*."

"Unless they were making a clean sweep," Watson objected. "There have to be millions of pretty girls on Wolfbane."

"And if they were making a clean sweep," Jasmine pointed out, "they would have wiped out his whole patronage network."

She shook her head. "There's no way to know," she added. "Talk to him, see what he says ...and then we can decide how to proceed."

"Getting out of the camp will be easy," Stewart said. "We just tunnel under the fence."

"Assuming they're not watching with sensors for us to start digging," Watson countered, darkly. "They might wait for us to pop up on the other side, then open fire."

"Then we will need a distraction," Jasmine said. She had thought about trying to dig a tunnel out of the camp, but the soaking ground would make it incredibly dangerous. And besides, the guards hadn't been fool enough to leave them any digging tools. "Something loud enough to keep their attention away from any sensors they might have."

"A riot would do nicely," Stewart said.

He broke off as the rain started to come to a halt. "The girl I mentioned - Kailee - is in Building 1," he said, quickly. "I think you should definitely talk to her."

Jasmine nodded, then glanced from Stewart to Watson. "We're going to get out of here," she said, firmly. "Whatever it takes, we're going to get out of here."

"Of course," Stewart said. "I never doubt it for a moment."

The rain came to a stop, leaving water dripping from the rooftops and splashing down to the muddy ground. Jasmine shook her head, cursing the prison uniform under her breath. It was bright orange, easy to see in semi-darkness ...and it clung to her skin in a manner that revealed each and every one of her curves. Being exposed didn't bother her - she'd been through worse in basic training - but it was yet another problem. They would be alarmingly visible if they happened to be caught tunnelling under the fence.

She nodded to them both, then headed towards Building 1. It was simple in design, nothing more than a long rectangular building. Judging by the jungle just outside the fence, Meridian was not short of wood; hell, clearing woodland was probably one of the first tasks the settlers had had to do, when they'd landed. And they'd thrown away a small fortune, if they'd been able to get the wood to Earth before the Fall …

Inside, it was no more elaborate than Building 8, where she'd been placed, but it had an air of despondency that suggested the inhabitants had been prisoners for much longer. They'd reached a stage, she realised, where they'd come close to giving up. A handful of bunk beds were occupied, mainly by women, either sleeping or just staring listlessly up at the wooden ceiling. There was nothing to do in the camp, save eat rations and sleep; there were no footballs, no board games, nothing the prisoners could use to distract themselves from the numb tedium of their existence. Given enough time, Jasmine had a feeling that the ennui would wear her down too.

You expected torture, she thought.

It was a galling thought. Conduct After Capture had warned her to expect torture, mistreatment, even rape. Admiral Singh's goons *had* tortured her, intent on trying to break her will to resist. But the POW camp was nothing except mindless tedium. There was no gloating enemy to resist, no leering torturer to fight …merely her own mind. Perhaps, just perhaps, the true intent of the camp was to erode her will to resist by depriving her of an enemy to fight. And it might just work.

"You're new, I see," a voice said. An older woman smiled at her, revealing broken teeth, although there was a hint of wariness in her expression. "What are you in for?"

"I'm looking for Kailee," Jasmine said, shortly. The woman sounded cracked, like so many of the older prisoners. "Where is she?"

"There," the older woman said, pointing towards a dark-haired girl lying on the bunk. "Be gentle, my dear. She's had a rough time of it."

Jasmine nodded, then walked towards Kailee. She was young, around twenty, although it was hard to be sure. Like so many other colonists, she would have aged rapidly during the battle to settle a whole new world. She turned to look at Jasmine as she approached, her dark eyes fearful.

Jasmine realised, grimly, that the girl had been through hell. No wonder she had refused to talk to either of the men.

"I'm Jasmine," she said, sitting down by the side of the bed. It reduced the height advantage, hopefully making it easier for Kailee to talk to her. "I understand you were born on Meridian."

"Earth," Kailee said. Her accent was definitely from Earth, although several years of being away from humanity's homeworld had weakened it. "I was born on Earth."

Jasmine frowned. "How did you wind up here?"

Kailee laughed, harshly. "I won a competition," she said. "I didn't enter the competition, but I won anyway. And they sent me out here, where I was happy after a while. And then they took me away and shoved me in the camp."

Jasmine frowned. She could understand imprisoning the planetary leadership, or anyone who might have military experience, but she rather doubted Kailee was either connected to the leadership or an experienced military officer. Indeed, Kailee held herself like someone from the lower classes of Earth, a sheep-girl who knew herself to be vulnerable. She wouldn't have survived an hour of Boot Camp, let alone six months.

"If you're from Earth," she said finally, "why are you here?"

"Because of Gary," Kailee said. "They want to keep him under control."

Jasmine felt her frown deepen. "Gary?"

"My…my boyfriend," Kailee said. "We came from Earth together and …and …I …"

She caught herself, then scowled at Jasmine. "There aren't many people here who like modern technology," she said. The bitterness in her tone was striking. "Gary's one of the few who do. And they wanted him to work for them, so they took me as a hostage."

"I see," Jasmine said. An idea was starting to flower at the back of her mind. "Tell me about him, please."

Kailee gave her a sharp look. "Why do you want to know?"

"Because it might be the key to getting out of here," Jasmine said. "And I need you to tell me everything you can."

Chapter Two

There was no distinction drawn between a previously-undiscovered human colony, that might object to being absorbed into the Empire, and members of an insurgency mounted against the Empire's overseers. They were all seen, legally, as being illegitimate combatants.
- Professor Leo Caesius. *The Empire and its Prisoners of War.*

Avalon, Year 5 (PE)
"It isn't going well, is it?"

Colonel Edward Stalker shrugged. "It's always darkest before the dawn," he said, seriously. "And the first impressions are always the worst."

President Gabriella Cracker eyed him sardonically. "And now we've gone through a whole list of clichés," she said, "it isn't going well, is it?"

Ed shrugged, again. "No one has fought a war like this for hundreds of years," he said. He looked around his office, morbidly. "We're still learning and so are they."

He sighed. "There are five worlds currently under occupation, but only one of them - Thule - is a significant issue," he added. "The remainder don't add much to our combat power …"

"But they look bad on the display," Gaby said. She pointed a sharp finger towards five holographic icons, all glowing a baleful red. "The Wolves seem to be advancing forward in an unstoppable wave."

"But they're not," Ed said. "There's a long way between the front lines and Avalon."

"You know that and I know that," Gaby said, tiredly. "But I have to convince the population that we're not losing the war."

Ed nodded, reluctantly. Avalon had always had a more stalwart population than Earth or any of the other Core Worlds, but even colonists, used to setbacks, could falter if they thought defeat was inevitable. Wolfbane had captured five worlds, after all, and Gaby was right; it did look bad. And yet, he knew the worlds were largely immaterial. The war wouldn't be won or lost until one side managed to destroy the other's fleet, planetary defences and industrial base.

"They're actually being quite cautious," he said, softly. "I was expecting a stab at Avalon itself as a way to open the war, but instead they're proceeding carefully, taking system after system as they advance towards our heartland. That gives us time to rally and mount counterattacks into enemy-held territory."

"And take out their supply lines," Gaby agreed. "Are you sure we can keep them from continuing the offensive?"

"Nothing is certain in war, apart from the simple fact that professionals still study logistics instead of tactics," Ed said. "They will need regular resupplies to keep their fleets advancing forward, everything from missiles to spare parts and replacement crewmen. And if we can impede that, they will be unable to advance further."

"I hope you're right," Gaby said, again. "The council isn't taking the latest loss too well."

Ed sighed, inwardly. It took nearly three weeks to get a message from the front lines back to Avalon, three weeks during which anything could happen. The Empire had had all sorts of problems because the Grand Senate had tried to issue orders from Earth, orders that were already long out of date before they reached the Rim. Avalon was closer to the war front, but three weeks was still far too long to do anything but allow the local commanders freedom of action. It was the only way to hold the line.

At least we can trust our commanders, he thought. *The Empire never felt it could trust anyone.*

"Tell them that we are rallying and readying our counter-offensive," he said. It was true, although he had a feeling that it would be several months before the Commonwealth could mount more than heavy raids behind enemy lines. Trading space for time was the only practical course of action, but it wasn't very heroic. "Is Travis still being a pain in the ass?"

"Travis isn't calling the war itself into question," Gaby said, "but he's insisting we need new leadership at the top."

Ed sighed, again. It was typical of politicians - opposition politicians - that they carped and criticised, while they had no power or responsibilities. Gordon Travis might have a point, but it was lost behind the simple fact that he could - and did - say whatever he liked. It wasn't *him* who had to make the plans work, or write letters to the families of men and women killed in action. And Travis blamed Ed for the death of his son.

"Tell him to wait for the next election," he said. "Unless he can put together enough of a coalition to rout you."

"I don't think he can, yet," Gaby said. "But if we lose more worlds, Ed, the councillors from those worlds will be out for blood."

Ed nodded, cursing under his breath. He'd trained as a Marine, not as a combination of Admiral, General and Politician. He'd had to learn to balance all three roles on Avalon, after they'd been abandoned by the Empire, but none of them really fitted. He wanted to get back into action, to get stuck into the enemy…not to remain behind while men and women under his command went into danger. Part of him had almost been glad when the peace talks had blown up in their face, when he'd had to command a force under siege on a primitive world …

He shook his head, angrily. It might have been better, in the long run, if they'd been able to make a firm agreement with Wolfbane. But, knowing what he did now, he was sure that Wolfbane wouldn't have honoured the agreement for long. They had simply far too much at stake to risk a firm peace.

"Then we hold the line, in the council as well as the war," he said. "I think …"

He broke off as his intercom buzzed. "Yes?"

"Colonel Kitty Stevenson is here to see you, sir," his current aide said. "She says its urgent."

Ed and Gaby exchanged glances. Colonel Kitty Stevenson had been stationed on Avalon long before Stalker's Stalkers had arrived, simply because she'd managed to get on the bad side of one of her superior officers. Ed wasn't sure of the details, but he'd never doubted Kitty's competence; she'd had almost nothing to work with, on Avalon, yet she'd built up the bare bones of an intelligence network from scratch. Now, she was in charge of both espionage and counter-espionage.

"Show her in, please," he ordered.

"I'll leave you to it," Gaby said. "I need to go soothe a few troubled minds."

Ed smiled. "Good luck," he said. "And I'll see you tonight?"

"Unless there's another late sitting in the council chamber," Gaby said. "I don't get to steer matters *all* my own way."

Ed watched her go, smiling inwardly at how the former rebel leader had matured. His instincts had told him that he could compromise with Gaby, work with her to establish a lasting peace…and he'd been right. But, at the same time, Gaby was as limited as himself when it came to building an interstellar government. The Commonwealth was a ramshackle structure in many ways, built from various planetary governments rather than something designed for genuine interstellar governance. It wouldn't be long before cracks started to show in the edifice.

But changing that will require careful forethought, he considered, as the door closed behind his friend and lover. *The Empire wasn't a very effective interstellar government either.*

The door opened again, allowing Kitty Stevenson to step into the room. She was a tall redheaded woman, wearing a naval uniform without any rank insignia. Her jacket was open, revealing a surprising amount of cleavage, something that would have gotten her in trouble if she'd been a genuine naval officer. Ed - and his fellows - had worked hard to ensure that the old patronage networks that had plagued the Imperial Navy found no root in the Commonwealth Navy. And trading sex for advancement had been a favoured practice for the Empire's senior officers.

"Colonel," she said, as she produced a bug-sweeper from her uniform pocket and started to sweep the room. "I'm afraid I have bad news."

Ed's eyes narrowed. "How bad? Should we go to a secure room?"

"This room appears clean," Kitty said. "I'm just feeling a little paranoid."

She returned the sweeper to her pocket and sat down facing him. "I think we have a rat."

Ed blinked. "A spy?"

"Yes, sir," Kitty said. "And someone quite high up."

Ed met her eyes, tiredly. "Explain."

Kitty looked back at him, evenly. "Since the start of the war, sir, Commonwealth Intelligence has been installing monitors on the various deep-space communications transmitters," she said. "It wasn't quite legal, but it had to be done."

Ed scowled. The Empire had been in the habit of insisting that all commercial encryption programs included backdoors, allowing Imperial Intelligence to read encoded messages at will. Unsurprisingly, bribes had changed hands and powerful corporations had developed ways to read messages sent by their rivals. And then pirates and news agencies had started cracking messages at will, too. It hadn't encouraged new businesses, already staggering under the weight of oppressive regulations, to enter the marketplace.

The Commonwealth had banned the practice. Businesses, even civilians, could use whatever encryption programs they liked, without ever having to leave backdoors for Commonwealth Intelligence. If someone realised that Commonwealth Intelligence had been quietly reading their mail *anyway*, it would cause a major scandal. And yet, Kitty was right. There were almost certainly spies on the planet's surface and those spies would have to send their messages back to Wolfbane *somehow*.

"I know," he said, finally. "Carry on."

Kitty's eyes never left his. "We were watching for signs of data being beamed into space that might be aimed at a spy ship somewhere within the system," she said. "Four days ago, we intercepted a communications packet that was heavily encrypted, so tightly bound that it took three days to unlock the encryption and scan the contents. It consisted of political intelligence from Avalon."

Ed smiled. "It took *that* long?"

"The encryption program was unfamiliar to us," Kitty said. "We've been checking message buffers to see if there were other encrypted messages, but if there were they were purged long ago."

She reached into her pocket and produced a datapad, which she passed to Ed. "As you can see, sir," she said, "most of the data is political in nature."

Ed studied the datapad for a long moment, skimming through the paragraphs one by one. It read more like a detailed letter than a spy report, but that wouldn't stop it being dangerous. Whoever had written the message had access to the council, or at least to a number of councillors ... he shook his head, then passed the datapad back to her. It was sheer luck they'd stumbled across evidence the spy existed before something far more sensitive was discussed in council.

And we thought the council was above suspicion, he thought, numbly. *Why did we choose to believe that again?*

"Very well," he said. "Do you have a suspect?"

"We've narrowed it down to several hundred possible suspects," Kitty said. "However, that list would include nearly every councillor on the planet, as well as their aides and perhaps even their families."

Ed swore. "If we started investigating them all, Colonel," he said, "we might well rip the Commonwealth apart."

"Yes, sir," Kitty said. "I attempted to trace each individual piece of information, but I wasn't able to narrow the suspect list further."

"There was too much in the message," Ed said. There had been no tactical data, which was *something*, but it was still worrying. Political intelligence - which councillors might consider surrender, which councillors wanted to fight to the bitter end - might be helpful to Wolfbane, particularly if Governor Brown started making peace offers. "Can you track where the message *went*?"

"To one of the asteroid mining facilities," Kitty said. "I suspect it was probably rerouted from there to a hidden monitoring station. Past then, we don't know."

"I see," Ed said.

He cursed under his breath. It would probably be impossible to track down the final destination. Five years ago, Avalon had had a RockRat colony and a cloudscoop ...and little else. Now, the entire system swarmed with mining stations and industrial production nodes. It would be easy for the enemy to hide a monitoring platform within the system, ready to intercept messages from Avalon and hold them until a starship arrived to take them home. As long as they took a few basic precautions, it would be impossible to detect the platform.

"A spy in the council," he mused. "Who?"

"Unknown," Kitty said. "It was sheer luck we stumbled across the message, sir."

Ed would have liked to believe it was Gordon Travis. The man had been nothing more than a headache since he'd been elected to the council, even though he had a respectable record as a businessman before and after the Cracker War. It was hard to blame him for being angry about the death of his son, but it didn't excuse outright treason ...

He shook his head. Travis might have disagreed with both Ed and Gaby, but that didn't make him a traitor. There was no *proof*, apart from personal dislike, and that wasn't enough to condemn a man to death.

"We have to find the spy," he mused. "Do you have a plan?"

"Yes, sir," Kitty said. "Now we have a handle on the encryption program, I have reconfigured the monitors to watch for more encoded messages. I intend to start distributing pieces of false or compartmented information around the list of suspects, then see which pieces of intelligence are passed to the enemy. Once we know what the enemy knows, we can narrow down our list of suspects considerably."

"It seems workable," Ed said. He sighed. The last thing the Commonwealth needed was a witch-hunt for a highly-placed spy. "Is there no way to cut down the number of suspects now?"

"No, sir," Kitty said. "I don't think it can be done, short of introducing arbitrary standards to the mix - like, for example, excluding everyone from Avalon. That would cause another political headache if it got out."

Ed nodded. "Yes, it would," he agreed. "The other worlds would be understandably furious."

"Yes, sir," Kitty agreed.

She shrugged. "I could also dispatch a team of investigators to the asteroid mining colony, but it would tip off the spy ...assuming, of course, the spy knows which route the messages take to leave Avalon," she added. "There might be an entire ring of spies on the planet's surface, like the agents who helped poor Mathew Polk get down to the ground."

"Wonderful," Ed muttered.

"But whoever put that report together is very highly placed," Kitty added. "I'd put money on it being someone from Avalon."

"But why?" Ed asked. "Why betray the Commonwealth?"

Kitty shrugged. "Money, power, revenge ...there is no shortage of possible motives," she said. "A councillor might believe that he'd be promoted to local ruler when Wolfbane wins the war, assuming he serves them well beforehand. Lots of people dream of power and probably shouldn't be allowed to claim it. Or he may believe that Wolfbane is going to win and he's doing what he can to make himself useful, just to save himself from the purge at the end of the war."

Her eyes darkened. "Or his child might be a prisoner, held hostage to guarantee his compliance, sir," she added. "I'm going to start looking into their families too, Colonel, but I am frighteningly short of manpower."

"I know," Ed admitted.

He'd never had much use for Imperial Intelligence, not as a Marine. Intelligence estimates had often been massaged to produce the answers the Grand Senate had wanted, not answers that happened to bear more than a passing resemblance to the truth. And there had been far too many intelligence officers ready to alter their reports ...which had ensured that military units had dropped into maelstroms because they'd been assured the enemy would break at the first sign the Grand Senate was prepared to use force. Han wouldn't have been such a disaster, he was sure, if the intelligence officers on the spot hadn't kept assuring everyone that there was no risk of an uprising.

And it had coloured his attitude towards Commonwealth Intelligence. The spooks could not be allowed to run amuck, develop their own agenda or start altering data to suit their political masters. But, at the same time, it had ensured that Commonwealth Intelligence was just too small to handle all of its responsibilities ...

"Hire more manpower, if you can," he said. It wouldn't be easy. Even now, five years after the war, there was still a shortage of trained manpower. The people Kitty would need were in high demand, while unskilled immigrants couldn't hope to work for Commonwealth Intelligence, even if they could be trusted. "But keep this as quiet as possible. I don't want to spook the spy before it's too late."

"Understood," Kitty said.

Ed glanced at his wristcom. "I have a meeting with Emmanuel Alves in an hour," he said, shortly. It wouldn't be a pleasant meeting. The reporter had been dating Jasmine Yamane before she'd been captured on Thule and he'd asked, every time, if there was word of his girlfriend. "This evening, I want a comprehensive plan for showing false information to part of the council. Let's see what the spy hears, shall we?"

"Yes, sir," Kitty said.

"I want this person identified," Ed added, "but you are not to attempt to arrest him without my permission. We might be able to use this spy to our advantage."

Kitty nodded, doubtfully. "It will be at least six weeks before his intelligence reaches Wolfbane," she said. "The situation will have changed by then."

"I know," Ed said. He smiled, openly. "But I think I have the bare bones of an idea."

CHAPTER THREE

This is, to some extent, a historical oddity. Very few states could reasonably claim to be the sole font of power and authority. Throughout history, mistreatment of POWs tended to backfire, particularly if the war was won and lost decisively.
- Professor Leo Caesius. *The Empire and its Prisoners of War.*

Meridian, Year 5 (PE)

"Brigadier," Watson said, as Jasmine entered the barracks. "Please let me introduce James Stubbins and Paula Bartholomew."

"*General* James Stubbins," Stubbins said. "I have not been stripped of my rank."

He eyed Jasmine doubtfully. "I must say you're awfully young to be a brigadier, young lady."

Jasmine eyed him back. Stubbins looked middle-aged, probably thanks to extensive biological engineering in his youth, but he didn't seem either fit or healthy. His brown hair was greying rapidly, while there was a hint in his expression that he was holding himself together by sheer force of will. If he'd been in the camp for over five years, Jasmine had a feeling that it was a wonder he'd lasted as long as he had. Maybe he was stronger and more resilient than he seemed.

"I was promoted quickly," she said, finally.

"Then I will have to assume command of the breakout," Stubbins said, firmly. "Do you have a workable plan?"

Watson opened his mouth, but Jasmine spoke first. "*I am in command of the CEF*," she said, sharply. "*I will command the breakout.*"

Stubbins scowled at her. "I was appointed to my rank by Admiral Waterford," he insisted. "A purely local rank does not, ever, take precedence over an Imperial rank …"

"The Empire is gone," Jasmine snapped. "Your rank is of no value in the camp."

"General," Paula said quietly, "it's been years since you commanded in the field."

Jasmine found herself studying Paula with some interest. She looked younger than Stubbins, almost as if the camp hadn't taken such a toll on her. Paula wasn't conventionally pretty - she had long brown hair and a freckled face - but she had a force of character that was, if anything, stronger than her commander. And she was clearly smarter than him too …

"Very well," Stubbins said. "I will allow you to continue to hold tactical command, young lady."

"Thank you," Jasmine said, sarcastically. She had a feeling she was going to have trouble with Stubbins, unless Paula managed to keep him under control. Perhaps she could …or perhaps she should simply tie Stubbins up in his bunk until they carried out their plan. "I would be honoured to keep the command I have earned."

She squatted down and motioned for the others to sit next to her. "Meridian has one major city and one spaceport," she said. Kailee had been quite informative, once Jasmine had started running gentle questions past her. Most of the information was out of date, but Jasmine rather doubted a stage-one colony world could change so quickly. "Most of the planet's population are hunters, farmers and stage-one industrialists. The handful of technical-trained people on the surface have either been taken away or forced to work for Wolfbane's occupation force."

Watson frowned. "Taken away?"

"Forced to work for Wolfbane elsewhere, I imagine," Stewart said. "They're probably quite short on technical experts, just like us."

"It was a major problem," Stubbins said, suddenly. "We had ships going into mothballs because we didn't have the men or spare parts to maintain them."

Jasmine wasn't particularly surprised. Between the Empire's jaundiced view of education and the limited opportunities for a technician to work within the system, the entire Empire had been having a major shortage of trained manpower before the Fall. Avalon had been lucky, in many ways; they'd been able to call upon the RockRats for technical training, while setting up their own technical schools. For a sector capital, the shortages in both manpower and industrial production nodes had to be disastrous. She couldn't help wondering just how many worlds had starved to death in the midst of plenty.

"I would have expected you to start training programs," she said, shortly. "Why didn't you?"

"Imperial Regulations forbade it," Stubbins said. "I could not defy the regulations."

Jasmine sighed, inwardly. All of a sudden, she was *sure* she knew why Governor Brown had sent Stubbins to Meridian, rather than simply having him quietly executed. Stubbins simply didn't have the imagination needed to be a danger to his superiors …but that same lack of imagination prevented him from tackling the problems facing his command. And to think, if he'd had any real imagination, he would have remained in power …

"Those regulations were killing your command," she said, dryly. "Didn't you see the dangers of blindly following them?"

She shook her head before he could answer. It was the way of the Empire. If someone defied regulations, his enemies would have all the ammunition they needed to bring his career to a shattering halt. No one would care if the victim had done what was necessary to save his command, not when there was political hay to be made by targeting him for breach of regulations. And, all over what remained of the Empire, starships and shipyards would be grinding to a halt for lack of maintenance and spare parts …

For want of a nail, a shoe was lost, she thought, morbidly. She'd been forced to memorise the poem at the Slaughterhouse. How had the poem ended? *For want of a battle, a kingdom was lost …all for the want of a nail.*

"They don't have a large force on the planet's surface," she said, instead. "All they really have are a handful of men in heavy combat armour, based on the orbital station. If anyone down on the surface poses a serious problem, they can just call in strikes from orbit and obliterate them. In fact, apart from the POW camps and the small garrison, they're not really oppressing the locals at all."

"But they don't have to have a soldier on every street corner to keep the locals under control," Stewart said, gruffly. "Not as long as they hold the high orbitals."

"No," Jasmine agreed. "There's a handful of locals who have been forced to collaborate, with their families held hostage in various camps to keep them obedient. Other than that …Meridian is largely immaterial to the war. There's no need to expend thousands of credits worth of resources on the planet."

"Right," Stewart said. "So our real problem isn't getting out of this shithole. The real problem is getting control of the orbital station."

"Yes," Jasmine said. "Once we're in command of the station, we can free the remaining prisoners and then decide our next step."

Stubbins snorted, loudly. "I think you're forgetting something," he said. "We're still trapped behind the barbed wire."

"Really?" Stewart asked. "I don't think we noticed."

Jasmine tossed him a sharp look. "Getting out of the camp will be simple," she said. "What's to stop us tunnelling under the barbed wire?"

Stubbins gaped at her. "It cannot possibly be so easy," he said. "They would have scattered land mines around, surely."

"I don't think so," Jasmine said. She'd spent two days watching the camp's routines before starting to consider ways to escape. "The locals come and go, bringing food and supplies to the camp, and they don't seem to watch their footing. There isn't even a second fence to keep outsiders away from a minefield."

"Careless of them," Stewart rumbled.

"They still have guards on the watchtowers," Watson offered. "Guards with guns."

"We need to distract them," Jasmine said. "If we stage a riot, or something else that will catch their eye, at one end of the camp, we can dig our way out at the other. And if we wait for rainfall, the guards will have far more problems tracking us once we get into the jungle."

"We'll have to be naked," Watson said. He pulled at his orange jumpsuit. "These things are far too visible in the gloom."

"It's why they made us wear them," Jasmine said. She couldn't help a thrill of excitement. Maybe they were still helpless prisoners, but at least they were planning their escape. "They want us to be visible."

"So we get out of the camp," Stubbins said. "And then ..."

"And then we proceed with caution," Jasmine said. Kailee had given her a few names and address, men and women she was sure were part of the resistance, but her knowledge was badly out of date. It was quite likely that the people she'd known were dead ...or worse. "I think we would need to get to Sabre City, then decide how to proceed from there."

"We can't all go," Stewart said.

"No, we can't," Jasmine agreed. She hesitated, then sighed. "Who do we have with us?"

Stewart closed his eyes and recited from memory. "There's a thousand people in the camp," he said, flatly. "Two hundred of them are prisoners from the CEF or Thule; the remainder are people Governor Brown sent into exile, rather than simply killing outright. I don't think we have any technical specialists among the prisoners ..."

"Of course not," Stubbins said. His voice was very bitter. "Technical specialists could be ...re-educated rather than simply sent into exile."

Paula leaned forward. "How many prisoners come from Meridian itself?"

"Just five," Stewart said. "They're all hostages, held here to ensure their relatives stay on good behaviour. I don't know if we could trust them."

Jasmine had to agree. Hostages could become dangerously unpredictable, either through Stockholm Syndrome or simply feeling responsible for their relatives. Kailee had sounded broken, rather than desperate, but who knew what would happen if she was offered a chance to escape? And yet, if she was right about *why* she was in the camp, she might be the key to winning their freedom.

"I think we three and Kailee will make a break for it," Jasmine said, finally. "We're the best suited to get back to the city, then plan our next move."

"Hold on," Stubbins said. "I want to leave the camp too!"

"Can you actually help us?" Jasmine asked. She didn't blame Stubbins for wanting to leave, but if Kailee was right they were several days walk from Sabre City. "You'd have to walk with us to the city, then blend in until we found out how to get to the orbital station."

Paula gave Stubbins a long glance. "You're not suited to a commando mission," she said, gently. "You really need to let them handle it, while you stay here and play dumb."

Watson snickered. Jasmine scowled at him and he converted it into a cough.

"The guards haven't bothered to count us since we were shoved in here," Jasmine said, carefully. "They're going to regret that, I think, but ideally we don't want them to think that anyone has escaped at all."

She smirked to herself. It was clear that Governor Brown hadn't bothered to assign his front-line troops to Meridian ...but really, why would he bother? Meridian was unimportant ...and even if the POWs did break out of the camp and scatter before KEWs could strike them from orbit, they wouldn't be able to get off the planet. She was mildly surprised he hadn't simply dumped them on the surface, without bothering with the camp. The locals could have found work for them, or simply shoved them away from settled lands, and there would be no hope of a return to orbit.

Unless he thinks of us as bargaining chips, she thought, grimly. *Who knows what he could do with us, if he thought he were losing the war?*

"We can try and keep them occupied," Stubbins said. "But how do you plan to get them looking in the wrong direction, without simply opening fire into the camp?"

"Let me handle that," Jasmine said. She glanced at Stewart. "Perhaps you could walk General Stubbins around the camp? See if it gives him any ideas?"

"Of course, Brigadier," Stewart said. He was smart enough to realise that Jasmine wanted to talk to Paula alone. "Carl will accompany us."

Stubbins looked as though he wanted to protest, but wisely said nothing as the two marines escorted him away. Jasmine watched them go, then turned to face Paula. The older woman - and she was sure Paula was older than she looked - was watching her with a mixture of amusement and respect. Maybe, Jasmine reflected, if she'd had a different life she would have made a good marine. There was something about her that suggested she would never give up.

"So," Jasmine said, "what's a nice girl like you doing with a scumbag like him?"

Paula shrugged, running a hand through her brown hair. Jasmine had never cared much for her appearance - there were stories of recruits fleeing in horror when they discovered they had to have most of their hair cut short - but she had to admit that Paula had done a remarkable job of keeping her looks, despite spending years in a POW camp. Indeed, she could have passed for someone on the streets, if she'd wanted.

"He's not actually that bad," Paula said. "All bark and no bite."

Jasmine gave her a sharp look. "Really?"

"Oh, yes," Paula said. "He let me run his life on Wolfbane and …and I just went into exile with him, when Governor Brown took over."

"Exile," Jasmine repeated. "Is that what you think of it?"

"James thinks he will return in triumph, one day," Paula said. "Governor Brown will run into trouble and need to recall him. On that day, he has grand plans for killing his enemies and securing his place once and for all."

She shook her head slowly. "I don't think much of his old patronage network remains, if any."

"Governor Brown has more competent subordinates," Jasmine said. Admiral Singh was working for him now and, whatever else could be said about Singh, she was a very competent Admiral. "There's no hope of a recall, I think."

Paula sighed. "I thought as much," she said. "But he did have a habit of putting friends in odd places. He might still have some contacts on Wolfbane."

"Keep him under control," Jasmine said. "His contacts might come in handy, later on. If they're still there."

"I'll do my best," Paula said. "But he sees you as his first real chance to make a break for it."

Jasmine rolled her eyes, rudely. Stubbins had been in the camp for five years; surely, he'd had enough time to spot the weaknesses in the defences. Maybe he just hadn't had the nerve to try to burrow under the fence while wearing his birthday suit ...or maybe he'd clung so tightly to the prospect of being recalled that he'd purposely not considered trying to escape. Or maybe he was just an idiot ...

"You stayed with him," she said. Someone as intelligent and capable as Paula could have found another posting, surely. "*Why* did you stay with him?"

"It was that or being reassigned," Paula said. She met Jasmine's eyes. "I had a feeling I would have been reassigned to the pleasure corps, if I were lucky. Staying with him seemed the better idea."

"I see," Jasmine said. *She* would never have whored for her postings, but perhaps she would have felt differently if she'd joined the Imperial Navy instead of the Terran Marines. "We will see how it will all work out."

She looked up as she heard Stubbins returning, escorted by the two marines. "I have a plan," he said. "I know what will distract the guards."

Jasmine lifted her eyebrows. "How do you plan to distract the guards?"

"Naked ladies," Stubbins said. He grinned, boyishly. "There are a number of women in the barracks. A couple of them can strip naked and try to seduce the guards ..."

"Except the guards will almost certainly be suspicious," Jasmine pointed out. She'd considered something similar, but her half-formed plans had always died when she'd realised the risks. A naked woman was an obvious distraction, while a dressed woman was simply not distracting enough. "They will think she's trying to keep them busy."

"Or she will be raped," Paula added, sharply.

"Then we modify the plan," Stewart said. "Have two naked ladies run out of the barracks, chased by a pair of half-naked men. It will look like a relationship gone badly wrong ...the guards will look and laugh, rather than think it's a distraction."

"Particularly if we do it in the rain," Jasmine agreed. "We'd want to do it in the clear, if it was a distraction."

She considered it, quickly. Nudity did tend to attract attention, unless the watchers had been brought up on worlds where public nudity was considered acceptable. But the women would be taking considerable risks, even if the guards were on the other side of the fence …she didn't like the idea, but she couldn't think of anything better. A riot might be ended, quickly and brutally, by the guards pointing their guns into the camp and opening fire.

"Very well," she said. She looked at Stewart. "Round up a couple of women willing to bare all for the plan, then organise a pair of men to serve as chasers. Tell them we want it to look serious, but slapdash. Make the guards laugh rather than cry."

"Of course," Stewart said. "When do you want to leave?"

Jasmine looked up at the sky. It was a pale blue, but based on past experience it would be raining within the hour, perhaps sooner.

"I'll get Kailee ready, then we can finalise our plans," she said. "We'll have to strip off too and be waiting near the fence. It will take some doing."

"And then we will wait for you," Stubbins said. "I will see you get medals for this."

Jasmine bit off the response that came to mind. "Thank you," she said. She exchanged a telling glance with Paula. "But let's keep them until we've actually escaped, ok?"

CHAPTER FOUR

> There were also practical considerations. If the only thing POWs could look forward to was slow torture, starvation and death, why would they want to surrender? Even if they were trapped in a hopeless position, fighting to the last might seem a better option than surrendering to certain death.
> - Professor Leo Caesius. *The Empire and its Prisoners of War.*

Meridian, Year 5 (PE)

"I hear thunder in the distance," Austin said. "My infallible intuition tells me we're going to be drenched in a few minutes."

Darrin snorted. Five years of practically being a brother to Austin and he *still* wasn't quite used to his friend's sense of humour. But then, five years of having to fend for himself on Meridian had taught him more than he'd ever dreamed possible. Earth had been a joke, a bad joke …and now it was nothing more than a fading dream. He tried not to think about Earth these days, even when the occupiers had offered rewards to anyone who could tell them what had happened before the planet died. There was no point in dwelling on the past.

"Maybe it's just someone farting in the distance," he said, as he crawled up to the vantage point overlooking the camp. "They were feeding the prisoners beans last time I checked."

He reached the vantage point and peered through the camouflage netting, down towards the POW camp. The occupiers had insisted, at gunpoint, that the settlers build the camp for them and, reluctantly, the settlers had done as they were told. They'd built it some distance from any settlement, just in case the POWs proved to be violent criminals. But none of the POWs the watchers had observed had seemed anything other than pathetic white collar criminals, if that.

It wasn't a very well designed POW camp, he knew. The carpenters hadn't wanted to spend more than the bare minimum of time on the barracks, so they'd built very basic transit housing and little more. But it would suffice to keep the prisoners relatively clean and dry, as long as they didn't spend too much time running around in the downpours that afflicted Meridian every three or four hours. And it would keep them in, as long as the guards remained alert and the prisoners remained listless. None of them, male or female, had seemed particularly bent on escaping ever since they'd been dumped on Meridian.

But now there were new prisoners. And they looked like soldiers.

"Makes you want to know what's happening out there," Darrin said, looking upwards at the rapidly darkening sky. "Where did these newcomers *come* from?"

Austin shrugged. He'd been born on Meridian and would probably die on Meridian, utterly unaware or unconcerned about the greater universe beyond the atmosphere. Darrin didn't really blame him; Meridian was a good place to live, but it demanded full attention from its settlers. The planet was nowhere near heavily populated enough to support a spacefaring civilisation or a space-based industry, assuming it ever got the chance. Wolfbane might have pre-empted any hope of Meridian becoming more than a stage-two or three colony world.

"It doesn't matter," Austin said. "All that matters is that they are *here*."

"I know," Darrin said. "But we need to know if we can find allies to get them out."

He shifted position, carefully spying on the watchtowers surrounding the camp. The guards seemed content to rotate between the watchtowers and a tiny set of barracks, rather than try to visit Sabre City or return to orbit. It made little sense to Darrin, but then he'd been born on Earth. Maybe the guards had come from yet another colony world, rather than Wolfbane or Earth. Or maybe they were just afraid of the consequences for leaving their posts.

"I make it fifteen guards within view," he said, after a moment. "You?"

"Sixteen," Austin said. "There's a guard walking around the edge of the fence."

Darrin followed his gaze, then nodded. "Still thirty guards in total, as far as we know," he said. "The remainder must be catching up on their sleep."

He smiled as a peal of thunder split the air. Once, it had been hard to sleep on Meridian, when the silence of night was frequently broken with thunder and lightning, but now he was used to it. The guards had been there for nearly a year, since the last prison drop; they'd probably grown used to it too. Another peal of thunder echoed over the valley, followed by a gust of wind that blew warm droplets of water into their faces. The thunderstorm was growing closer.

"Must be," Austin said. "And do you have any bright ideas for getting them off our planet?"

Darrin shook his head. Everyone was armed on Meridian, from five-year-old children to old grannies and granddads …and it hadn't made the slightest bit of difference when the Wolves had arrived. The settlers could overwhelm the POW camp and the spaceport any time they liked, but what would it get them, when the Wolves held the orbital station in their clutches. They'd wiped a couple of farm settlements off the map when they'd first arrived, just to make it clear who was in charge. And they could destroy much of the settled lands in short order, if they wished.

"All we can do is wait and watch," he said, finally. "There's nothing else we can do."

He thought, briefly, about Gary, one of the handful of people forced to work for the occupiers. Gary and he had never really been friends, but he'd hoped that Gary would work with them against the occupiers. Someone working in the spaceport would have been in a good position to spy on the Wolves, yet the bastards had been one step ahead of the settlers all along. They'd taken Kailee as one of their hostages and Gary wouldn't do anything to risk her life.

And that shouldn't be a surprise, he thought, as rain started to patter down around them. *Who would have expected him to wind up with her?*

"So it would seem," Austin said. The rain grew stronger, obscuring their vision. "Let's get down to the shelter and wait."

Darrin nodded and followed his friend back down to the hidden shelter. There, they could wait out the storm and then get back into position until relieved. And then ...

He shook his head. Watching the guards had taught them a great deal about just how careless they were, even on a harmless planet, but none of the intelligence was any use. They'd been idiotic enough to fall into routine patterns, all of which could be used against them ...if the goddamned Sword of Damocles hadn't been hanging over their heads. All they could do was wait, watch and hope that someone bigger and nastier than Wolfbane threw them off the planet before it was too late.

Dropping into the shelter, he leaned against the wall and closed his eyes.

"Wait," Austin said. "What's that?"

Darrin looked up, sharply. Austin had far better hearing than him, as well as a handful of other minor genetic modifications; it was quite likely that Austin could hear something over the downpour, even though Darrin himself could hear nothing. The deluge seemed to be overpowering everything, hammering the shelter so hard that it might collapse, if it hadn't been built by expert carpenters. And yet, Austin could hear something ...

"Come on," Austin said. "Hurry!"

He opened the hatch and led the way into the pouring rain. Darrin sighed, then followed him back towards the vantage point, feeling water cascading down from the skies and soaking his jungle camouflage until it clung to his skin. Lightning flashed high overhead as they reached the vantage point and peered down towards the camp.

"And what," Austin said, "is that?"

Private Victor Toal hated Meridian. It rained all the time, particularly when he was on guard duty, and there was absolutely nothing to do in their free time, apart from watching porn on his datapad and pacing around the edge of the camp. He'd hoped they would be permitted to visit the nearest city, or at least have some fun with one of the prisoners, but they'd been told, in no uncertain terms, that they were to do neither. They weren't even allowed to hire a woman or two from the city to cook, clean and serve them while they were off-duty. And, to add insult to injury, the lucky bastards on the orbiting station had far more leeway to do as they pleased.

But he knew better than to question orders. He'd been inducted into the army after he'd lost his part-time job on Wolfbane and he'd seen enough examples of just what happened to people who questioned orders to keep his mouth firmly closed at all times. The sergeants who'd trained him had forced anyone who dared ask questions to perform hundreds of push-ups, while later officers had shot men who'd asked questions on active duty. All he could do was carry out his orders and hope the next posting, wherever it was, had beaches, babes and no actual enemies.

He reached the top of the tower and nodded to Private Guzman, who passed him the binoculars with a smirk. Victor glowered at him; the lucky bastard could go back to the barracks and have a lie-down, before cooking something inedible for dinner. The settlers had plenty of food, he knew from bitter experience, but the guards weren't allowed to eat any of it, just because it might be poisoned. Victor knew it was nonsense - the POWs had eaten heartily without getting ill - yet, again, he dared not question orders. He'd just have to put up with rations until they were finally sent home.

"Most of the buggers have gone inside," Guzman said, in his horrible accent. Victor had no idea where he'd come from, before he'd been conscripted into the army, but it had to be somewhere right off the beaten track. "Just a couple of fuckers at the edge of the fence, staring at the jungle."

Victor looked ...and sighed. They weren't women and that was all he cared about. A downpour turned the shapeless prison outfits into clingy bathing costumes, but there were no women in view. If they couldn't touch, at least they could look ...he shook his head, then half-heartedly scanned the barracks for signs of trouble. The prisoners hadn't tried anything in five years, but he knew better than to slack off *too* much. If the CO saw him taking a nap in his tower, or ogling women for longer than a minute or two, he knew he would be in for a beating.

A scream split the air, dragging his attention towards one of the nearest barracks. A naked woman - *two* naked women - were running out of the barracks, screaming as though the hounds of hell were after them. Victor stared, watching in awe as their breasts bounced, trying to catch a glimpse of the space between their legs. The women were trying to cover themselves as they ran …a man appeared, running after them, his pants hanging down around his knees. Victor couldn't help laughing as he tripped over his pants and fell face-first in the mud. Another man, wearing a pair of orange underpants and nothing else, followed the women, screaming something incoherent about strip poker and bets being bets. He tripped over the first man and fell on top of him, while the women ran, screaming and giggling, towards the end of the fence.

Idiots, Victor thought, as he adjusted his binoculars as the women ran past him. They didn't look bad for girls who had been trapped in the camp for five years; their buttocks still looked shapely, as if they'd been working out constantly. He followed them as the men picked themselves up and gave chase, still screaming about bets. No doubt they'd been playing games with the women, Victor decided, and now the bitches were trying to welsh out of the agreement. Maybe they'd offered to put out if they lost the game.

He watched the men as they chased the women in and out of the next set of barracks, alternatively helped and impeded by other prisoners as they stepped out into the open air, despite the falling drizzle. The other guards were watching too and calling out bets, trying to guess when the women would be caught and what would happen to them *when* they were caught. Victor wasn't sure *what* the guards should do if the prisoners started to fight each other; their orders were to keep the POWs safe, but also never to go into the camp itself.

"Get a hose," he said, as one of the women slipped on the mud and fell to her knees. Mud clung to her skin as she scrambled upwards, just before one of the men caught her and started to drag her back towards the barracks. "We might need to separate them before it goes too far."

"Or we could just watch," another guard said. "This is better than porn!"

"That's because you've watched everything a million times over, wanker," Victor said. The CO would not be happy if they woke him for anything short of a mass break-out, but he was starting to feel there was no alternative. "Get some more the next time you go home."

He snickered as the woman kicked her captor in the chest, then broke free and started to run again, mud slipping down her chest and clinging to her breasts. The other woman appeared at the far end of the barracks, shouted something rude about the man's lack of manhood, then vanished again as the other man gave chase. Victor laughed and settled down to watch the show.

Kailee had always been scared.

It was something she had had to learn to live with, growing up on Earth. There was no such thing as safety for a teenage girl - or anyone else, for that matter. A person could be attacked, raped or even murdered in the giant CityBlocks and no one would really give a damn. She had known girls in her class who had been forced to have sex by boys and others who had just vanished one day, with only rumours to mark their passing. All she had been able to do was dream of escape …

…And she had escaped, only to wind up in another nightmare.

It didn't seem fair, somehow. She had survived a crash, a thug who had raped her and a gang of bandits who might have done worse, only to wind up a hostage for her boyfriend's good behaviour. They'd told her, when they'd taken her into custody, that she would be unharmed as long as Gary behaved himself, but she'd known they were lying. Even if they never touched her, the certainty that she'd lost control of her life once again had destroyed her fragile stability. She'd dated Gary, she'd fallen in love with Gary, because he would never attempt to control her. She'd studied with Austin's sister, she'd learned to shoot and look after herself …and none of it had mattered because, once again, she was a helpless pawn.

And now a new woman had arrived, offering her the chance to escape.

She wasn't sure what to make of it. On one hand, she didn't want to stay in the camp; on the other hand, she hated the idea of risking her life once again. Life might be bad, but it could easily be worse. The guards might decide to use her for sport, the other prisoners might turn on her

...or they might escape, only to be killed for being collaborators. She could easily imagine the locals turning on her, calling her a Dirty Earther who had never truly adapted to Meridian. They had thought of her as a liability long before Wolfbane had arrived.

"It's time," Jasmine said quietly, as she slipped into the barracks. There was a blithe confidence in her movements that Kailee couldn't help admiring - and envying. "Get undressed."

Kailee eyed her, doubtfully. She understood the logic, but she hated the idea of being naked. It made her feel hopelessly vulnerable, when she already felt far too vulnerable for her own peace of mind. If the guards caught them, or a bandit gang ...God alone knew what had happened on the outside, after she had been taken into the camp. It was vaguely possible that Gary and her friends were dead and no one had ever bothered to tell her. Nothing she'd heard from the moment she'd entered the camp had reassured her that Wolfbane was practical enough to release her once her value had dropped to zero...

"Get undressed," Jasmine repeated. She shucked off her own prison outfit at the same time, revealing a lithe muscular body. "Hurry."

Kailee stared, even though she knew it was rude. Jasmine was built like a small man, not a woman. Her breasts were barely larger than a man's, while there wasn't a hint of fat or wasted meat on her body. Hell, if she hadn't been completely naked, Kailee would have wondered if she was looking at a man pretending to be a woman. But she was very definitely female, just ...unfeminine.

"All right," she said. "But can we do this quickly?"

Jasmine shrugged. Kailee nodded back, then removed her outfit and dropped it on the ground. It didn't smell pleasant - she washed and changed as little as possible - but she'd seen it as a way to defend herself, even in the camp. Besides, they'd always been hectored to save water on Earth...

"Come on," Jasmine said. Outside, Kailee could hear someone shouting and screaming loudly. "Leave your shoes and hurry."

Kailee hesitated, then followed Jasmine out into the rain.

CHAPTER FIVE

In addition, the victors of the war would almost certainly seek to try the losers in court, if only to bolster their own claims. Mistreating prisoners, therefore, would come back to haunt the leaders of the losing power.
- Professor Leo Caesius. *The Empire and its Prisoners of War.*

Meridian, Year 5 (PE)
Jasmine heard Kailee gasp behind her as Stewart and Watson, wearing nothing more than their birthday suits, appeared out of the rain. They'd covered themselves with mud, in the hopes it would provide some additional concealment, but the rainwater was washing it off their bare skin at terrifying speed. She glanced at them both, then nodded towards the place they'd picked beside the fence. One way or the other, they were committed.

"Get digging," she muttered, as the sound of female screaming grew louder. There was no way to be *sure* what the guards would do, even if the whole event looked more like fun and games rather than a rape in progress. They *might* have orders not to let the prisoners have too much fun. "Hurry."

Kailee hung back as Watson started to dig, pulling mud out of the ground with his bare hands. Water pooled around him as he kept digging, slowly widening a passage under the wire. Jasmine and Stewart knelt behind him and started digging themselves - it struck her, suddenly, that she must look terribly undignified - until the passage was wide enough for her to slip under the wire. She crawled underneath, careful not to actually touch the metal, then beckoned for Kailee to follow her out of the camp.

The girl had frozen, staring at nothing. "Force her," Jasmine hissed, as the rain started to lighten. "Hurry!"

Stewart grabbed Kailee's arm and pushed her towards the hole, then into it. Jasmine grabbed her arms as soon as she was within reach, then pulled her through a gap that was rapidly filling with muddy water. Stewart followed her, with Watson bringing up the rear; they paused long enough to push more mud into the gap, then hastened towards the jungle. Mud dripped off them as the rain washed their bodies, leaving them bare and alone. Jasmine glanced back at the camp, making sure that no one had seen them, then led the way into the foliage. There was no sign of any pursuit.

Kailee staggered as soon as they were safe, half-falling to the ground. Jasmine sighed impatiently, then nodded to Stewart, who hefted the girl up and over his shoulder. Kailee looked alarmingly thin, even by the standards of the other women in the camp, but then women on Earth had been expected to be pencil-thin. It hadn't been remotely healthy, Jasmine knew, yet fashion had a life and a logic of its own. And besides, someone had probably thought it saved resources.

"No sign of any pursuit," Stewart said. "I think we made it."

"Let us hope they don't count heads," Jasmine agreed. If *she'd* been running a POW camp, she would have held headcounts every morning, noon and night, just to make sure that all the prisoners were where they were supposed to be. "For the moment, we'd better keep moving."

Stewart nodded, then looked at Kailee. "Should we keep carrying her?"

"For the moment," Jasmine said. Kailee didn't seem to be much of a fighter, but that too was a legacy of Earth. It was astonishing how wimpy most of Earth's citizens, male or female, had become. But then, she'd been told that the brave and the bold had set out to conquer a galaxy. "She's our only hope of making contact with the resistance."

She took a long breath, then peered up at the overcast sky. The rain was finally coming to an end - she could see chinks of sunlight burning through the cloud - and once the skies were clear, they could start navigating away from the camp. It was impossible to be sure, but they had seen aircraft flying over the complex, heading south, and it seemed likely there was *something* there, either a farm or a small settlement. Once they made contact with the locals, their options would get better.

Or we will simply be betrayed, she thought. Conduct After Capture had focused on denying as much as possible to her captors, but Escape And Evasion had warned of the dangers of making their way through hostile territory. The civilians might be friendly, or hostile ...and they might be afraid to do anything but call the enemy to catch them. She'd had to make her way through enemy-held territory on the Slaughterhouse and she'd been caught far too many times. They'd all been caught before they'd learned not to take too many chances.

"We move on," she said. "I want to put some more distance between ourselves and the camp before they decide to check for any missing prisoners."

She sighed, inwardly, as they started to walk. It had been too long since she'd carried out a route march, but at least she'd managed to stay in shape. How long had it *been* since she'd run the two kilometre run she'd had to do when she'd entered Boot Camp? They'd been told that the only easy day was yesterday, but she hadn't understood what it meant until she'd realised that the Drill Instructors were upping the pressure every day. She'd joined a class of one hundred recruits, male and female; by the time she'd been accepted at the Slaughterhouse, only nineteen recruits had made it through. And seven of them had quit once they'd seen the Slaughterhouse ...

The mud squelched below their feet as they kept moving, looking around for signs of possible threats. Meridian was a stage-one colony world, Jasmine recalled; the Empire probably wouldn't have cleared it for settlement if there had been any real dangerous native animals living on the planet. But the settlers might easily have imported something dangerous, something that might have developed a taste for human flesh ... her lips quirked as she recalled tales of biological catastrophes, caused by introducing Earth-native vegetation into undeveloped biospheres, but few of those had involved anything dangerous to humans. Rabbits and cockroaches had done more damage than lions and tigers.

"Ouch," Kailee said. "What happened?"

She needs a proper doctor, Jasmine thought. She normally had no time for headshrinkers, but Kailee probably needed therapy. *And perhaps a chance to strike back at her enemies.*

"We made it out," Jasmine said. Kailee probably didn't *like* being carried by a man, but she wasn't protesting. It took her a moment to realise that the girl was too scared to protest. "Do you think you can walk for yourself now?"

Kailee looked down nervously, then smiled weakly. "I think so," she said. "Please."

Stewart put her down gently, then gallantly looked away as Kailee remembered she was naked. She wouldn't have lasted a day in the barracks, Jasmine thought mischievously, as Kailee struggled to cover herself. Modesty went out the airlock on the very first day, along with any illusions about going into Boot Camp on Monday and becoming a super-soldier on Tuesday. It was astonishing just how many would-be Rambo-types never completed Boot Camp, let alone the Slaughterhouse. Becoming a Marine was hard work.

"Take the lead," Jasmine ordered Stewart, who nodded. "I'll bring up the rear."

Kailee eyed her doubtfully, but didn't attempt to suggest that *she* should bring up the rear. It wouldn't have mattered if she had; Jasmine knew she could keep up with the two men, but she didn't dare let Kailee fall behind. Route marches had been hellish until the recruits had gotten into the swing of them …and this was unexplored territory. She nudged the girl forward as Stewart started to walk, then followed her slowly. There was no point in trying to run, not now. They'd just exhaust themselves for nothing.

The rain came to an end, gusts of wind blowing final splashes of water into their faces before fading away into nothingness. Jasmine let out a sigh of relief as she looked up at the blue sky, then at the mountains in the distance. Navigating by the stars would have been impossible, even at night time, but she knew where the mountains were relative to the POW camp. It would allow them to make their way towards the settlement - *possible* settlement, she reminded herself - without delay.

She stopped as *something* ran across the path, then vanished into the undergrowth. It looked like a large mouse or rat, she decided; she wondered, absently, if they tasted good when cooked and eaten. They might have to stop and harvest something to eat, which would have its own risks. It was quite possible that fruit or seeds that looked edible would actually be deadly poison. They'd have to carry out tests, all the time getting hungrier and hungrier ...

"Kailee," she said, slowly, "do you know what's safe to eat?"

"Not everything," Kailee said. "It's been too long since they told us what we could eat."

Stewart glanced back at her. "You live here and you don't know what you can eat?"

Kailee staggered, as if he had struck her a physical blow. Jasmine caught her and held her steady, studying the younger girl thoughtfully. Everything she'd undergone had broken her, piece by piece, until there was no strength or determination left. The merest rebuke would have her in tears, if only because she could fear worse in the future.

"People on Earth don't know where food comes from," she said. It still seemed absurd to her that Earth's citizens couldn't draw a line between the cattle in the farming zones and the beef they ate for dinner, but people could believe anything if it was hammered into their heads from a very early age. Besides, most of Earth's population would have eaten algae-based foodstuffs rather than real meat or vegetables. "It must have been a surprise when you tasted real meat for the first time."

Kailee smiled, slightly. "I threw up," she said. "It was not my proudest moment."

"I imagine it wasn't," Jasmine agreed. She'd known a girl, back home, who had been violently allergic to chicken. No one had taken it seriously, apart from her parents, until she had almost died. Normally, allergies could be treated, but this one had proven surprisingly resistant to all kinds of treatment. "What do you eat normally, when you're at home?"

"I try not to think about it," Kailee said. "How do you cope?"

Jasmine shrugged. She'd grown up on a farm. Her family had learned, quickly, never to get attached to any of the animals, if only because they were eventually slaughtered and turned into dinner. They'd been allowed to keep dogs, but they'd been regarded as part of the family. It hadn't been until she'd gone to Boot Camp that she'd tasted algae-based foods and she'd considered them rather bland. The Marines had practically drowned them in spicy sauce.

"Tell me about Earth," she said, instead. Talking would keep Kailee's mind off their predicament. "What happened towards the end?"

"I didn't see anything special," Kailee said. "All we really know is that Earth ...Earth fell shortly after we left. And that was the end. My family ..."

She shook her head slowly. Jasmine understood. Kailee was clearly lower-class, at best; it was highly unlikely that any of her family had made it out before the end. Just what had happened on Earth was something of a mystery, although the Commonwealth had collected hundreds of thousands of rumours, most of which were contradictory. The only thing known for certain was that Earth had died roughly six months after Stalker's Stalkers had been exiled from the planet.

The Grand Senate did us a favour, she thought, recalling their last nightmarish battle on Earth, against the Nihilists. *We could have been there when the shit hit the fan.*

"My aunt ...I used to think my aunt hated me," Kailee confessed. "She was always telling me off for every little thing, while her husband was a freaking peeping tom. But she gave me credits before I left and told me to enjoy myself. I don't understand her at all."

"She wanted the best for you," Jasmine said. "You should have heard what the Drill Instructors had to say about me, when I started. And everyone else."

"Yeah," Watson said. "My first day at Boot Camp, I managed to run out of the barracks without any trousers on. The Drill Instructor was *very* sarcastic."

Kailee glanced at Jasmine. "Is that true?"

"Probably," Jasmine said. God knew that she'd forgotten pieces of clothing when she'd been awoken and forced to dress at breakneck speed. She still recalled one particularly unlucky recruit being lectured for forgetting to wear her bra. "The first day of Boot Camp is *always* hectic."

"Oh," Kailee said. "How did you handle it?"

"You get used to it," Jasmine said. "You learn to sort out your uniform before you go to bed, then you can just get dressed very quickly when the whistle blows in the morning. And then you learn to get your weapon ready for use, and then …"

She shrugged. "By the time you leave Boot Camp," she added, "all of these little things are second nature to you."

"Or you get your head torn off until they are," Stewart said. "Do you know how long it took me to learn to field-strip my rifle?"

"I read your file," Jasmine said. "You won the shooting award for your class."

"But I still took days to learn how to strip and clean it properly," Stewart said. "The Drill Instructor practically stood over me and glared until I had it down pat."

"They treated you like that?" Kailee asked. "Is that allowed?"

"We all signed up for it," Jasmine said. Part of the reason Earth had so many problems was that no one was actually permitted to discipline children, who rapidly grew into unruly and unemployable teens. She wondered, absently, just how many Marines had come from Earth, before it fell into chaos. Colonel Stalker had been born on Earth, she knew, but she couldn't think of any others. "And if we really couldn't take it, we could just quit."

She looked up as another rumble of thunder echoed out in the distance. "There were times when I thought about just ringing the bell and leaving," she admitted, softly. "But I kept going."

"It doesn't seem fair," Kailee said. "Don't you have altered standards?"

"The universe isn't fair," Stewart pointed out. He nodded to Watson. "I am more experienced than Carl, but Carl is stronger and faster. I'd be wise to take that into account if I had to spar with him, rather than moaning about fairness."

Kailee looked at Jasmine, who nodded. "I'm faster than both of them," Jasmine said, although she wasn't sure if that were still true. "But I dare not try to grapple with them at close quarters. They'd break my neck."

"The enemy doesn't give a damn about any concept of fairness," Stewart said. "If we hamper our own forces, out of a misguided attempt to make the universe fair, we only make it easier for them to hurt us."

Jasmine smiled. "Keep walking," she ordered, as another peal of thunder split the air. "How often does it rain here?"

"Every two hours or thereabouts," Kailee said. "Austin used to say the planet was too close to the sun and there was more water entering the atmosphere, but I wasn't paying close attention."

Jasmine frowned. Did that make sense? She struggled to recall what she knew of how rain was produced, then shook her head. The world wouldn't have been settled if there had been a long-term threat to the colony's survival. Given how intent the Empire had been on saving money, they wouldn't have risked having to evacuate the planet at a later date. Unless there had been corruption involved ...she made a mental note to check on it at a later date, then put it out of her mind. There was no point in worrying about it now.

"I think we should keep going for another hour, then take a break," she said. They could have travelled further, without Kailee, but she didn't want to risk exhausting themselves. "And then ..."

She froze as something changed. Instincts honed at the Slaughterhouse, then strengthened on a dozen different worlds, were screaming, warning her that they were no longer alone. Stewart and Watson were glancing around, their fists balled and ready to fight, while Kailee was staring at her in confusion. Jasmine heard something - or someone - moving behind them, coming up the trail. She cursed mentally, then motioned for Kailee to get down on the ground. The foliage was making it hard for her to see who was coming. Guards? Or someone else who'd make a daring escape? Or ...

Stewart slipped to one side, using hand signals to indicate that he was going to try to flank the newcomer. Jasmine nodded back, ordering Watson to accompany him. If there were guards following them, their only hope was to fight, rather than surrender. The guards wouldn't be so careless a second time. Their superiors would be furious with them for allowing even one escape from the camp.

"Quiet," she hissed at Kailee. It was unlikely the Earth-born girl could escape, even if she had spent the past six years of her life on Meridian. But she had to try. "Stay as low as you can and get ready to run ..."

The figure stepped into view, holding his hands in the air. Jasmine tensed, bracing herself for fight or flight. He was young, the same age as

Kailee, wearing what was clearly intended as jungle camouflage of some kind. There was a nasty scar on his right cheek.

Kailee gasped. "Darrin?"

The newcomer stared. "Kailee?"

CHAPTER SIX

Therefore, all sides benefited, to some extent, from treating POWs reasonably well.
- Professor Leo Caesius. *The Empire and its Prisoners of War.*

Meridian, Year 5 (PE)

Darrin wasn't quite sure he believed his eyes.

It had taken them some time to realise that the entire show in the POW camp was a diversion - and if he was forced to be honest, he would have to admit that it had been Austin who had realised the truth. They'd hastily scanned the rest of the camp, just in time to see a pair of figures slip under the fence and make their muddy way into the jungle. And then they'd given chase, watching carefully for any signs the guards had also noticed …

And then they'd caught up with the escapees and realised that they *knew* one of them.

"Kailee," he said. "It's good to see you again."

Kailee looked paler than he remembered from when she'd been seen as an unattainable ice princess, her naked body alarmingly thin. She'd never put any real weight on, even after growing accustomed to the idea that she didn't have to be thin to be pretty, but now she was thinner than ever. He looked at her companion and found himself staring, despite the presence of two other men. Kailee's companion looked thoroughly odd, even by local standards.

"Darrin," Kailee said. "I …"

She clutched at her companion and tried to hide herself. Darrin looked away, embarrassed and ashamed. Life on Meridian had taught him that some of Earth's social mores were not only disgusting, but wrong … and actively dangerous, when every teenage girl carried a gun.

"My name is Jasmine," the companion said. Her accent was impossible to place; it wasn't Earth's slurred speech or Meridian's clipped precise tones. "We made it out of the camp."

"We saw," Austin said. "I don't think they noticed you were gone, but it's impossible to be sure."

"They're friends," Kailee said, from where she was still hiding her face. *That* was odd, Darrin considered, although he had no idea what had happened to her since she'd been taken hostage. "We can trust them."

"We're part of the resistance," Austin said, as he stepped into view. "And yourselves?"

Jasmine exchanged glances with one of her male companions. "We're former prisoners of war," she said. "Can you escort us somewhere safe?"

"Yes," Austin said. "There's a hidden settlement not too far from here."

He strode past Jasmine, then started to walk onwards. One of the men followed him, showing no difficulty in matching his pace, while the other hung back, watching Darrin without ever quite seeming to look at his face. Darrin couldn't help feeling a little intimidated, remembering Yates and some of the other ex-military personnel he'd met on Meridian. For what was universally regarded, at least on Earth, as a pool for losers, the military seemed to have a habit of turning out competent and dangerous men. But then, Earth had been safe until the crunch came. Meridian forced people to rely on themselves, rather than help from an all-powerful government.

But the government wasn't all-powerful, he thought, as he walked after Jasmine and Kailee, trying to keep his eyes firmly fixed to the ground. *If it had been, Earth would never have fallen.*

"Tell me," Jasmine said, without looking round. "What's the situation in Sabre City?"

It was Austin who answered. "The Wolves don't have many people on the surface, at least not in the city," he said. "But they have us under firm control."

"They must not consider you to be very important," Jasmine said, slowly. "Have they been taking more people hostage?"

"A handful of people from various families," Austin said. "They asked for volunteers for work on the orbital station, but rejected all the applicants we tried to send them."

"Interesting," Jasmine said. "Why did you pick them?"

It was nearly an hour before they approached the hidden settlement, concealed within the jungle. Darrin had been there when the colonial militia had cleared the bandits out, either killing the bastards or sending them to a labour camp; now, the resistance had turned it into a base for their operations. The settlement had already been very well hidden, but the resistance had brought in camouflage netting and hundreds of other surprises, just to keep it safe and secure. A handful of scouts, male and female, were charged with gathering food for the settlement, without leaving any trace of their presence. Darrin had never quite stopped envying the children who'd been *born* on Meridian …

"Into here," Austin said. "I'm afraid we are going to have to ask a doctor to look at you."

"I quite understand," Jasmine said, as they stepped into a large building. "I think you should check Kailee first, though."

"Of course," Austin said.

Darrin smiled as he saw the interior of the building. The scouts had laid blankets on the floor and turned it into a sleeping cabin, then installed a table at one end of the room. A stove sat at the other end, where a young man was cooking stew; there was no point in risking a fire when orbital sensors might pick up on it and wonder why someone was using a fire, hundreds of miles from any known settlement. Austin motioned for Jasmine to put Kailee down on the blankets, then headed over to the cook. They exchanged a few brief words, then the cook passed Austin the spoon and headed out of the building at speed.

"We should be safe here, for the moment," Austin said. "Kailee can have one of the blankets, if she wishes to cover herself. We may also have some clothes for you all to wear …"

"Never mind that now," Jasmine said. She was pacing around the interior of the building, like a caged tiger. "We need to plan our next move."

"Food first," Austin said, firmly. "Darrin, can you get some bread and cheese from the storehouse? And tell the doctor and Scoutmaster Clarence that we need them."

"Of course," Darrin said.

He headed out the door and down towards the storehouse, passing a handful of scouts on the way. It shamed him to realise that the young men and women - the oldest was fourteen, he thought - knew more about survival than he did, even now. Earth hadn't had a Boy Scout Chapter for centuries, ever since the drive for more and more safety had forced the scouts to cut back on their activities until there was nothing left. He couldn't help feeling that it had been a dreadful mistake. Earth wrapped its children in cotton wool - or at least tried to - while Meridian gave them adult responsibilities from a very early age. And Earth's crime rate had been appallingly high, while crime was almost unknown on Meridian. It hadn't taken him long to realise that there was definitely a connection there.

Scoutmaster Clarence looked up at him as he entered the storehouse. He was a tall man, wearing a pair of spectacles and a uniform that couldn't disguise his heavyset bulk. On Earth, he might have been considered overweight, if he'd felt like claiming disability benefits for himself; on Meridian, it was clear that most of his size was muscle. Darrin had wondered, at first, why he led the scouts. It hadn't taken him long to realise that Clarence was respected as well as liked by his followers.

"Darrin," Clarence said.

"We need bread and cheese, then you and the doctor have to come meet our guests," Darrin said. "They made it out of the camp."

Clarence's eyes narrowed. "You're sure they actually escaped?"

"I believe so," Darrin said, and explained what they'd seen. "It would be a great deal of effort to fake such an escape, if they were intended to infiltrate us."

"True," Clarence said. "Still, we must be careful."

The stew smelled very good, but tasted better. Jasmine practically inhaled the first bowl, then took a second and ate it more carefully. Beside her,

Stewart and Watson ate their own stew, while keeping a wary eye on their new friends. There was no doubt that the resistance was inclined to be friendly, but they knew to be careful. The Wolves might threaten an entire city if the former POWs were not returned to the camp, which would force the resistance to surrender their guests at once. And that would be the end of any hope of escape.

She looked up as an older woman, carrying a medical kit in one hand, stepped into the building and smiled at them. "I'm Doctor Cavendish," she said, as she placed the kit on the ground and snapped it open. "I need to give you all a brief check, I'm afraid."

"Treat Kailee first," Jasmine said. It wasn't just kindness; it would let her get a sense of the doctor's competence before she started to inspect the marines. "She's had a rough time."

"The entire planet has had a rough time," the doctor said. She knelt next to Kailee, then started to wave a scanner over her body. "How are you feeling, my dear?"

"Tired," Kailee said. "Do you *have* to poke and prod me?"

"I need to check everything," the doctor said. She pushed a scanner against Kailee's forearm, then frowned at the datapad in her hand. "You've not been eating very well, have you? I'm surprised you managed to walk this far without falling apart."

"I did fall apart," Kailee protested.

The doctor ignored her. "You'll need to take supplements every day for the next two months," she said, firmly. "I'll write you a prescription, then send someone down to the city to get it filled. Make sure you eat three full meals a day, even if you don't feel particularly hungry. You really need to rebuild your strength."

Jasmine concealed her amusement at Kailee's expression with an effort. Someone born on Earth would have been conditioned, from a very early age, to eat as little as possible, all in the name of saving the environment. The schools would have fed the bare minimum, perhaps not even that, while the parents might not have been able to obtain enough food to compensate. To eat three full meals a day would seem an impossible dream.

"Do as she says," she advised. "You are really in a mess."

Kailee sighed, but nodded.

Jasmine allowed the doctor to poke and prod at her, then the other two marines. The doctor didn't have much to say, beyond a concern that Jasmine might be incapable of having children in the future. Jasmine had honestly not thought about the prospect; like other female marines, she'd had eggs removed from her body and held in stasis when she'd made it through Boot Camp, but those eggs had been on the Slaughterhouse. God alone knew what had happened to the training world.

"You should really take better care of yourself," the doctor reproved her, afterwards. "A woman's duty is to produce children to populate the world."

"Depends on where you sit, I suppose," Jasmine said, waspishly. *Her mother had had seven children; her older sister had had five. A woman on Meridian would probably be expected to have as many children as possible, but a woman on Earth would be actively encouraged to sterilise herself.* "And my duty is to get back home."

"I suppose," the doctor said. She looked down at the scanner for a long moment, then smiled at them. "You're healthy, but make sure you eat plenty over the next couple of weeks too. I hate to imagine what the crap they were feeding you was doing to your insides."

"Producing poison gas," Watson said, with a wink. "We had beans for breakfast, beans for lunch and beans for tea. I'm sure that violates some convention on the use of torture on prisoners."

Jasmine shrugged. Under the circumstances, Wolfbane had treated its POWs remarkably well. The Marine Corps had built up the determination never to let someone remain in enemy hands through a grim awareness that any prisoner was likely to be brutally tortured, then murdered. Insurgents throughout the Empire had known, after all, what was likely to happen to any of *them* who fell into enemy hands and they'd been happy to return the favour.

And Admiral Singh tortured you, her own thoughts reminded her. *You've been very lucky this time around.*

"Probably," the doctor said. She paused. "On a different note, you don't seem to have been stung with any tracking bugs, but the gear I have isn't too advanced. I may be wrong."

"I know," Jasmine said. She *thought* they hadn't been stung, but there was no way to be sure without mil-grade scanners and some luck. A bug could be so tiny it could only be seen with a microscope..."We'll just have to take our chances."

"And so you will," the doctor said. She turned towards the door, then stopped. "I'll have some clothes sent in for you, then assign you to one of the huts. I assume you want to stay together?"

"Yes, please," Jasmine said.

"Then you shall," the doctor said. "I'd recommend a day of rest, but if you're anything like Old Hans, you won't want to stay still for a moment."

She walked out of the door. Moments later, Darrin walked in, accompanied by a heavyset man who looked as if he was running to fat. Jasmine eyed him carefully and noted that, despite his girth, he was definitely surprisingly quick and strong. And he had a stance that suggested he knew he was both liked and respected. In some ways, he reminded her of Colonel Stalker.

"Jasmine, this is Scoutmaster Clarence," Darrin said. "He's in charge of the local section of the resistance."

Jasmine rose to her feet, then held out a hand. "Pleased to meet you," she said. Clarence took it and shook her hand firmly. "It's always a pleasure to meet a scout."

Clarence smiled. "And were you ever a scout?"

"Many Marines have been scouts," Jasmine said. She'd never been one herself, but her homeworld hadn't really liked the creed of the Imperial Boy Scouts. "I was a Survivor myself."

"Ah, our dread rivals," Clarence said. He gave her a smile that suggested he hadn't taken offense, then motioned for her to sit down. "As interesting as it would be to compare notes, I don't think we have time. We need to talk, instead, about just how you wound up on this world - and why."

Jasmine nodded. "It's a long story," she said, "but I will do my best."

She hesitated, then started by outlining how the company had been exiled to Avalon - and how they'd started to build the Commonwealth to take the Empire's place, now it was dead and gone. Clarence listened carefully, without interrupting, as she talked about the peace talks that had ended in failure, then the war on Thule. When she finished, he leaned forward and looked her in the eye.

"Your Commonwealth," he said. "Can it liberate our world?"

"I think so," Jasmine said, although in truth she knew it would be hard to be sure of anything now. Perhaps, once the POW camp was liberated, she would sit down with Stubbins and Paula and try to work out some hard numbers for Wolfbane. How many ships had been in the sector when Governor Brown had taken control? "But it may take years."

Clarence's eyes narrowed. "How long?"

"I don't know," Jasmine said. "The war was just starting when we were captured, sir. I don't think the Commonwealth will win or lose quickly; it may take years before one side gains a decisive advantage. The front will probably surge backwards and forwards hundreds of times before then."

She sighed. "I wish I could give you a timetable for the liberation of your world," she added, "but I can't. All I can do is plan our escape and do it in a manner that ensures you can't be blamed for helping us."

"I see," Clarence said. "And what if we decided that it was too dangerous to risk allowing you to make a try for escape?"

"We would respect your decision," Jasmine lied. She knew she couldn't find a place to live on Meridian and stay out of the war, but she couldn't blame the resistance for having second thoughts about allowing them to risk the entire world. "If you truly wanted us to do nothing, we would find work here and stay out of sight."

Darrin took a step forward. "Wouldn't that get you in deep shit when you got home?"

"Maybe," Jasmine said. There was no *maybe* about it. Failing to try to escape could be considered a court martial offense. "But I won't endanger your world without your permission."

"We will discuss the matter and make our decision known to you," Clarence said. He rose to his feet. "Austin will show you to your hut. I would ask you to wait there until we have made up our minds."

Jasmine rose. "Of course," she said. "We need to rest anyway."

She allowed Austin to lead her through the settlement and into a smaller hut, with a handful of blankets lying on the floor. There was no sign of anything else, apart from a primitive shower and toilet in the rear. She guessed that the scouts probably cleaned up their campsites pretty thoroughly, like the Marines had been taught during Escape And Evasion.

"We'll make sure Kailee is fine," Austin promised as he turned to leave. "And I'll have clothes sent to you."

"Please," Stewart said. "My ass is going red from all the stares."

Austin smiled. "We don't normally have guests here," he said. "You're the first since this settlement was converted into a base camp."

Jasmine watched him go, then sighed. "Get some sleep," she ordered. They were in seemingly friendly territory, but there was no point in taking risks. "I'll take the first watch."

CHAPTER SEVEN

> However, this tended to run into other problems. For example, the early attempts to codify the laws of war found it hard to identify soldiers. They wore uniforms, true, but what happened when they didn't wear uniforms?
> - Professor Leo Caesius. *The Empire and its Prisoners of War.*

Avalon, Year 5 (PE)

When I come to write my memoirs, Ed thought, as he stepped into the briefing room, *I will leave this year out completely.*

He pasted a smile on his face as the councillors rose to greet him. It seemed that he spent half his time in meetings and the other half attending or giving briefings, either to councillors who didn't understand what he was talking about or reporters who - if considerably better than the reporters who had infested the Empire - seemed to think they had a need to know absolutely everything. At least the Commonwealth had some pretty strong penalties for reporters who learned something they shouldn't and told the entire universe. God alone knew how many enemy intelligence operations back in the old days had consisted of nothing more than scanning the Empire's newspapers.

"Thank you for coming," he said, keeping his voice level. He'd dealt with worse people, including the Grand Senate, and most of the Commonwealth's politicians had some real experience of the outside universe. They might be stubborn and suspicious of interstellar alliances, but they had some common sense. "If you will take your seats, we can begin."

He slid the datachip into the room's processor, then turned to look at the councillors. None of them *looked* guilty, but one of them had to be a spy. Who? He glanced at Gordon Travis, who looked back at him with cool regard, then at Marilyn Morrison. The latter had a good record of keeping small businesses going, despite the wars with both the bandits and the Crackers. It seemed unlikely that she would betray her homeworld, but God knew just how many seemingly-loyal people had turned their coat. And then there was Thomas O'Rourke and Howard Malevich …Ed honestly couldn't say he knew either of them very well.

O'Rourke is a farmer, he reminded himself, *and not someone to take much interest in the outside universe. Malevich is a builder threatened by competition from the rest of the Commonwealth. Might they each have a separate motive to turn traitor?*

He sighed inwardly as he keyed the processor and displayed a holographic starchart in front of the assembled councillors. He'd trained to fight in battle, from stand-up encounters with the enemy to the far more common insurgencies launched in the midst of a civilian population, not to track down an enemy spy. No doubt whoever he was seeking was skilled in deceit …he wished, suddenly, that there had been more time to assemble a counter-intelligence service before the war had started. But it was far too late for regrets. He'd played his cards the best he could and now all he could do was muddle through and hope for the best.

While preparing for the worst, he thought, sardonically. *And who knows what a witch-hunt will do to us?*

He could trust his fellow Marines, he knew. He could trust Gaby; if she'd wanted to sell out the Commonwealth, she could have done it without slipping information to the enemy. But who else could he trust? The remains of the Civil Guard? The Knights? Assorted local militia who felt they'd been overridden by the Commonwealth? The Traders? There were just too many places for a spy - or even a *rumour* of a spy - to cause havoc. It made him wonder if they'd been *allowed* to pick up the message, just to spread distrust and paranoia among his people …

Stop that, he told himself, firmly. He'd definitely been away from the battlefield for too long, even if he *was* needed on Avalon. *Any more paranoia and you will go mad.*

"I am obliged to warn you that the following data is considered classified and must not be shared," he said, without any other preamble. "Please don't talk about it, even amongst yourselves, outside a sealed room. We cannot allow word to spread to the enemy."

He paused, then began.

"The war front appears to be stabilising," he said, although he knew that most of the reports were three weeks out of date. So far, no one - not even the Trade Federation - had been able to enhance FTL speeds, let alone send messages from star to star without a starship to carry them. "We lost control of Elder, councillors, but we regained control of Preston and successfully contested Elision. In Preston's case, the Wolves were unable to secure control of the system before we evicted them."

He watched the councillors carefully as he went on. "There were two more long-range exchanges of fire between our respective task forces," he continued, "but both engagements were inconclusive. In the first encounter, the enemy decided we had the advantage and saw fit to retreat; in the second, both sides were apparently evenly matched. There were several volleys of missile fire before both sides broke contact.

"However, there have been signs that the Wolves have been probing the Harper system," he said. That was true. "As we have stationed a mobile foundry in the system, to support our war effort, I have ordered the dispatch of an additional squadron to the system to provide cover if the foundry needs to be withdrawn."

And that, he knew, was *not* true. Harper was largely useless, at least until someone invested in a cloudscoop and several hundred thousand new colonists. There was nothing particularly special about the asteroid belt, while the settlers were largely farmers who paid their Commonwealth dues in food and drink. Any CO who stationed a mobile foundry in the system, particularly one on loan from the Trade Federation, would be swiftly relieved of duty for gross incompetence. It wasn't as if Harper could afford the bribes it would take to convince an Imperial Navy CO to declare the system important ...

But it would be interesting to see if that particular titbit of information made its way to the transmitter .

It was an opportunity, he knew. The Wolves would have only a couple of weeks to take advantage of it before the mythical squadron arrived. They'd need to send a small task force of their own to the system, in hopes of catching the foundry before it was withdrawn ...and, as there was nothing to find, it would tie up one of their task forces for a few weeks. But the opportunity would be very limited ...

"Colonel," Gordon Travis said. "I was under the impression that the treaty we signed with the Trade Federation specifically states that the foundry ships are not to be risked."

Ed kept his expression blank with the ease of long practice. It was a shame that Travis was on the other side, a political opponent if not an outright enemy. He was smart, perceptive and alarmingly competent. God knew the Commonwealth's industrial base wouldn't be as strong without him and his fellows, businessmen who had been able to expand now the dead hand of the Empire's rules and regulations was gone. But he was also determined to wrest control of the Commonwealth away from Gaby and her allies.

"The war has changed some of our agreements," he said, instead. The Trade Federation wasn't exactly fighting by their side, but it had gone a long way to help the Commonwealth fight the war. "The foundry ship is required to produce war material that can be shipped directly to the front, rather than produced here and forwarded to ships and bases that may no longer be there."

"That is understandable," Travis said. "But surely the risk of a diplomatic incident isn't worth the advantages of keeping the ship there?"

Ed gritted his teeth, then forced himself to relax. Was Travis merely trying to make political hay out of a controversial decision ...or was he standing up for Avalon's industrial base, which stood to lose a considerable amount of money if the Trade Federation handled most of the industrial production? In the long run, they had nothing to fear; in the short term, it might be disconcerting.

"With all due respect, Councillor," he said, "the consequences of losing the war will be a great deal worse than a minor diplomatic incident."

He waited to see if Travis would disagree, but the councillor didn't seem inclined to say anything further. Instead, he just waited.

"Training programs have been accelerated on all threatened worlds," Ed continued. *They* were no secret, not if the Wolves were monitoring the Commonwealth's media. "I do not expect local resistance cells to be able to force the enemy off their planets, but it will force Wolfbane to tie down its armies to keep the planets under control. Furthermore, we have organised evacuation programs for skilled manpower …"

"Which causes no end of disruption," Councillor Bunche muttered.

"Better that than losing their services," Travis sneered. He looked at Ed. "Has there been any change in the reports from Thule?"

"No, Councillor," Ed said. "The Wolves are still rounding up every scrap of trained manpower they can find. Those who can't help to rebuild Thule's industrial base are being shipped back into enemy territory."

"Stands to reason we should be probing enemy territory," Travis said. "Is there a reason you're not?"

He was right, Ed reflected, sourly. The Commonwealth *was* probing enemy territory. But it wasn't something he wanted to discuss, not when he didn't know who he could trust. The enemy had to know the Commonwealth was trying to locate their worlds - or at least identify which ones had become industrial powerhouses - but they wouldn't be certain which worlds had been surveyed.

"The navy is hard-pressed at the moment," he said, which was true. "Our plans to survey enemy space have been badly delayed."

He paused. "With your permission, I will continue," he added. "Military production levels …"

When he finished, he was surprised by a question from Councillor Morrison.

"Colonel," she said, "has there been any news regarding POWs?"

Ed winced. He knew, all too well, that several hundred Commonwealth personnel had gone into enemy captivity after the Battle of Thule … and countless others had been scooped up as the Wolves advanced into Commonwealth territory. The Wolves had promised to treat them well, but he had his doubts. Governor Brown was a product of the Empire, after all, and the Empire's normal attitude to POWs had never been kind.

"No, Councillor," he said, bluntly. "We have attempted to open discussions regarding either an exchange of prisoner lists or a direct exchange of prisoners, but we have been rebuffed on both counts. I suspect they have calculated that holding so many of our prisoners not only gives them leverage, it gives them a definite advantage. Their manpower levels may well be much higher than our own."

Morrison frowned. "Is there no way we can force them to give up their POWs?"

"Not until we win the war," Ed said. "That's the only way we can force them to the negotiating table."

Colonel Kitty Stevenson knew she was competent, although the entry her superior officer had entered into her permanent record had been enough to ensure she would not only never see promotion again, but be exiled to the very edge of explored space. The asshole had seen her as an easy lay, as someone who would trade sex for a promotion …and when she'd declined, he'd set out to make an example of her. Maybe he'd succeeded, the nasty part of her mind thought, but there was a good chance he'd been stuck on Earth when the end came.

And part of her rather liked Avalon. It wasn't as sophisticated as Earth, or any of the Core Worlds, but it was a decent place to live. She'd set out to do her duty, even before the Marines had arrived, hoping to embarrass her former superior. Even now, knowing she would never see the man again, part of her enjoyed *proving* her competence. Spy-catching was long slow work, but it was fun.

"Colonel," she said, when Edward Stalker stepped into her office. "Did you record the meeting?"

"I did," the Colonel said. "There were twelve people in attendance, not including me."

Kitty allowed herself a tight smile. There had been hundreds of possible suspects, but - if the tale about the foundry ship reached the transmitter - there would be only twelve. And the story *was* urgent, if the Wolves planned to take advantage of it. They would have to send the message off-planet within two days if they didn't want it to be anything more than a historical curiosity.

"I understand you're giving another briefing tomorrow," she said, after a moment. "Can we insert another false fact into the briefing?"

"Of course," the Colonel said, dryly. "Just make one that will definitely attract attention."

Kitty nodded, then looked down at the transcribed message they'd intercepted. She'd tried to narrow the suspect list down still further, but she had to admit she'd failed utterly. The spy seemed to have an odd set of priorities; there were some military titbits buried in the message, yet most of it was centred on politics and political relationships. Apparently, Councillor Hammond and Councillor Burton were having an affair. It would be embarrassing if the affair was revealed, Kitty was sure, but it would hardly be disastrous ...

Or would it? Hastily, she pulled up the voting records and ran a comparison check. Councillor Hammond and Councillor Burton had voted together seven times in the last four months, which meant ...what? Did they agree with each other or was one changing his vote to please the other? And if so, what did his constituents think of it? Hammond was married, if she recalled correctly, and colonists tended to be more intolerant of adultery than Earthers.

Maybe the information is meant to imply blackmail, she thought. *But it wouldn't really cost them anything beyond their posts if it became public ...*

Colonel Stalker cleared his throat. "Do you have anything else for me?"

Kitty blinked, feeling her face heat. She always lost track of everyone else in the room when she was considering the puzzle in front of her.

"I've been working on trying to eliminate as many suspects as possible," she said, "but I have not been able to eliminate more than a handful. Councillor Martin's son *may* be a POW, sir, but as we have no way to exchange prisoner lists with the Wolves there's no way to be sure."

"Councillor Morrison asked me about the POWs," Colonel Stalker said, slowly. "Could she have been influenced by him?"

"She may well have several constituents who have lost people to POW camps," Kitty said. It wasn't something she'd considered, but she made a mental note to add it to her list of possibilities. "Someone with a potential hostage in enemy hands could be our spy."

Colonel Stalker frowned. "How many people would that include?"

"From the senior leadership? It depends on the factors," Kitty said. "There's several politicians who have relatives who may be in POW camps - I can give you a list, if you like. Then there's people who have friends ... you would be on that list, sir. Brigadier Yamane was your protégée."

"I see," the Colonel said, tightly.

He looked down at the transcribed message, then shook his head. "I have work to do, so I will be back tomorrow," he added. "Let me know if you manage to isolate a suspect."

Kitty looked at the files as he left the office, closing the door behind him. The encrypted message still struck her as odd, as if the writer was more used to thinking in terms of politics than military affairs. But there were only a handful of people on the council who had any pre-independence political experience, if one counted the Crackers as politicians ...

But they weren't, she thought, *not really. Internal insurgency politics are very different from the Empire's politics ...*

"Maybe it isn't someone on the military oversight boards," she muttered. "Just someone on the political side alone."

She turned to her list of suspects and started to work her way through the facts. The Commonwealth had never bothered to collect vast amounts of data on each citizen, which left her with tantalisingly little to go on. Her handful of agents were collecting information as fast as they could, but there were simply too many gaps in the datafiles for her to say anything for sure. She wasn't even certain just how many of her suspects had children, let alone where those children actually were ...

"It must be someone who thinks he can benefit from us losing the war," she mused, slowly. It narrowed the list of suspects, slightly. "Someone who thinks he can make himself useful to the enemy. Someone in a good position to collaborate."

One by one, she worked out a list of suspects. Gordon Travis had a good reason to hate the Commonwealth ...and, as a wealthy and capable businessman, had a proven track record Wolfbane could use. So did Morrison and Malevich ...and around thirty more, all of whom had to be considered suspects. All she could do was wait and see which false piece of information was forwarded to the enemy. That would allow her to narrow the list of suspects considerably.

She shook her head, tiredly. Until then, she could keep tracking their movements. Perhaps one of them would make a covert visit to a data centre, one suitable for inserting a message into the transmitters. It would be nice if one did …

But she had a feeling that it wouldn't be anything like that easy.

CHAPTER EIGHT

This caused problems for anyone intent on following the laws of war. Was the man looking at the advancing troops from a distance, wearing civilian clothes, a spotter calling in long-range fire or merely a curious civilian? How were they meant to respond when it was clear that the opposing side was pretending to be civilians right up until the moment they opened fire?
- Professor Leo Caesius. *The Empire and its Prisoners of War.*

Meridian, Year 5 (PE)

"There are worse places to stay, I suppose," Stewart said.

"I suppose," Jasmine agreed. They'd spent two days in the hut and, despite herself, she was growing impatient. The longer they remained at large, the greater the chance someone would notice they were missing from the camp. "But I would like to be on our way home."

She sighed, then looked at the paper books they'd been given to read. The scout manual was tame, compared to the marine survival guides they'd been forced to memorise as recruits, but the guidebook to Meridian had contained a great deal of useful, if outdated, information. In some ways, she could see the attraction of settling down on a colony world, well away from the Empire's mainstream. But it wouldn't have lasted indefinitely.

"They're checking us out, I suspect," Watson said, from where he was leaning against the wood. "They may feel we're spies ourselves."

Jasmine nodded, ruefully. If two days weren't enough to convince the resistance to help them, she wasn't sure what she could do. They'd have to break free, then make their own way to the spaceport, something that would ensure they'd be hunted by both the resistance and the occupation force. And the resistance would know the lay of the land much better than any of the Marines. She hadn't failed to note that they hadn't been given precise maps of the countryside.

"Or trying to determine if they dare help us," she agreed. "They're totally naked if the bastards decide to start dropping rocks from orbit."

She gritted her teeth. She'd always felt sorry for civilians caught in the midst of war zones, particularly the ones who had come out of hiding to help the Empire's forces. They tended to be abandoned to the tender mercies of their fellows, once the Empire had completed its mission - or at least claimed the mission was completed - and withdrew its forces. There had been times, early in her career, when she'd wondered why *anyone* dared help the Empire, knowing they would be left to their fate. Perhaps they'd dreamed of a better life without the insurgents who'd made their lives hell.

"It could be worse," Stewart said. "We could be running around the countryside, completely naked."

Jasmine had to laugh. "Yeah," she said, as she heard someone at the door. "We could be naked."

She rose to her feet as the door opened, revealing Darrin. He'd spoken to them once or twice since they'd been asked to stay in the hut, but he hadn't known anything particularly useful or informative. As a first-gen immigrant from Earth, he probably wasn't trusted completely by the locals, no matter how much he'd done to prove himself. The planet's home-grown culture would probably have responded badly to newcomers from Earth, particularly someone they regarded as useless.

But they made him part of the resistance, she thought. *They must have some faith in him.*

"Clarence will be along in a few minutes," Darrin said. "I think he finally received word from higher up the chain."

Jasmine nodded. She wasn't surprised that there was more than one resistance cell on the planet - and that the lines of communication were rather vague. The Empire had plenty of experience in cracking resistance networks that were strictly hierarchical, simply by capturing one member and then working their way up the chain. A diffuse network had more chance of remaining intact, once the counter-intelligence goons got to work.

But they might also have differences of opinion, she thought, sardonically. The Crackers had split after the peace talks, with some factions deciding to fight on rather than accept a share in power. *One cell might want to go in one direction, while another might have different ideas.*

"That's good to hear," Stewart said. "And Kailee?"

"She's recovering, very slowly," Darrin said. "She didn't have an easy time of it here."

Jasmine was mildly surprised. In her experience, the Earth-born tended to be immensely selfish and utterly lacking in empathy. For Darrin to concede that someone had had a hard time ...it said good things about him, she decided. But then, if half of Kailee's story was true, he and his friends had all had to grow up in a hurry. And one of them hadn't made it.

"Being trapped for so long couldn't have been good for her," Stewart agreed. "Make sure she gets plenty of support and encouragement."

The door opened again. Clarence stepped into the room, looking tired. "There was some disagreement on how to proceed," he said. "The short and final answer was that you could proceed, as long as we are not implicated in your scheme. We won't risk the planet just to get you and your fellows home."

"You have a choice between helping us and having the Wolves breathing down your necks for the rest of your lives," Watson said, sharply.

Clarence gave him a sharp look. "When your side has a fleet of starships in the system, you can talk to us," he said. "Until then, I am disinclined to risk my family and friends on a mad scheme to break us free of an interstellar power."

Jasmine nodded. "We understand," she said, shooting Watson a warning glance. No matter what they did, Wolfbane would eventually notice that *something* was wrong and send a ship to investigate. At that point, if the Wolves decided to blame the planet's settlers, Meridian would be hammered into rubble from orbit. "We will make them think we were acting alone."

"Good," Clarence said. "It's a minimum of five days from here to Sabre, assuming we stay away from the main roads. We'll escort you down to the city and then let you sort out your own plans."

"We will need Kailee's help," Jasmine said, after a moment. There was just too much to learn in too little time. "And her boyfriend too."

"If they are willing to help, they can," Clarence said. "But again, we cannot risk being implicated in your actions."

"Blame everything on the Earthers," Darrin said.

"I intend to," Clarence said. "And I am sorry."

He looked back at Jasmine. "We have food, drinks and packs for you," he said. "I think you should depart as soon as possible."

Jasmine nodded. They hadn't seen the sun since they'd been asked to stay in the hut, but she was fairly sure it was early morning. Good; they could make a solid start on the march before they holed up for the night. It wouldn't be anything like as bad as route marches and death trails on the Slaughterhouse, she was sure. They'd need tents to keep the rain off their heads while they slept, but they had practice in carrying plenty of weight.

"I'll get them organised," Darrin said. He smiled at Jasmine. "Kailee and I will be coming back to the city too."

The settlement looked deserted when Jasmine emerged, blinking rapidly, into the sunlight and looked around. There had been young children, all scouts, playing in the village; now, they were all gone, along with most of the adults. A pair of men wearing jungle camouflage watched them closely, Clarence and Austin were standing with the doctor, but no one else was in sight. It was clear the resistance had largely decided to abandon the settlement, just in case. Jasmine felt a pang of guilt, which she ruthlessly suppressed. Meridian's only hope for freedom lay in help from the Commonwealth.

"I should have an intelligence packet waiting for you when you arrive," Clarence said. "We have been gathering intelligence on the enemy, but … most of it is arguably useless."

"We'll see," Jasmine said. She'd been taught there was no such thing as useless intelligence, but she had her doubts. Information on enemy terrain or political geography was always useful, yet other intelligence briefings had been definitely useless. Who gave a damn about the environmental impact of an engagement two years ago? "It might be quite helpful."

"Check the packs," Clarence ordered, as he indicated where they were lying on the ground. "If there's anything else you need, let us know now."

Jasmine nodded, then picked up and opened her pack. It felt surprisingly light to her, after a lifetime of carrying full combat loads from place to place, but it held everything she could imagine needing. There was a small selection of ammunition, plenty of ration bars, flasks of water and purification tablets, just in case they needed to drink from streams or ponds. At the bottom, there was a small medical kit. It was surprisingly comprehensive - and packed in waterproof packaging. She had a feeling they were going to need it.

"We arranged for a number of rifles to …go missing from a nearby farm," Austin said. "The owners have gone into hiding, so if anyone checks it should look as though you raided the farm, killed everyone and took whatever you needed. I would advise you not to talk about that with anyone else, though, if it can be avoided. Shooting bandits on sight is considered perfectly legal."

Jasmine made a face as she took the hunting rifle and checked it, carefully. Living off the land was one thing, but stealing from civilians quite another. They'd been told, more than once, that there would be times when they would have no choice, but she'd never liked the idea. They might wind up stealing seed corn or vital - and irreplaceable - supplies from helpless men and women. And, once they got into the habit of stealing, they might never be able to break it.

"Thank you," she said, instead. She pulled her pack over her back, then tested it carefully. It definitely felt lighter than a standard combat load. "Shall we go?"

"One moment," Darrin said. "Kailee's just getting ready."

"Make sure she takes her pills, every time," the doctor warned. "She's on the verge of simply giving up completely, something made worse by her lack of proper food. I think she will get better once she has a few dozen meals inside her, but right now she has little to live for."

"Gary will be glad to see her," Darrin said. "I know he hasn't strayed in the years since she was taken."

Jasmine smiled as Kailee appeared, looking thin and pale in her jungle outfit. Her eyes were firmly fixed on the ground, as if she didn't dare look anyone in the face. Jasmine sighed inwardly, noting how she shied away from the men. It might well be a long time before Kailee recovered from her imprisonment.

"Walk with me," Jasmine said. She had to seem appallingly unfeminine to the younger girl, but at least she was a woman. "The others can lead the way."

"Of course," Austin said. "I will take point; Darrin can bring up the rear."

Jasmine kept a sharp eye on Kailee as they walked out of the settlement and down a half-hidden trail, concealed from orbital sensors by the jungle canopy. The gloom descended rapidly, casting the trail into shadow; she couldn't help glancing around, even though the guidebooks had reassured her that there were few dangerous animals apart from packs of feral dogs. Austin set a good pace, but she'd been forced to walk harder and faster on the Slaughterhouse. But then, they weren't being chased by an opposition force this time.

"I could almost enjoy this walk," Stewart muttered, as he dropped back to pace beside Jasmine. "But we could go faster."

"I think Kailee won't be able to keep up with us," Jasmine said, practically. If worst came to worst, someone could carry the girl, but it wasn't something she would have preferred to do. "Besides, we are going to be walking for several days."

She glanced at Kailee, then withdrew into her own thoughts. There were plenty of options for when they reached Sabre, but she didn't know enough about the situation on the ground to pick one. What were the occupation forces doing? Did they know four of their prisoners had escaped? In truth, she knew it would be impossible to answer those questions until they reached the city.

And if they are on the lookout for escapees, she thought, *our task will become much harder.*

High overhead, she heard the sound of thunder. Darkness descended rapidly, followed by a pouring shower that rapidly drenched all of them. Jasmine took Kailee's arm as she started to slip and slide as the ground turned to mud, then helped her along the way as the rainfall grew heavier. Small animals appeared from nowhere, running around their feet, then vanishing back into the undergrowth as the rain finally came to an end. She glanced up and saw chinks of sunlight peeking through the canopy.

"They should call this world Rainfall," Stewart muttered. "Or simply Wet."

"Wetter Than Thou," Watson offered.

"There are supposed to be places where it doesn't rain," Darrin said. He looked to be coping with the walk better than Jasmine had expected, for someone from Earth. "But most settlements were built in the tropical zone."

Stewart glanced back at him. "Do you know why?"

"Some of the earlier settlers preferred to use boats and fish rather than farm," Austin said, "or so I was told. There was definitely some confusion over the best place to set up farms and settlements. But we actually have two harvests in a year and plenty of other advantages, living here. There's just an awful lot of rainfall."

They stopped long enough to eat ration bars and take a drink of water, then resumed the hike as water splashed down around them. Jasmine found herself almost enjoying the march, despite the weight on her shoulders and the need to keep a constant eye on Kailee, who seemed to have withdrawn completely into herself. It was surprisingly like her homeworld, apart from the ever-pouring rain. She felt a touch of homesickness, which she pushed away savagely. She'd known she might never see her home and family again even before she was sent to Avalon.

"We're approaching the first campsite," Austin said. "Do you want to set up here for the night or carry on for another hour?"

Jasmine glanced at Kailee. "Stay here, I think," she said. The Marines could have gone on for several hours, but Kailee was not in a good state and Darrin didn't look much better. "We can press on tomorrow."

"No campfire, of course," Darrin said. He gave Austin a tired smile. "Do we at least get to sing songs?"

"Yep," Stewart said. He threw back his head and started to bellow. "Oh, up in the north, there lived a great …"

"I think they're not old enough to hear that song," Jasmine interrupted, quickly. It started out as rude and went downhill from there. "And besides, you can't sing."

"Of course I can," Stewart objected. "I'll have you know the Drill Instructors wanted to turn my singing into a training tool. They were going to play it to young recruits who weren't showing enough enthusiasm."

"And there I was thinking it was going to be played to prisoners," Watson said, as they entered the clearing. "A few hours of hearing your caterwauling and they'd be begging us to let them confess."

Jasmine concealed her amusement as she unslung her pack, then started to dig out the tent while Kailee collapsed to the ground. She'd have very sore feet in the morning, Jasmine suspected, remembering her first week at Boot Camp. There had been odd bruises popping up all over her body until she'd grown used to pushing herself to the limits. And Kailee hadn't had a chance to walk for nearly five years.

"We can't set up a fire," Austin said, once the two tents were erected. "There's too great a risk of attracting attention. But I suppose we could sing, if you wanted."

A loud peal of thunder split the sky. "I think God is saying no," Watson said, with a rude snicker. "And some of us should really get some sleep."

"True," Jasmine agreed. She dug more ration bars out of her bag and ate one, then practically force-fed a second bar to Kailee. The younger girl looked unhappy, but reluctantly ate and then took a swig of water and a handful of pills. "I'll put Kailee to bed, then get some sleep myself. Carl, if you take watch, wake me up in four hours and I'll take over from you."

"Understood," Watson said. He hefted his rifle, then sat down outside the larger tent. "Do you think we're in any danger?"

"There used to be quite a bandit camp up here," Austin said. He picked up a shovel, obviously intent on finding somewhere to answer the call of nature. "There may still be stragglers, if they escaped the sweep afterwards."

Jasmine leaned forward. "What happened to them?"

Austin shrugged. "Most of them were indentured prisoners who fled rather than work off their debts," he said. "I have a feeling that any survivors would have tried to hide, rather than attack the newer settlements. But I honestly don't know for sure."

"Keep a sharp eye out," Jasmine ordered, as the rain started to fall once again. She urged Kailee into the tent, then sighed. They were going to have a damp night. "And wake me in four hours."

The following morning, after eating a brief breakfast, they started on their way again.

CHAPTER NINE

And when this happened, civilians died. They were shot down by advancing troops, who believed them to be insurgents or terrorists.
- Professor Leo Caesius. *The Empire and its Prisoners of War.*

Meridian, Year 5 (PE)
There were few times in Gary's life that he could honestly say he'd lived without fear.

Maybe he had felt no fear as a newborn baby, when he'd been too young to realise the dangers of growing up on Earth, but that time had passed too quickly. No one had defended him at school, no one had stood up for him …not when it was safer to side with the bullies, instead of the unpopular loner. He'd never gone a day without someone doing something to him and he had known, one day, that eventually they would kill him. And he'd worked hard to escape, only to find himself on Meridian.

There had been a time when he'd felt safe, after Barry's death. But it hadn't lasted. The Wolves had taken Kailee from him, using her as a hostage to force him to work for them, which had made him a collaborator with an occupying force. It wouldn't be long before someone put a bullet in him, thinking they were striking back against the Wolves. The looks of hatred he received every time he went to the city were quite bad enough.

He looked around the spaceport control room, feeling bitter hatred as he stared at the equipment. None of it was remotely modern; Meridian had never bothered to invest in a large spaceport, not when there was only a small stream of colonists coming down from the Empire. They'd even thought they would be completely isolated once the Empire had collapsed, leaving them alone. But the Wolves had had other ideas. Meridian could work for them ...or it could be bombarded into ruins. And then they'd taken hostages to force people to collaborate.

There had been times when he'd considered destroying the equipment and killing himself, but he'd known he wouldn't be able to do that to Kailee. She'd been the only girl to show any real interest in him, after they'd arrived on Meridian. And he'd been happy in her arms, even when she cried at night, until she'd been taken away. He couldn't condemn her to death by refusing to follow orders ...

He pulled himself to his feet and glared out of the window. There was really nothing to the spaceport, apart from a pair of wooden hangers, a tank of shuttlecraft fuel and a tiny control tower. One man could handle most of the spaceport's operations by himself, if he was prepared to work hard; Gary had found it quite satisfying, before the Wolves had arrived and forced him to work for them. Now, he was effectively their slave.

Shaking his head, he walked to the door and clambered down the ladder to the ground floor. The building had always struck him as incomplete - there were arrival halls that were nothing more than bare rooms, not even painted to welcome newcomers - but it wasn't as if anyone was interested in finishing the job of preparing the spaceport. Meridian didn't want new settlers and had been trying to discourage them, before the Empire had fallen into ruins and their final links to Earth had been severed. At least the Wolves hadn't done more than set up POW camps and insist the prisoners be fed regularly. They hadn't dumped more settlers on Meridian.

That will come, he thought, morbidly. Meridian had excellent long-term prospects, once the current unpleasantness - whatever it was - settled down. Wolfbane could dump a few hundred thousand settlers on the planet and to hell with what the prior settlers wanted. There would be resistance, of course, but what would it matter? Wolfbane could just hammer the planet from orbit until the battered survivors surrendered and begged for mercy.

He peered into the empty hanger, then started the walk to his cabin, on the edge of the spaceport. He'd moved in shortly after Kailee had been taken, both to be closer to the spaceport and to be well away from the city. Darrin and Austin visited, from time to time, but no one else did, not when they distrusted him on principle. Even if he hadn't been *evil*, they knew he had someone held hostage for his good behaviour. How could they know how he would react to finding someone in his house?

A gust of warm air blew into his face, followed by a scattering of raindrops. The sky was clouding over rapidly, once again. He hoped, sadistically, that one of the Wolves was flying a shuttle through the planet's atmosphere, even if the odds of a crash were very low. There would be some turbulence, he was sure, which would make the flight unpleasant. But then, the flying doctor might have to fly to a medical emergency ... and that would be very far from pleasant.

He paused at the gate, then peered inside. Darrin was standing by the doorway to the cabin, waiting for him. Gary hesitated - part of him would always be scared of Darrin, even though he'd never been the worst of Gary's tormentors - and then pushed the gate open, striding into his garden. There had actually been next to no time to actually take care of the garden; he was mildly surprised that anything grew, given his lack of attention.

"Gary," Darrin called. "I have a surprise for you inside."

Gary blinked. The settlers believed, firmly, that a man's home was his castle. No one, but no one, stepped inside without permission. He would have been quite within his legal rights to shoot anyone who entered, even if they had only come to beg for a cup of sugar. For Darrin to put something inside his house without permission ...Darrin might have been born on Earth, like Gary himself, but it was still odd. He should have learned better even before Barry had met his final end.

"You put something inside my house?" He asked. "What?"

"Come and see," Darrin said. "I think you'll like it."

Gary eyed him suspiciously - the last time he'd been told anything like that, it hadn't been remotely pleasant - then stepped through the door and into the house. It was a tiny cabin; the living room and the kitchen were combined, while the bedroom was tiny and the bathroom was barely large enough for a shower. But it was large enough for him ...he looked at the sofa, then stopped dead. Kailee was sitting there, staring back at him.

"Kailee," he said. "I ..."

He ran across the room and enfolded her in his arms. For a moment, she didn't respond, then she hugged him coolly, almost robotically. Gary hesitated, unable to avoid thinking that she had fallen out of love with him, then held her gently. Her entire body was quivering slightly, as if she were terrified.

"I brought another guest," Darrin said. "She's waiting around the back."

Gary wanted to talk to Kailee, but he suspected Darrin wasn't going to wait. "Show her in," he said, as he slowly let go of his lover. "I'll put the kettle on."

Darrin nodded and slipped out of the door. Moments later, he returned with another newcomer, a dark-skinned woman with very unfeminine features. If Gary hadn't known better, if Darrin hadn't told him, he would have taken the newcomer for an oddly-shaped man, rather than a woman. Her face wasn't conventionally pretty and her body was surprisingly masculine. And her arms, what little he could see of them, were heavily muscular.

"My name is Jasmine," she said. Her accent clearly wasn't local - or Earther. It didn't sound like anything he'd heard from the Wolves either. "I think we need to talk."

"Dear God," Gary said. It all made sense now. "You're from one of the camps!"

"I told you he was smart," Darrin said, mischievously.

Gary shot him a sharp look, then busied himself making a pot of hot tea. Real tea was rare on Earth, but it was surprisingly common on Meridian and everyone drank it throughout the day. Even making tea had become a ritual, something that gave him time to think. He picked up a packet of biscuits, then looked around for cups. Luckily, he had a handful of mugs he'd taken from his old home, enough for all four of them. He poured the water into the teapot, then placed it on the table in front of the sofa.

"I would have preferred not to drop in on you like this," Jasmine said. "However, given your position, we need your help."

Gary nodded, then started to pour the tea. He had a feeling he knew what was coming.

"I have sugar as well as milk," he said. "What would you like in yours?"

"Just milk," Jasmine said. She gave him a soft smile. "My mother was always very fond of tea too."

Darrin cleared his throat. "When do you have to be back at the spaceport?"

Gary shrugged. "There's supposed to be another supply shuttle in a week," he said. "Before then ...me being there is more of a formality than anything else. There's nothing to do, but study manuals and tinker with the computers."

Jasmine sipped her tea thoughtfully. "And can you do much with the computers?"

"Not enough," Gary admitted. "They might have been designed for bad weather, but there are limits. I think we will start losing them within a couple of years."

Darrin scowled. "You can't fix them?"

"No," Gary said, flatly. "I have neither the tools nor the expertise to fix the computers, should they suffer any physical problems."

He shook his head. What was the point of explaining, to Darrin, just what it took to build a computer? Meridian's industrial base was laughable; it produced farm tools, a handful of primitive vehicles and little else. Even the dump of HE3 would have to be resupplied, eventually, from off-world. When - if - the fusion plant near the city failed, that would be the end, unless it could be replaced. It wasn't designed to allow someone to repair it in place.

"I thought you were good with computers," Darrin said.

"Not *that* good," Gary admitted. "I can do basic programming, which is more than I could do on Earth, but I certainly can't replace missing components."

Jasmine held up a hand. "Let me be blunt," she said. "We need to know everything you know about the enemy, then we can start making plans."

Gary looked her in the eye. "And if I don't help you, Kailee suffers?"

"No," Jasmine said. Oddly, Gary believed her. "But there will come a time when they realise she's not in the camp."

"I see," Gary said.

He swallowed, nervously. The idea of risking Kailee was anathema to him, but now ...he might succeed in doing nothing more than implicating them both in resistance activities. If they were caught, the best they could hope for would be immediate execution …if, of course, the Wolves didn't decide to make an example out of a small farming village or two.

"You said you could read their traffic," Darrin said. "Do they know she's escaped?"

"I don't think there was any reference to escaped prisoners," Gary said, after a moment. "But they don't *have* to route their messages through the ground-based transmitter."

"We can, but hope," Jasmine said. "Tell me about the enemy."

Gary took a breath. "They have seven POW camps scattered over the continent," he said. "Each of them has around thirty to forty guards, none of whom seem very happy to be living there. There's almost no contact between the guards and the local settlers, apart from food shipments. They're searched thoroughly before being allowed into the camp."

Jasmine nodded, impatiently. She'd probably heard it already from Darrin.

"They have the orbital station under their complete control," Gary continued. "The station was actually powered down and left in a stable orbit shortly after the Fall of Earth - I believe the original crew went elsewhere. They powered it up again, attached a bombardment module to the underside and turned it into a base. I believe there are forty or so crew stationed there, along with a handful of …slaves."

"Sex slaves," Jasmine said.

"I think so," Gary admitted. The thought of Kailee being added to someone's harem had horrified him. Barry had gloated, openly, about his long-term plans. They had been completely impractical, Gary knew now, but they would still have been brutally unpleasant for both Gary and Kailee. "They took a number of girls from the planet when they first arrived."

"Don't they always do that," Jasmine muttered. "What about the other technical experts?"

"I think they were just shipped right out of the system," Gary said. "They certainly haven't managed to get back in touch with me."

Jasmine took another sip of her tea. "Do they have anyone stationed here, in Sabre City?"

"Not as far as I know," Gary said. "They issue orders over the communications net, such as it is, and expect us to carry them out. I don't think they cared enough to station an occupation force in the city itself."

"So it would seem," Jasmine agreed. "What else do they do?"

"Every two weeks, they send down a shuttle which we load with food," Gary said. "I imagine they check the food before eating it ..."

"I would imagine so," Jasmine mused. "Is the shuttle crewed or automated?"

"Crewed," Gary said. "There's actually an advisory against using unmanned shuttles in the planet's atmosphere. The weather changes too rapidly for autopilots to handle easily."

"That's a safety regulation, not a practical concern," Jasmine said, shortly. "How many people crew the shuttle?"

"Two," Gary said. "They stay in the cockpit while we load the craft."

Jasmine looked at him, sharply. "And you never thought to include a large bomb in the supplies?"

"It was considered," Darrin said, before Gary could say a word. "The resistance decided there was no way we could guarantee destroying the orbital station ...and besides, they get a ship here every couple of months. They'd know what we'd done."

Gary nodded. The orbital station might have been tiny, compared to the giant battlestations that had surrounded Earth, but it was large enough to be dangerous, should pieces of debris start to rain down on the planet below. And even if it was blown to atoms, the Wolves would eventually send a ship to find out what had happened to their garrison. Darrin was right; they might score a short-term victory, but in the long term it would be disastrous.

Jasmine shrugged. "What make of shuttle?"

It went on and on. Gary felt exhausted at the end, as if he'd had every last piece of knowledge pulled out of his head, but he couldn't help feeling that he was finally doing something to strike back at the enemy. He sat next to Kailee and forced himself to relax as Jasmine paced the room, muttering to herself. She clearly had some kind of plan, but what?

"I'll need to check your emergency supplies," she said, shortly. "Did you keep everything the law insisted you keep?"

Gary shrugged. Legally, every colony world was to have two shuttles held in reserve at all times. Practically, one of Meridian's shuttles had broken down years ago and the other had been confiscated by the Wolves. The secondary supplies *might* still be functional, but he wasn't sure how to check them. He'd just have to lead her to the underground storage dump and hope she knew what she was doing.

"Right," Jasmine said, once he'd explained all that. "You can take me there this evening?"

She jerked her head at Darrin, who rose and took Kailee's arm. Kailee rose at once, wordlessly allowing Darrin to lead her out of the room. Gary stared after her, torn between horror and a terrifying sense that his life was about to change once again. Kailee had held herself together before, when they'd faced Barry together, but now ...

"She's had a very hard time," Jasmine said, catching his eye. "You will have to grow used to the fact that she isn't the person you knew, not any longer. I think she can recover, but ...but it will probably take years before she's feeling any kind of confidence in herself. You have to make allowances for her."

"I will try," Gary promised. "But ..."

"But nothing," Jasmine said. "People cope with trauma in different ways. Kailee seems to have largely zoned out of the world, not helped by problems with her diet. You will take care of her and try not to push her too far."

Gary nodded, wordlessly. He didn't dare disagree. There was something about Jasmine he found terrifyingly intimidating. He'd never really met a girl he'd thought could stand up for herself before, not when the only true protection for a girl on Earth was to ally herself with a strong man and pray he defended her against all comers. No one had ever looked to *him* for protection, of course. The whole idea was laughable.

And you owe Kailee more than that, he reminded himself, firmly.

"I'll do my best," he said. "I assume she will be kept out of sight?"

"We have her in a boarding house at the other side of the city," Jasmine said. "A doctor will take care of her, from time to time. I do hope she recovers, but ..."

Gary nodded. He'd seen plenty of people on Earth just give up. There had been nothing to live for, not even children and grandchildren. He'd had his own escape plan, but ...in hindsight, being forced to travel to Meridian had saved his life. He would have died on Earth.

"Me too," he said. He took one last swig of his tea. "I'll show you the emergency supplies now?"

Jasmine smiled. "Why not?"

CHAPTER TEN

> The laws of war, thus, insisted that soldiers had to be seen to be soldiers, if they were to be treated as soldiers. A soldier who wore civilian clothes could, legally, be shot out of hand as a spy. Furthermore, the moral blame for atrocities committed against the civilian population rested with the defender, rather than the attacker.
> - Professor Leo Caesius. *The Empire and its Prisoners of War.*

Meridian, Year 5 (PE)

Jasmine had learned to loathe the Empire's bureaucracy from a very early age.

It was maddening to have to do battle with both the enemy *and* people who were supposed to be on your side. Her father, the farmer, had known far more about running a farm than any of the bureaucrats, yet he'd sometimes had to account for everything he'd done to them, while allowing the bureaucrats any influence over military affairs was asking for trouble. The Commonwealth, at least, had managed to slim down the bureaucracy, although she had no idea how long that would last. Bureaucracies spread like cancers.

And it galled her, as she looked around the storage room, to actually have to feel *grateful* to the bureaucrats.

Imperial Law stated that colonies were to maintain a reasonable supply of expensive emergency gear at all times. On paper, it looked like a sensible idea, but the settlers - and not the development corporation

- were responsible for paying for and maintaining the supply, something that only pushed the planet further and further into debt. They had to take out loans to pay for it ...

But now it might have worked in her favour.

"This gear hasn't been touched," she said, as she examined a standard spacesuit. "Do you know if anyone bothered to maintain it?"

"I think it was never used," Gary said. "The Wolves certainly never demanded we hand it over to them."

Jasmine nodded, absently. There were thirty spacesuits, a small collection of deep-space survival gear and an emergency power generator, plus enough spare parts to be reasonably sure she could get at least ten of the spacesuits working. The medical kits, stowed at the rear of the compartment, were modern; she was surprised they hadn't been taken and put to use long ago. God knew the doctors on Meridian had to make do with primitive equipment and self-produced medicines. The collection of ration bars - enough to keep a small army fed for several months - was just the clincher.

"We'll have to come back and check everything," she said. "Do they ever search the spaceport?"

"They did once, when they arrived," Gary said. "I don't think they've bothered to be concerned with anything we did after that, once they reassured themselves that we weren't a threat."

"I see," Jasmine said. There were no weapons in the chamber, merely a handful of tools that could be converted to weapons with a little imagination. The hoplophobic bureaucrats had probably refused to consider insisting that everyone keep a supply of weapons. "We can use these, I think."

"Good," Gary said. "But how do you plan to get up to the station?"

Jasmine smiled. "We will have to ride their shuttle."

Gary looked doubtful. Jasmine wasn't too surprised. Gary and Kailee both clearly had long-term problems stemming from their upbringing on Earth; it was unlikely, she suspected, that Gary was truly capable of bravery. People who were bullied relentlessly - and Darrin had made it clear that Gary *had* been savagely bullied - either snapped and tried to kill someone, or lost all hope they could direct their own lives. In hindsight, it was that lack of competence that might have attracted Kailee to Gary. He wouldn't have the nerve to force himself on her.

"It sounds like madness," he said, finally. "Are you serious?"

"Yes," Jasmine said. She had hoped there would be a shuttle on the ground, one they could use, but the Wolves had moved it to orbit. Besides, even if they had access to a shuttle, the station was permanently in place to spot anyone trying to get off the surface. A half-imagined scheme for transporting a shuttle to the other side of the planet had been nothing more than a pipe-dream. "There's no other way to get to the station."

She eyed Gary's back as he turned back to the door. Would he try to betray them? He had no reason to love the Wolves, but Stockholm Syndrome - and simple fear for Kailee's life - might lead him to do something stupid. She'd been told, more than once, that there would come a time when she would have to make a decision between taking an innocent life and risking her mission, but she'd never had to do that. Now …she feared that time might have come.

You need him, she reminded herself. *You cannot take his life now*.

"I hope you know what you're doing," Gary said. "They're due here in a week. How do you plan to take control of the shuttle?"

"Wait and see," Jasmine said. "Now …I want to see your databases."

Gary hadn't been kidding, she discovered, when he'd described the computers as outdated and cumbersome. Someone had done their level best to prepare them for life on a very wet world, but it was clear the systems were on the verge of breaking down completely. Jasmine took the codes Gary gave her, then started to probe through the files. Most of them were completely useless - she rolled her eyes when she discovered the porn stash - but some of them were interesting. The Wolves had adapted a Mark-VIII heavy-lift shuttle for their supplies, rather than anything newer.

"That's the shuttle they took from us," Gary said, peering over her shoulder. "But we don't have anyone who could fly it."

"I could," Jasmine said. She'd never had the chance to fly a Mark-VIII shuttle before, but it didn't matter. The Empire had standardised everything years ago. There were few differences, at least in the cockpit, between a Marine Assault Shuttle and a standard civilian model. "All I'd need are the control codes and some practice. But I would also need someone to speak to them on my behalf."

"Hold a knife to their throat," Gary advised. There was an odd tremor in his voice. "A person will say anything if you threaten them with immediate death."

"It depends on who you threaten," Jasmine said. When had *Gary* been threatened? A school bully? Knives were banned on Earth, if she recalled correctly, but it wasn't as though it would be hard to smuggle one into a school. A bit of imagination, used correctly, would make it easy. "Someone intent on being a hero at the wrong moment could get us all killed."

She looked up at him. "Do you know the pilots? Personally?"

"No," Gary said. "They never really talk to me."

Jasmine nodded. It made sense; the Wolves wouldn't want their people to form any kind of attachment to the settlers, not when it would make them reluctant to strike the planet if necessary. She had wondered why the guards - and she knew now that there was more than one POW camp - had been so isolated, but it did make sense. The only real question was why they hadn't abused the prisoners.

They may think they can get some use out of us, she thought. *Keeping us unharmed would be part of the deal.*

She checked the last few files, then stood. "I'll go back to our base now," she said, glancing at her reflection in the mirror. She looked like a teenage boy, rather than any kind of woman, but she had to admit it would probably draw less attention. "I will contact you later to discuss our plans."

Gary looked pale. "And Kailee?"

"We'll keep her safe," Jasmine said. She knew, no matter how she chose to justify it, that she was effectively keeping Kailee as a hostage for the second time. Gary would know, of course, what she was doing. But she suspected they had no choice. "She will be fine, I promise."

"She won't be fine if they turn the planet into ash," Gary snapped. "Will she?"

"They won't destroy the whole planet," Jasmine assured him. "It would be pointless devastation."

Of course they won't, her own thoughts mocked her. *It would be much easier to drop a rock on the largest city, then wait a few years. Everyone will either die or be reduced to barbarism. And then they will just drop a few hundred thousand new settlers on the other side of the planet.*

"They don't seem to give a damn about anything, apart from power," Gary said. He pointed upwards, towards the peeling ceiling ...and the stars beyond. "What's happening out there?"

"War," Jasmine said.

She told Gary everything she could about Avalon, the Commonwealth and Wolfbane as they made their way back to the cabin. Gary listened, asking questions from time to time, although he didn't seem to know much about the outside universe. Jasmine wasn't really surprised; Earthers weren't encouraged to learn for the sake of learning, while Meridian's settlers had too much to do to worry about affairs light years from their homes. In many ways, the universe had become much bigger with the fall of Earth. Star systems that had once been known elements were now strangers...

I need to sit down with Stubbins, she thought, *and go through everything, piece by piece.*

"Thank you for your help," she said, when they reached his cabin. "We'll get back in touch with you."

Rain was starting to fall, once again, as she walked down the road towards the city. It was the sole modern road she'd seen, although it was clear that it had suffered from a lack of basic maintenance. Water gushed down the gutter, heading to the sea, but levels were rapidly rising and muddy liquid was starting to splash against her boots. She looked behind her as she heard the sound of hoof beats, then smiled as she saw the horse and cart approaching from one of the side roads, the rider sitting under a makeshift canopy. It looked uncomfortably primitive, but horses were much easier to maintain on a primitive world - and self-reproducing too.

"Hey," the rider called. He was a young man, barely sixteen. "Do you want a lift?"

Jasmine smiled. "Why not?"

She scrambled up next to the rider and chatted to him, trying to keep her voice low. He didn't seem to have realised she was female, but there was no point in taking chances. It was clear that she didn't *look* typical, at least for a woman on Meridian, and being known as female would cause comment. She was quite happy to stick with the cover story - that she had grown up on an isolated farm - and politely deflect his questions.

"My father wants more wood for the new barn," Gavin said. He'd told her his name, along with so many biographical details that it was clear he was starved of company on the farm. "He's planning a barn-raising this week. Will you be coming?"

Jasmine shrugged. She'd done barn-raisings on her homeworld, back before she'd left for good, and they'd always been special occasions. The men would raise the barn, while the women would cook a feast and the children ran around getting in the way. It was a tradition she rather wished the Empire had seen fit to spread, although the cynic in her understood why the Empire had done nothing of the sort. Anything that caused unity among the population - a unity that could be easily turned against the Empire - was discouraged on general principles.

"I'd like you to come," Gavin said. "It would be fun."

"I'm sure it would be, but it depends on my father," Jasmine said. "He really hates being in the city."

She sat back and watched as Sabre City came into view. It didn't look very impressive, not compared to Camelot on Avalon, but she had to admit it had style. The wooden buildings were designed to let water flow off them as quickly and efficiently as possible, while the gutters were deep enough to keep water flowing down to the sea without flooding the streets or washing against the sides of the buildings. They'd been treated, she suspected, to prevent rot, but it still struck her as an unsafe place to build. But then, the settlers might not have been given much choice.

"You can drop me off here," she said, as they drove into the city. "I'll try and make it, but no promises."

She couldn't help feeling a flicker of guilt as she watched Gavin drive away, then turned and made her way towards the tiny house. It had surprised her when Austin had told her they could use the house, but she'd understood when she'd seen it. Sabre City often played host to visitors from the rest of the settlement, who would hire a house for a few days or weeks, then go back to their homes. And then there were transit barracks around the edge of the city ...she pushed the thought aside as she stepped up to the house, then tapped on the door. It opened moments later, revealing Stewart. Watson was sleeping on the sofa, one hand resting on a pistol he'd been given by Austin.

"Kailee is in the next room," Stewart said. "Did you find anything useful?"

"We're going to have to take a ride on the shuttle," Jasmine said, bluntly. She coughed loudly to wake up Watson. "There's no other way to orbit."

"Bollocks," Watson said. "You're sure?"

"The only way up is in their shuttle," Jasmine said. "Unless you have a plan to build a shuttle we can actually fly?"

"I don't think we can, not here," Watson said, sourly.

Jasmine shrugged. She'd once heard a story about a primitive world that *had* managed to build a spacecraft, but it had been insanely risky and probably mythical. By her most optimistic estimate, it would be at least two hundred years before Meridian was capable of producing even a primitive space rocket, assuming that Wolfbane just sat back and let them get on with it. The shuttle that had been stripped for parts was effectively useless, leaving them with one option. She could see no alternative.

"Then we need a plan," Stewart said. "They're unlikely to let us stow away with the fruit and veg."

"I know," Jasmine said. "That's why we're going to be riding on the outside of the shuttle."

Watson smiled. "I like it."

"You would," Stewart said. "Brigadier, with all due respect, we're not Pathfinders."

Jasmine winced, inwardly. "I know," she said. Pathfinders could survive in space without spacesuits, if the rumours were true. "But there are spacesuits in the storage dump, ones we can adapt for our use. Give us a handful of days and we should be able to prepare three of them. If worst comes to worst, we can simply patch them up and jury-rig an oxygen tank."

"It would work," Watson said. "But wouldn't they notice the extra weight?"

"They don't seem very concerned about the precise weight of food," Jasmine said. "All they really want is enough of it to feed forty-odd men and women. They don't insist on it being *precisely* one hundred tons of crap."

"We'd have to disable the exterior sensors," Stewart warned. "Or spoof them, somehow."

Watson smirked. "If it isn't a military-grade shuttle, we wouldn't have to worry about sensors," he said. "Civilians don't normally monitor for any vague bumps on the hull."

"Better to be careful," Jasmine said. She paused, then outlined her plan. It was vague, but she couldn't think of anything better. "We will need some help from the resistance to make it work."

"They would definitely have to help us," Stewart agreed, once Jasmine had finished. "And it could easily explode in their face."

"No, we could do it without them," Watson said. "There are spaceport workers who will help load the shuttle, in any case. We can get them to do what we want without involving the resistance."

"They'd have to be walking up and down and around the shuttle," Stewart said. He tapped the table, thoughtfully. "They're not going to be doing that without a reason. We'd have to give them one."

"Yeah," Jasmine agreed. "I'll speak to Austin later tonight. If he agrees, we can start modifying the spacesuits and tools tomorrow."

"Better hurry," Watson said. "I think they were actually trying to sell us on the virtues of staying here."

Jasmine shrugged. "How long could we stay here once the guards realise we're missing?"

"Besides, it would mean breaking our oaths," Stewart rumbled. "I, for one, have no intention of just surrendering. Staying here after I retire would be nice, but for the moment ...we need to get back home. The Colonel is waiting for us."

"They may also be thinking about keeping us here by force," Watson warned. "We are a danger to them, just by existing."

"They're already in trouble," Jasmine commented. "Us leaving might not be suspicious, as we know little about the planet, but Kailee will lead them back to Gary. They were committed the moment they chose not to call the Wolves and have us thrown back into the camp."

"Make sure they know that," Stewart said. "Covering up their involvement won't be easy."

"Yes, it will," Watson said. "We evacuate the POW camps, then bombard them from orbit. It will look like we blew up every last trace of Wolfbane, then vanished. As far as they will know, the POWs would be dead."

"Let us hope they believe that," Jasmine said. Would the Wolves really believe she'd been ruthless enough to slaughter the prisoners she couldn't take with her? "And for now, I'm going to get some rest."

CHAPTER ELEVEN

> This may seem absurd. If a school were to be hit by gunfire and destroyed, killing hundreds of children, it seems self-evident that whichever side fired the fatal shot was responsible for the disaster. But was that really the case?
> - Professor Leo Caesius. *The Empire and its Prisoners of War.*

Meridian, Year 5 (PE)

"Are you sure," Gary asked, "that this is a good idea?"

"I think we have no choice," Austin said.

"Nothing is certain in war," Darrin intoned, "save that the enemy will be the enemy, that the good guys will be the good guys, and the politicians will find a way to snatch defeat from the jaws of victory."

Gary snorted. How long had it been since they'd watched that entertainment? The show had been nothing more than mindless, yet curiously sterile violence, naked girls and endless sex scenes. In hindsight, he understood it was intended to keep the population distracted, preventing them from thinking about their lot, but it was still surprisingly anti-establishment.

Years, he thought. *There are no viewscreens on Meridian.*

"Their shuttle will be here within an hour," Gary said, instead. They'd worked out the loading schedule carefully, but there had been no way to rehearse properly. "Once it arrives, we will be committed."

Austin nodded. "I think we need to take a gamble," he said. "And risk everything on one throw of the dice."

Gary nodded. Kailee had been taken from him ...and now she was back, he wanted revenge on her captors, even if he knew he didn't have the bravery to face them himself. But the risks were horrendous ...the Wolves might rain fire and death on Sabre, or settle merely for blasting a hundred farms from orbit, ensuring that the population would starve. Who knew *what* they would do to keep order on their conquered worlds?

"It is risking everything," Darrin said. "But the alternative is remaining under their thumb until the end of days."

"Then we are committed," Gary said. He checked his watch, thoughtfully. "I have to get back to the control tower. I'll see you afterwards ..."

"Yeah," Darrin said. "See you then."

Jasmine checked and rechecked the spacesuit as she waited, knowing that both Stewart and Watson would be doing the same with theirs. Some of the equipment had decayed over time, unsurprisingly, and cannibalising some of the suits to ensure that three were operational had been a major headache. She was privately relieved they'd been able to do it themselves, as bringing more people from Meridian into the conspiracy would have increased the risks of detection. Who knew if the Wolves had a couple of spies on the surface? It was what she would have done, if she'd been in their place.

But all the collaborators have been accounted for, she told herself firmly. It was odd to realise that the collaborators and the resistance actually *collaborated*, but perhaps it shouldn't have been a surprise. The collaborators weren't *willing* collaborators and the resistance knew better than to lash out at the collaborators, forcing them to give themselves wholeheartedly to their unwanted masters. *None of them know we're here.*

She took a breath, then pulled the spacesuit over her head. It felt cumbersome, compared to a Marine-issue shipsuit, but it hadn't been specifically tailored for her. She was just lucky, she decided, that she didn't have larger breasts. Whoever had come up with the standardised designs for spacesuits hadn't thought to account for wearers who had breasts ...or were excessively fat, for that matter. It was just another way the endless intrusion of bureaucracy had weakened the Empire.

"I feel like a penguin," Stewart complained, as he waddled around in his suit. "And the air smells like bat barf."

"As long as you can breathe, it should be fine," Jasmine said, dryly. She activated her own life support system and took a breath. The oxygen smelled worse than Stewart had suggested, but it would keep her alive. No doubt one of the filters in the reprocessors had decayed since the suits were last checked. "Carl?"

"My air smells like fairy dust," Watson said. "I think I need to replace the life support box."

"Then do it," Jasmine said, sharply. She glanced at the clock on the wall and frowned. There was less than an hour before the shuttle landed, before they knew if they were going to succeed or die trying. "Hurry up."

She started to walk around in the suit, cursing the way it constrained her vision and movements. Heavy combat armour would have been preferable; it could be just as irritating, but it was effectively bulletproof and carried enough weapons to make up for any minor inconveniences. But they would have to rely on the suits, at least until they reached the station, where they could be discarded.

Unless they blow the hatches, she thought. *But will they be expecting an attack?*

There was no way to know. Everything she'd seen suggested the Wolves weren't too worried about being attacked, but the station was the key to their control of the system. Losing a POW camp or two would be annoying, losing the station would free Meridian from their control …at least until a warship arrived to find out why the station wasn't responding. They had to take it more seriously, unless the Wolves really *had* sent all their Category-Z manpower to Meridian. She found it easy to believe that all the POW guards were classed as expendable.

"I still feel like a penguin," Stewart muttered, as he picked up their makeshift tools and started to practice manipulating them in the suit. "We really need skin-tight gloves."

"We're not going to get them," Watson said, curtly. He fiddled with a modified processor, then dropped it on the ground. "We'll just have to learn."

Jasmine nodded. They had no choice.

"They're coming," Gary said. "ETA ten minutes."

"I'll let the Marines know," Austin said. "Good luck."

Gary shrugged. In truth, there was very little for him to do, beyond monitoring the enemy's flight path. There was almost nothing in the air, save for an emergency aircraft flying far to the north; there was no real risk of the shuttle ramming another aircraft or being forced to crash by a sudden burst of turbulence. He'd been reassured, more than once, that no matter how bad it seemed, it was almost always minor. It would have been more reassuring if his first flight in an old-style aircraft hadn't ended in a crash.

But, for once, he half-wished the turbulence was vile enough to knock the craft out of the sky.

The Wolves didn't bother to send him updates as they dropped down towards the spaceport, unsurprisingly. They could have landed there - or anywhere - without his help. Gary rose to his feet and peered through the window as the shuttle came into view, a boxy shape that hung in the air over the spaceport, seemingly defying the planet's gravity. He couldn't help feeling a pang of regret for lost opportunities - his life would have been very different if he'd gone with the Traders, instead of landing on Meridian - which he pushed aside, savagely. If he hadn't landed on the planet, he would never have started a relationship with Kailee.

"Attention," a voice snapped, through the radio. "We're landing, now."

Gary rolled his eyes. They always felt the urge to make such announcements, even though they were pointless. Nine days out of ten, there was no one on the spaceport save him ...and even now, with the loading crew getting ready to go to work, there was no one on the landing pad. It was just another petty exercise in intimidation, like so much of what he'd faced on Earth. But it was also backed with overwhelming force.

He strolled back to the console and tapped a switch. "Welcome to Meridian," he said, in what he hoped was a neutral manner. "We have your supplies ready for you."

The voice changed, slightly. "Anything special?"

"I'm afraid not," Gary said. The resistance *had* tried to find ways to bribe the pilots, but nothing had worked. They only seemed to be interested in flying and fucking. "Just food and drink, the usual."

The pilot sighed. "No porn?"

"None," Gary said. Earth had produced thousands of terabytes of porn daily - yet another way to keep the population distracted - but Meridian didn't have either the inclination or the equipment to even begin producing porn. "We could find you board games, if you like."

"Bah," the pilot said. "Boring."

Gary shrugged. Once, he would have agreed. What was Chess or Risk or Monopoly compared to a 3D game? But now, he found himself appreciating the simplicity of such games.

"The hatches are open," the pilot said. "Start loading now, if you please. We have to get back up there as quickly as possible."

"Understood," Gary said. "Your supplies are on the way."

He closed the channel, then headed down the ladder to the hanger, where the food and drink had been stored. The heavy wooden boxes looked fragile, but he knew from experience that they were strong enough to support the food indefinitely. He nodded to the loaders, who started to pick up the first set of boxes and carry them out the door. As long as they were carried carefully, there should be no way for the shuttle's crew to see that there were three people in spacesuits, hanging to the rear of the crates. He prayed, silently, that the plan actually worked. Discovery now, while everyone was still on the ground, would be disastrous.

Godspeed, he thought.

Jasmine held her breath as the crate was carried up to the shuttle, then put down in front of the loading ramp. There were cameras scattered around the shuttle's hull, she knew, but there were blindspots ...and, if everything had gone perfectly, they were now in one of them. The crew shouldn't be able to see them scrambling away from the boxes and fixing themselves to the hull. She briefly considered slipping *into* the hull, but it was too risky. There was no connection between the cargo hold and the cockpit, ensuring they could be caught like rats in a trap.

And they could have scattered sensors inside the hold, she thought. It was what she would have done, if she'd been forced into depending on the locals to load her shuttles. Someone trying to stowaway would be the obvious way to reach orbit. *We just need to be careful.*

She checked that she was securely linked to the hull, then forced herself to wait. Her first parachute jump had been far harder, in many ways; no matter what she knew about safety, it had been hard to step over the edge and plummet down towards the ground. There was no way she could talk to either of the others, not without risking detection; the only thing she could do was wait. But at least she'd learned patience the hard way too.

The shuttle rocked suddenly as the ramp closed, then she felt the hull start to shiver as the pilots powered up the drives. *She* would have insisted on making a visual inspection of the hull before take-off, but then she also knew what was coming. A garrison on occupation duty, light years from the front, might well grow lazy and careless. Even Marines could succumb to ennui, if given a chance. It was why there was never any shortage of duties to perform, even well away from a war zone.

Here we go, she thought, as the shuttle rocked, then launched itself off the ground. She turned her head and watched the planet falling away behind her - Meridian truly was a beautiful planet, save for the eerie dark rainclouds gathering in the distance - then looked back at the shuttle's hull. The temperature, according to her HUD, was falling rapidly as the shuttle kept gaining height. It wouldn't be long before the repaired spacesuits were put to their first real test ...

"Well?"

"They're gone," Gary said. He glanced at his console, then back at Austin. "They should be at the station within twenty minutes."

Austin nodded. "Is there any way we can track them once they're onboard?"

"No," Gary said. The spaceport should have had a live feed from the orbital station, but the Wolves had disconnected it as soon as they'd taken control. They probably hadn't wanted him spying on them. "We're committed."

"Yeah," Austin said. "And we don't even dare signal for evacuation."

Gary stared at him, finally grasping just how large a risk Austin had taken. Meridian was his home, the settlers his people ...and yet, he'd risked them all. There was no time to evacuate the city, if the shit hit the fan. Hundreds of people were likely to die if the Wolves started shooting, once they realised they'd been boarded. And Austin had done it without a second thought.

He cannot give up, Gary thought, remembering how they'd first met. Austin had seemed like a boy from another world, which in a sense he was. Their life experiences had been so different that talking to him had been like talking to an alien. *And he cannot compromise himself, even for his life.*

"So we wait," he said, instead. There was nothing else they could do. "We wait and see."

Jasmine saw the orbital station come into existence as the shuttle turned, shining with reflected sunlight against the blue-green orb of Meridian. As Gary had told her, it was a fairly standard orbital station, designed to make unloading bulk freighters and shipping their cargos down to the ground much easier. There was certainly nothing elegant about its design, nothing like the spinning wheels that housed the Empire's richest families well away from the maddening crowds. It was nothing more than set of boxy modules tied together, just like the orbital station at Avalon. The only real difference was a KEW pod hanging below the station, ready to launch projectiles at the planet.

We know how to navigate inside, she thought. She'd been one of the Marines who had boarded Orbit One, when they'd first arrived at Avalon. *And we know how to take down its computer network.*

The shuttle quivered, then altered course again, heading towards a large docking port. It looked inefficient, Jasmine saw, but without gravity there would be nothing stopping the Wolves from floating the crates up and out of the shuttle, one by one. She braced herself as they flew closer - if someone insisted on making a visual inspection of the shuttle, they were doomed - then relaxed as the shuttle slowed to a halt. The crew were clearly practiced, she noted; they inched towards the docking port, then made contact so gently that she barely felt the craft shudder.

She glanced at Stewart, then nodded towards the station's hull. Stewart crawled forward, over the shuttle, then across the docking port and onto the station itself. A civilian-designed station wouldn't have sensors intended to track people on the hull, Jasmine knew, but the designs were intended to be heavily modified. Someone could have easily rigged up a few sensors once the station was turned into an orbital fortress, if they'd wanted to secure their position against all possible threats. But nothing happened as they crawled onwards, towards one of the access hatches. Thankfully, even the Wolves hadn't seen fit to override the bureaucratic insistence that *all* hatches be accessible from the outside.

Better just hope they don't have anyone watching the other side, Jasmine thought, as she started to fiddle with the hatch. Civilians or not, there would be an alarm when the hatch opened, unless she managed to isolate it from the computer network. But if she screwed it up, there was a good chance she would actually trap herself in the airlock. *Or someone monitoring the computers at all times.*

She turned to look at Stewart. *Me first*, she signalled, using her hands. *Give me five, then assume the worst.*

Stewart looked doubtful, from what little she could see of his face, but nodded. Jasmine nodded back, then opened the hatch and ducked inside. It was nothing more than a standard ingress-egress hatch, without any stored spacesuits or tools. She shrugged, then keyed the other hatch, bracing herself as gravity slowly reasserted itself. It seemed as though the station's operators had deliberately set the gravity to Luna-norm, rather than standard Earth-norm. She puzzled over it for a moment, then glanced out as the inner hatch opened. There was a surprised-looking man on the far side.

He opened his mouth, but she hit him in the throat before he had a chance to say a word. The force of the impact broke his neck and he crumpled to the deck, dead. Jasmine scowled down at the body, then hastily recycled the airlock. Moments later, both Stewart and Watson had joined her inside the station.

"Nothing of interest on the body," Stewart muttered, after a brief search. "Just a handful of datachips and a set of multitools."

"Bring them with us," Jasmine said. If she recalled correctly, there should be a computer node further down the passageway, unless the locals had reconfigured the station at some point. "And shove him in the airlock, then jam it."

"Understood," Stewart said. He hefted up the body as the other two kept watch, dumped it in the airlock and then sealed it by jabbing one of the multitools into the control panel. "You do realise that jamming an airlock is a court martial offense? You could be shot."

Jasmine snickered, humourlessly. She'd lost the Battle of Thule and seen over two hundred prisoners taken into enemy hands. By any reasonable standard, she was due a court martial by the time she returned home, assuming Colonel Stalker didn't summarily strangle her on the spot. Compared to that, jamming an airlock in an enemy facility and cutting off their line of retreat was a minor offense.

"Come on," she said. She couldn't hear anyone else, but that meant nothing. "We have to hurry."

CHAPTER TWELVE

It depends. Was the school being used as a military installation? If yes, the school was a legitimate target and the moral responsibility for the atrocity rests with the defenders.
- Professor Leo Caesius. *The Empire and its Prisoners of War.*

Meridian, Year 5 (PE)

"Two people in the compartment," Stewart signalled, as they reached the half-open hatch and peeked inside. "Take them both?"

"Without letting them get a word off," Jasmine signalled back. "On three …"

She used her fingers to count down, then led the way into the compartment as soon as she reached zero. The occupants, two young men in slovenly uniforms, barely had a moment to realise they were under attack before they were yanked out of their chairs and forced to the deck. Jasmine covered her target's mouth with her hand, then pressed her fingers into his neck. Moments later, he was unconscious and helpless. Stewart dealt with his in the same way, while Watson scrambled to the console and sat down.

"They were playing games," he said, with some amusement. "*Turbo Nuke-Them*, Volume III."

Jasmine snorted. She had a feeling that any marine caught playing games on active duty would wind up wishing they'd been nuked, once the sergeants were through with them. But, on the other hand, the men hadn't had any reason to expect attack. They'd assumed they were safe from everyone on the planet below.

"Never mind that," she said. She vaguely recalled Blake Coleman talking about *Turbo Nuke-Them*, but she hadn't been paying attention at the time. "Can you hack into the station network?"

"I think so," Watson said. He reached for the processor he'd carried up from the surface, then plugged it into the console. "Give me a moment ..."

There was a long pause as his hands danced over the console. "I can shut down most of their systems, but not enough to prevent a counterattack," he said, finally. "The civilian designs won't let me vent the atmosphere without blowing all the hatches at once."

Jasmine silently cursed civilian bureaucrats under her breath, then leaned forward. "What *can* you do?"

"I can reroute power from everything, but bare life support," Watson said. "I'm not sure what that will do to the bombardment module, though. It doesn't seem to be directly connected to the station's power grid."

"Wonderful," Stewart muttered. "The one time they show a lick of competence and it has to be at the worst possible moment."

Jasmine nodded. If the KEW launcher had been tied to the station's network - the lazy way to handle it - they could have simply shut it down, preventing any chance of a final strike on Meridian. But it wasn't ...she briefly considered going EVA to knock it away from the station, then dismissed the thought. They would just have to take the station's command centre before it was too late.

"Rig something so we can crash the network, if necessary," she ordered. "We'll secure these two idiots and then make our way to the command centre."

She checked the men for weapons - neither of them were carrying anything more dangerous than a computer datapad - then tied their hands and feet with their own clothes. They'd be humiliated when they awoke, she was sure, but it wouldn't matter. The geeks would either be prisoners or explaining themselves to their commanding officer. Being near-naked would be a minor issue.

Watson rose, tiredly. "I rigged up an emergency switch," he said. "It won't crash the network completely, but it will make life difficult for them."

"Good," Jasmine said. She opened her spacesuit, then climbed out of it. The mask would have to suffice if someone tried to vent the station. "Let's go."

The interior of the station seemed quieter than she had expected, although she'd only seen one other station of the same design. It puzzled her until she realised that the crew were probably busy unloading the shuttle and transferring the supplies into the cargo holds, below the habitation modules. If Gary had been right and there were forty people on the station, though, they couldn't all be there. Or were they trying to get first dibs on anything lifted up from the surface? She puzzled over it in her head as she passed a half-open door, then glanced inside. Several crewmen were lying on bunks, snoring loudly.

"Close the hatch, then seal it," she ordered. There were seven men in the room; locking them in, even for a few hours, would make taking the station easier. "The control compartment is just down the corridor."

She left Stewart to seal the hatch and walked down to the control compartment. A warship would have had a guard standing at the hatch, but the Wolves didn't look to have bothered with any formalities. It seemed odd, Jasmine thought, yet it might make sense. There was no real threat from the planet and any warship, even a tiny frigate, would be more than enough to destroy the station and take the planet for itself. It would be pointless to try to resist.

"They're trapped," Stewart muttered, catching up with them. "I think they'll have to break down the hatch to escape."

Jasmine nodded, then pointed to the hatch ahead of them. "We'll go in together, weapons ready," she said. She wished, bitterly, for stunners. Firing bullets in an enclosed compartment was likely to damage something. "But no shooting unless we have no choice."

"Understood," Stewart said. Beside him, Watson nodded. "Open the hatch?"

"Yep," Jasmine said. She keyed the hatch - it opened with a grinding hiss, suggesting poor maintenance - and stepped into the compartment. "EVERYONE FREEZE!"

The five men in the compartment stared at her in disbelief. They had *known* they were safe, right up until the moment she'd walked into their room and held them at gunpoint. There had been no reason to expect trouble...

Idiots, she thought, as she motioned for them to move away from the consoles. *I was taught to always expect trouble.*

"All right," she said, as the prisoners were bound. "Which one of you is in charge?"

"I am," one of the prisoners said. "I ..."

"You will tell the remainder of your people to surrender," Jasmine said, cutting him off. "I want them all in our hands within five minutes, or I will have to use deadly force."

The man glared at her. "How do I know you'll treat them well?"

"I'll treat them as well as you treated us," Jasmine said. There was no point in mistreating helpless prisoners, none of whom had been in any place to issue orders. "And that really wasn't too bad, apart from the endless boredom. I'll even throw a football and a handful of board games into the camp, if you behave."

There was a long pause. "But if you don't cooperate, I will have to use more stringent methods to enforce your cooperation," she added. It wasn't an idea she liked, but there was little choice. They'd been committed from the moment they'd attached themselves to the shuttles. "Make your choice quickly."

The man sagged. "I want their safety guaranteed from everyone," he said.

"Very well," Jasmine said. If the locals wanted them, too bad. She could just dump them on an isolated island and make them wait for the war to end, before they were repatriated home. "But only if you tell them to surrender now."

"I will," the man said.

Jasmine helped him to a console, then listened carefully as he issued his final set of orders to the men. They acknowledged, although they sounded astonished; Jasmine didn't blame them for being surprised. But without a security network, it was hard to be sure they were complying with their orders, instead of planning a surprise. Of all the oversights, it was that one that puzzled her the most.

"My superiors intend to use this station to land additional colonists, once the war is over," he said, when Jasmine asked. "They're planning to establish a purpose-built garrison station in the system at some point."

"I see," Jasmine said. It made sense, she supposed. No matter how many weapons one bolted to the hull, the orbit station was horrifyingly vulnerable to a single spread of missiles or a single kinetic strike. "We'll deal with your crew, then decide where to put them until the end of the war."

It took nearly an hour to round up every last one of the Wolves - and their slaves. There were seventeen girls on the station, Jasmine discovered, all recent immigrants to Meridian from Earth. It was obvious they'd been volunteered for the task, rather than volunteering themselves; she wasn't sure if she hated the locals for sacrificing them or understood their point of view. Oddly, the slaves hadn't been badly hurt - they'd actually been treated decently, apart from being kept as slaves in the first place - but that didn't lessen the horror.

"I have to keep my men entertained," the Wolf said. His name had turned out to be Colonel Halcyon. "Otherwise, they get restless."

Jasmine snorted, rudely. "Did you run out of decking to polish?"

She shook her head as Halcyon was marched off to his private cells. The girls would have to be moved down to the planet, then ...she'd have to lean on the resistance to care for them. And the resistance wouldn't be too pleased with her for keeping the Wolves, even though they'd committed crimes against Meridian itself. Maybe she could just tell them she'd executed them all on sight ...no, that wouldn't work for long. She'd just have to explain she'd made a deal and hope they accepted it with nothing more than token protests.

"I've got them all in the hold," Stewart said, finally. "They're bound, but I don't think we can keep them indefinitely without help. We need manpower from the surface."

"Get the shuttle and prep it to go pick up some help," Jasmine said. Stewart would have to fly the craft on his own, unfortunately. She just hoped that nothing would go wrong. "Carl?"

"I've been looking at the schedules," Watson said. "Everything is imprecise, of course, but it looks as though they're expecting another load of prisoners within two weeks. There's certainly *something* scheduled for that day."

"We'd better prepare Halcyon to assist us," Jasmine said, slowly. "If it's a freighter, we can take it and get out, but if it's a warship ..."

She shook her head. She'd captured pirate ships in the past, but pirates were notoriously careless and cowardly. A genuine warship, crewed by an experienced crew, would be much harder to take intact. The crew would either rally and repel the intruders, or slow the attackers up long enough for the CO to hit the self-destruct. She could only pray she managed to lure it in close enough to plant a barnacle mine on its hull, then force the crew to surrender.

And they would definitely notice a missing warship, she added, in the privacy of her own mind. *They'd start wondering what happened ...and then send something bigger and nastier to take a look at us.*

"I dare say we can convince him to cooperate," Stewart said. "I'll go see to the shuttle now."

Jasmine nodded. "Do we have control of the bombardment package?"

"Aye," Watson said. "Halcyon was kind enough to give us the codes ... not that it would have taken long to hack it, seeing they used a very primitive system. They didn't want to waste a more advanced weapons package on this world."

"Good," Jasmine said. She mentally outlined their next few steps. Get a crew up from the surface to assist with the prisoners, drop the prisoners somewhere safe ...then recover the rest of her people from the POW camps. And then destroy the POW camps, just to hide the evidence of what they'd done. "Deactivate it for the moment. We won't be using it until after we take a starship."

"Of course," Watson said. "I'll get right on it."

Jasmine nodded, then sat down at a console and brought up the station's backlog of classified files. There wasn't much, beyond a simple list of notations of when and where prisoners had been taken, but none of it was good news. Most of the prisoners had come from Thule - or worlds she assumed to be within Wolfbane's space - yet a number had come from Commonwealth worlds along the border. The war might not be going well.

They won't have told anyone here more details, she thought. Wolfbane seemed to be as careful about sharing information as the Empire, which had insisted that only it could determine who had a need to know. In the end, it had cost the Empire dearly. *We may have to make guesses about just what's happening out there.*

The intercom buzzed. "I'm ready to go back down to the surface," Stewart said. "They managed to get most of the crap out of the shuttle before we took the station, so there will be room for newcomers."

"Good," Jasmine said. "Have a safe flight."

She turned back to the list of bases on Meridian and shook her head, ruefully. There were fourteen prison camps - including two so far from Sabre that the resistance hadn't known about them - but not much else. The Wolves hadn't bothered to establish a garrison, beyond the POW guards, let alone a shore leave resort. Maybe Halcyon hadn't wanted to risk his men having unguarded conversations with the locals ...or maybe he'd just been worried about the potential for incidents. She knew just how much trouble young men could get into on shore leave, both with the local law enforcement and their superior officers. And, of course, someone could bribe or seduce them.

"We could try seeing if any of the guards want to defect," Watson offered. "They can't have enjoyed being out here."

"Worth a try," Jasmine agreed. She pulled up a star chart and examined it, thoughtfully. It might have been outdated by at least a decade, but stars remained firmly in place even if political boundaries were incredibly fluid. They were at least nine weeks from Avalon, assuming a modern phase drive. "But the locals will want their scalps and ..."

She hesitated, then pressed on. "Leave it until we have this place secure," she said. They'd have to search the entire station for unpleasant surprises, a task that would be far from easy without skilled manpower. "We can make them an offer afterwards, once we know where they're going."

"Understood," Watson said.

———

Gary let out a sigh of relief as the shuttle landed neatly in front of the control tower, then broke character and ran out to greet the marine as he opened the hatch. Thomas Stewart - if that was his real name - had always intimidated him on some level, yet he'd also had a sense of abiding decency that reminded him of Yates. Maybe it was something marines were taught to project, he wondered, as he came to a halt. Being trusted by the people they served would be very helpful for them.

"Success," Stewart said. "The station and fifty-seven prisoners are in our hands."

"Thank God," Gary said. He waved to Austin, who was standing at the edge of the spaceport, then turned back to Stewart. "I think the troops are five minutes away, waiting in the jungle. Can you fly them back to orbit?"

"Yep," Stewart said. He sounded distracted, rather than pleased, as if he were occupied by some greater thought. "We also need technical experts, if you are hiding any of them."

"Just me," Gary said. The handful of other technical experts on Meridian were long gone; as far as he knew, none had been hidden in time. "And I was never …never that much of an expert."

"Needs must when the devil pisses on you," Stewart said, crudely. "Can you come join us?"

Gary hesitated. Part of him would love to go back into space, he knew, but the rest of him was nervous. Being around so many people, all stronger and tougher than him, was not a pleasant thought. But then, it had defined so much of his life.

"I will," he said, finally. He was damned if he was going to give Barry's shade one last crude laugh. "But I don't know how much help I will be."

Austin came up behind them before Stewart could make a response. "The troops will be here in a minute," he said. "Should we pass the word to hit the camps? I don't know how the guards will react to losing the station."

"I'll check with the boss," Stewart said. "But you're right. You probably should move now."

Gary swallowed, thinking of the scouts who made up the resistance army. He'd done his fair share of learning to shoot, but he knew he would never make a soldier. He simply didn't have the nerve to stand up for himself, let alone others …and he hated the thought of pain and suffering. One would have thought he'd get used to it, but he never had.

And those scouts were going to put themselves on the line for the POWs, for men and women they'd never met. It wasn't something *he* could have done. If he'd ever had any bravery in him, it had been battered out of his soul by Barry ...and just about everyone else he'd ever met. He could never have hoped to become someone like Stewart ...

...And *that* thought tore at his mind, mocking him.

Stewart stepped away and tapped his radio. There was a brief discussion, too quiet for Gary to hear, then Stewart looked back at Austin.

"Tell your people to move," he said. "And once we get the others up to orbit, we can start shipping the prisoners down here."

CHAPTER THIRTEEN

Idealists would say otherwise. But idealists have no practical understanding of the battlefield. It is simply unrealistic for the attacker to allow the defender to hide behind the laws of war, not when the laws of war are slanted against the attacker.
- Professor Leo Caesius. *The Empire and its Prisoners of War.*

Avalon, Year 5 (PE)

"Colonel," Kitty said. "Do you have a moment?"

Colonel Stalker looked up from his data terminal. "I have nothing but moments for you," he said, tiredly. "The paperwork can wait."

Kitty shrugged as she stepped into the office and closed the door behind her, then reached for the bug detector in her belt. Colonel Stalker eyed her with some irritation as she swept the room for unexpected listeners, but said nothing. She understood his irritation - she would have disliked someone checking her office - yet she could do nothing about it. A bug in the right - or wrong - place could be far more dangerous than a single spy.

"We caught a second message last night," she said, slipping the detector back onto her belt and dropping into a hard wooden chair. "It was ... odd."

Colonel Stalker frowned. "How so?"

Kitty met his eyes evenly. "We spent the last week inserting pieces of false information into political briefings," she said. "Group One was told about a mythical foundry ship; Group Two was told about a planned reinforcement of Base Zero; Group Three was told about an encounter with another successor state on the other side of Wolfbane's territory … there were ten pieces of information in all. No one should have had access to more than one piece of information."

"I know the theory," the Colonel said, impatiently. "Am I to understand that more than one piece of information leaked its way into the message?"

"*Four* pieces of information appeared in the message stream," Kitty confirmed. "That gives us fifty-seven suspects, all of whom should have known only one."

The Colonel scowled. "Are you suggesting we're looking at an entire ring of spies, including at least four senior politicians?"

"That's one possibility," Kitty said. "But I would have thought that such a development would have been impossible. It would only take one badly-handled approach to reveal the existence of the spy ring. They would have to be incredibly lucky to pick four people, *all* of whom were willing to commit treason."

"I see your point," the colonel said. "What - exactly - does it mean?"

"I wish I knew," Kitty said. She sighed, resting her head in her hands. "I've got people breaking down the lives of all of the suspects, looking for common strands, but nothing quite seems to make sense. They can't *all* imagine they're going to be made rulers of Avalon if Wolfbane wins the war."

"People have been stupider in the past," Colonel Stalker said.

"This isn't Earth, Colonel," Kitty said, more sharply than she'd intended. "The politicians and businessmen here had to *work* to earn their places. I don't think stupidity is part of their mindset. They might be greedy bastards intent on squeezing the last credit out of a trade deal, but they have to understand the dangers of betraying the Commonwealth."

"True, I suppose," the Colonel said. He didn't seem to take offense at her tone. "But one of them might think he can put a lock on politics or the market permanently."

"That didn't do the Empire any good," Kitty said. "And I highly doubt it will do Wolfbane any favours either. *And* we would have to have at least four people making the same, highly-stupid decision, at more or less the same time."

"Too many coincidences," Colonel Stalker agreed.

Kitty nodded. She had been taught, during training, that most people were self-interested rather than selfish. A man could be relied upon to follow his own self-interest, as he saw it, rather than acting out of altruistic motives. And while she could understand Wolfbane being willing to make all sorts of offers to get a highly-placed spy on their side, someone smart enough to carve out a business or political empire in the Commonwealth would want something more than empty promises. She did have teams looking for sudden displays of wealth, but she had a feeling that would be *too* obvious.

"This leaves us with a problem," Colonel Stalker said. "Do we start narrowing down the focus by providing false information to more people, or do we start compartmentalising information more than we already do?"

"I would prefer to do nothing, for the moment," Kitty said. "There's a chance, now we have a smaller number of suspects, that we can turn up something useful."

"There's also a chance that the bastard will transmit something dangerous to the Wolves," the Colonel snapped. "What happens if they learn something they can use to win the war?"

Kitty met his eyes. "The vast majority of the data we intercepted was political information, rather than military secrets," she said. "Whoever is behind the spy ring, I suspect, is a politician. Maybe even a *conventional* politician."

"You mean someone from the pre-Commonwealth council," Colonel Stalker said. "Are there any of them left?"

"Not in power," Kitty said. "But the old council did have a number of teenage children who were deemed not to be involved with their parents."

"Some of them were lucky to escape," the Colonel pointed out. "Their parents were not the nicest of people."

"True," Kitty agreed. "But others might have considered them good parents."

"And one of them might be in a position to hear something," the Colonel mused. "It's too thin."

"I know, sir," Kitty said. "I would prefer to continue data-crunching, for the moment. Now we have a smaller number of suspects, we can do proper work-ups of their lives. There may be something they have in common ..."

"Or three of them might be bragging and the fourth might be the spy," the Colonel said. "But even bragging could get someone in trouble for releasing classified information."

"Yes, sir," Kitty said. "With your permission, sir, I will return to my office."

The Colonel nodded, curtly, then picked up his datapad. Kitty rose to her feet, then left the compartment and slipped down the corridor to her own office. The guard outside nodded to her, then ran a DNA scan even though he knew who she was. Kitty waited patiently - she would have sacked him if he *hadn't* carried out the checks - then stepped into her room. The terminal was lit up, indicating that yet another package had arrived from her agents.

And I still need more manpower, she thought, sourly. Avalon hadn't had many detectives, police officers, marshals or anyone else with experience that could be used to detect and identify a spy. The handful of agents she *did* have had no time to serve as training officers, not when she needed them on the streets. *But I'm not going to get it, am I?*

Shaking her head, she sat down, poured herself a cup of coffee and started to read through the reports. Luckily, most of the suspects were public figures; privacy laws or not, it was hard for them to go anywhere in person without being noticed and leaving a trail. Councillor Sims had spent the week alternating between the various offices under the council chamber and his own business office ...hadn't he been reported for abusing his power by granting contracts to his cronies? A quick check revealed that Sims *had* been sharply rebuked by the council and was unlikely to remain in office for long, once his constituents finished organising a recall election. There was self-interest and then there was greed and most people on Avalon could tell the difference.

Did that make him the spy? It was possible, but any spy worthy of the name wouldn't do anything to threaten his own position. She shrugged, then checked his movements. A number of reporters had followed him every time he'd left his rooms, showing her where he'd gone in considerable detail. The only place he'd gone that stood out was a party, four days ago, at Governor Brent Roeder's mansion. Reporters were largely barred from attending, unless they had been cleared by the former Governor personally ...

Her eyes narrowed. Governor Roeder had no power; hell, it was questionable if he still had any real right to the title. The Empire he'd served was gone. He'd had a courtesy seat on the first post-Empire council, but after that he'd voluntarily stepped aside. Reading between the lines, Kitty had a feeling he'd been privately told he wouldn't be allowed to remain on the council, now there was a new generation of politicians coming into the public eye, and he'd chosen to claim to leave of his own free will. Not that she could really blame him; leaving willingly would be less humiliating than simply being outright forced off the council.

"Do a cross-reference," she muttered, as she hastily pulled up the other records. She would have liked an AI to handle it, but Imperial Intelligence had never been able to produce one that matched a human's ability to draw conclusions from isolated snatches of data. "See how many others went to his party."

It took her far too long to crunch the data manually, but she finally had her answer. Of the fifty-seven suspects, seventeen had attended the party ...and, collectively, they would know all four pieces of falsified information. It could be a coincidence - she'd been an intelligence officer long enough to know that damning, and completely inaccurate, patterns could appear in the data if one looked hard enough - but she had a feeling she'd stumbled across a very important clue. If all four pieces of information had been at that party, they could have been scooped up by the spy, either through simply bugging the rooms or listening to politicians showing off just how important they were.

The Governor might be tempted, she thought. *He was denied power by the Old Council and then by the New. What if Wolfbane offered him Avalon as his private fiefdom?*

She sighed. It didn't sound right. She'd met the Governor once or twice, but he'd never struck her as insanely ambitious. Being Governor of Avalon - or at least the pre-independence Avalon - wasn't *that* important a job. It made him a big fish in a very small pond ...and still left him a tiny fish, in the Empire's *colossal* pond. He'd have known that Avalon was a dead end, if he'd wanted to become a Sector Governor ...unless he'd had some sense the Empire was doomed. The Old Council had had their own thoughts on the matter too.

It *was* unlikely, but she had to admit it was possible. And she knew she would need to talk to someone who *had* attended one of the parties. She looked down at the list, hunting for familiar names. Only one stood out.

Bastard, she thought, unsure if she was directing the frustrated curse at the Governor or God Himself. *The only person I can talk to is a goddamned reporter.*

Emmanuel Alves had never really expected to work for Commonwealth Intelligence, rather than the *Avalon Central*. He was a reporter, nothing more; he wasn't a dashing spy or cold-hearted counterintelligence agent. Indeed, if he hadn't been deeply worried about his lover, who might be a POW or dead, he would have thought twice about accepting the invitation to Commonwealth Intelligence. Having a good record would be helpful, later, when the government was trying to locate reporters interested in embedding with the troops, but it also risked compromising his neutrality.

And you're dating a Marine, he reminded himself, sharply. *Just how does that tie in with your neutrality?*

He pushed the thought aside as he entered the building and allowed two guards to search him thoroughly, confiscating everything from his datapad to his wristcom. There was no point in protesting; he wasn't allowed to take electronic devices into a secure room, no matter how much he complained. Once the guards had finished their search, leaving him feeling uncomfortably as if they had explored every last inch of his body, they showed him into a barren meeting room. There was nothing inside, but a pair of chairs, a tiny table and a coffee machine.

"Please, be seated," a voice said. Emmanuel turned to see a redheaded woman, entering through another door. "Thank you for coming."

"It's a pleasure," Emmanuel lied. He had a feeling that prisoners weren't searched so thoroughly before being shoved into a cell. "May I ask to whom I'm speaking?"

"Kitty," the woman said. She didn't offer any surname or rank, leading him to suspect it was a false name. His sole contact with Imperial Intelligence had taught him that they used false names as a matter of course. "Please, be seated."

Emmanuel sighed, but obeyed as the woman poured them both cups of coffee. His eyes narrowed as he realised that she'd prepared his perfectly, in line with his preferences, then recalled that his tastes might have been noted during the disastrous mission to Lakshmibai. But for anyone else, it might have seemed like a disconcerting hint of CI's omniscience, its ability to see all. They would find it more than a little worrying.

"I was surprised to be called," he said, trying to take control of the meeting. "Does this have something to do with Jasmine …with Brigadier Yamane?"

"No, at least not as far as I know," Kitty said. She sat down facing him and crossed her long legs, then settled back into her chair. "There has been no word about her or any of the other POWs, I'm afraid. We know nothing about their current status."

Emmanuel nodded, bitterly.

Kitty gave him a brief sympathetic look. "I need to pick your brains, Emmanuel," she said. "If you agree to keep it to yourself until the investigation is completed - and we do have ways to get at the truth - you will have an exclusive."

"I understand," Emmanuel said. "What do you want from me?"

"I understand that you attended a party at the Governor's mansion last week," Kitty said. "Tell me about it."

Emmanuel blinked. He'd expected questions about Jasmine, or about reporters being embedded, not …not this. "Can I ask why?"

"Not yet," Kitty said. Her voice was calm and composed, but there was an undertone that bothered him. "Tell me about the party."

"I can try," Emmanuel said. "The former Governor has been arranging …ah, meetings, places for people with up and coming business or political interests to meet their fellows in a neutral setting. Quite a bit of business is supposed to be done there, away from the lights and cameras of the media. There's also a great deal of social networking among partners and others ...and a surprising amount of fun, too. Last week, he hired a team of acrobats to put on a display for the guests."

Kitty frowned, as if a thought had struck her. "Where does he get the money?"

"I believe his wealthier guests pay a small stipend for their invitations," Emmanuel said, slowly. It wasn't something he had ever considered, but ...in hindsight, he should have at least considered the question. "I don't think he has any other source of income."

"Sounds a little rude," Kitty said, although her eyes were hard. "Asking your guests to pay for cocktail weenies and whatever else they get served at the parties."

"I think they consider it an investment," Emmanuel said. "There have been quite a few business agreements made at the various parties that are worth millions, literally, to their investors. Just one wealthy guest - Gordon Travis, for example - could pay for everything and never notice the loss. And it would work out in his favour."

Kitty shrugged. "I shall have to check up on that," she said. "Does he even own his mansion?"

"One could claim that he owns it by squatters rights," Emmanuel pointed out. The laws intended to deal with the disposition of the Old Council's money and property had granted ownership to whoever lived on it. A mansion was a little larger than a small apartment in one of the giant apartment blocks on the edge of Camelot, but the principle was the same. "Or no one has the heart to take it from him."

"Perhaps," Kitty said. She looked down at the ground for a long moment, as if she were making up her mind about something. "Do you have an open invitation to his parties?"

"The office has one," Emmanuel confirmed. "I can use it if I wish."

"Then I would like you to take me as your date," Kitty said. "I believe they're held every Saturday, right?"

Emmanuel blinked. "Yes, but ..."

"It's quite simple," Kitty said. She rose to her feet and started to pace. "No one ever looks twice at the arm candy. I will be on your arm, wearing a low-cut dress and a short skirt and they won't take me seriously."

"Some of them will try to lure you into bed," Emmanuel said. "And they will be staring at your assets."

"But they won't notice the brain housed inside this body," Kitty said, placing a finger between her breasts. "They will think of me as nothing more than a sex object, perhaps someone you hired for the night. I don't think they will consider me a potential threat."

"Thank you," Emmanuel said, sourly. He'd never lowered himself to hire *anyone* for the night, even though it was perfectly legal on Avalon. "You *do* know I'm in a relationship?"

"I know, but how many others know?" Kitty asked. She went on before Emmanuel could say a word. "And this is important, Emmanuel. I need you to cooperate."

"I'll charge you for it later," Emmanuel said. "Now, what exactly is going on?"

Kitty smiled, then started to explain.

CHAPTER
FOURTEEN

Like so much else, this harks back to the age-old problem of enforcing the laws.
- Professor Leo Caesius. *The Empire and its Prisoners of War.*

Meridian, Year 5 (PE)

"I cannot say that I am pleased at the agreement you made," Clarence said, a day after the station had been captured. "Those bastards should be put on trial, then executed."

"I understand how you feel," Jasmine said. "But they surrendered and should be treated decently. More to the point" - she held up a hand before he could say another word - "Wolfbane will return to the system and you don't want to be responsible for something they *will* see as an atrocity."

Clarence scowled at her, then sat down. "Very well," he said. "We will - reluctantly - accept the agreement. They can be dumped somewhere well away from the rest of the settlement and remain there, at least until the end of the war."

Jasmine nodded, relieved. "The POWs present another problem," she said. "You liberated all the camps?"

"Yes," Clarence said. "But can you lift all the prisoners?"

"It depends on what ship we capture," Jasmine said. "But unless we get very lucky and they send a whole fleet of colonist-carriers, probably not."

She looked down at the datapad in some irritation. The Wolves had kept fairly good records of just who they'd locked up on Meridian, but most of them were largely useless to her, at least when it came to plotting the next stage of their escape. There were former CEF personnel mixed with political prisoners like Stubbins and hostages like Kailee. Some of them, she was sure, would be useful in the later stages of the war, particularly if they could be secretly reinserted onto their homeworlds, yet for the moment they were merely a logistic headache.

"I think most of them will definitely have to be hidden here," she said, finally. "Can you provide hiding spaces?"

"They'll have to work," Clarence said, "but we can hide them. Unless, of course, the entire planet is turned to ash. *That* would kill them."

Jasmine smirked. Only an idiot - or a Grand Senator - would suggest searching an entire planet for a handful of fugitives. Meridian might be a grain of dust in the everlasting cosmic sea, but on a human scale the planet was still incomprehensibly huge. As long as the former POWs kept their heads down and refrained from emitting any betraying signatures, they should be effectively impossible to locate. They could stay on Meridian until the end of the war, if they chose.

"There are places they can hide," Janet Livingstone said. She was a former Imperial Army officer, someone who had remained out of sight until the station had been taken. Jasmine had had the impression she was actually quite senior in the resistance's ranks, but no one had bothered to either confirm or deny it for her. "We do have quite a few camps that are completely primitive, without anything that could attract attention."

"They'll hate it," Clarence predicted.

Jasmine smiled. *She'd* had plenty of experience roughing it and she had to admit it gave one an appreciation for the wonders of modern civilisation. Who would want to live, permanently, without hot and cold running water, or modern medicine, or any of the other marvels of technology? The former POWs would have no choice, however; they didn't dare let any of them be recaptured. It would prove disastrous.

"They can like it or lump it," she said, flatly.

She sighed. "There's a ship due soon," she said. "By then, we have to be ready to capture her and then decide our next move."

"That's your call," Clarence said. "Are you sure you can destroy all the physical evidence?"

"I think so," Jasmine said. She shrugged. "As far as anyone will be able to tell, Kailee accompanied us to the city, then made contact with Gary ... all without any help from the rest of you. The destroyed camps will suggest we smashed everything we could before we left, along with the prisoners. They won't be able to tell any different, as long as your people keep their mouths shut."

"They will," Clarence assured her. "They know the score."

Jasmine hoped he was right. In her experience, civilians could be remarkably stupid about keeping their mouths shut all the time. They might have largely avoided notice in the city - or so she hoped - but flying so many shuttles to and from the station could not have gone unremarked. All it would take to betray the secret would be to have one person open his or her mouth at the wrong time. And then Wolfbane would wreak a terrible revenge.

"Good," she said, instead. "I hope you don't mind us borrowing Gary and Kailee."

"They wanted to go with you," Clarence said. He smiled, rather dryly. "Not everyone can hack it down here."

"I know," Jasmine said. "But that doesn't make them bad people."

"Not elsewhere," Clarence said. "But here it could make them a burden."

Jasmine rather suspected that wasn't particularly fair. Gary would have gone far, with the proper education and support, while Kailee had never really had a chance. Given the help they needed, they might have grown into something remarkable; hell, Kailee could certainly have had children, to help the next generation of settlers grow. But she also understood Clarence's attitude. Meridian simply didn't have the resources to tolerate freeloaders, or useless mouths. Few stage-one colonies did.

"They will be fine with us," she said, shortly. She took a final look at her datapad, then rose to her feet. "Do you have any other volunteers?"

"I will come, if you need me," Janet said. "But I would prefer to stay."

Jasmine nodded, making a mental note to have a proper chat with Janet when they were alone. Being a female Marine was hard - she had no illusions about just how many women washed out during Hell Week alone - but being a female soldier in the Imperial Army could be a foretaste of hell. And yet Janet didn't look either broken or useless. If she'd lived on Meridian for five years, at least, she had to be tougher than she seemed.

"We'll see what we have," she said. The CEF had never anticipated having to fight in space, let alone repair a space station and prepare to grab a freighter. If she had, she would have insisted on more of her people collecting space-capable MOS badges. "We may just have to patch together the station with spit and bailing wire."

"I can provide the lemons," Clarence said. Jasmine looked at him blankly. "To provide lots of saliva."

Jasmine snorted. Blake Coleman would have made the same joke, she was sure, and probably added something about blood, sweat, tears and semen. But she didn't really feel like laughing.

"We'll see," she said. "I have to go back to the station in an hour, anyway. Is there anything else before we go?"

"Just wishing you good luck," Clarence said. "And asking if any of your people want to stay permanently."

"Wait until after the war," Jasmine said, tartly. She might have liked to retire to Meridian, but she had her duty. Besides, if the war came to an end, she might even be able to return to her homeworld, if her family was still alive. "I think a few of us might like to settle here."

"It feels strange to be here, doesn't it?"

Gary looked at Kailee, sharply. She'd been acting oddly ever since they'd been flown to the station, alternatively being the girl he remembered and a stranger who eyed him with fear in her eyes. He hadn't dared touch her, knowing she might react badly, but he couldn't help wanting to take her in his arms and hold her tightly. She'd been put through hell merely for daring to fall in love with him.

But *was* she in love with him? He'd clung to her, at least in part, because he had *known* that no local girl would be interested in him. What was he compared to Austin, or even Darrin? But would Kailee have stayed in love with him when she'd endured five years in a POW camp, just to keep him under control? He could understand why she might have decided to hate him, now. If it hadn't been for him, she would never have been imprisoned.

"It's different," he agreed, finally. "This is a modern station."

He opened a hatch and peered inside, then pressed the diagnostic tool to the installed components. The Wolves hadn't been keen on basic maintenance, he'd discovered, not when they'd considered the station a temporary home. So far, he'd encountered a number of components that would have to be replaced, if they wanted to keep the station operational for a few more years. It was sheer luck the life support systems hadn't suffered a catastrophic failure. Cleaning out the vents wasn't a pleasant job, but it had to be done.

"No trees," Kailee said. "No insects. No animals. No smell."

Gary wrinkled his nose. It was true there was no natural smell in the air, but he could smell everything from overheating components to a tangy metallic scent that bothered him, if only because he didn't know where it was coming from. Stewart had told him to be grateful - he'd claimed that pirates defecated everywhere, when they crewed ships - but he wasn't sure he believed the Marine. Who would be stupid enough to think a ship would remain operational when they were knee-deep in human waste?

"It's different," he said, again. "I might have liked staying here."

Kailee frowned, fastidiously. "Are you going to stay here?"

"I think I will be going with them," he said. "It won't be safe to stay here."

He gritted his teeth in bitter helpless rage. Darrin and Austin understood he'd had no choice, but to collaborate …but somehow he doubted everyone else on Meridian would feel the same way. They might kill him for collaborating and then kill Kailee too, just for daring to be close to him. He'd always been picked on at school and he saw no reason that would change, not now.

"I don't know," Kailee said. She stared down at her long fingers, tanned after spending so long on the planet. "It won't be safe anywhere."

"I know," Gary said. "It never was, was it?"

He sighed. As a child, he'd envied the men and women who had earned enough money to create their own safe environments. They'd lived on giant space stations or asteroid colonies where anyone who caused trouble could be evicted, without a second thought. He'd hoped to earn that much money himself, once, before he'd been sent to Meridian. Now ...all he could do was keep his head down and hope not to be noticed.

"No," Kailee said. "It wasn't."

She sat down by the bulkhead, resting her head in her hands. Gary hesitated, then closed the hatch and sat down next to her. She froze as his arm brushed hers, then visibly forced herself to relax and lean against him. Gary shivered, wondering just what she might have endured in the POW camp, knowing it would be a long time before they could touch each other intimately once again. Kailee hadn't just worn an overall, she'd buttoned it up so tightly he couldn't see anything below her chin.

"I was always scared," she said. "Scared of being caught, scared of being alone, scared ...scared of being *used*, like a dishrag. And now, I am *still* always scared."

Gary nodded, cursing the Wolves - and Barry - under his breath. He'd known life wasn't easy for girls, but he'd hated them too, hated them for sticking together and trying to protect one another when no one had ever protected him. In hindsight, he saw it for what it really was, just another way to divide and rule the population of Earth. If everyone was at everyone else's throats, they weren't going to be uniting against their masters.

"I don't know what I want to do," she admitted. "Would it bring an end if I stepped out the airlock?"

"It would be the end," Gary agreed.

He swallowed. He'd tried to commit suicide twice, but he'd failed; the knives he'd been forced to use were poor at cutting human flesh, while he hadn't been able to find enough pills to end his life. Or had that been his own reluctance to end his life? Now ...there was no shortage of weapons on Meridian, yet would he be able to pull the trigger if he put the gun to his head?

"That's the point," Kailee told him, waspishly. "It would be the end."

Gary stared at her, trying to think of something - anything - he could say that wouldn't be either useless or condescending. But what *could* he say? There was no real hope for either of them. Kailee wasn't strong enough to make it on Meridian, nor was she technically inclined to work in space ...what *could* she do? And even if she tried, she would still be at the mercy of bastards, bullies and assholes. What could he say to convince her that life was worth living? What could he say when he was half-convinced his *own* life wasn't worth living?

"There's always hope," he said. "You're young and pretty ..."

"Not *that* young," Kailee snarled. "And am I pretty on Meridian?"

No, Gary thought.

He kept that to himself. Meridian loved girls who were competent and capable, rather than decorative. Austin had even said as much, when he'd pointed out that beauty faded, but the ability to do everything required on a farm just got better and better. His girlfriend hadn't been pretty, by Earth's standards, yet she'd had a zest for life that Gary knew Kailee would never be able to match. Kailee's dark hair, slim body and pale eyes didn't pass muster on Meridian. It made her look like someone who couldn't stand up for herself.

"You're not stupid either," he said. "You could learn to teach in school or ..."

"I wouldn't be able to stand up to the children," Kailee said. "Could I?"

"I don't know," Gary said. He had a vague idea that schooling on Meridian was different to schooling on Earth, but he wasn't sure how. "What else can you do?"

"Nothing," Kailee said. She laughed, bitterly. "I couldn't hope to become a movie star, could I?"

Gary sighed. He'd known Kailee had dreams of stardom - every girl did - but there was no point in clinging to that dream on Meridian. Hell, from what Darrin had told him, there had been little hope on Earth too. Yates had pointed it out to Darrin, coldly and precisely; Kailee's dreams had been almost certainly beyond any hope of coming true. But on Meridian, they weren't even faint hopes. The only people who acted were amateurs who put on plays during the winter months.

"I don't think so," Gary said. He paused. "There *is* a teaching machine here, isn't there? You could use it ..."

Kailee looked at him. "And do what?"

"Find something you're good at and do it," Gary said. "We're in space now. You might not have to return to Meridian ..."

"Janet was a soldier," Kailee said. "And so is Jasmine."

Gary blinked. Janet had always intimidated him, while he had some problems wrapping his head around Jasmine's femininity. If she hadn't been introduced by name, he would have thought she was definitely a young teenage boy, not a grown woman. But where had that come from? Janet had barely had any time for any of them since the Wolves had landed; she'd gone undercover at once, hoping to remain undiscovered.

"I should ask them," Kailee said. "They might be able to suggest something."

"Maybe," Gary said. Greatly daring, he put an arm around her. Kailee froze, again, and remained still until he removed his arm. "Kailee ..."

"It's not your fault," Kailee said. "It's me."

She rose to her feet, her body's curves hidden behind layers of clothing. "I'm useless, Gary, utterly useless."

"No, you're not," Gary said. "I ..."

"*You* can do repair work," Kailee said. The bitterness in her voice shocked him. "I can't do anything, beyond looking pretty. And I'm not even pretty on Meridian!"

"You are pretty to me," Gary said, thinking hard. Kailee needed help ... but who could give it to her? There were no therapists on Meridian, where the locals prided themselves on handling their own problems. "Kailee ..."

"You're not to blame," Kailee said. She placed a hand on his shoulder for a long second, then marched towards the hatch. "But I need to talk to someone else."

Gary watched her go, unable to work up the nerve to go after her or even to call her back. He honestly didn't know what to do ...he'd never understood girls and women, despite the hundreds of thousands of texts available in the school's database. It hadn't taken him long to realise that most of the texts were contradictory, as if the writers had disagreed on just about everything under the sun. They certainly hadn't been any help to him.

He stared down at the deck, feeling helpless. What could he do? The cold-blooded part of his mind insisted that Kailee was right; she *couldn't* do anything. Only a handful of schoolchildren on Earth ever had any real potential to become anything more than the parents of the next generation of useless children. But the idealistic part of his mind knew better. Kailee wasn't useless, merely ...having problems finding her vocation. She might stumble across something tomorrow that would determine the rest of her life ...

I'm sorry, he thought, *but I don't know what to do.*

CHAPTER FIFTEEN

A law can only be enforced by a power both capable and willing to enforce the law. A law against gambling, for example, only holds force if the local police are willing to enforce it. If the police are unwilling to enforce the law, either through corruption or fear, gambling may proceed unmolested.
- Professor Leo Caesius. *The Empire and its Prisoners of War.*

Meridian, Year 5 (PE)

"Most of the station should last long enough for us to capture a freighter," Watson said, once Jasmine had entered her new office. Halcyon hadn't been a decent commanding officer, not by her standards, but at least he'd kept his private office neat and tidy. "After that ...I think we should probably blow the station once we leave."

"Understood," Jasmine said. They'd moved forty of her people from the camps to the station, but the remainder would have to wait until the freighter arrived. "There's no point in leaving it intact."

She sighed. The station would need to be replaced, once the war was over, but that wouldn't be difficult. Wolfbane would have to replace it themselves, if they wanted somewhere to tranship POWs to the surface; the locals had little interest in the station, certainly not enough to demand that Jasmine should leave it intact. Besides, even if they had, they certainly understood that the station was useless until the war was over.

"I'll be happy to see to it," Watson said. He'd earned a MOS in demolitions while he'd been on the Slaughterhouse and had lots of fun on active service, putting his training to good use. "I think we'd be better off shattering it - or hurling it out of orbit into the sun. We don't want to leave pieces of debris raining down on the planet and doing damage."

"Plan out a way of launching it into the sun," Jasmine ordered. Chunks of hullmetal probably *would* hit the planet's surface - and if they were large enough, they might do real damage to the settlement. "But make sure you don't actually set the charges until we have a starship."

"Of course," Watson said. "I ..."

The doorbell chimed. "You have a visitor?"

Jasmine shrugged, then tapped the switch on her desk. The door hissed open, revealing Kailee, looking rather out of place. "Excuse me," she said. "Do you have a moment to talk?"

Jasmine eyed the stack of paperwork she needed to go through - mainly older files from Wolfbane - then nodded. "I'll speak to you later," she said to Watson. "Let me know if anyone else from the surface volunteers to join us."

"Stubbins is coming up on the next shuttle," Watson said. "I bet *he* wants to join us."

He saluted, then turned and walked out of the hatch, which closed smoothly behind him. Jasmine looked at Kailee, who was wringing her hands together nervously, then pointed to a comfortable chair placed in front of her desk. Kailee sat, reminding Jasmine of Mandy Caesius in a way she didn't really like. Mandy had been a brat when they'd first met, but Kailee ...was a traumatised soul. It wasn't really the same at all.

"I may not have long," Jasmine said. There was too much to do that required her direct attention, even though she trusted both Stewart and Watson implicitly. She would have sold her soul for a team of technical experts from the Commonwealth - or the Trade Federation. "What can I do for you?"

Kailee looked down at the deck. "I want to become a Marine," she said. "How do I join?"

Jasmine stared at her, shocked speechless.

"I mean it," Kailee insisted. "Please."

"I see," Jasmine said, schooling her voice to remain calm. She'd never been a recruiting sergeant, nor had she ever really *wanted* to become one.

Even if she had, she would have needed at least ten years service and a surviving Empire. "May I ask why?"

Kailee met her eyes. There was something in her eyes that suggested she was on the far end of her tether. "Because I want to be useful," she said. "And because I am *sick* of being so scared all the goddamned time."

"I've been scared," Jasmine said. It wasn't something she would have admitted normally, certainly not to one of her comrades, but Kailee needed to know that Marines weren't fearless. "I ..."

"You were dumped in a camp," Kailee said. "I was there for five years; you were there for four *days*. You managed to put together a plan to get out, then actually *did* it while I sat there uselessly. I want to be like you."

Jasmine sighed, inwardly. It was tradition that no one was turned away, if they arrived at a recruiting centre and signed on the dotted line. Boot Camp and Hell Week did an excellent job of rooting out the people who simply weren't suited for military life, while ensuring that seemingly unprepossessing recruits were allowed a chance to shine and grow into their roles. Indeed, relatively few committed offences that *would* get them kicked out. They tended to quit themselves before matters got out of hand.

But a recruiting sergeant had an astonishing amount of discretion, if he thought there was something genuinely wrong with the would-be recruit, or if he thought the recruit didn't have a hope of surviving the first day. Kailee ...the more Jasmine looked at her, the more she was sure that Kailee wouldn't last the first day at Boot Camp. She wasn't built for the role, nor was she in the best of health. The facilities that would have helped her to build up her muscles - and confidence - no longer existed.

"Kailee," she said, slowly. "How old are you?"

"Twenty-one," Kailee said. "I think ...somewhere around twenty-one, anyway."

Jasmine frowned. "The youngest we can take someone is eighteen, without parental permission," she said. It was, in theory, possible to take a sixteen-year-old, but she'd never actually heard of it being done. "There's no upper limit, but ..."

She sighed, then told herself to be gentle. "Kailee, right now, we don't have the facilities to train new Marines," she admitted. Rebuilding something akin to the Slaughterhouse, along with centuries of traditions, would take years. "Even if we did ...I would have grave doubts about recommending you for training."

Kailee's eyes flashed. "Because I came from Earth?"

"Because you're not suited to the life," Jasmine said, honestly. "The purpose of Boot Camp is to separate the quitters from those who just won't quit, no matter what is thrown at them."

"I won't quit," Kailee said.

"Listen," Jasmine said, sharply. "Do you know what I had to do?"

She took a breath. "They made us march eight miles from one hidden marker to another," she said. "Then they made us march another eight miles. And then they made us march *yet another* eight miles. Can you imagine how tired, sore and pissed off we were when we found the fourth marker?"

Kailee glowered at her. "I've walked long distances before," she insisted.

"Carrying a full combat load?" Jasmine asked. She went on before Kailee could answer. "So there we were, at the fourth marker, watching as the Drill Instructor rode up in a truck and smiled at us. And he told us that we needed to do *another* fucking eight miles. Some of us quit on the spot! I kept going. And going. And going."

She met Kailee's eyes. "You have to keep going whatever gets in your way," she said. "Your feet will be covered in blisters, your legs will be aching, your arms will feel numb, your eyes will be in pain and your vision will be dimming out ...and you will still have to keep going, because you have to complete your mission. And at the end, you will be expected to deploy, attack your target and then retreat the way you came, knowing the hounds of hell will be snapping at your heels. You will go through hell.

"It gets worse. You will be expected to follow orders that will make no sense, or seem dangerous or pointlessly humiliating. You will be yelled at every time you fire your rifle and miss a shot. You will be beasted every time your rifle is inspected and found to be less than one hundred percent completed. You will be dropped in a swimming pool and expected to swim miles in full combat uniform. You will be taken up in an airplane and tossed out, hoping and praying that the parachute doesn't fail on the way down. You will go into space and be exposed to hard vacuum, or worse. You will be trapped and cuffed to a chair and beaten halfway to death to harden you against interrogation techniques. You will ..."

Jasmine met Kailee's eyes. "By the time you have that Rifleman's Tab pinned to your shoulder," she concluded, "you damn well will have earned it."

"I can do it," Kailee said.

"I don't think you can," Jasmine said. "Kailee, I understand the impulse. I understand what you're trying to do. But it won't help you to take on an impossible challenge, even if you could."

Kailee looked downcast. "Is there no hope?"

"There's always hope," Jasmine said. It was a belief that had kept her going, even when she'd been trapped in a foxhole all night and she was wet, cold and miserable. "But there's also such a thing as taking on too great a challenge."

She met Kailee's eyes. "Why didn't you try anything on Meridian? The Scouts let girls join, don't they?"

"I was too old," Kailee said. "I ...they thought I was stupid."

Jasmine winced. A child on Meridian would be expected to know how to hunt, shoot and countless other skills that were practically unheard of on Earth. To them, Kailee had to seem a silly and ignorant girl, someone absurdly focused on the immaterial over the material. It wasn't unknown for recruits to arrive at Boot Camp with a similar degree of ignorance, but the Drill Instructors knew how to deal with it without making the recruits feel stupid or useless.

She closed her eyes and thought, rapidly. She wasn't a training officer of any stripe, let alone someone capable of turning a raw recruit into a marine. Kailee would be hard to train in any case, if only because her life had taught her that if something was too hard, either someone would give it to her or it wasn't worth having. She might well give up at the first hurdle because she couldn't see it as being attainable.

And I couldn't have passed the Crucible the day I entered Boot Camp, Jasmine thought. *I wasn't anything like as fit as I became.*

"I may need someone to serve as an aide," Jasmine said, slowly. It wasn't something she wanted - and she would have needed someone with more technical expertise - but it was something Kailee could do. "In exchange for that, I will give you some basic training - and, if you manage to stay the course, recommend you for training when we get back to Avalon."

She held up a hand before the girl could say a word. "This won't be easy," she said. "You will find it immensely difficult. If you want to quit, you can quit at any time."

"I won't," Kailee said.

Jasmine had her doubts. Kailee had almost no confidence at all, something that would drag her down more than physical issues. Hell, Jasmine was fairly sure Kailee would have hurt herself at Boot Camp, even if she hadn't given up and quit in disgust. She just didn't have the body to become a Marine.

"You'll get a fair chance," Jasmine said. "But one chance is all you will get."

"Thank you," Kailee said. She sounded nervous, rather than elated. Jasmine recalled all the recruits who'd been homesick, their first night in barracks, and sighed again. At least Kailee was used to being away from home. "Um ...what do you want me to do as your aide?"

Jasmine groaned, inwardly. Now she would have to think of something for the girl to do.

"Look through these files," she said, finally. She picked up a datapad, then downloaded the personnel files from the station's computers. "I want you to mark any POW with either qualifications or experience to work in space."

"I thought people had to have qualifications," Kailee said, as she took the datapad. "How else would employers know who could do the job?"

Jasmine pointed a finger at her. "*That*, Kailee, is one of the lies you were told at school," she said, sternly. "A person who spends all of their time passing exams will not be good at anything beyond passing exams. The ability to do the job matters far more than a piece of paper *saying* you can do the job ...particularly when the exam is often tied up with other exams, none of which are important to the job. Besides ...I'm pretty sure Gary doesn't have anything saying he can work in a spaceport."

"He doesn't," Kailee confirmed. "But this is different ..."

"No, it isn't," Jasmine said, shortly. "I ..."

The doorbell chimed, again. "There's an empty room to the left," Jasmine said, as she opened the door. It had once housed a pair of slaves, who had divided their time between housekeeping and servicing the Wolves. "Start reading through the files and let me know what you find."

She looked past Kailee to see Paula standing in the door. "Come in," she said. "I trust they got you out of the camp without problems?"

"They captured the guards, then tore down the fence and walked off with us," Paula said. She stepped to one side as Kailee walked past her, then sat down as the door hissed closed. "I didn't believe it."

Jasmine's lips curled. "Why not?"

"It just seemed impossible that three people could capture a space station by themselves," Paula said. "No matter what help you had …"

"Nothing is impossible if you try hard enough," Jasmine said. She'd learned that lesson as a child, although age and experience had led her to temper it a little. "How is your boss?"

Paula sighed. "He's planning a coup."

Jasmine blinked. "Is he mad?"

"He spent the last couple of days trying to organise support from some of the other political prisoners," Paula said. "Basically, he plans to unseat you, take the station, take the next ship that arrives …and then head back to Wolfbane, where he will be welcomed in triumph."

"He's delusional," Jasmine said, sharply. She doubted Stubbins could organise a piss-up in a brewery, let alone taking a space station …but then, the space station had already changed hands once in the last week. "All he'll do is get a great many people killed."

She slapped the table. "And if he *does* manage to get back to Wolfbane," she added, "all he'll do is get *himself* killed."

"So it would seem," Paula said. She looked up at Jasmine. "You might want to dissuade him first."

Jasmine looked back at her, evenly. "*You* can't dissuade him?"

"When he gets an idea into his thick head, it is rather difficult to get him to give it up," Paula said. "It was hard enough to steer him when he was a General in truth, rather than merely in name. Being tough-minded kept him going through some pretty dark moments …"

She made a face. "Suffice it to say that my steering skills aren't going to be enough," she admitted, ruefully. "All I can really do is warn you and hope you can deal with him."

"I see," Jasmine said. "Why have you stayed with him, anyway?"

Paula shrugged. "Being the secretary of a powerful man made me powerful," she said, "but it also made me enemies. I was seen, rightly or wrongly, as his hatchet woman. There were people just licking their lips on Wolfbane at the mere prospect of my fall from grace. I would have been lucky to wind up selling myself to stay alive."

"So you said," Jasmine remembered.

"It seemed better to go into exile with him," Paula added. "But right now, he's not going to listen to me and he's just going to get me killed. Or dumped on Meridian again ...I want to go home. I think it's time to start looking after my own interests."

"I can try and get you to Wolfbane," Jasmine said. "And, whatever happens, you won't be dumped on Meridian."

"Thank you," Paula said. She looked down at the deck. "Are you going to let him commit himself before you move?"

"No," Jasmine said. She could see the logic in allowing a suspect to run free, just to see what he would do, but it wasn't something she was inclined to try. "I think I don't want to take the risk. Who has he suborned so far?"

"Just a handful of political prisoners," Paula said. "He was reluctant to approach anyone who might feel loyal to you personally."

Jasmine felt a flicker of relief. Most of the political prisoners were harmless, or at least not on the station. She could handle the affair by arresting Stubbins, then interrogating him ...there was no need to purge everyone who *might* have been touched by him. And if Paula hadn't told her about the plan, it might have ended badly for everyone.

"I'll deal with him now," she said, flatly. "Do you want him to know that you came and told me?"

Paula hesitated, then nodded. "It might shock him into actually being helpful," she said, slowly. "I don't think I'll be going to bed with him for a while."

"No," Jasmine agreed. She reached for the intercom and called Stewart and Watson, then looked back at Paula. "He might try to strangle you in your sleep."

CHAPTER SIXTEEN

> When it comes to the laws of war, where a whole country may be the criminal, enforcing the laws almost certainly requires war. This would require outside powers to invade the offender's territory, if all other methods of persuasion failed.
> - Professor Leo Caesius. *The Empire and its Prisoners of War.*

Meridian, Year 5 (PE)

"Go," Jasmine said, as General James Stubbins stepped into her office. "Now."

Stubbins blinked, then gasped as Stewart and Watson grabbed him, forced his hands behind his back and snapped on the cuffs, then searched him roughly. Somewhat to Jasmine's amusement, he wasn't carrying anything apart from an automatic pistol he'd probably picked up on Meridian. Given his lack of shooting practice - it was rare to see a general in the shooting range - Jasmine had a private suspicion he wouldn't actually have managed to hit her, even if he had drawn it before he'd been grabbed. But she wasn't inclined to give him the chance.

"This is outrageous," Stubbins protested, as he was forced into a chair. "I ..."

He stopped as his gaze fell on Paula. "You! You ..."

"That will do," Jasmine said, sharply. She hated to do it, but it was important to make it clear to Stubbins that he was completely in her power. "You were plotting to take over by force, General. I could not allow that to happen."

She rose from behind the desk and paced around to face him. "I have every intention of getting us back to friendly space," she added, "but your coup plot would have gotten us all killed. There was no choice."

Stubbins glared at her. "I have to go back," he said. "My people ..."

"Have done nothing for you in five years," Jasmine said. "If you had the connections you claim to have, they would have sent a ship to pick you up by now. Instead, you were left here to rot. Now, if you cooperate with me, I will ensure that you have your chance to go back to Wolfbane. If you don't, I will drop you back on the surface and let the locals deal with you."

She winced, inwardly, at his expression. It was never nice to hurt a person - and Wolfbane hadn't bothered to supply any truth drugs, lie detectors or anything else she could have used to ensure the interrogation was reasonably pleasant. Hell, it was quite possible Stubbins had implants designed to make it impossible to force him to talk. He was certainly convinced of his own importance ...

At least we know Wolfbane wasn't planning to interrogate any of us, she thought, savagely. *They were just going to leave us here to rot.*

Stubbins sagged, visibly. "You can get me back home?"

"Yes," Jasmine said. She doubted Stubbins would find anything beyond a quick death when he reached Wolfbane, unless he had a fleet at his back, but he could have his chance. "Tell us everything you know and we will get you home."

Stubbins stared at her, then shot a glance at Paula that promised later mayhem and murder. "What would you like to know?"

"Start with Governor Brown," Jasmine said. The files were vague - Governor Brown hadn't been considered *that* important - but she knew enough, she hoped, to catch him in a lie. "Tell me about him."

Stubbins scowled. "Corporate rat," he said, bitterly. "The damn corporations put him in power to make it easier to squeeze the last bit of blood out of the sector. He did a damn good job of it too, dispensing patronage to make sure his people were in important places. And then the news from Earth reached us and he just took over. He had troops on the streets and in key positions before anyone else quite realised what had happened."

Jasmine nodded, slowly. That accorded with what she knew of Governor Brown.

"He started telling everyone that such measures were only temporary," Stubbins continued, slowly. "I thought we'd make contact with whoever took command in the Core Worlds and then reassume contact with the rest of the Empire. But all hell broke loose there instead and ...and Governor Brown just took power for himself. I didn't have time to protest before it was too late."

"I see," Jasmine said. "All hell broke loose?"

"There was a conference on Terra Nova, according to the reports we got," Stubbins said. "I think it was to try to sort out the post-Earth universe. It failed, spectacularly, and everyone started to go to war. That was the last we heard from the Core Worlds."

Jasmine sighed, inwardly. There was so little reliable news from the Core Worlds. Hell, they hadn't known anything about the Fall of Earth until the first encounter with Admiral Singh ...and then only the barest details. There was no shortage of rumours, of course, but they ranged from unlikely to impossible. What sort of idiot would believe a giant bird had been incubating inside Earth and it's birth had cracked a planet like an eggshell?

"I see," she repeated. "There's nothing else?"

"Not as far as I know," Stubbins said. "But the Governor might have kept something to himself. He always was a devious bastard."

"Yeah," Jasmine said. "Tell me about the fleet. How many ships does he have at his disposal?"

Stubbins gave her a sharp look. "He had seven squadrons of battleships and over three hundred smaller ships," he said. Stewart let out a low whistle. "Half of the battleships were being cannibalised for spare parts to keep the remainder going ...I think most of the smaller ships were in full working order. The Governor had enough industrial capability to keep them maintained."

Jasmine resisted the urge to swear. The Commonwealth had only three squadrons of battleships, all captured from Admiral Singh. True, there were quite a few pieces of advanced technology that might tip the balance in the Commonwealth's favour, but Governor Brown still had a major advantage. Clearly, the only thing that kept him from winning the war outright was his own natural caution, perhaps made worse by bruising encounters with new technology.

"We're going to have to go through it in some detail," she said. Stubbins had been in the camp for five years, after all. Governor Brown could have repaired the remaining battleships by now, if he was prepared to devote the resources and manpower to keeping them in active service. "Can he build new ships of his own?"

"Everything up to and including battlecruisers," Stubbins said, flatly. "He had a shipyard even before the shit hit the fan. By now, it could be a great deal larger."

Jasmine's eyes narrowed. "A shipyard?"

"A military-grade shipyard, in the Wolfbane System," Stubbins said. There was something almost taunting in his voice. "Quite a big industrial base too. I fancy he dragged nodes from every system for fifty light years, just to keep them all under his personal control. Thousands of workers too, all from shitholes like Meridian, working hard for the greater glory of the corporate rat."

"Said rat thoroughly outmanoeuvred you and dumped you here," Jasmine pointed out, tartly. "And if he hadn't, you wouldn't be here."

She gritted her teeth, thinking hard. The more she thought about the news, the less she liked it. Wolfbane might have a numerical superiority that would off-set anything the Commonwealth could put up against it. Given five years, and the combined industrial base of every system within fifty light years of Wolfbane ...the odds didn't look good. She needed to get the intelligence back to Avalon, but how?

"There will be more questions," she said, tiredly. Maybe Kailee could sit down with Stubbins and write down his answers, perhaps with someone from the CEF to supervise. "And you will answer them."

Stubbins looked at her, sardonically. "Don't you wish you let me go back to Wolfbane?"

"In five years," Jasmine said, "you never even *tried* to escape. Now, when someone else comes up with a plan, you try to take control. And you don't even have a ship that will get you back to Wolfbane. Surely, you should have waited until you had a ship!"

She sighed. "We will endeavour to get you back to Wolfbane," she added, "*provided* you answer our questions. If we catch you in a single lie, you're going to be hurt."

"I'm a General," Stubbins protested.

"The Empire you served has gone," Jasmine said. "And I think whatever titles you had afterwards were taken by Governor Brown."

She nodded to Stewart, who marched Stubbins out of the cabin and down to the cell they'd prepared. He would be under guard at all times, with no one permitted to talk to him without Jasmine's express permission. Hopefully, her precautions would be enough to keep him from doing something else stupid. And if they weren't ...she thought wistfully about airlocks, then pushed the thought aside. She didn't want to kill him when he could spend the rest of his life on a penal farm, on the planet below.

"Good God," Watson said. "Are all Generals so self-centred?"

"They do tend to have large egos," Paula confirmed. "And a certain reluctance to recognise reality does keep them going, when lesser souls have given up."

Jasmine scowled. If the generals on Han had realised that the planet was about to explode, hundreds of thousands of lives would have been saved. Instead, they'd fiddled while the arsonists prepared to burn the planet to the ground. She hated to think of just how many lives had been lost, both civilian and military, or ruined by the uprising. Millions had been killed and millions more had been driven away from their homes, or forced into refugee camps where they had been abused, raped and sometimes murdered. And yet, if the Core Worlds had exploded into war, the death toll on Han would merely be a drop in the bucket.

"I will have him interrogated, time and time again," she said, reluctantly. Paula might not be able to supervise, but she could write down his words and summarise them. "We need to know everything he knows about Wolfbane."

"Everything he knows will be five years out of date," Watson warned. "If they really have been collecting every industrial node for light years around ..."

Jasmine nodded. Wolfbane would be powerful ...and probably capable of training up new manpower in a hurry. She didn't know enough to calculate how long it would take to repair the battleships, but the Commonwealth had started to produce its own fleet of ships within two years of being abandoned. Wolfbane had definitely had a head start on the Commonwealth, even if they stuck to tried and tested technologies.

And going after Thule did considerable damage to our long-term plans, she thought, morbidly. *We didn't have that many worlds with solid industrial bases.*

"I should talk to him," Paula said. "Maybe I can calm him down ..."

"Or he will want to beat you to death," Watson said, dryly. "He'll see what you did as a betrayal, not as you saving him from himself."

"You could protect me," Paula said, batting her eyelashes at him. "I can hide behind you ..."

Jasmine coughed, loudly. "Wait outside," she said, shortly. "Carl, I need a quick word with you."

Watson waited until the door had firmly closed, then snapped to attention. "Yes, boss?"

"I would suggest you didn't let her try to seduce you," Jasmine said, "but I know better than to give an order I know won't be followed."

"I don't think she's trying to seduce me," Watson said.

"You mean she's *succeeding*?" Jasmine asked. "Carl, do you remember what happened to Blake?"

Watson smirked. Everyone knew the only reason Blake Coleman had missed the Battle of Camelot had been the fact he'd been seduced by a pretty girl, then drugged and held prisoner by the Crackers. He hadn't told them anything, but his fellows hadn't let him forget it until the day he'd died. There were easier ways to take a pratfall.

"Just watch yourself," she said. "That woman is a woman on the edge."

"I'll behave," Watson said. "But ..."

"Be careful," Jasmine said. "Make sure she gets a room on the station, but try not to spend *too* much of your time with her. She should be kept away from her former boss, I think; he probably won't be pleased to see her again. And good luck."

She watched him leave, then tapped the terminal on her desk, replaying everything that had happened since Stubbins had entered the room.

Nothing he'd said sounded encouraging, save for the simple fact that most of Wolfbane's industry was concentrated in a single system. It suggested a point failure node, save for the fact she was sure the system would also be heavily defended. The Empire had massed staggering levels of firepower around its critical industrial nodes and there was no reason to think Wolfbane would have done any differently.

Reaching for a notepad and pen, she started to scribble down other questions she needed answered, even though Stewart was right. Most of what Stubbins had to say would be out of date. The exact size of the system's industrial base, plus that of the rest of the sector. The condition of the smaller ships in the fleet. Security threats on Wolfbane and the other planets in the sector. Possible rebel groups who might sign up with the Commonwealth ...coming to think of it, how many of the political prisoners would be willing to help? Governor Brown's inner circle - who did he trust, who did he suspect, who else had been exiled? Did he have a wife? A husband? A mistress?

He's a corporate rat, she thought. *He wouldn't have been encouraged to develop any tastes beyond doing his duty.*

The thought alternatively chilled and amused her. It was chilling, because she hated the idea of anyone being able to dictate like that to anyone; it was amusing, because it showed just how far someone would go for power. But she knew, all too well, that someone who amassed enough power could do literally *anything* within the Empire. They were above the law, no matter what they did. There was no one who could hold them to account, not even their peers. It was far more important to reinforce the *status quo*.

She put the notepad down and sighed. If she'd known she would be interrogating a prisoner, she would have gone for the interrogation MOS at the Slaughterhouse. As it was, she would have to find someone on the surface who had both the background knowledge and experience to set questions for Stubbins, then catch him in a lie. She rather doubted there was *anyone* who could have done the work. It would need a full team and the closest team she knew was on Avalon.

We can interrogate some of the other prisoners too, she thought. Some of them had been dumped on the planet only recently, less than a year ago. *See if we can corroborate their stories ...*

She shook her head as she picked up the notebook again and scribbled the last set of questions. They would just have to wait and see. Perhaps she could study some system information sheets, then start asking Stubbins to fill in the blanks. Or maybe she should ask him to tell her what he thought she should know. A sense he had power over her might help push him to be more helpful.

The doorbell chimed. Jasmine opened it and Kailee stepped into the room, carrying a datapad.

"I finished reviewing the reports," Kailee said. "I have a list of possible candidates here."

Jasmine took the datapad and glanced at the list. Kailee hadn't done a bad job, she had to admit; she'd spotted everyone Jasmine had already earmarked for service in space, if they wanted the job. A handful of question marks lay next to a couple of names, both without any experience in space. Jasmine frowned, then tapped the names and waited. It would be interesting to see how Kailee justified her choices.

"They have experience in fixing vehicles on the ground," Kailee said. "They *might* be able to work in space."

"Good thought," Jasmine said. It *was* a good thought. She'd have to see if they were needed ...and, if they were, get them onto the station. "Now, for your first day ..."

She smiled at Kailee's expression. "I need to exercise," she added, darkly. "Do you know how to do push-ups?"

Kailee looked doubtful. "I don't think so," she said. "How do you do it?"

"I'll show you," Jasmine said, as she rose to her feet. "There's a gym down the corridor. I expect you to use some of the equipment every day, at least once you're checked out on it. Don't stop when your body starts to ache - that's a sign you're starting to push yourself."

"Oh," Kailee said. "What's a gym doing on a space station?"

"Helps keep the crew nice and healthy," Jasmine said. "On a Marine Transport Ship, you would have Marines running around the central corridor and jumping over bottomless pits in the middle of the compartments."

Kailee blinked. "Bottomless pits?"

"No one ever came out of them," Jasmine teased. Rumour had had it that the hatches were connected to the waste disposal system and anyone who fell in landed in the shit, but she had a feeling that wasn't true. "But we learned to jump pretty well."

"But why?" Kailee asked. She stopped at the hatch leading into the gym, looking doubtfully at the pieces of exercise gear. They looked like torture devices. "Why brutalise yourselves?"

Jasmine shrugged. "Hard training, easy mission; easy training, hard mission," she quoted, softly. Her first Drill Instructor had answered the same question the same way. "And that explains why this station was so easy to take, doesn't it?"

CHAPTER SEVENTEEN

But they would fail, for two reasons. First, the offender may feel that he has no choice, but to break the laws as a matter of national survival. Second, it would be hard to come up with a genuine case to support a war of enforcement.
- Professor Leo Caesius. *The Empire and its Prisoners of War.*

Avalon, Year 5 (PE)

"Tell me something," Kitty said. "Just how large a contribution do the Governor's backers *make*?"

Emmanuel shrugged. "A big one," he hazarded. The more he thought about it, the more he was sure he was right. "A *very* big one."

"It must be," Kitty said, as they walked up to the gate. "Just how much does it cost him to host these parties?"

Emmanuel shrugged, again. The Governor's Mansion was large, large enough to house both the Governor's family and a whole series of offices to actually run the planet, but maintaining it had to cost a fortune. If he'd been given the house, *his* first thought would have been to sell it as quickly as possible, knowing it would cost most of his income to keep the house in a decent state. But the Governor had not only kept his mansion, he'd managed to set it up to host a succession of fancy parties. The building practically glowed with light.

They stopped at the gates, where a guard checked their IDs against a list of invited guests and then ran a scanner over their bodies. Emmanuel wasn't surprised when the guard insisted on confiscating his datapad; it was configured to covertly record everything in the vicinity, even when placed in a sealed pocket. Kitty had nothing apart from a wristcom, which the guard left alone. Emmanuel would have bet good money that her wristcom was designed to covertly record conversations too.

Inside, he could hear the sound of music as they walked up to the mansion. Children were playing on the lawn, tossing balls as they ran around, while a handful of sulky-looking teenagers supervised them. Emmanuel felt a brief moment of envy - the children had no need to worry about the rest of the world - which he rapidly suppressed. Children were also helpless victims when the shit hit the fan, unable to influence events or even understand what was going on, why their lives had suddenly collapsed. Kitty glanced at several of the teenagers without going out of her way to make it noticeable, then allowed him to lead her into the mansion itself. The sound of music grew louder as they stepped through the doors.

"There's normally a dance down in the ballroom," Emmanuel muttered. A waiter appeared and held out a tray of drinks, then bowed and retreated when they both shook their heads. "Or we can make the rounds, see who's worth talking to."

"Let's see where the councilmen are," Kitty said, after a moment. "And then the Governor himself."

Emmanuel nodded and led her through a set of corridors. The ballroom was heaving with people, mostly the partners and children of men and women who had earned their places among the planetary elite. He couldn't help feeling that there was something more energetic about it, unlike the parties the Old Council had used to hold. *They* had been ruthlessly obsessed with protocol and penalised anyone who put so much as a single foot wrong on the dance floor. And they probably would have found the new dancers terribly vulgar.

He snickered, quietly. Maybe the newcomers *were* lacking in social graces, maybe they didn't have the time or patience to learn the social steps. But they had an energy, and a drive to succeed, that would have terrified the Old Council. They would have known they couldn't compete on even terms. It was why they had worked so hard to keep everyone else firmly under their thumb.

Kitty elbowed him. "Credit for your thoughts?"

"This party is very strange," he said, "but far more productive."

His smirk grew wider as they passed the buffet table. Once, the Old Council would have demanded the finest of everything, from roasted mice to fish eggs and paper-thin ham, just because they could. Their wines would have been so expensive that each bottle would have cost more than his annual salary, perhaps more than most people expected to see in their lives. And their suits and dresses would be carefully tailored, each one so expensive that only someone who had no worries about money could hope to wear one without shame. But now ...

He looked at the table and smiled. The food was distinctly plebeian, without any of the absurdities that had characterised the Empire's elite in the years before it fell. Great casks of beer were placed on the table, besides piles of good, but simple foods. Maybe it was just a subtle insult, from the Governor or his wife, or maybe it was just a victory dance. The new councillors - and businessmen - wouldn't care to adopt the habits of a bygone age.

"You think?" Kitty asked. "Why?"

Emmanuel nodded towards a handful of young women, all in their early twenties. He recognised one of them as the daughter of a new shipping magnate, so he assumed the others were from similar families. They were all wearing fancy dresses, showing off enough of their breasts and legs to draw the eye, but he was experienced enough to tell that the dresses weren't *that* expensive, or exclusive. Their fathers and mothers placed their money elsewhere.

He took Kitty's arm and nodded, very lightly, at the girls. "They look good, don't they?"

Kitty nodded, puzzled.

"Their dresses aren't worth more than a hundred credits apiece," he said. "And notice how two of them have the same dress, just in different colours. In the old days, there would have been a major screaming fit if two women had spent hundreds of thousands of credits on the same dress, even if both of them had been the very best of friends the previous day. The Empire wasn't just about concentrating all the wealth in as few hands as possible, it was about conspicuously consuming that wealth. There was so much of it that there was little real prospect of it running *out*."

He shook his head. "Now, wealth is reserved for reinvestment and no one is complaining," he said, as they moved away from the table and down a long corridor. "And *that* is far more productive than wasting it on expensive dresses."

"I see," Kitty said, slowly. "I never knew you for a commissionaire of dresses."

"They had me on the fashion beat, once upon a time," Emmanuel said. "I never thought anyone actually bothered to read my articles."

Kitty smirked. "Because they were too busy gaping at the pictures?"

"...Probably," Emmanuel said. "Damned if there was anything else worth looking at in that old rag."

The next room held a handful of men in ill-fitting suits, smoking heavily as they discussed the war and how it was affecting their businesses. Emmanuel listened carefully, picking up a number of titbits for later consideration, then followed Kitty as she walked towards one of the councillors she'd mentioned. Councillor Johan Cagier turned to face them as they approached, then nodded politely to Emmanuel. He didn't pay any real attention to Kitty, apart from a quick glance at her breasts. As far as anyone knew, she was just an intern being shown the ropes.

"It's been quite some time," Cagier said, as he caught Emmanuel's arm and led him towards a corner. "I liked the piece you did on the Battle of Basting's Reach."

"Thank you," Emmanuel said. It hadn't been a particularly detailed piece, but he always liked to be told when he had caught someone's attention. "I trust it helped convince a few people to stay the course."

"Oh, you know what it's like," Cagier said. "The news from the front is good - wonderful, victory is in our grasp! We will crush Wolfbane, capture their women and divide the spoils amongst ourselves. The news from the front is bad - horrors! We're going to lose the war! Our women will be raped, our children will be brainwashed and our businesses will be sold to the highest bidder. Horror upon horrors!"

Emmanuel smiled politely. He had never been particularly sure why Cagier had been elected into office in the first place. Clearly, whatever district he represented must have had only a few choices, although he *did* have to admit that Cagier had an excellent war record. He'd kept his resistance cell running right up to the bitter end, making the Old Council's goons miserable, before the Marines had arrived. Even then, he'd managed to keep the vast majority of his cell intact.

"I know what it's like," he agreed, as another waiter approached. Cagier took a glass of wine and motioned for Emmanuel to take one too, but he declined. "Why did you come to the party?"

"The Governor always throws the most interesting shindigs," Cagier said. He winked, mischievously. "And it's a good place to meet others."

He raised his voice and waved to a tall man, who had just entered the room. "Jim! Come and tell us about your recent business agreement!"

Jim's face was impassive as he strode over to meet them, but Emmanuel could tell he was annoyed. "We will be operating three new cloudscoops before the end of the year," he said, shortly. His accent suggested an off-world origin. "Stockpiles of HE3 will continue to rise dramatically."

"Which tells others to invest in more fusion plants," Cagier said. He leered cheerfully at Kitty. "Buy stock in fusion companies, if you want to make a quick buck."

"I'm not allowed to buy stock," Emmanuel said, drawing the half-drunk councillor's attention back to him. "It would compromise me."

"You'll never be rich with an attitude like that," Cagier proclaimed. "Take the opportunities as they come, seize the day! Raise the Jolly Roger and prepare to board! Right, Jim?"

"Correct," Jim said. His voice was expressionless, but - if anything - he looked more irked at having to talk to Cagier than ever. "If you will excuse me, I have an appointment with Councillor Travis."

He bowed and retreated. "We need to head onwards too," Emmanuel said, before Cagier could say a word. "If you'll excuse us ..."

"By all means," Cagier said. He took another swig from his glass, then smirked. "I have a bet going that Lucy's dress is going to slip off by the end of the day. See if you can get a picture of that."

Emmanuel nodded, then walked through the door and into the corridor. Kitty caught his arm as soon as they were out of earshot, then rolled her eyes at him when he turned to look at her.

"Tell me," she said. "How much of that was just an act?"

"Hard to tell," Emmanuel said. "Someone who is good at *acting* drunk might pick up a few pieces of information no one would say otherwise. Or it could be a real piece of drunken stupidity. Or ..."

He shrugged. "Most of the people here are hard-bitten bastards, even if they're not outright pirates," he added. "Don't expect them to give a sucker an even chance."

Kitty's eyes narrowed. "Would they do anything to compromise the Commonwealth?"

Emmanuel frowned. "Probably not," he said, after a moment's thought. "They know what happens to planets overrun by Wolfbane. Their undoubted competence might help push Wolfbane into keeping them, but the Wolves will also want to share out the rewards of conquest to their people. Better to fight by the Commonwealth than try to desert it."

The next hour passed very slowly. They moved from room to room, keeping an eye on a handful of suspects, while watching the entertainments the Governor had laid on for his guests. Surprisingly, they were tasteful; Emmanuel had expected something considerably more rude, like strip shows and even private lap dances. Maybe the Governor's wife had moderated him, or maybe he'd been reluctant to cater to the worst impulses of his guests. It was impossible to find out without asking and Emmanuel rather doubted he'd get a straight answer if he tried.

"That's odd," Kitty mused, as they returned to the ballroom. "Councillor Travis and Councillor Muncie have both disappeared."

"We can ask," Emmanuel said. He strode over to a bored-looking waiter, who was carrying a large tray of burgers wrapped in floured buns around the edge of the room. "I'm looking for Councillor Travis."

The waiter nodded, then keyed his headset. "He's currently in a meeting," the waiter said. "I don't think he can be interrupted unless it's urgent."

"I can wait," Emmanuel said. A meeting? "Do you know who he's meeting?"

"I am not authorised to divulge that information," the waiter said. He didn't sneer, but he looked very much as though he *wanted* to. "We take the privacy of our guests very seriously."

"Ah, Emmanuel," a voice said from behind him, before he could start trying to bribe the waiter. "It's good to see you here."

Emmanuel turned to see Paul Valentine, a very wealthy businessman who'd started creating his business shortly after the defeat of the Old Council and rapidly become one of the most important and powerful people within the Commonwealth. He was short, in his early forties, yet there was something about him that warned people never to take him for granted. Emmanuel knew he wasn't a criminal, but Valentine had flown right up to the edge of the law, such as it was. He didn't know any more ruthless men in the business world.

"Mr. Valentine," he said. "What can I do for you?"

"Talk elsewhere," Valentine said. He glanced at Kitty. "This your intern?"

"Yes," Emmanuel said. "She comes with me."

"Don't trust her alone, do you?" Valentine said. "I don't blame you."

He led the way up to a private room, then motioned for Emmanuel to step inside first. It was a relatively small room, with a handful of chairs, a table and a dumbwaiter; the walls were barren, save for a handful of photographs of Avalon from orbit. Emmanuel took the seat on one side of the table, then watched impassively as Kitty performed a covert bug-sweep with her wristcom. If Valentine noticed, he said nothing.

"My daughter will be getting married in three weeks," Valentine said, flatly. "I would like you to cover the wedding."

Emmanuel blinked. He'd expected a session of trading information, or probing questions designed to elicit snatches of data that could be worked into a whole. Instead, Valentine was demanding something altogether different. Was Valentine's daughter actually getting married? Emmanuel didn't know, but it would be easy enough to check.

"I'm normally on the politics and military beat," he said, slowly. "I'd have to get my editor to okay me going instead of ..."

Valentine smirked. "Someone less important?"

"Yeah," Emmanuel said.

He studied Valentine for a long moment. The man was a pirate, no doubt about it ...and yet, he wanted his daughter to have the finest wedding money could buy. But why would he want a reporter? Emmanuel knew, without false modesty, that *he* wouldn't want a reporter at *his* wedding ...apart from him, of course. It might end badly ...

"I can make it worth your while," Valentine said, quietly. "Do you realise that a couple of councillors have been trading favours to help their business partners? I could give you their names."

It was important to him, Emmanuel realised. And yet it made no sense. Or did it? He'd wondered, earlier, about the newcomers not seeking conventional acceptance, yet ...did Valentine want conventional acceptance? Did he want the sort of coverage that would be given to a Grand Senatorial wedding on Earth, or as near to it as Avalon could provide? It would be the ultimate proof that he'd arrived ...

"The names would be a good start," he said. If he was right, Valentine might be prepared to up the ante a little. "What else can you offer me?"

They haggled backwards and forwards for several minutes, then agreed a date to meet and share information. Valentine nodded once he had his agreement, then rose and left the room.

"I was hoping we could go home," Kitty said. She battered her eyelashes at him in a manner that was too crude to be seductive. "Please?"

Emmanuel blinked, but nodded. They walked out of the room, said their farewells to the Governor's wife, and then made their way back down to the gates and out onto the darkened streets. He waved cheerfully to a handful of militiamen on patrol, then allowed Kitty to lead him back to his apartment. If there were any watching eyes, they would see him taking Kitty home for the night.

Because we're reporters and we shit where we eat, he thought, crossly. The Empire's media had been famous for gross immorality, as well as never running a story that threatened the powers-that-be. He was trying to do better, but it wasn't easy. *Everyone expects me to cheat on Jasmine with my own intern.*

"That was interesting," Kitty said, once she had sweep his apartment for bugs. "Didn't you think?"

"I thought we saw nothing, apart from people sharing information," Emmanuel said. "What did you see?"

Kitty tapped her wristcom. "The private room was bugged," she said. "Mil-spec gear, very advanced …they actually rigged the privacy generator to serve as a bug. I've seen it done before, but never so well."

Emmanuel blanched. "You mean …every discussion in that mansion is recorded?"

"I would imagine so," Kitty said. She started to pace the room, lost in thought. "Certainly, they'd have audio …perhaps visual, if they were careful where they placed the pickups. And the Governor has been encouraging people to use his mansion as a private meeting place, where they can hold confidential discussions away from prying eyes."

"And everything they say goes directly to Wolfbane," Emmanuel said. "Does that prove the Governor is the spy?"

"I don't know," Kitty said. "But we need to find out *quick*."

CHAPTER EIGHTEEN

Therefore, idealists who believe that war can be civilised are dreaming. The seeming laxness of the laws of war are a reflection of the conditions that formed and shaped them, a compromise between preventing atrocities and respecting the rights of both parties to the conflict.
- Professor Leo Caesius. *The Empire and its Prisoners of War.*

Meridian, Year 5 (PE)

"I think I hate you," Kailee said.

Jasmine snorted, rudely. "You haven't done anything yet," she said, as Kailee stepped off the exercise machine. Her pale skin was shining with sweat. "You really haven't."

Kailee scowled at her. "Are you sure?"

"Yes," Jasmine said. "Do you know how many exercises I have to do, every day, just to keep myself in fighting trim?"

Kailee groaned, then rubbed her arms. "Do I *have* to continue?"

"You can just walk away," Jasmine said. "*I'm* not going to stop you leaving."

She kept her face impassive as she watched the younger girl. It wouldn't have been hard to force her to keep going, either with threats or corporal punishment, but that wouldn't have helped Kailee develop the internal stubbornness she needed. She had to force herself to carry on, not allow someone else to force her into shape …and relax, the moment that person turned her attention elsewhere.

"I am doing better, aren't I?" Kailee asked. "Really?"

Jasmine shrugged. "What do you think?"

Kailee looked downcast. On Earth, children were praised for every little achievement, no matter how miniscule it was in reality. Or, sometimes, even for failing. But it was different on Meridian and *very* different in the Marines. Jasmine wouldn't have expected her to complete the Crucible the day after she started training - she'd never met a recruit who could do that - but it was important that she understood just how far she had to go.

"Not that much better," Kailee said, finally.

"True," Jasmine said. "I would measure your advancement in millimetres, myself. But if you don't stop, if you keep going, we might just move to inches."

She shrugged, then fought down the impulse to climb onto one of the machines herself and just start exercising. It wouldn't help Kailee to watch her exercise, knowing it would be years before she ever came close to Jasmine. But she felt oddly unhealthy just standing and watching as Kailee did her exercises. Perhaps she should try some of the tougher exercises while she waited ...

Her wristcom chimed. "Brigadier?"

"Yes," Jasmine said, picking it up from the table. "Report."

"We just picked up a message from a freighter," Stewart said. "She crossed the phase limit two hours ago, judging by the timing. ETA currently estimated at seven hours."

"They're not rushing, then," Jasmine said. If the freighter had dropped out of phase drive so far from the phase limit ...it was odd, unless they had problems with their drive. The cost of flying through normal space would be prohibitive to any commercially-operated starship. "Send back the planned message, then continue to monitor their approach."

Kailee looked at her as Jasmine put the wristcom down. "You're not going to the command centre?"

"Not yet," Jasmine said. "There's seven hours before they arrive, you know. Plenty of time to finish exercising and have forty winks."

She sighed inwardly as she motioned for Kailee to get back on the machine. If Wolfbane had sent a warship to escort the freighter, and they might, they were thoroughly screwed. She had no illusions about the ability of the sensors on the orbital station to track any warship that was maintaining even basic stealth procedures. There would be no point in trying to snatch both ships too. She would have no choice but to surrender ...*again*.

Thirty minutes later, Kailee was dripping with more sweat and had clearly pushed herself as far as she could go. "Get a shower," Jasmine advised, as the younger girl stumbled off the machine. "We'll pick this up again tomorrow."

She watched Kailee go, marvelling at just how absurd Earth's fashions had become. Kailee was almost a perfect hourglass, with large breasts and buttocks, but very thin waist and long legs. It was easy to see why she'd had so many problems on Meridian ...and why she would probably never be more than an amateur martial artist. She simply didn't have the endurance for long sprints ...

Probably didn't want the girls able to either fight or run away, she thought, sardonically. *Can't have them thinking they might be able to stand up for themselves, can we?*

There was a knock at the hatch, which opened to reveal Watson. "Can we use the room now?"

"Only if you don't mind sharing it with me," Jasmine said. "Kailee can go and have a nap."

"We could spar," Watson offered. "Let her see what she could become."

Jasmine eyed him, darkly. "That would just intimidate her," she said. She wouldn't have minded, but there wasn't time for a proper spar. "Kailee needs to feel that something is attainable, not that it will be forever beyond her reach."

"You could be wasting your time," Watson said. "How many Earthers do you know who became Marines?"

"Colonel Stalker," Jasmine said. She thought for a long moment. "Major-General Kratman. General Carmichael."

"Two of whom are in the past," Watson said. "Only one of them is actually alive now. And I believe he joined the Marines at sixteen."

"It's something to do," Jasmine said. She remembered one of her Drill Instructor's favourite sayings and smiled. "And besides, you never know who might be a diamond in the rough."

"True," Watson agreed. He strode over to the side of the room and began to remove his tunic. "But how many rocks do you have to polish before you find a diamond?"

Jasmine opened her mouth to answer, then closed it as Kailee stepped out of the shower, wearing a long bathrobe that had seen better days. She gave Watson a surprised look, then glanced at Jasmine for reassurance. The devil in Jasmine was tempted to agree to the spar after all, perhaps ordering Watson to take a fall to convince Kailee that he *could* be beaten, but she knew it would be futile. Kailee would either accept it or rationalise it as being the result of better training, experience and build.

"Go get some rest," Jasmine said, instead. There wasn't much for Kailee to do, save transcribe the notes from Stubbins interrogations. "I'll see you later."

Kailee nodded and fled the room.

"Nice looking girl, but weak in body and crippled in mind," Watson said. "Do you *really* think you can toughen her up?"

"We shall see," Jasmine said. Watson was right; Kailee's main enemy was her lack of confidence in her ability to shape her own life. It remained to be seen if basic training could make a difference. "Don't do anything to discourage her, not yet. See how she goes first."

She clambered onto the exercise machine, upped the level to maximum and went to work. Watson nodded, then climbed onto his own; Jasmine watched him grimly, then returned her gaze to her own machine. It wasn't quite built to Marine specifications, but it was suitable, barely. An hour later, she scrambled off the machine, feeling uncomfortably flabby. It hadn't been enough to raise a sweat.

"We should definitely spar," Watson said, as Jasmine grabbed a towel and headed for the shower. "There just isn't time for anything else these days."

Jasmine shrugged and stepped into the shower. One definite advantage of the orbital station was an unlimited supply of hot water, something that was kept artificially low on marine transport ships. She stripped off her shorts and shirt, allowed water to wash down over her body, then dried herself before walking back into the exercise compartment and pulling her uniform back on.

"I'll see once we're on the freighter," she said. "Did you hear anything from young Gary?"

"Nothing," Watson said. "I think I scare him."

"You probably do," Jasmine said. "It's the look on your face."

"Hey," Watson protested.

Jasmine smirked, then sobered. Gary had been raised to fear men of violence, both the bullies he'd encountered in school and the media's portrayal of policemen and soldiers. It didn't help, she knew, that most of the Civil Guardsmen *were* power-mad buffoons who shouldn't be allowed anywhere near a loaded weapon. To Gary, Watson and Stewart had to look like monsters, while *she* was a freak of nature. It was just another legacy of Earth's attempts to emasculate its children.

"If he does, be encouraging," Jasmine ordered. "And give him what training you can."

She sighed, inwardly. On her homeworld, men were encouraged to be men; it was considered a badge of honour to be strong, determined and able to support one's wife and family. There was endless competition to be the best shooter, the best swimmer, the best at everything ...and there was honest pride taken in winning. Her brothers had taken her being better at them at *anything* as a personal challenge.

But Gary? How would he react to Kailee starting to learn how to defend herself?

What a screwed-up world, she thought, remembering her last term on Earth. It felt like decades ago, even though she knew it couldn't be more than six years. *Gary might join her, just to keep up, or he might resign himself to being an eternal butt monkey.*

"He had five years on Meridian," Watson said. "And really, do I look like a Drill Instructor?"

Jasmine shrugged. "Eat sour lemons morning, noon and night," she said. "That should make you look mean enough. And I can have one of the hats made for you if there isn't one on the planet below."

"And then I would scare him away," Watson said. "I don't think he has the confidence to go forward."

"I know," Jasmine said. "But ...diamonds in the rough ...blah, blah, blah."

She smiled, then walked out the hatch and down the long corridor. It had been cleaned, since she'd moved some of her people to the station, but it still managed to look rather grimy. The only places the Wolves had bothered to clean were their sleeping quarters and a handful of loading bays, which they'd used regularly. It was just another sign that no one considered Meridian very important. Governor Brown - or one of his subordinates - had probably classed it as a place to dump anyone they couldn't be bothered to fire.

"Hey," a voice called. "Is there a ship approaching?"

Jasmine turned and saw one of the former slaves, looking up at her nervously. Compared to pirates, the Wolves had treated their captives surprisingly decently, but they'd still been slaves, still at the mercy of their captors. Most of the slaves had been among the last shipment of legitimate colonists, before the Empire had lost contact with Meridian; they'd probably been rated as expendable. Meridian might be a decent place to live - it *was* a decent place to live - but it also had the colonial mentality that suggested some people had to be sacrificed to save the remainder.

"Yes," she said, gently. She'd always felt sorry for slaves; hell, it was something she would have gladly stamped out, given the chance. "There's a ship coming."

The girl leaned forward, her pale eyes haunted. "Will it take us back to Earth?"

"I don't think so," Jasmine said. "Earth is gone."

She nodded to the girl, then walked past her to the command centre. A CEF soldier was standing on guard outside, just in case the former prisoners started to cause trouble. Jasmine nodded to him, then walked through the hatch and into the compartment. A display - no holographic projectors for the orbital station - showed a single red icon approaching the station, while a line of text underneath noted that the freighter was five hours away.

"Thomas," she said, as Stewart rose to his feet. They'd rehearsed the operation several times, but she knew from bitter experience that the real thing would be different. "What's the latest?"

"They sent us a manifest," Stewart said. "Apparently, they have one thousand prisoners from various places. Most of them seem to have been purged from occupied territories, but a handful are definitely from the Commonwealth."

Jasmine frowned. "Any specific instructions?"

"They just want them in the camps," Stewart said. "There wasn't much else in the statement ...oh, the freighter's captain was asking about shore leave for his crew."

"That's odd," Jasmine said. They'd reviewed all the old files, but there hadn't been any definite procedure for approaching the station. "What did you tell him?"

"That there weren't any facilities," Stewart said. "I don't know why they didn't set up a camp or something they could have used for shore leave."

"Probably thought they wouldn't be staying," Jasmine said. "Like that crew on Firebase Qing."

Stewart winced. Firebase Qing had been established in a hurry by a team of Civil Guardsmen, who had been told they would be pulled out within a week. Instead, their departure date had been put back, and then put back again, until they had wound up staying there for two months. But they hadn't bothered to start any long-term projects to put the firebase in shape to stand off an attack, which was why it had almost fallen within days after the uprising on Han had finally begun. Only the rapid addition of a company of marines had saved it from falling anyway.

She shrugged. "Maybe they were expecting time with the slaves," she added. "Go get some rest. We can't do anything until they dock, anyway."

Stewart saluted. "See you in four hours," he said.

Kailee looked ...exhausted.

Gary eyed her nervously as she stumbled into the cabin they shared - she had one bed, he had the other - and dropped her bathrobe on the deck. Her pale skin was marked and bruised, suggesting she had been beaten ...and yet, there was something odd about the bruises. Gary had been bruised far too many times to count and they'd looked different, somehow. It was almost as if Kailee had been stretching her skin too far.

"Kailee," he said, nervously. He wasn't sure he wanted to talk about her plans with anyone, even her. "Are you sure this is a good idea?"

"I don't know," Kailee said. "But I have to try."

Gary swallowed. "But you're in pain!"

"I know," Kailee said. She looked down at him for a long moment, then sat down on her bed and wrapped the towel around herself. "I have to try to push on."

Gary swallowed, again. He understood the urge, but life had taught him that no matter what he did, he would always be dumped on. There was no *point* in trying to get better at anything when there were people who would always be better than him. What was the point in playing if the game was rigged?

"I have to try," Kailee said. "All I could do was run from Barry …and that didn't work, did it? And then they put me in the camp …"

Her voice trailed off. Gary felt another stab of helpless rage. Barry could have killed him at any moment - and he had done far worse to Kailee - and yet he'd never been able to muster the nerve to fight back. It was if, at some point, he'd just become accustomed to being life's bitch. Life had taught him that fighting back was pointless. He only got hurt and he lost whatever he was trying to save anyway.

And yet, what if Kailee *succeeded*? What if she *did* learn to stand up for herself?

It wasn't a pleasant thought. He couldn't protect her from the outside world, but she didn't *expect* him to protect her. She'd chosen him, he suspected, because she knew he didn't have the nerve to push it, if she said no. The other boys at school had said that girls only said no because they were testing the boys, that they would surrender if pushed, but he'd never been able to force himself to take that step. And now, he knew all too well, that there was no difference between pushing a girl to open her legs and outright rape.

He shuddered. If someone tried that on Meridian, he knew from the stories he'd been told, the rapist would be lucky to survive the experience.

But what if she did learn to stand up for herself? Would she see him as pathetic, like so many others, and dump him? He'd stayed loyal to her for five years, while she'd been in the camp, but he'd done nothing to help the resistance find and free her. What would she make of him once she was strong?

You're an asshole, he told himself, savagely. *She stayed with you when she could have had her pick of men on Meridian.*

And yet she wouldn't have been welcome there, his own thoughts mocked him. Kailee was beautiful, by earthly standards, but weird-looking on Meridian. *Who else did she have who might have been interested in her?*

"You shouldn't," he said. "It's hurting you."

Kailee stood up, so quickly her blanket almost fell to the deck. "Do you think it didn't hurt when Barry fucking fucked me!"

Gary recoiled at the naked rage in her voice. He hadn't thought about it. In truth, he hadn't *wanted* to think about it.

"I need to do this," Kailee said, calming down. "And I think you should join us."

"I can't," Gary said. He felt tears prickling at the corner of his eyes. "There's no point!"

"Yes, there *is*," Kailee said. "I need to be able to defend myself and so do you! You're joining us if I have to drag you there myself!"

"…Fine," Gary said, reluctantly. "But don't blame me if it doesn't work."

"At least you will have tried," Kailee said. "And that's all that matters."

CHAPTER NINETEEN

> Matters become more complex, however, when one or more of the parties involved isn't a nation-state.
> - Professor Leo Caesius. *The Empire and its Prisoners of War.*

Meridian, Year 5 (PE)

"I make her a modified *Blackbird*-class bulk freighter," Stewart said, as the freighter closed in on the orbital station. "Modular interior; easy to turn into a POW transport without needing to rip the life support system open and reengineer the hull."

"Looks that way," Jasmine said.

She frowned, thoughtfully. The freighter could charitably be described as ugly - she was nothing more than a set of metal boxes, attached to a phase drive - but ships like her were the backbone of interstellar commerce. Judging by her lack of markings, she probably had started life as an independent freighter, rather than a corporate transport. But she was definitely large enough to transport a thousand men in cramped conditions.

Shaking her head, she tapped her wristcom. "Carl? Are you in position?"

"Yep," Watson said. He sounded confident, despite the timing problems. "Team One is ready and raring to go."

"Just don't move until the freighter has docked," Jasmine said. "We don't want them getting shy and starting to run."

"Understood," Watson said.

Jasmine sucked in her breath. There was still no sign that the freighter had an unseen escort - and she knew, reasonably, that there was no point in the Wolves assigning a destroyer or a frigate to escort the POWs to their new homes. But what if she was wrong? What if they *did* have an escort?

Then we're all about to die, she thought, sharply. *All we can do is wait and pray.*

"Send the signal," she ordered. "Tell them the docking ports are open and ready to receive them."

"She's coming in," Stewart said. "Docking ports cycling ...now."

Jasmine felt a dull quiver echoing through the station as the freighter docked, its drive field fading away into nothingness once it had latched on. Stewart rose to his feet, as planned, and hastened towards the hatch. Jasmine watched him go, wishing she dared leave the command centre long enough to take point herself. The freighter *had* to be secured before her crew realised they were in deep shit.

"Carl," she ordered, tapping her wristcom. "Go now."

She forced herself to relax as Team One swarmed up from its hiding place on the station's hull and jumped over to the freighter. If the freighter's crew had realised that something - anything - was wrong, they'd react now. But nothing happened as Team One found the hatches, forced their way inside and swarmed the ship, while Team Two captured the airlocks and advanced into the ship.

"Captain," she said, keying the link to the freighter. There was no point in trying to hide any longer. "Your ship is being boarded. If you surrender without further ado, you have my word as a Terran Marine and Commonwealth officer that you and your crew will remain unharmed. Resistance is futile."

There was a long pause. She knew, all too well, just how attached some captains and crews could become to their ships. It was quite possible that her commanding officer would consider trying to blow the ship, rather than allow it to fall into enemy hands. And if that happened, Jasmine was sure the explosion would take out the station as well as the freighter ...

The radio buzzed. "Who are you?"

"That doesn't matter," Jasmine said. There was no live update, but she could tell her two teams were racing through the freighter, stunning everyone they met. They didn't dare allow anyone a chance to resist. "All that matters is that you have to surrender now or face the consequences."

"Very well," the enemy officer snarled. He sounded furious ...but there was a hint of panic behind his anger. "I will surrender, if you keep your word."

"I will," Jasmine said. "Open your hatches and unlock your computers, then offer no resistance. My people will take you into custody."

Her wristcom buzzed. "They're surrendering," Watson said. "We're taking the ones who remain awake into custody now."

"Good," Jasmine said. All things considered, it could have been much worse. "I'm on my way."

She waited for Stewart to return to the command centre, then headed down to the airlock and through the docking port. A handful of freighter crew, mostly teenagers, were lying on the deck, stunned before they had a chance to fight back. She glanced at their outfits - they didn't look like Wolfbane's soldiers - then walked past them, deeper into the ship. Watson met her just outside the bridge, looking grim.

"I think this is a family ship," he said. "There are even children among the crew."

Jasmine frowned, then stepped onto the bridge. It was small and cramped, compared to a marine transport ship, but it was definitely functional. Six people sat against one bulkhead, their hands zip-tied behind their backs; two adults, three teenagers and one young boy who couldn't have been older than seven. The adults looked grim, while the teenagers looked sullen and the child looked oddly excited. To him, Jasmine realised, it was all a big joke.

"I am Brigadier Yamane," she said, addressing the Captain. "For the moment, you are in my custody."

The Captain eyed her bitterly. "Captain Jim Frazier," he said. "Owner-Captain of *Passing Water*."

Jasmine nodded, curtly. "I have some questions for you," she said, "once we have your crew off the ship. You and your family will be moved down to the planet, where you will be held until the end of the war. I'm sorry to take your ship, but ..."

"You don't need our ship," one of the teenagers said. She was a red-headed girl, eying them with open defiance. "You just want to throw your weight around."

"I have no other way to get home," Jasmine said. She looked at Watson. "Move them to the POW quarters on the station, then we can prepare quarters for them on the planet. I'll speak to the Captain before we move them down."

She watched as the prisoners were hustled off the bridge, then looked down at the consoles and keyed in a command. The system had been unlocked, as she'd hoped; *Passing Water* lay open before them. A quick check revealed that she was over four hundred years old, with several extensive refits in the last two centuries. But her drive had a worrying flutter that might eventually spell disaster. No wonder they'd come out of phase drive so far from the limit.

"The POWs are in their compartments, just as we were," Watson reported, when he returned to the bridge. "Should we move them to the planet?"

"Unless there's anyone we can use, yes," Jasmine said. She already had too many people to move off Meridian, including Stubbins, Kailee and Gary. "We will have to get the Commonwealth to assign a couple of freighters to pick them up."

She sighed, then reviewed the latest entries in the ship's log. Captain Frazier and his crew had picked up the POWs, then transported them to Meridian. There wasn't much detail in the logbook, which didn't really surprise her. Most independent freighter captains preferred to be as vague as possible, even when working for corporations or governors. The only real surprise was a mention of two older teen girls who hadn't been found when the ship had been boarded.

"I think I want to ask Captain Frazier some questions now," she said. "Start moving the POWs to the camps, then bring up our own people. I want to be able to clear out at very short notice."

"Understood," Watson said. "We can be ready to depart in less than a day, if we push things."

Jasmine nodded. "I leave it in your hands," she said. "Good luck."

She nodded and walked back to the station. Captain Frazier was already sitting in her office, cuffed to a chair, while two soldiers were keeping a close eye on him. Kailee was leaning against the bulkhead, ready to write down whatever he said. Frazier glowered at them all impassively, then relaxed slightly when he saw Jasmine. It couldn't be easy to know that his children were prisoners as well as himself, particularly when those prisoners included a young and nubile teenage girl. His imagination had to be working overtime to come up with hundreds of horrifying possibilities for her future.

"I have one question," Jasmine said, as she sat down in front of him. "Where are your other daughters?"

Frazier glared at her. "Hostages," he admitted, finally. "They took them off the ship when they caught us trading without permission."

Jasmine lifted her eyebrows. "Explain."

"We used to move from world to world, selling our wares," Frazier said. "We kept doing it even when the Empire vanished. It was *such* a relief not to have to worry about their bureaucrats ruining our lives. And then we were arrested for trading on Rangel without a licence …we didn't know anything about Wolfbane! They took my daughters, then told me that I would be working for them if I wanted to see my children again."

And now we have ensured the girls will be killed, Jasmine thought. It made a brutal kind of sense; hell, it was theoretically legal to take hostages at any point. She just couldn't recall any episode when the marines had actually gone ahead and done it, let alone killed the hostages when their parents renounced them. It wasn't done. *At least that explains why the freighter was alone.*

"And they turned you into a glorified prisoner transport," Jasmine said. "*That* must have stung."

"It did," Frazier said. He sagged against the cuffs. "What are you going to do with us?"

Jasmine considered it. "I was going to abandon you on Meridian," she said. "Do you have any other ideas?"

"We can help you," Frazier said. "I …but what will happen to my children?"

"I will tell the Wolves that we took the ship by force," Jasmine said. She had no idea *what* would happen to the girls. Certainly, at some point, the Wolves would realise the ship was overdue and take steps, but ...but what? Kill the girls? Throw them into a brothel? Or simply decide they were worthless and let them go? "An alternative ..."

She sighed, then shook her head. Taking Frazier with them might be helpful, but he would have a very strong motive to betray them. A single codeword to alert the Wolves that the ship was under enemy control would be disastrous. No, she couldn't take Frazier and his family, even if they *did* have some useful knowledge. Unless it was *very* useful ...

"I know something you can use," Frazier said. "I'll trade it for the safety of my family."

Jasmine frowned at him. "What do you know?"

"The location of a Trade Federation base," Frazier said. "Somewhere you can go and make contact with your allies."

"...*That* would be useful," Jasmine said. "But why didn't you go there and seek help?"

"My daughters would have been killed," Frazier said. He met her eyes. "Take my family with you and I will show you to the base."

Jasmine took a moment to consider all the angles. The base, assuming it was still there, would definitely let her send a message back home. But it was quite possible the Wolves already knew about the base, while she knew Frazier would always put his children first. Did she dare keep him with her, knowing he could turn on her at any moment?

"If we keep you and your family on the ship," she warned, "you will be under *very* close supervision at all times. One step out of line and I will pitch you out the airlock."

Frazier swallowed. "I understand."

"Good," Jasmine said.

She looked up at the soldiers. "Take him back to the prison compartment for the moment," she ordered. "We can move him back to the ship later, once it's been thoroughly swept for unpleasant surprises."

Kailee coughed as soon as the hatch was sealed. "Are you not going to help his daughters?"

"I have no idea where to find them," Jasmine said. The Wolfbane Consortium might be far smaller than the Empire at its height, but it was still vast enough to contain over two hundred star systems. She had a feeling the girls would be kept on Wolfbane itself, along with anyone else deemed a useful hostage. "They could be anywhere."

"They could be on Meridian," Kailee pointed out. "*I* was kept as a hostage on Meridian."

Jasmine blinked. She hadn't thought of that.

"It's worth checking," she said. She rather doubted it would be the case, not when Frazier and his remaining crew were regularly flying between various collection facilities and Meridian, but it was a good thought. "Other than that …"

She shook her head. "It's something you never get told by the flicks," she added. When the flicks weren't portraying marines and soldiers as blood-thirsty monsters, they were busy creating an image of war where no one got hurt. "Being a Marine sometimes means having to make hard choices."

Kailee's eyes narrowed. "Like what?"

Jasmine picked up a datapad and glanced at it, absently. "There's a man who walks down the road past the firebase, half an hour before the insurgents drop a hail of mortar fire on your head," she said. "Is he a dicker spying on you or is it just a coincidence? Should you shoot him on suspicion or take him into custody?"

She went on before Kailee could say a word. "There are people in the city too scared to do anything, but support the insurgents," she added. "Should you treat them as potential enemies or should you treat them lightly, even though they're helping the bastards who are trying to kill you? There's a religious building being used as a sniper perch. Should you blow up the building, pissing off the locals and the media, or should you let them snipe at you without any comeback?

"And there's a child running towards you," she concluded. "Do you shoot the child or give her a hug?"

Kailee stared. "Shoot a child?"

"The child is carrying a bomb," Jasmine said. She shivered inwardly; she'd faced the threat herself on Han. Whatever else could be said about the Crackers, they'd been reasonably decent insurgents. "Do you shoot her before she gets close enough to you to blow your entire platoon up … or do you let her kill you all?"

"No one would do that," Kailee protested. "Really."

"They have," Jasmine said, flatly. She didn't blame Kailee for being doubting. There were levels of horror, like her life on Earth, then the nightmares unleashed by monsters who wanted to terrify their foes into submission. "The enemies of civilisation have done far worse than turn children into portable bombs."

She shook her head. "Go see what sort of supplies were loaded onto the freighter," she ordered. "I need to give the resistance a call."

Kailee nodded and left, looking shaken.

Jasmine sighed, then keyed her terminal. It was nearly ten minutes before Clarence replied.

"Brigadier," he said. "Congratulations."

"Thanks," Jasmine said. "I'm sending you about nine hundred prisoners - can you take them all to the camps?"

"They should be fine," Clarence assured her. "And the remainder of your people are ready to go."

Jasmine nodded. "Get the last of your teams out of the POW camps," she ordered. "Once we have the freighter loaded, we're going to hit them from orbit, as planned. Let me know if there's anyone still there in nine hours."

"You're moving quickly," Clarence said. "Janet wants to know if you need her to come with you."

"I don't think so," Jasmine said. She'd checked Janet's record, but she didn't have anything Jasmine desperately needed. "If she would prefer to remain on Meridian, she can stay with you."

"I'll see what she says," Clarence said. He took a breath. "Make sure you get clean away before they come looking for their missing ships, Brigadier. I would hate to have all this be for nothing."

"Me too," Jasmine said. It would be bad enough for her, but worse for Meridian. The Wolves would definitely take their anger out on a defenceless civilian population. "Me too."

She closed the channel, then took a moment to gather herself. They had a ship; they had a destination, if Frazier was telling the truth. And then ...they could get a message out, even if they didn't set course directly for the Commonwealth. And then ...

It was tempting to just head straight home. She had a duty to report in to the Colonel, to take her licks for losing Thule. Maybe it would mean the end of her career, or an assignment to train soldiers for future deployments, or even a deployment to a frozen world, but whatever it was she would endure. And yet ...they were behind enemy lines, without the enemy having the slightest idea they were alive and free. Who knew what they could do with such an opportunity?

Get a message to the Commonwealth, she thought, carefully. *The Trade Federation can do that for us, if we make contact. Or snatch another freighter and send* that *ship to the Commonwealth. And then ...*

She keyed her wristcom. "Carl, Thomas, once the freighter is loaded, I want to see you both," she ordered. She would need to talk to Frazier and probably Stubbins - and Paula - as well, but if her fellows thought she was pushing her luck, she wouldn't take it any further. "I have had an idea."

"Understood," Watson said. "There's still at least eight hours before the freighter can depart, though."

"No worries," Jasmine said. She smiled and stood, then stretched. "I think we will have plenty of time to lay our plans."

CHAPTER TWENTY

A nation-state can be held responsible for its actions. Furthermore, soldiers can be ordered to wear uniforms and generally comport themselves under the laws of war. A terrorist group, however, cannot be relied upon to wear uniforms or do anything else to honour the laws of war. Nor can an insurgency.
- Professor Leo Caesius. *The Empire and its Prisoners of War.*

Passing Water, **Year 5 (PE)**

"We're in position, Brigadier," Stewart said. He paused, mischievously. "Should I be calling you Captain now?"

"No, thank you," Jasmine said, primly. She might have been in command of the *Passing Water*, but she was damned if she was stealing a title that properly belonged to Colonel Stalker. "Do we have KEWs locked on target?"

"Damn right," Watson said. "I have nine projectiles locked on each camp, and a final two on the spaceport. There won't be anything left of them, but a hole in the ground."

"Fire at will," Jasmine said.

"Failing that, fire at the camps," Watson said, wryly. He tapped a switch on his console, then looked back at her. "Firing."

Jasmine watched, silently, as the KEWs fell through the atmosphere and struck the camps with staggering force. She'd been far too close to orbital bombardments on Han, years ago, and she knew just what it was like to be targeted from orbit. Watson was right; the evidence the camps had been emptied before they were destroyed would be utterly wiped out, along with all traces of the POWs. The Wolves should have no evidence that she had evacuated the camps before she destroyed them.

It was a risk, she knew. The Wolves could easily use it to justify an atrocity on a Commonwealth world. But, at the same time, it would give Meridian plausible deniability, allowing them to claim they knew nothing of the breakout. Let the Wolves blame her for everything, Jasmine figured. It would save countless lives.

"Bombardment complete," Watson reported. "All targets smashed flat, then pulverised. I say again, all targets ..."

"I heard," Jasmine said. "You may boost the station out of orbit now."

Watson grinned, then tapped a set of commands into his console. On the display, the station's orbital thrusters - and a handful of spares her people had taped to the hull - activated, slowly pushing the station up and away from the planet. She watched its hull start to crumple under the sudden acceleration, half-expecting to see it shatter, then allowed herself a moment of relief as it moved further away from the planet. Watson tapped a second set of commands into his console and the station picked up speed, heading directly towards the sun. It would be years before it reached its destination, but there was no doubt it would make it.

"The charges are primed," Watson said. "Request permission to detonate."

"Granted," Jasmine said.

The station disintegrated. She kept a wary eye on the display, but most of the pieces of debris were still on a course that would take them - eventually - straight into the sun. By the time the Wolves realised that something had gone wrong, there would be little hope of using the debris as anything other than a source of raw materials. They would need to put together a whole new orbital station if they wished to send more POWs to Meridian.

Unless they start using single-shot capsules, she thought, morbidly. *The Empire had used similar devices to dump new prisoners on penal colonies. But that would mean losing track of the prisoners afterwards.*

She pushed the thought aside, then glanced at Stewart. "Are we ready to move?"

"The drive is online," Stewart said. "ETA Phase Limit; nine hours, thirty-seven minutes."

"Then take us out of orbit," Jasmine ordered. They'd set a course that shouldn't intersect with a warship coming from Wolfbane, but she had no illusions about their ability to win a stern chase. "Best possible speed."

She sat back in what was laughingly called the command chair as Stewart activated the drives, then forced herself to relax. One way or the other, they had escaped from Meridian and now they were heading to a place where - she hoped - they could pick up intelligence and decide what to do next. The inescapable prison had proven to be rather less than secure, after all.

We got lucky, she reminded herself. *We couldn't have done it without Gary and Kailee - and the locals.*

Meridian fell behind as the freighter picked up speed, eventually reduced to nothing more than an icon in the display. Jasmine watched it fade, then picked up a datapad and began to read through more of the interrogation records. Stubbins had been surprisingly talkative once he'd realised they'd actually captured a ship, but there was no way to know just how much of his information was badly outdated. Jasmine had tried to take a stab at guessing, only to decide it simply wasn't possible. Some details were largely set in stone, but others were very changeable.

"Show me the rest of the system," she ordered. "Is there any sign of a technological presence?"

"None," Stewart said. "Although with these pieces of shit" - he kicked the console - "I would be surprised if we picked up a bunch of loudmouths caterwauling the Imperial Anthem over every radio channel in the universe. Someone could probably sneak up on us and have a boarding party on our hull before we knew they were there."

"It can't be that bad," Watson objected.

"Oh, yeah?" Stewart asked. "How exactly did we take this ship again?"

"Keep a sensor watch, as best as you can," Jasmine said, firmly. It was a shame they didn't dare trust the ship's original crew, but there were too many dangerous variables. "And alert me the moment you pick up something, anything."

Stewart nodded. "Meridian does have a reasonable chance of becoming a profitable system," he said, after a moment. "They have a gas giant and a small asteroid belt ...maybe not quite on the same scale as Avalon, but they could definitely make a go of it."

"They could do with one of the start-up loans," Jasmine said. Professor Cassius had talked the Commonwealth into offering new member worlds loans to establish cloudscoops and small industrial nodes for themselves. She didn't understand the economics behind it, but she had to admit that cheap HE3 had paid off in a big way. "But that will have to wait until the end of the war."

"True," Stewart agreed. He looked down at his console. "But if there's anyone else in the system, I don't think they're keen to reveal themselves. And who could blame them."

"Survivalists wouldn't," Jasmine said. The Commonwealth had encountered several tiny settlements, each one planning to ride out the collapse of civilisation and then restore order on their own terms. Most of them had gratefully joined the Commonwealth, but a handful had insisted on remaining independent. They still thought the worst was yet to come. "But wouldn't they have been better off on Meridian?"

"No way to know," Stewart said. "They might have assumed Wolfbane would survive the chaos - or *someone* would have - and then set out to build a whole new empire."

Jasmine frowned, then returned to her chair and waited. Hours ticked by slowly, too slowly, before the freighter finally crossed the Phase Limit. Stewart tapped his console, then keyed the switch that triggered the Phase Drive. The ship shuddered violently - it was clear the drive needed more than a little maintenance - but dropped into phase space without hesitation. Jasmine let out a breath she hadn't realised she'd been holding, then relaxed completely. They had made it away from Meridian.

"Course to Saltine laid in," Stewart said. "I think we're looking at five days of transit, assuming the drive holds out."

"And if it doesn't, we're screwed," Jasmine said, dryly. There were no shortage of tales about starships limping home at STL speeds, but most of them were purely fictional. The old generation ships hadn't lasted long, once humanity had developed the phase drive, and no modern ship could support its crew indefinitely. "Even if we did manage to limp somewhere, it would be Wolfbane territory."

"Too true," Stewart said. He rose to his feet. "Do you want me to remain on watch?"

"It should be me," Watson said. "You two go and get some sleep. I'll stay here and mind the store."

"Keep an eye out for trouble," Jasmine ordered. She stood, then walked to the hatch. "And wake me if anything happens, anything at all."

Watson nodded, then sat down in the command chair. "I'll scream like a little girl if I need you," he assured her. "Just come relieve me after you've had a nap."

Gary would have given his fortune, which wasn't that much, to have had a teaching machine on Meridian. There were so many skills that he'd needed, as the sole spaceport operator, that he hadn't had a chance to learn, if only because there had been no one on Meridian able and willing to teach him. Now, he sat in front of the teaching machine on the starship and studied, hard. There was so much he had to learn.

"Hey," Kailee said, as she stepped into the compartment. "It's time to go exercise."

"Later," Gary said. He hadn't realised just how easy it was to navigate a starship, if one had the right computer programs. Or, for that matter, how parts could be replaced with jury-rigged systems, if necessary. "I need to do this."

Kailee stepped forward, then caught his arm and pulled. Taken by surprise, Gary stood up and stared at her. "I ..."

"You're coming with me," Kailee said, firmly. "You can come back to the machine later, I promise."

Gary opened his mouth, then saw the glint in her eye and closed it again. Kailee held his arm, gently but firmly, as they walked down a short corridor and into a large empty compartment. Jasmine was doing push-ups on the deck, her body going up and down with an almost hypnotic regularity, her skin dry and unmarked by sweat. Her sparse outfit - a shirt and a pair of shorts - showed muscles rippling over her body, and a handful of nasty-looking scars. One of them looked as though someone had tried to cut her open with a knife.

"There's an outfit for Gary over there," Jasmine said, without stopping her push-ups. "Get him into it, then run on the spot for a few minutes. I'll be with you afterwards."

Gary hesitated - he hated getting undressed in public, even with Kailee - but did as he was told. Gym class - he hadn't been one of the lucky ones who had managed to claim exemption from legalised torture - had taught him there was no point in trying to delay. It was better to get changed rapidly, then get out before Barry or Moe or one of the others decided to start playing games with him. The shorts felt loose against his body, but he knew better than to complain. Gym teachers had always had more latitude to mistreat students than anyone else, particularly the ones they felt were slackers. God alone knew how Jasmine would react to any hesitation on his part.

"Run on the spot," Jasmine ordered. She *still* hadn't stopped her push-ups, merely placed one hand behind her back so she was using only one hand to go up and down. "It will warm you up."

"Like this," Kailee said. "Do as I do."

She started to run, lifting one leg then the other. Gary's eyes were drawn to her breasts, bouncing under her shirt, then looked away, embarrassed. Someone like Barry could stare without any consequences, but a nerd like him would be mocked relentlessly for allowing himself to forget his place. Instead, he started to run on the spot, feeling his heartbeat start to race as he pushed himself forward. It sounded as though someone was letting off a gun inside his head.

Jasmine stood up in one smooth motion and looked at him, her dark eyes studying his body in a cold dispassionate manner. He couldn't help thinking of the first doctor he'd visited, the asshole who'd made his mother sign all kinds of papers before agreeing to take a look at Gary. Gary had read the papers later and, as far as he could tell, they indemnified the doctor for everything, up to and including a patient dying on the examination table. Given how many students he knew who hadn't survived medical treatment, he had a feeling the doctors had needed such paperwork.

"You have a lot of work to do," she said, shortly. "I would actually recommend you learned to use a gun, but there are plenty of worlds that don't allow people to own or carry weapons."

Gary stopped running. His arms and legs were aching. Normally, he hadn't walked for more than a kilometre or two each day and he'd never had to run. He tried to stand upright, but found himself sagging into himself. Jasmine shrugged, then held out her hands.

"We don't have any proper exercise machines here," she said, as she dropped to the deck. "I think you should start with push-ups. Lie down on the deck, then put your hands down like *this*."

Gary looked at her, then did as he was told. The deck felt cold against his chest, but he could feel a dull *thrumming* echoing through it that he recalled from his first trip on a starship. His heartbeat was still racing terrifyingly fast, no matter what he did. Just how many people died of heart failure on Earth anyway? He would have bet good money that hundreds of thousands of people had similar problems.

"Lift up your body, like so," Jasmine ordered. She moved upwards without any difficulty, the muscles in her arms showing no sign of strain. "Lift yourself up and hold position."

Gary did as he was told, but his arms started to hurt almost at once. His chest hurt too, as if it were trying to pull him back to the deck. He gritted his teeth and held position, somehow.

"Now lower your body until you are *almost* touching the deck," Jasmine said. "You don't want to actually touch the deck, because that costs you some of the benefits ...no, *don't* touch the deck."

Gary cursed. Lowering his body without going all the way down wasn't easy. The pain in his arms was growing worse, much worse. He forced himself to hold position, somehow, then collapsed onto the deck. Jasmine snorted, then told him to get back up and lower himself once again. This time, Gary managed to hold the position.

"Better," Jasmine said. "Now ...up and down. Up and down. Up and down."

"I'm trying," Gary gasped. Getting back up once hurt; lowering himself again was acutely painful. Somehow, he managed to do a second push-up, then a third …and then he fell back on the deck, his arms hurting so badly he feared he'd broken something. "I can't do it."

"You will," Jasmine said. "Pain is weakness leaving the body."

She stood, then helped him to his feet. "Move like this," she ordered, demonstrating a series of movements that flexed his arms and legs. "You need to work your muscles to develop them, no matter what sort of background you have."

Gary groaned. "I thought Marines had drugs for physical enhancements."

"That damned *Psycho Bloodlust Marine* flick has a lot to answer for," Jasmine muttered, irked. "They didn't get a single thing right in the entire movie, you know. Even if we did have performance-enhancing drugs, we wouldn't risk using them."

She caught his eye. "I suppose you could get a body like Carl's if you went to the body-shops," she added. "But tell me …would you keep up with the exercise needed to maintain it in peak condition?"

"Probably not," Gary said. He slowed to a halt, then caught the warning look in her eye and started again. "But it would be easy to go back again and again, wouldn't it?"

"It wouldn't be *your* body," Jasmine said. "You wouldn't feel you owned it."

Gary scowled, then poked at his chest. "Do you have any idea how much I hate *this* body?"

"The Imperial Army takes everyone," Jasmine said. "There was a woman on the firebase who was stuck in a wheelchair. You can't discriminate against cripples, they said, so they gave her some basic training and put her in front of a computer, where she could do *something* useful. I thought she was a silly bitch until the base was attacked, whereupon she pulled a pistol out of her chair and opened fire. She killed four of the attackers before the *slow* reaction force arrived."

She looked Gary up and down, then smiled coldly. "If she can do something useful, if she can learn to fight back, so can you," she said. "Kailee will take you for a shower, then the two of you can continue exercising later today. I expect you to get up to ten push-ups at a time within a few days, then we will just keep piling them on and on."

Gary groaned. *Three* push-ups had left him in pain. And yet, Jasmine had been doing push-ups since before they'd arrived in the compartment. How many had she done in front of him before he'd managed to get changed?

He swallowed, then asked. "How many push-ups do you do each day?"

"Hundreds," Jasmine said. She gave him an evil look. "Do you know what the Drill Instructors say when you do something stupid?"

Gary shook his head. "What?"

"Drop and give me fifty," Jasmine said. "It's a very efficient process. You get some exercise and you learn not to do whatever you did wrong again. Trust me - if you keep going, you will be doing hundreds of push-ups a day too."

CHAPTER
TWENTY-ONE

This creates a moral headache for the defenders. Terrorists and insurgents, by not following the laws of war, put themselves outside their protection. They can, on one hand, be legally shot, enslaved - or interrogated in any manner that seems necessary.
- Professor Leo Caesius. *The Empire and its Prisoners of War.*

Avalon, Year 5 (PE)

"You took a *reporter* with you?"

"Yes, sir," Kitty said. "And he was helpful in identifying the leak."

Colonel Stalker glowered at her. "This isn't some embed on a starship where we control the communications," he said, sharply. "Do you feel you can trust him to keep his mouth shut?"

"This isn't the Empire, sir," Kitty said, "and he isn't really a fatheaded piece of shit from Imperial News. Even aside from his ...*choice* of girlfriends, he understands what is at stake and just what will happen to him if he leaks ahead of time. And besides, this will be a stepping stone to future stories for him."

"Right," the Colonel said. He leaned forward, putting the issue aside. "What have you found?"

"There was a bug hidden in the private conference room we used," Kitty said. "The device was actually concealed within the privacy generator, an old trick used to render a room unsafe while conveying the impression that one can talk freely. Given how many important people were at that party, it is logical to assume that many of them discussed official and corporate secrets near the bugs."

"And every room could be bugged," the Colonel mused.

"Yes, sir," Kitty said. "If one room was bugged, they could all be bugged. I had a look at the mansion's plans on the city database and it's clear the inbuilt processor would be capable of handling the task of monitoring and cataloguing the intake from thousands of bugs. Given even a few names of interest, their conversations could be recorded for later scrutiny at any time."

The Colonel sighed. "And you're sure it is the Governor?"

Kitty hesitated. "He does seem to have a high turn-over of staff," she said. "There's only a couple of long-term employees in the building, so this may not have been set up under his nose."

"With him as an innocent dupe," the Colonel concluded. "He must be involved somehow ..."

"I fear so," Kitty agreed. She shook her head. "Imperial Intelligence has a lot of experience sneaking bugs into places they shouldn't go, sir, but a coup on this scale would be damn near impossible. The Governor would have to be stupid not to have the mansion swept for bugs on a regular basis, no matter how confident he is in his privacy generators. And my sweep picked up the bug almost at once."

"Damn it," the Colonel said. He took a breath. "How do you propose we proceed?"

Kitty met his eyes. "I understand why you might want to have this channel cut off as quickly as possible," she said. "But I would prefer to leave it open for a few weeks, just to see what pieces of false information we can feed through the bugs and directly to the enemy."

"They'll realise they're being played, sooner or later," the Colonel pointed out.

"Yes, they will," Kitty agreed. "But they won't know *when* we caught on to their scheme. I think they would have to assume the worst, that we always knew about it and we were feeding them shit when it suited us to do so. They will have to throw out everything they learned from the bugs, knowing it could be compromised."

"Unless they can verify the information," Colonel Stalker said.

"They can't verify all of it," Kitty said. "And even if they could, they might think we were lulling them into a false sense of security."

"This is precisely why I hate intelligence work," the Colonel said. "Everything becomes a shadowy world of absolute confusion."

Kitty smiled. "I understand the feeling," she said. "For the moment, I would like to use the channel to feed them some crap, while feeling out just what the Governor is thinking."

The Colonel looked her in the eye. "And the alternative? We could arrest the Governor straight away."

"We would lose any chance to manipulate the conduit," Kitty said, flatly. "I would understand if you wanted to shut it down, but it is my duty to inform you of the possibilities involved in using it to our own advantage. Furthermore, we do not have an ID on anyone helping the Governor pass information to Wolfbane. If we move too quickly, the rest of the spy ring will go undercover and vanish."

"For the moment," the Colonel said, "leave it in place. However" - he held up a hand - "I want you to be ready to shut it down at a moment's notice, if necessary. There's a limit to how far we can keep data to ourselves."

"We could warn people to be more careful what they say," Kitty said. "Or engage in a little kabuki play to convince them that there are spies everywhere."

"I will have to see what can be arranged," the Colonel said. "Continue with your plan, Colonel. I will expect to see a progress report by the end of the week."

Kitty nodded, then rose to her feet.

"One other thing," the Colonel added. "I will expect you to be careful just *what* you share with your reporter friend. There are limits to how far we can afford to trust anyone."

"Understood," Kitty said.

She stepped out of the door, then walked down to her office. The guard outside checked her ID, as if he hadn't seen her leave the room thirty minutes ago, then stepped inside to allow her to enter the compartment. Emmanuel Alves was sitting on the sofa, reading a datapad with a curious expression. He'd been warned, in no uncertain terms, not to attempt to move further into the complex.

"Kitty," he said. "How was the Colonel?"

"Concerned," Kitty said. "Did you see anything interesting in the papers?"

"I downloaded copies of all the gossipy rags," Emmanuel said. "Most of them raved about the latest party, then bragged about who the reporters sat next to when they were at dinner. Nothing too important, really; someone sat next to the Governor's wife and claimed she made a great conversationalist."

Kitty sighed. "Nothing important, then?"

"Not unless you look carefully," Emmanuel said. "There's a very definite hint that several business marriages are being contemplated, as well as relationships between two mining corporations and a new industrial start-up. Oh, and some of them are planning to lobby for an end to start-up loans to businesses on Avalon. There should be a story there."

"There probably will be," Kitty said. She sat down, facing him. "The leak is in the Governor's Mansion. There's no rational alternative, unless we're prepared to believe that over a third of our political and corporate leaders are planning to sell the Commonwealth down the river. This leaves us with a problem. How do we identify the link between the mansion and the other spies? And what can we do with it?"

Emmanuel considered it. "I had an idea," he said, finally. "I could offer to do a puff piece on the parties. They *are* quite famous, really. A chat with the Governor might be enough to write a story - and give us insight into his mind."

"He isn't going to confess to you," Kitty pointed out. *That* only worked in bad flicks. "I think he'd just talk about nothing."

"I know," Emmanuel said. "But you'll be with me when he does."

Emmanuel had expected some resistance when he'd sent the message to the Governor's Mansion. In his experience, most politicians and corporate leaders on Avalon were reluctant to talk to the press, not when they couldn't expect the press to either suppress an inconvenient truth or toe the political line. But the Governor agreed almost at once, much to his surprise; he'd even offered the use of his mansion as an interview site. Emmanuel had grabbed his equipment, ensured that Kitty looked like a low and naive intern, then set off to the mansion in his car. The guards allowed him to enter without doing more than a basic check.

The former Governor was waiting for them, flanked by his wife. Governor Brent Roeder had been middle-aged when he'd been dispatched to Avalon, while Hannalore was a few years younger - and looked, thanks to the miracle of cosmetic surgery, young enough to be his daughter. Her body looked teenage, definitely, but her eyes were hard and cold. Emmanuel couldn't help wondering if he was looking at the true brains behind the Governor's life. She would hardly be the first woman to be quietly driving her man on from behind.

"It's always a pleasure to meet a gentleman of the press," the Governor said. He might have little or no effective power, but one wouldn't have known it from his stance. "I've enjoyed reading some of your articles."

"And so we were surprised when you contacted us, requesting an interview," Hannalore added, sharply. Her voice would have been sultry if it hadn't been so icy. "You are not known for reporting on social engagements."

"I was informed by several of my contacts that your parties are actually more than mere social engagements," Emmanuel said, as they stepped through a side door and into a large sitting room. A waiter appeared, carrying a tray of steaming mugs of coffee. "They believed that some business deals were made here, out of the public eye."

The Governor smiled as he sat down. "I was lost for quite some time," he said, as the waiter handed out the cups of coffee. "What can a former Governor do when the state he serves no longer exists? There was nothing to be gained from trying to remain on the council, I thought; the new state had no time for me. My three years on the council were wasted."

Emmanuel nodded. *He'd* heard the Governor had jumped before he'd been pushed, but he didn't blame the man for trying to put the best possible spin on events. Being fired was never easy to handle, particularly when whatever had happened wasn't one's fault.

"And then my wife had an idea," the Governor continued. "We still owned the mansion, so we could use it as a place to encourage social mixing. The new would mix with the old and both would emerge stronger."

"Social mentoring was always one of my interests," Hannalore said, icily.

Kitty leaned forward. When she spoke, her voice was almost painfully naive. "What is social mentoring?"

Hannalore eyed her for a long moment. "High Society is a jungle with many different rules," she said. For a long moment, her accent was very definitely aristocratic, enough to make the hackles rise on Emmanuel's neck. "A newcomer, presented at court, will not know how to handle herself without giving offense. A society mentor ensures that she avoids making any major mistakes until she finds her footing."

"That society is gone," Emmanuel said, lightly.

"The basic idea is still the same," Hannalore said. "People of ...wealth and achievement, if not family, meet in a neutral location to talk. Some of those talks lead to business alliances and success. The society we are building is developing its own rules, but eventually those rules will start to shut out newcomers, unless they are carefully mentored into learning the ropes."

Emmanuel leaned forward. "Do you believe that to be possible?"

"High Society was very exclusive on Earth," Hannalore said. There was a trace of underlying bitterness in her voice. "And true newcomers were very rare."

"And the corporations will eventually reach a point where they discover that suppressing competition is easier than trying to compete openly," the Governor said. "They will soon discover their self-interest drives them towards closing ranks, rather than embracing the new and feeding on change."

"You may be right," Emmanuel said. "How do your parties help keep that from happening?"

"We encourage the older, more established interests to meet with the new," the Governor said. "I - we - aim to develop a society where the new is always embraced, rather than rejected or excluded. Strong habits of learning from the new will build on themselves, eventually excluding those who *refuse* to learn from the new. There will be no opportunity to close ranks."

"The Trade Federation has something comparable," Hannalore added. "Families take newcomers as marriage partners, to ensure that they remain part of the family. The principle is the same."

"So it would seem," Emmanuel mused. Privately, he had his doubts; the Commonwealth was barely five years old, while the Empire had endured for centuries before it collapsed. "How did you get started?"

"We invited everyone who had earned wealth," the Governor said, "and others who might do as well, given time. And then we went on from there."

"It must have cost money," Emmanuel said. "How did you pay for it, originally?"

"My wife sold her jewels," the Governor said. He gave Hannalore a fond look, even though she didn't seem happy at the admission. "That brought us enough money to pay for the first couple of parties, then we sold a handful of subscriptions."

"Another way to keep people invested," Hannalore said. Her voice was very cold. "They do tend to place more value on something they pay for themselves."

Emmanuel kept his face impassive, somehow. If the Governor had been an observer on the council for three years, he had to have left just after the Commonwealth had encountered Admiral Singh - and then Wolfbane. Was that a coincidence? And if Hannalore had sold her jewels …he swore mentally as he realised it was unlikely the sale had brought in more than a few thousand credits. Avalon's society beauties wouldn't place much value on jewels from Earth, while anyone who had actually earned money would draw the line at buying them.

She couldn't have earned that much from selling her jewels, he thought. *Did she take money from Wolfbane?*

It wasn't a pleasant thought. He'd largely overlooked the Governor's wife, considering her nothing more than an appendage to the Governor. But he should have known better. She had a motive to betray the Commonwealth - it had destroyed her social position - and the means, given that she controlled the mansion. And she'd clearly had the nerve to push her husband into carving out a new role for himself.

"That is true," he agreed. "Do *you* feel they have been a good investment?"

"They pay for themselves," the Governor said. "Being a mediator isn't quite like being a Governor, really. I find it quite relaxing."

"I imagine," Emmanuel said.

"It's quite romantic how Holily Brennan and Roger Mortimer have fallen in love," Hannalore said. "*That* started at one of our parties."

Emmanuel grinned. "And how do you benefit from that?"

"Good vibes," Hannalore said. "And we get to charge for using the mansion for the wedding."

"I'd like you to talk up how people come together here," the Governor said, as the interview started to draw to a close. "They have to understand that we're giving birth to a new era and parties like the ones we hold only help reshape people into a united civilisation."

"I will quote you on that," Emmanuel promised. "Do you have anything else you wish to say to the readers?"

"Just that the Commonwealth will survive, prosper and eventually overcome," the Governor offered. "And you can quote me on that too."

Emmanuel nodded, then allowed the Governor to show them back out of the house and into the car. He didn't say a word until they were out of the gates, then Kitty had performed a quick check for bugs. There were none in the car itself, but he took the precaution of activating his privacy generator before he dared say anything. He didn't want to take unnecessary risks.

"It's the wife," Kitty said, flatly. "She's the brains behind the operation, I bet you."

"I thought as much," Emmanuel agreed. "I doubt she could have got more than a few thousand credits for her jewels, even if she had the Crown Jewels of Prince Roland hidden under her mansion. There aren't many people here who would buy them at their old value."

"I need to check up on her," Kitty said. She cursed under her breath. "I was fixated on the Governor...it never occurred to me that his wife might be involved."

"It's a common mistake to make," Emmanuel said. "I'm pretty sure she wasn't much more than a hostess when her husband actually held real power."

He sighed. "All her talk about social mentoring," he added, rolling his eyes. "I'd bet good money that she's been regretting coming out here, ever since she found out the truth about Avalon. Wolfbane probably didn't have to work hard to convince her to work for them. Hell, given how many contacts she has now, she might even be an acceptable collaborator leader for them."

Kitty ran her hand through her long red hair. "I need to take this to the Colonel," she said, slowly. Colonel Stalker would have to make the final decision. "And then we need to decide what to do."

She shrugged. "We still have to identify the link back to Wolfbane," she added. "Perhaps one of her permanent employees…or perhaps someone else. Still, we know who to follow now."

"Unless there's something more out here," Emmanuel said, pessimistically. That was Kitty's problem, really. He had other things to worry about. "I'd better get on with writing that damn puff piece."

"It might get you a few more invitations, so make it as sweet and gentle as you can," Kitty said. Her lips curled into a grim smirk. "And they might come in handy, when we make her an offer she can't refuse."

CHAPTER
TWENTY-TWO

But, on the other hand, promising harsh punishments to any captured member of the terrorist organisation guarantees that there will be few surrenders.
- Professor Leo Caesius. *The Empire and its Prisoners of War.*

Saltine Asteroid, Year 5 (PE)

"This is neutral territory," Captain Jim Frazier said, as they stepped through the airlock into Saltine Asteroid. "Try not to pick a fight."

Jasmine nodded, then took a deep breath as the atmosphere struck her face. Like many asteroid settlements that lacked eco-caves, Saltine smelled of too many humans in too close proximity, mingled with the scent of machinery and foodstuffs. The handful of people in view wore everything from shipsuits to colourful outfits that seemed to come from another era. Most of them were armed, she noted with some concern, and many of them looked deadly, as if they were determined to fight to defend themselves.

But it would be pointless if a warship arrives, she thought, as Frazier led her down a long corridor. *They could simply blow the asteroid apart with a well-placed nuke.*

She took another breath as they stepped into a cavern, which was crammed with stalls and people trying to sell their wares. It looked distressingly familiar; she'd seem similar displays on pirate-operated asteroids, where there was no law and order and the strong bullied the weak mercilessly. No one seemed to be selling slaves, which was one mercy;

she frowned as she saw a sign advertising a brothel. The whores might be selling their own bodies or they might be being sold, the helpless victims of emotionless pimps. There was no way to know.

"You could try to sell some of your supplies for credits," Frazier offered, as they made their way past a set of stalls. "Or you could just wait and see what happens."

"I will," Jasmine said. "I don't think we would get much for anything we have on the ship."

"Trade the fresh food," Frazier said. "You could probably get quite a bit in trade, if you try."

Jasmine put the thought at the back of her mind, then followed him up to a solid airlock. It was unmarked, save for a simple scratch that looked too precise to be natural. Frazier tapped on the hatch, then waited; two minutes later, it hissed open, revealing a small office. A dark-skinned woman, her skin far darker than Jasmine's looked up and frowned as they entered, then waved to a pair of seats. Frazier sat down, then nodded to Jasmine. She had to do the talking.

"I understand you're the Trade Federation representative here," Jasmine said. "Is that true?"

"Yes," the girl said. She looked around the same age as Jasmine, but her eyes suggested she was considerably older. The Traders had never had any compunctions about using semi-legal biological treatments to extend their lives. "And you're a marine, unless I miss my guess."

Jasmine nodded, shortly. "We need help," she said. "Can we ask for it?"

"They've escaped a POW camp," Frazier said, helpfully. "And she isn't sure if she should trust your agreement with the Commonwealth."

Jasmine shot him a sharp glance, then looked back at the girl. "He's right," she admitted. "We did escape a POW camp."

"I see," the girl said. "My name is Mary, by the way. And I think you'd better tell me the full story."

She listened, impassively, as Jasmine told her a very basic outline of their escape from an unnamed world. It was possible they would eventually realise that it was Meridian, but for the moment she would prefer to keep the world's name to herself. Mary waited until Jasmine had finished, then keyed a switch below her desk. Jasmine tensed, one hand crawling towards the pistol at her belt, as a hidden door hissed open. Two men, both unarmed, stepped into the room. They looked so alike she was sure they were clones.

"We have an alliance with your Commonwealth," one said. He made a show of stroking his beard before continuing. "I believe we are obliged to honour it, although I should warn you that our presence here is very limited. They would not tolerate a military base in their rear."

Jasmine gave them a sharp look. "They know you're here?"

"Of course," the second clone said. "Trade trumps everything, young lady."

"And it's a good source of intelligence," the first clone offered. "We have learned much about the Wolves and passed it to our superiors."

Mary cleared her throat. "The Andrews are the supervisors here," she explained. "We just call them One and Two."

Jasmine shook her head. Cloning a living person had been illegal under the Empire, although she'd heard rumours that some of the Grand Senators had cloned themselves more than once, perhaps to provide transplants for medical purposes. Given how easy it was to clone a single organ in a cloning tank, she had her doubts. But, unlike some rumours, it was actually technologically possible.

"Very well," she said. "How much help can you give us?"

Andrew One smiled. "What do you want to do?"

"Either take advantage of being here," Jasmine said, "and strike them somewhere in the rear, or simply head home. I have over a thousand POWs on my ship and most of them need to be back on Avalon."

Andrew Two smiled, in a manner precisely identical to Andrew One. "We can provide you with another bulk freighter or two," he offered. "But getting behind their lines …it would be quite risky."

"We're already behind their lines," Jasmine pointed out. "And they don't know we're here."

"Sabotage teams could have been launched directly from the Commonwealth," Andrew One countered. He paused, then exchanged an identical look with his twin. "However, we may be able to help you. Our only stipulation is that you do nothing to draw their attention here."

"We will do our best," Jasmine said.

"Glad to hear it," Andrew One said. "I can have a second bulk freighter prepped for you in a couple of hours, along with a crew. I'd expect you to replenish the tanks if nothing else …"

"I dare say the Commonwealth will make it worth your while," Jasmine said. The crew would need to be paid, if nothing else. "What information do you have on Wolfbane?"

"Plenty," Andrew Two said. "I will have it readied for you. We would advise you to remain on your ship, unless you wish to trade. This is not a secure location."

They bowed, then retreated through the door, which hissed closed. Jasmine had expected more of an argument, but perhaps it had been foolish. The Trade Federation was a loose structure, very much a flattened hierarchy, yet it did honour agreements …

"They're a strange bunch, but they're decent people," Mary said. "I rather like working with them."

Jasmine blinked. "Are they clones?"

"Yep," Mary said. She gave Jasmine a sharp look. "Is that a problem?"

"I'm just surprised," Jasmine said. "I've never seen a full-body clone before."

"There's several clone-families along the Rim," Mary said. "Their genes are dominant, so every child they sire is another clone. The Andrews have been working for the Trader Queen since the Trade Federation was established. No one doubts their loyalty or competence."

She paused. "This isn't Earth," she added. "There are lots of …people out here whose mere existence would be considered illegal, in the Core Worlds. Clones, half-human hybrids, enhanced cyborgs …there's a rumour going round about people who have been assimilated into a giant hive mind. No one gives a damn about the Empire's hypocritical morality here."

Frazier smiled. "How often do you have to give that speech?"

"Too often," Mary said. "There are worse people out here than the Andrews."

Jasmine didn't doubt it. Saltine looked civilised, compared to a pirate asteroid, but there was very little distance between accepting individual quirks and rationalising something truly awful. Pirates gleefully engaged in looting, rape, murder and slave trading; it was astonishing just how many activities could be deemed acceptable, if it suited someone to make that determination. If Kailee had been shocked at the number of hard choices Jasmine had had to make, in her seven years of active service, she would be horrified if she knew just how many compromises were made by people who lived on the Rim.

"We'll go back to our ship," she said. "And then we will decide what to do."

Frazier followed her out of the office, then stopped. "I was serious when I said that fresh food would go far," he said. "If you like, I will try to sell some of your stockpile for you."

"I'll have to arrange for you to be escorted," Jasmine said. "I'm sorry, but ..."

She winced inwardly at the look on his face. His children were hostages; one set hostage to Wolfbane, one set hostage to Jasmine and her team. Frazier could please one of the hostage-takers at the price of pissing off the other, ensuring that he'd lose at least two children. It was an awful place to be, Jasmine privately conceded. But she had no choice. She *had* to keep him aware of the consequences of betrayal.

Her thoughts mocked her. *What would Blake, friend to all female things, think of you?*

"I understand," Frazier said. "Please ...please send the other children back to the Commonwealth."

Jasmine gritted her teeth. If she did, it would be hard to hold the threat to them over his head; if she didn't, she would keep the kids in a dangerous situation. Blake would have spat on her, she was sure; there were limits to how far anyone could go without losing any claim to the moral high ground.

"I can try," she said. But if she did, she would have to watch him *very* carefully for any sign of betrayal. Done properly, he would be able to save both sets of children ...at the cost of Jasmine and her entire team. "We will see."

They walked back to the ship in silence. Once they were onboard, Jasmine placed Frazier in his locked cabin, then made her way to the bridge, feeling like an old bitter woman. She'd mocked the asteroid's dwellers for compromising their principles and rationalising the worst sins humans could commit, but how was she any different? She was the one holding hostages to secure a single person's good behaviour.

"Boss," Stewart said. "I just picked up a message from the asteroid's command network. There's a freighter being docked in the next airlock, for us. Her file says she can take all of the POWs, no problem."

"There shouldn't be any problems with range either," Watson added. "She's got enough fuel and supplies to take us all back to Avalon without risking interception."

Jasmine nodded. "Ask for volunteers among the soldiers; I think we won't need more than a couple of dozen," she ordered. "The remainder are to transfer to the new ship as soon as it is ready to go."

"Understood," Stewart said, curtly. "Do you want to hold anyone else back?"

"General Stubbins and Paula," Jasmine said. "Gary and Kailee, if they want to stay."

Watson smirked. "You must like me."

It took Jasmine a moment to realise what he meant. "I hope you're keeping your eyes open," she said, tiredly. "Someone like Paula should be watched carefully."

"Of course," Watson said. "I was watching her *very* carefully last night."

"Going back into barracks is going to be a strain, isn't it?" Jasmine said, ruefully. She had a feeling that summary demotion was waiting for her, when she finally returned to Avalon. "I won't find it any easier."

"Maybe," Stewart said. "Am I to assume you have a plan?"

"I have half of one," Jasmine said.

She sighed, then turned to the hatch. "I'm going to study the intelligence, then see if I can put together a workable plan," she added. "Alert me if anything changes."

"Of course," Stewart said.

"And put Frazier's children on the other ship," Jasmine added. She briefly considered sending Frazier too, but she had a feeling she'd need his contacts. "Tell them they have a few minutes to say goodbye, then make it happen."

Neither of them said anything. Somehow, that only made it worse.

"I don't understand," Gary said.

"It's quite simple," Watson said. The marine eyed him with barely concealed disdain. "You can take a freighter back to Avalon, where you can join the Commonwealth Navy or find something else to do with your time, or you can stay with us. I think you have around five or six hours to decide."

"Thank you," Kailee said, before Gary could say a word. "We'll let you know when the time comes."

Watson nodded curtly, then turned and stepped out of the compartment, closing the hatch behind him. He *still* intimidated Gary, all the more so now he knew how badly his arms ached after doing twenty press-ups a day. Jasmine had told him that it would take time for him to develop the muscles to do more, but Gary honestly couldn't wait for the day it was completely painless. He would have given up if Kailee hadn't made it clear she wouldn't let him change his mind.

"There's little we can do here," he said. He'd made progress with a proper teaching machine, but he knew he had a long way to go. "We could take the freighter …"

"*No*," Kailee said, flatly. "I am not going to leave this ship."

Gary peered at her. "This ship …or *her*?"

Kailee gave him a nasty look. "This is an opportunity I will not surrender," she said. "And I will not let you surrender either."

"I know," Gary said. She'd told him that if he wanted to keep seeing her naked, he had to do his exercises. He would have been furious if she hadn't grown better at massaging his sore muscles after each bout. "But what can we do to help?"

"I don't know," Kailee said. "But we have to try."

Gary wanted to roll his eyes. Kailee's mood swings were becoming increasingly alarming; she moved from being weak and helpless, unwilling to clamber out of bed, to being utterly bombastic, as enthusiastic about exercise as any half-mad gym teacher. There were times when he honestly wondered if she was the same person he'd known - vaguely - on Earth.

But he had few illusions about how little they could be of help. He could handle the ship, to some degree, but he was very far from an expert. Besides, the ship already had a set of pilots: the Frazier Family. They didn't need him clowning around with their ship.

"I'm not an action hero," he said, reluctantly. He would have liked to tell himself otherwise, that he had the nerve to do something useful, but he knew it would be a lie. "And neither are you."

He held up a hand before Kailee could say a word. "We will go to Jasmine," he added, "and ask her if she would like us to accompany her. If she says yes, we stay with her; if she says no, we go to Avalon. Is that all right?"

Kailee sighed, furiously. "It will do," she said, in a tone that suggested he wouldn't be seeing her naked for a week. "Let's go."

Gary followed her as she stood and strode out of the compartment, then hurried down the corridor to Jasmine's cabin. The hatch was closed - Gary was tempted to suggest they came back later - but Kailee tapped on the hatch until it opened. Inside, Jasmine was seated on a half-made bunk, studying a datapad. There was something in her expression, for once unguarded, that sent chills down Gary's spine.

"Kailee," Jasmine said. She sounded tired, rather than angry, but her tone still made Gary want to run. *He'd* never dreamed of a woman who could snap his neck like a twig. "And Gary. What can I do for you?"

"I would like to stay with you," Kailee said, flatly. "But Gary was wondering if we would be any use."

"I do not know, yet," Jasmine said. "However, I would advise you to make your own choices. You could go with the freighter and there would be no hard feelings. I wouldn't expect you to come with us."

Gary worked up his nerve and asked a single question. "Are you expecting to come back?"

Jasmine lifted her head and gave him a long, considering look. "I don't know," she admitted, finally. "I have always known that one day my luck would run out and I would die. This time may be my final swan song. But you two? You don't have to come with me."

Kailee stepped forward. "We *are* going to come with you."

Jasmine gave her a tired smile. "Why?"

"Because I'm tired of being helpless," Kailee said. "And if you have a use for us, it will be my pleasure to serve."

"Very well," Jasmine said. Her gaze moved to Gary's face. "And you, Gary?"

Gary swallowed. He wanted to run, but he didn't want to desert Kailee; he wanted to drag her with him, yet he knew it would be futile. Everything in his life had taught him that there was no point in trying to fight. Kailee would get herself killed and he would die right alongside her ...

But she was right. He was tired of being helpless too.

"I'll stay," he said. Oddly, making the decision felt like a load off his mind. "I might be able to do something useful for you."

"We shall see," Jasmine said. "I won't be with you this evening, so do your exercises alone - and don't miss a single push-up. Or you will regret it tomorrow."

Gary frowned. *That* didn't sound pleasant. "You'll hit us?"

"Your body will ache more the following day," Jasmine said, nastily. "Efficiency."

CHAPTER
TWENTY-THREE

> This grows more complex as one realises that terrorism can be a criminal act, instead of an act of war. Should terrorists be treated as criminals, with full access to legal resources to defend themselves, or illegal combatants, who can be legally shot?
> - Professor Leo Caesius. *The Empire and its Prisoners of War.*

Saltine Asteroid, Year 5 (PE)

"We have a unique opportunity here," Jasmine said, the following morning. "I do not intend to waste it."

She glanced around the makeshift conference room. Watson and Stewart sat next to her, flanked by Stubbins, Paula, Kailee and Gary. Behind them, Frazier looked thoroughly unhappy, while Robert Gouette - who had been a CEF trooper before the Battle of Thule - kept a sharp eye on him.

"We are here, behind enemy lines," she continued. "It's two weeks to Wolfbane. There, we might have a chance to do real damage to their infrastructure before making a dash to the Commonwealth. We have enough intelligence to know that there *are* weaknesses, weaknesses that a small team can take advantage of. A direct attack would give the Commonwealth a much-needed breathing space."

There was a long pause. "It could also get us killed for nothing," she added. "I need you to tell me if you feel we can actually accomplish something."

She sucked in her breath as the words echoed in the air. Colonel Stalker wouldn't have asked for advice - or, at least, he wouldn't have effectively handed his subordinates a veto over his next decision. But she'd been doubting herself ever since she'd been dropped into the POW camp. Was she intent on hitting the enemy because she believed it possible ...or was she looking for make up for her mistakes? The hell of it was that she wasn't sure herself.

"I have contacts in the system," Stubbins said. "We would have some degree of access, once we arrived."

"Your contacts may no longer be there," Paula pointed out. "And even if they were, they might not be inclined to risk their lives by helping you."

Stubbins gave her a nasty look. "My people are not defeated so easily."

Jasmine fought the urge to rub her face with her palm. "Carl? Thomas?"

Stewart smiled. "I think we should go," he said. "You're right; this is a unique opportunity and we shouldn't waste it."

He held up a hand before Jasmine could say a word. "I know, there's a case to be made that we should report in to the Commonwealth," he added. "But there isn't much hope of getting there and then getting back before they realise they've lost a few prisoners. If nothing else, we can expect them to take a sharp look at their security arrangements."

Jasmine nodded. The files they'd captured had proven that the Wolves hadn't been particularly concerned about the POWs, beyond dumping them in a camp on a world at the very edge of settled space, but that would change. Losing the camp alone would have been irritating; losing the station and then a starship would be embarrassing. She was sure there would be a review, eventually, of security arrangements. It might end with a complete reshuffle of everything they knew.

"We'd be looking at a three-month round trip," Watson warned. "I think the decision rests in your hands."

"I know," Jasmine said. She took a long breath. "I'm going to trade some of our fresh food for supplies, then we will depart - hopefully, by the end of the day. By the time we reach Wolfbane, I want to be ready for anything."

Gary looked at her, nervously. "How do you know there will be a way in?"

"There's an entire system," Jasmine pointed out. She'd managed to insert an entire team onto Corinthian before, back when she'd first encountered Admiral Singh. Slipping into a star system would be child's play by comparison. "I suspect there will be no shortage of ways to slip in at the edges."

She paused, then went on. "The other freighter will be departing in an hour," she added. "If any of you want to record messages for people on Avalon, do it now. The crew will take them home."

"Understood," Stewart said. "But there's only the Colonel there."

"You should have spent more time socialising," Watson said, sardonically. "I have friends back there who probably miss me."

"So you want to give them another shot," Stewart said.

Jasmine groaned. "Record your messages and send them to the freighter," she ordered. She had the private feeling that Watson probably intended to record messages for a dozen different girls, perhaps telling each one that *she* was the only one he'd thought about while he was in the POW camp. "Gary, Kailee; you'll come with me to the asteroid. If you want to record messages yourselves, do it now."

Gary shrugged, expressively. Jasmine understood; there was no one, save perhaps Darrin and Austin, who Gary might want to contact. She knew nothing of his home life on Earth, but humanity's homeworld was gone. Anyone he'd known in his CityBlock was probably gone too. Kailee merely looked at the deck, then nodded once. God alone knew who *she* wanted to record a message for. As far as anyone knew, Gary and Kailee only had each other.

She rose to her feet. "Meet me in the airlock in thirty minutes," she ordered the two youngsters. "Dismissed."

Back in her cabin, she took a moment to review the report she'd written for Colonel Stalker, then uploaded it to the other freighter. It was as complete and comprehensive as she could manage, including everything they'd learned about Wolfbane and copies of the files she'd drawn from their computer networks. The station's datacores had been removed prior to its destruction, ensuring that techs on Avalon would have a chance to search them for anything useful, file by file. Jasmine doubted there was anything useful left undiscovered, but Commonwealth Intelligence might find something they could use against the Wolves. It was worth a try.

She hesitated, then opened the second message. God alone knew what Emmanuel thought had happened to her; it wasn't clear if Wolfbane had attempted to pass the POW details to the Commonwealth or not. There was no way to know what he was doing, back on Avalon, or how long he would wait for her. And if he thought she was dead, he might well have moved on. She braced herself, then uploaded the message and rose to her feet. It was time to go to the asteroid and do what trading she could.

Gary and Kailee met her at the airlock, both looking tired and wan. Jasmine smiled to herself as she picked up the crate of fresh food, then opened the airlock and walked through the hatch into the asteroid. Both of the youngsters gasped when they smelled the atmosphere, as if they hadn't been expecting the sudden change. Jasmine wasn't too surprised. Groundhogs rarely realised that starships could smell quite unpleasant to a newcomer, while each planet and asteroid had its own unique smell. It wasn't a coincidence that one of the less pleasant nicknames for people from Earth was dirt-foot.

"Be polite as long as you're here," she said, firmly. She turned to see their reactions to her next words. "Justice here can be even rougher and readier than it was on Meridian."

The two youngsters exchanged nervous glances, then followed her down the corridor and into the marketplace. Jasmine suspected there were similar places on Meridian, where farmers sold their produce to the townsfolk, but this was very different. One stall was littered with refurbished spare parts, another was covered in datachips, datapads and large posters advertising pirated flicks and audio tracks. Jasmine glanced at the names of the stars, then rolled her eyes in dismay. None of them had proven very popular on her homeworld.

"I remember them," Kailee said, pointing to a datachip box covered in pictures of scantily-clad women. "They were very popular on Earth."

"I'm not surprised," Jasmine said. The actresses looked disturbingly young and innocent, yet they were dressed in shirts that looked as though they were going to fall off at any moment. "The only thing that kept their outfits on are the eyes of every young man in the chamber."

Kailee blinked. "Are you always so cynical?"

"Better to be a cynic than a deluded optimist," Jasmine said. She shook her head as Kailee picked up the box hopefully. "Anyone who looks that innocent on Earth probably has a great many secrets buried in her closet."

"I never believed they were what they seemed," Gary said. "They're not real, are they?"

Jasmine shrugged and led them onwards. "You can do remarkable things with computers," she said. "If there hadn't been laws saying that every flick had to have live actors, the producers would have replaced them all with computer-generated simulations. *They* don't complain, they don't get into trouble with law-enforcement, they don't start demanding extra money because they've made a number of good flicks ..."

Kailee snorted. "You seem to know a lot about this," she said. "Did you want to be an actress too?"

"Perish the thought," Jasmine said. Her parents would have disowned her if she'd tried to become an actress. "I just know how easy it is to put together simulations for training purposes. The civilians who run across our positions aren't real, but they *look* real. There's no technical reason you couldn't produce a completely computer-generated flick that would be impossible to distinguish from the real thing."

"Even ...even a pornographic flick?" Gary asked. "They're not real?"

"I think most of them are done by very skilled actors," Jasmine said, snidely. It had shocked her, when she'd entered Boot Camp, to see just what some people considered erotic. "Most people can't do half the positions you see in the flicks, not without injuring themselves."

She stopped outside a hatch, then knocked once. It opened, revealing an assessor's office, complete with a grim-faced man sitting in front of a pair of scales. He rose to his feet as they entered, then bowed. Jasmine took a moment to read the handful of rules pasted on the bulkhead - the sellers got ten percent commission on every sale - and then placed the box on the table.

"Fresh fruit," she said simply, as she disengaged the stasis field. "Apples, oranges, slices of cooked ham and turkey ...all ready to be eaten now."

The man inspected the box thoroughly, then looked up at her. "Cash or commission?"

Jasmine considered it. "How much are you prepared to offer?"

"Five thousand traders, straight up," the man said. "Or ten percent commission, depending on the sales."

Gary whistled. Food was cheap on Meridian, where fruit and vegetables were grown everywhere. A bag of fresh apples could be so cheap that a child could buy one with a tiny fraction of his chore money. But on Earth, the same bag of apples could be so expensive that most families wouldn't have a hope of being able to afford one unless they were prepared to make real sacrifices. Fresh meat, if it was authorised for shipping, was solely the preserve of the upper classes. Most people had to make do with algae-based foodstuffs.

"Ten thousand traders," Jasmine said. She'd taken the opportunity to check prices as they walked through the marketplace and knew they would need at least six thousand to get everything they needed. "I think you should be able to do more than recoup your losses."

"I very much doubt it," the man sneered. "Six thousand traders."

They haggled backwards and forwards for a long moment, then compromised on seven thousand, five hundred traders. Jasmine took the credit chip without delay, checked it carefully and then inserted it into her pocket. They *might* have earned more by allowing the office to sell the fresh produce on commission, she knew, but they simply didn't have the time to waste. Instead, she nodded politely to the man and led the way back out of the office.

"I have a shopping list," she said, once the hatch had slid closed. "I'm afraid we don't have much money to waste, so try not to pick up anything we don't need."

Gary nodded, then stared in disbelief as a pair of hairy monsters strode past. "What ...what are those?"

"They had their genes modified for some reason," Jasmine said. "Their homeworld was probably very cold and their founders decided to go for modification, rather than doing anything to warm the planet's atmosphere. It's not very common."

"I thought they were aliens," Gary said. He looked up at her. "*Are* there real aliens?"

"No," Jasmine said. Once, there had been hundreds of thousands of stories about humans encountering other forms of intelligent life. Now, with nearly half the galaxy explored and colonised, it was clear that humanity was alone. The highest form of life anyone had encountered anywhere apart from Earth was a creature roughly akin to a tiger. "There's just us out here."

She shrugged, then led the way to the first stall and started placing her orders. The stallkeeper haggled for a few minutes, then handed over the tools Jasmine wanted. Another stall provided various forms of advanced weapons, while a third offered a number of military-grade spacesuits. Jasmine carefully *didn't* speculate on where they might have come from as she purchased a round dozen, then concluded her dealing by picking up two automated hacking kits and user manuals. Someone in Imperial Intelligence, she decided, had been making money by selling equipment on the sly. It was an old tradition when there wasn't actually a war on.

Kailee caught her arm as three men stepped past, walking in mechanical unison. Jasmine watched them without much interest, even when one of them paused and looked at her with cold inhuman eyes. Gary shrank back against her, then relaxed slightly as the strangers walked onwards. Jasmine sighed inwardly, then made arrangements to have her purchases shipped back to the freighter.

"You sent everything back," Gary said. "Do you trust them?"

Jasmine grinned. "Money talks in a place like this," she said. "You will see great inhumanities here, and you can expect people to try to haggle as much as possible, but you won't see anyone try to steal anything you leave with them. It would destroy their reputation."

Gary snorted. "Is that really important?"

"Of course," Jasmine said. "No one would ever trust them again."

She paused, once she'd picked up the final pieces of equipment. "There's some time left," she said. "Do either of you want to do anything while you're here?"

Gary and Kailee exchanged glances. "I don't know," Kailee said, finally. "Is there anything to do here?"

Jasmine made a show of considering the question. Most of the entertainments on the asteroid were geared around spacers, who tended to want cheap food, booze and sex, perhaps not in that order. She doubted that either of them would want to go to a brothel …they *could* go catch a flick, if they wanted, but most of the flicks on offer would be mindless pap. It was true of just about everything the Empire had produced in its final years, she suspected.

"Not much," she admitted, finally. "But it would get you off the ship for a while."

"No, thank you," Gary said. "I don't feel safe here."

"You probably won't be mugged," Jasmine reassured him. *She* would have killed, back when she'd been a raw recruit, to get out of the barracks for a few hours. "Just make sure you don't sign any contracts. They will be held against you."

"No, thank you," Gary repeated. "I would prefer to go back to the ship."

"I have work for you to do there," Jasmine said. She stepped over to a food stall and bought several bags of sweets, which she stuffed in her jacket pocket. "By the time we get to our destination, I want you to have mastered the ship's computers ...and a handful of other computer packages."

Gary looked torn between confidence and fear. Jasmine had reviewed his work with the teaching machines and noted that, while Gary had an insight into how the systems worked, he was lacking in both practical and theoretical knowledge. And he probably expected a beating for every failure ...Jasmine shook her head, mentally. If he screwed up in the Wolfbane System, a beating would be the least of anyone's worries.

"And me?" Kailee asked. "Do you have something for me to do?"

"You said you wanted to be a nurse," Jasmine said. "I think you should keep studying what you can, if you still want to do anything. And ...I may have something else for you to do."

Kailee looked doubtful, but said nothing. Jasmine understood; they didn't have a medic with them, leaving them dependent on what the marines knew of battlefield medicine. There was no way they could train Kailee, not enough to make a difference. But it would keep her busy, at least until they reached Wolfbane. By then, Jasmine's plan might have proved itself workable ...or useless.

She led them back to the freighter, then sent them to their cabin while she walked back to the bridge. Stewart greeted her and confirmed that the other freighter had departed on schedule, carrying most of the POWs - and their messages - back to the Commonwealth. Jasmine, oddly, felt freer, now they were no longer her responsibility. She could take the initiative for herself.

"Once our supplies have arrived, unpack them and check everything," she ordered. No matter what she'd told Gary, there were limits to her trust. "And then we cast off as planned."

"Understood," Stewart said. He paused. "And might I recommend some rest?"

"I'll rest when I'm dead," Jasmine said. It was an old saying, passed down from the legendary first marines. "Until then, I have work to do."

CHAPTER TWENTY-FOUR

And it grows even more complex when one reasons the terrorists might even have a point. If they follow the laws of war, they will be crushed easily. Does this serve as an excuse for avoiding the laws of war?
- Professor Leo Caesius. *The Empire and its Prisoners of War.*

Passing Water, **Year 5 (PE)**

"I think that's thirty push-ups," Gary said, as he slumped to the deck. The aching in his arms refused to fade. "Isn't it?"

"Twenty-nine," Jasmine said, from where she was leaning against the bulkhead. "Do another ten for luck."

Gary groaned. His body felt unwilling to move, no matter what he did. The deck, hard and cold, seemed almost as welcoming as his bed. Jasmine had said, time and time again, that it got better, but he found it hard to believe her. And yet, even twenty-nine push-ups would have seemed impossible, four days ago.

He gritted his teeth and forced his body up again. His joints screamed in pain, but somehow he managed to do another five before he lost control of his body and thudded hard against the deck. For a long moment, he just lay there, seriously thinking about staying there for the rest of his life. And then Jasmine reached down and effortlessly lifted him to his feet.

"You're getting better," she said. "You just need to keep working on it."

"Thanks," Gary said, bitterly. He honestly had no idea how he was going to keep working on the computers if his body ached so much the following morning. "Does it get really get easier?"

Jasmine smiled. "How many push-ups were you doing when you started?"

"Five," Gary said. He shook his head, feeling sweat falling down his body and soaking his shirt. "But ...but it *hurts.*"

"It's time to try something new," Jasmine said. She nodded to Kailee, then led the way into the next compartment. Gary exchanged glances with Kailee, who was sweating so badly that her shirt clung to her breasts, and followed Jasmine into a larger room. A large bag hung from the ceiling, decorated with a crude representation of a human face. "This is a makeshift punching bag."

Gary frowned. "It is?"

"The problem you have - that you both have - is that you are reluctant to actually hit out at someone," Jasmine said. "You are neither naturally violent nor trained to unleash violence at the right moment. When threatened, you either freeze or flee rather than try to fight back."

"I know," Gary said. He'd been attacked more times than he cared to think about, yet he had never even been able to work up the nerve to defend himself. Hitting Barry had seemed an impossible task. "But ...but I can't ..."

"And that is what you will have to overcome," Jasmine said. "I'm not interested in turning you into violent monsters, if you're wondering; I'm interested in training you to unleash violence whenever you need to fight back."

She motioned for them to stay back, then walked up to the bag. "You will have seen hundreds of flicks that purport to show fights," she said. "They are almost always unrealistic, because realistic fights make bad cinema. The idea is to take the enemy down as fast as possible, not engage in an elegant dance. Flying kicks and roundhouse punches, in real life, are just a good way to get seriously injured."

Gary frowned, then stared as Jasmine pulled back her hand and punched the bag with staggering force. He'd barely seen her arm move before the bag was thrown backwards by the force of the impact! Beside him, Kailee gasped. Neither Barry nor Darrin - or even Austin - had been able to move so fast. Gary swallowed hard, then forced himself to watch as Jasmine caught the recoiling bag and steadied it. He had a feeling that not paying attention would be dangerous - or painful.

"If I had struck your neck, or your chest, or your balls, or even your skull, with such force, you would be dead," Jasmine said. "I was always taught to go for the weakest parts of the human body. It wouldn't look spectacular, but it would work."

She paused. "Did either of you watch gladiator fights?"

"A few," Gary admitted. Kailee just shook her head. "They were awful."

"They were also unrealistic," Jasmine said. "The gladiators were trained to spin things out as long as possible, just to keep the audiences entertained. I wasn't taught to play games with my targets. *Real* fighting is all about disabling or killing the target as fast as possible, before they have a chance to fight back. Ideally, you *want* to win with a single blow."

She drew in a breath, then slowly cocked her fist. "We'll worry more about proper technique later," she added. "For the moment" - she nodded at the bag - "I want you to hit the bag as hard as you can. Just imagine it has the face of your worst enemy."

Gary hesitated - his arms were still aching - and then stepped forward. The bag hung in front of him, mockingly. Jasmine twisted it so the crude face was staring right at him, then smiled. It was suddenly all too easy to imagine Barry standing there, laughing at him. Bitter memories - of being debagged in public, of having something poured down the back of his neck, of being humiliated time and time again - rose up in front of his eyes. He drew back his fist, then stopped. It was hard, so hard, to throw a punch …

"Hit him," Jasmine snapped. "Now!"

Gary threw the punch. The bag shuddered under the impact, but barely moved. Gary shivered, feeling his legs buckling under his weight. If he'd tried to punch any of the bullies, they would have laughed at him before giving him yet another beating. And yet, he'd hit the bag. Maybe next time he could hit it harder.

"Try again," Jasmine said. "Focus all your strength on your arm and hit it!"

Gary drew back his fist and hit it again, and again. Cold rage rose up within him as he slammed his fist into the bag, feeling his knuckles start to hurt under the impact. It felt almost as if he *was* punching Barry …

"Not bad," Jasmine said. "You'll find it easier in future, I fancy."

"Oh," Gary said. "But it isn't the same as hitting a person, is it?"

"No," Jasmine agreed. "We'll come to that later."

She nodded to Kailee. "I want you to try something different," she said, as Gary stepped backwards and started to massage his hands. "I want you to aim for his balls."

Kailee shuddered. "I wouldn't want to touch his balls," she said. "I …"

Jasmine snorted. "Would you rather hit his balls hard enough to put him out of commission or have him force those balls into you?"

Kailee shuddered. "I …"

"That's not a fair question," Gary said. "She …she went through hell and …"

"The universe isn't fair," Jasmine said, cutting him off. She turned to face him. "Unless I miss my guess, you were taught in school that men and women are equals, right? Tell me …does your experience tell you that is actually true?"

Gary hesitated. "No," he said, finally. "The girls always needed protectors."

"Yes, they did," Jasmine agreed. "When it comes to raw strength, boys are generally stronger than girls. Obviously, there are some girls who are stronger than most boys, but the general rule is that boys are stronger than girls. Telling *all* girls that they are equal to *all* boys in *all* ways is nothing more than a flat-out lie."

"But you're a strong woman," Kailee protested. "You could have killed anyone with that punch …"

"I'd still be in deep shit if I had to face a male marine," Jasmine said. "Yes, I should be able to outfight anyone without similar training and experience …but that doesn't make me unstoppable. The trick for women, as a general rule, is to use what advantages we have to defeat the boys quickly. Aim for the balls, aim for the neck, aim for weak spots and keep moving. Don't let them pin you down or you're dead."

She shook her head. "But you also need to be proficient with weapons," she added. "Most rules of sporting fights have been devised to ensure fairness. In reality, there's nothing wrong with bringing a knife to a fistfight and a gun to a knife-fight. Having a weapon, and being able to use it, will even the odds between you and any attacker, no matter how strong he is."

"Oh," Kailee said.

Jasmine nodded at the bag. "Hit it," she said. "He's a bastard coming to rape you. Hit him!"

Kailee hit the bag, lightly. Gary winced. It wouldn't have hurt much, he suspected, even if the bag had been a real boy.

"Not hard enough," Jasmine said. "He's knocked you to the ground and is currently having his way with you. You're dead."

"I'm sorry," Kailee said, "but …"

"You have to learn to project violence if necessary," Jasmine said. "Hit him again."

Gary leaned forward. "Are boys more naturally violent than girls?"

Jasmine considered it. "It depends how you look at it," she said, finally. "I've heard a great many different theories, but they range from plausible to absurd or insulting. All you really need to know is that most people can become violent, under the right circumstances."

"I never did," Gary muttered.

"You had learned helplessness battered into you," Jasmine said. "And even then, I imagine you might have snapped one day."

She nodded to the punching bag, then sighed. "I want both of you to add this to your daily exercises," she added. "Punch the bag at least ten times a day, as hard as you can."

Gary groaned. Jasmine supervised his press-ups, but Kailee insisted on going through everything else, from running on the spot to exercises designed to stretch his muscles further than they'd ever been pushed before. It just wasn't fair …he shook his head, knowing what Jasmine would say if he said that out loud. The *universe* wasn't fair.

He rubbed his aching muscles as Jasmine strode out of the room, then looked up at the punching bag. The face seemed almost to be leering at him, as if it were daring him to take another swing. Suddenly, furiously, he drew back his fist and lashed out, hitting the bag as hard as he could. It wobbled violently, but stayed in place.

"You're getting stronger," Kailee said. She looked downcast. "I couldn't hit the bag, not properly."

"I had problems too, at first," Gary said, reluctantly. It was hard to overcome a lifetime of conditioning. Jasmine had told him that a marine had been born on Earth, but Gary didn't believe her. "But we are getting there."

"I hope so," Kailee said, as they stepped into the next compartment. Someone had rigged up a bath, complete with hot and cold running water. "This has to be done, Gary."

"So you keep saying," Gary said, as he reached for her sweaty shirt and pulled it over her head. "So you keep saying."

Kailee smiled tiredly at him as her bare breasts bobbed free, hauntingly lovely despite the red scars on her pale skin. They had alarmed him at first, but Jasmine had assured them that they were nothing more than stretch marks, signs her skin was expanding to cope with her developing muscles. Her arms were still smooth to the touch, yet he was sure it wouldn't be long before she grew stronger. She was more determined to proceed than *he* was.

He sighed, then pulled off his own shirt and held her closely. "I don't have the strength," he admitted. Her breasts felt wonderfully soft against his skin. "It's hard enough to hold you."

"Oh," Kailee giggled. In that moment, she sounded more like her old self than ever before. "I think I'm offended."

Gary shivered. In *his* experience, girls giggling was never a good sign. They were always giggling at him, not the muscle-bound morons who were actually *dangerous*. It was *safe* to laugh at meek little Gary, who wouldn't hurt a fly ...*he* wouldn't slam them against the wall for daring to show their amusement. He *hated* it when they giggled ...

And then her hand reached down and slipped into his shorts. He felt himself stiffen against her, despite the aches and pains ...and then she kissed him and all rational thought faded away.

"They've got a long way to go," Stewart observed, as he paced out a circle on the deck. "I think they may still be lost causes."

"They have hope," Jasmine said. "Besides, it helps to pass the time."

Stewart nodded, then used a crayon to sketch out the circle. "You should invite them to watch us," he said. He looked up at her, then winked. "Does that look suitable?"

Jasmine silently estimated the circle's dimensions, then nodded. "It's fine," she said, as she checked her shirt and shorts. "Have you had a chance to warm up?"

"Yeah," Stewart said. He gave her a dry look. "You really should invite them to watch us."

"It would just scare them," Jasmine said, flatly. "They're not ready to see *real* combat."

She stepped into the circle, then ran through a series of warm-up exercises. Her body was far fitter than Kailee's - indeed, it was highly unlikely Kailee would ever match her physically - but she had let herself go a little, back when she'd been trapped behind a desk. She might be teaching Kailee and Gary, yet she also had to take care of herself. Shaking her head, she stood upright and watched as Stewart stepped into the circle and bowed to her.

"Normal rules," he said. "And damned be the one who fucks up first."

Jasmine smiled. A sparring match could be lost in two ways, either by being beaten ...or by accidentally stepping out of the circle. Hell, *pushing* one's opponent out of the circle was considered a legitimate way to win. Blake Coleman had been large enough to use it regularly, once he caught hold of someone, but she'd never been able to make it work against an equally skilled opponent.

"Of course," she said. "On three?"

"On three," Stewart confirmed. "This will hurt you more than me."

Jasmine rolled her eyes, then dropped into a crouch. "Three ...two ...one," she said. "Go."

Stewart didn't hesitate; he came forward, readying himself to launch a dizzying series of kicks and punches at her. Jasmine ducked backwards, careful not to step over the circle, and punched back, aiming at his weak spots. Stewart hissed, then lashed out with stunning speed, hoping to catch her before she could get in close. Jasmine darted backwards, then closed in, hitting out at him. He caught her blows and kicked her in the chest, hard. Jasmine staggered backwards, then fell over the circle. Stewart instantly stopped and raised his hands.

"Damn it," Jasmine said. She looked down at her shirt, then lifted it to see a nasty bruise. If she hadn't been moving backwards when he'd kicked her she probably would have broken a few ribs. "Too slow."

"Too much paperwork," Stewart said. He held out a hand, offering to help her to her feet. "I think you need more practice."

Jasmine brushed aside the hand and rose to her feet. "I know," she said. "I trust you will be ready to spar every day?"

"Of course," Stewart said. "There's ten days to go before we get there."

He paused. "I'd recommend a return to active duty, myself," he added. "I was pretty flabby when I returned to the company, after two years on detached duty."

"We'll see what happens when I get home," Jasmine said.

Stewart held her eyes. "Do you want to talk about it?"

"I don't know how the Colonel does it," Jasmine admitted. "He's handling everything without showing any sign of strain."

"I think they teach officers never to show weakness to the lower ranks," Stewart said, affecting a plumy accent. "You never went through OCS, did you?"

Jasmine scowled. "How could I?"

"There's a lot you probably needed to learn that you had to pick up on the job," Stewart said, as he led the way into the shower. "Your career has been a little eccentric since we were exiled, hasn't it?"

"Yeah," Jasmine said. She stripped off her shirt and examined the mark, then pulled off her shorts and stepped into the shower. "Rifleman, Platoon Commander, Mission Commander, CEF Commander, Prisoner of War ...you could say that."

"And you were tortured on Corinthian," Stewart added. "And then you were taken prisoner for a second time. I'm not surprised that you're doubting yourself. Your confidence would have been gravely shaken."

Jasmine nodded, wordlessly, then scrubbed herself down thoroughly. She hadn't had a chance to build up a layer of sweat, but she'd been taught to wash herself from a very early age. Her hair felt odd under her fingers, now it had had a chance to grow out again. She made a mental note to have it cut as soon as she could, if only because it would get in the way when she tried to don a helmet. There was no way she could grow shoulder-length hair like Kailee.

"I wasn't much better off," Stewart admitted. "To be taken prisoner ... it was quite humiliating. Part of me doesn't want to go home, to explain to everyone else that we were the dumb bastards who got ourselves captured. But we have no choice. Once we hit Wolfbane, we head home."

"I know," Jasmine said. She stepped out of the shower, then reached for a towel and dried herself. "And then ...the Colonel will be the one to decide what happens to us."

CHAPTER TWENTY-FIVE

> The problem can be argued both ways. In the end, matters are settled by victory. If the terrorists lose, they are terrorists; if they win, they are freedom fighters. To paraphrase an old saying, terrorism never prospers, because if it prospers, none call it terrorism.
> - Professor Leo Caesius. *The Empire and its Prisoners of War.*

Avalon, Year 5 (PE)

The key to following someone covertly, Kitty had learned long ago, was not to make it blindingly obvious. Ideally, a small team of operatives should be assigned to the mission, alternatively picking up and discarding the subject before the subject realised that she was seeing the same faces time and time again. Imperial Intelligence had practically made a game out of shadowing someone on Earth, although it was a great deal harder on less-developed worlds.

She kept one eye on Hannalore Roeder as she made her way through the shopping district, popping in and out of dozens of shops. There was no way to know if she was trying to shake off any tails or if she was merely enjoying a day out on the town, but it was hellishly difficult to keep an eye on her. Kitty had five men and seven women assigned to the task and even then it was hard to watch her at all times. She was grimly aware that Hannalore might well have some counter-surveillance training of her own.

"This is One," she whispered, keying the subvocal processor in her mouth. "Target has gone into Motherwell's; I say again, target has gone into Motherwell's."

"Understood, One," Three said. "I'm following her now."

Kitty sat down on a bench and watched as Three, who looked like an elderly lady, walked across the road and into the shop. Motherwell's specialised in producing baby clothing, although there were quite a few offerings for infants and young children too. There didn't seem to be any reason for Hannalore to be interested in the shop - as far as anyone knew, she had no children - but it was possible she just wanted to browse. Or she wanted to see who might follow her into the shop.

Twenty minutes later, she emerged, carrying a bag under her arm. Kitty watched her unobtrusively as Three followed, then headed down the road in the other direction. If Hannalore was suspicious, she probably would find Three's departure reassuring. Besides, Three looked old enough to start nagging younger women about their duty to have children.

"She bought a couple of outfits for children," Three said, through the communications network. "I didn't get near enough to have a close inspection, but they looked like spacer suits. I'd say they were for children no older than six."

"Noted," Kitty said. "Four; take point."

"Understood," Four said. "She's heading down towards the orphanage."

Kitty rose to her feet and hurried into the alleyway, flanking Hannalore without ever letting her see her shadow. Four kept her updated as Hannalore walked up to the orphanage and knocked on the door, then stepped inside as soon as the door opened. Kitty cursed under her breath, thinking hard. Hannalore probably had some charitable reason to visit the orphanage, but what? It wasn't as if it was hard to find foster families for children who had been orphaned by the war.

"Check the records," she ordered, slowly. She had never paid much attention to the orphanages, save for keeping an eye out for children who might be worth training into something useful. "Who lives in that orphanage?"

"Most of them are kids from the Old Council," her coordinator said. "The babies could be adopted, but the middle-aged kids had nowhere to go. They were having some problems getting employment, according to the files."

And probably little chance of being adopted, Kitty thought. She couldn't help a stab of sympathy. *If they picked up bad habits from their parents, no one would want them.*

She drifted past the orphanage, eying the building darkly. It hadn't been intended to be a permanent residence for anyone and it showed. Chances were, the entire district had been marked for demolition and only the orphans stood in the way. Kitty sighed inwardly - something had to be done about the kids, even if it was just a homestead somewhere well away from civilisation - and then frowned as she saw a young man hastening out of the orphanage. Her instincts told her she should pay attention to him.

"Here's a picture," she subvocalised. "Tell me who he is."

"William Garston," her coordinator said, after a long moment. "Nineteen years old; his tax return claims he works at the Rodeo Dwell. That's a datanet cafe ..."

"I know it," Kitty said. She kept walking, thinking hard. "Five, Six; go after Garston and keep a sharp eye on him. I want to know what he's doing."

"Understood," Five said. Six echoed him a moment later. "We're moving after him."

"Target has re-emerged from the orphanage," Four put in. "She's heading back towards the heart of town."

"Good," Kitty said. "Is she still carrying her packages?"

"Negative," Four said.

Kitty frowned. The youngest kid in the orphanage had to be at least fourteen by now, unless more had slipped through the cracks than she'd realised. It had been six years, more or less, since the Old Council had been defeated. Their children couldn't have been so badly contaminated that it was better to keep them in an orphanage, could they? Or was there something else going on?

"See if you can find an excuse to take a look at the orphanage," she ordered. Perhaps Emmanuel could do another puff piece, if she couldn't organise an official inspection. The hell of it was that it was unlikely she could, unless she placed her cards on the table and prayed for a sympathetic judge. Avalon's laws were designed to prevent official busy-bodies poking their noses into private affairs. "And see if you can also give me a complete list of its occupants."

She walked back towards town, thinking hard. Hannalore had gone to an orphanage, dropped off a set of clothes that were really too small for any of the children, then made her way straight home. The bit of her mind that was prejudiced against the great and the good had no trouble believing that Hannalore was stupid enough to buy the children clothes that were far too small for them, but the rest of her had too many doubts. Hannalore simply wasn't that stupid.

"One, Garston has entered his workplace," Five sent. "He's taking a computer and going to work."

"His boss looks a little surprised to see him," Six added. "You want me to go sit next to him?"

"Please," Kitty said. Six looked young enough to be a teenager - and was wearing an outfit guaranteed to lower the male IQ to single digits. "But keep your voice down until he leaves."

She hesitated, then hurried around until she could cross Hannalore's path as she walked home. The woman barely looked at her, unsurprisingly. It was astonishing just how much difference a wig and a change of clothes could make, particularly when the human eye was lazy enough not to look under the facade. Kitty got a long look at her and frowned, inwardly. It looked very much as though Hannalore had relaxed a little, which suggested she'd done whatever she'd set out to do.

There was another party last night, she thought, grimly. If the enemy spies followed their standard practice, there would be yet another message beamed to outer space the following day. *She takes the recordings, puts them on a datachip and carries them to the orphanage ...Garston takes them there, then passed them onwards ...to whom?*

She altered course as soon as Hannalore was out of sight, walking back towards the apartment they'd taken over near the Governor's Mansion. It wasn't perfect, but the landlady wasn't the type to ask questions and the other lodgers were out most of the day. Kitty had run a check on each of them, just in case; none of them had anything in their files that raised red flags. They were all just immigrants coming to try and find long-term employment on Avalon.

Her radio buzzed. "He asked me for a date," Six said. There was a hint of amusement in her voice. "I'm scheduled to go dancing with him in an hour; I just begged time to powder my nose."

Kitty rolled her eyes. "What happened?"

"He plugged a datachip into a computer, then fiddled with it for a few moments," Six said, slowly. "Once he was done, he dropped the chip into the disintegrator and asked me out."

"Have fun," Kitty said. There was no harm in taking advantage; besides, it was starting to look as though Garston was definitely involved in the operation. They'd have to open up a file on him too. "There's no hope of recovering the chip?"

"He stood over the disintegrator until it was atomised," Six said, flatly. "There's nothing left of it, but dust."

Kitty swallowed a curse. It was astonishing just how much could be recovered from a datachip, even if the data was wiped and the entire chip rewritten several times in a row. Anyone who really wanted to keep something a secret would make sure the chip was destroyed, smashed down into dust. Even a commercial disintegrator would be more than sufficient to destroy all the evidence.

"Very well," she said. "Go with him, but be careful."

Nine entered the conversation. "One, target walked through the mansion gates and straight up to the house," he said. "I can't go any further."

"Understood," Kitty said. "Get back to base. We can leave the monitoring of the mansion to the probes now."

She finished her walk to the apartment, then poured herself a mug of coffee and sat down for a think. It seemed likely that Garston was the link in the chain between Hannalore and Wolfbane, unless there were others involved. She rather doubted it; Hannalore was in a good position to spy, but also in an excellent place to get caught. Garston would probably have no connections to anyone else, just in case he was snatched by Commonwealth Intelligence or slipped up badly enough to be arrested through sheer dumb luck. It had happened in the past.

"Get me a workup of Garston," she ordered, picking up her terminal. "Who is he and what is he doing?"

There was a long pause. "He's the son of Councillor Garston," her coordinator said. "He was arrested briefly after the Battle of Camelot for throwing stones at the militia; he spent two years on a work farm, then was released with a warning. There were a handful of minor jobs since then until he got the place at the Rodeo Dwell, two years ago. He's been there since then."

At roughly the same time Hannalore started having her parties, Kitty thought. The file blinked up in front of her and she skimmed it, quickly. *He certainly has a motive to want to betray us.*

The file wasn't that detailed, beyond a note that Gaston had probably been beaten by the militiamen before they'd handed him over to the judges. There had been hundreds of cases at the time, so no one had bothered to do more than the bare minimum; they'd charged him with resisting arrest, then sent him to the work farm. He might have thought he was defending his family, but the militia had other views. Kitty couldn't help a flicker of sympathy; Gaston's father had been executed, his mother had been exiled and his younger sisters had been happily adopted. He hadn't seen any of them since the day he'd been arrested.

But it doesn't matter why someone chose to betray us, she thought, as she sipped her coffee thoughtfully. It was beyond her to correct every little injustice, every little incident that would leave someone seething with resentment. *All that matters is that he did.*

"I think he's definitely linked," she said. "Can you see if he had any known contacts with offworlders?"

"Unknown," her coordinator said. "I don't see any records suggesting he might have met someone from off-world, but that proves nothing."

"Assign Five and Seven to monitor Garston and his date with Six," Kitty said. She wondered briefly if Six would go home with Garston - it would be an excellent chance to look inside his apartment - but pushed the thought aside. If Six went, she would be pleased, but she drew the line at forcing someone to put out on demand. "If it turns up nothing, I want him to be followed for the next few days; draw additional people from the Hannalore watch, if necessary."

She rubbed her forehead, then sat back in her chair.

"Colonel, I have some information from local files," another operative said. "There are only thirteen official residents at the orphanage, not counting the five caregivers. The youngest is fourteen, so they may be hoping the place can be closed in a few years. However, two of the caregivers are married and have young children. The suits she bought might have been intended for them."

Kitty nodded, slowly. "Why are the children still there?"

There was an embarrassed pause. "The files suggest that the children have …severe behaviour problems," the operative said. "They're only allowed to remain there on sufferance; five of them have arrest records, while three of them …may have been abused while they were younger. I don't know for sure, but I suspect the problem was just swept under the rug."

He swore, just loudly enough for Kitty to hear. "These things don't *happen* on Avalon!"

"Evidently they do," Kitty said. "If five of the children have arrest records, why weren't they sent to work camps?"

"I don't know," the operative said. "The files are sealed; I don't think I could get inside without a court order. They may have been flogged instead, or simply given stern warnings and sent home. Their exact legal status is a little vague."

"And so we allowed this problem to fester," Kitty mused. She shook her head. "Get in touch with a judge and put in a request for a court order. I think they should grant it for us."

She closed the channel and looked at the files. There was little there, beyond a series of incident reports, but reading between the lines it was clear they hadn't been arrested. Avalon had a tendency to hold parents responsible for their children, yet the orphans *had* no parents, not any longer. She sighed, tiredly, then settled down to wait. There would be time to attend to the injustice later.

"Garston and Six are heading to the Disco Infernal," Five reported. He snickered, none too politely. "They look like a happy young couple."

"Good," Kitty said. "Keep an eye on them."

She turned her attention to her work, but listened with half an ear to the stream of reports from the disco. Garston and Six danced for nearly two hours, then headed back to his apartment. It was another two hours before Six emerged, looking tired, and hailed a cab, which took her directly back to base. Kitty was waiting for her with a mug of coffee and a questioning expression.

"He's not bad," Six said, with a grin. "He …"

"I wanted to know about his work, not how good he is in bed," Kitty snapped. "What did he tell you about himself?"

"Very little," Six said, "but his apartment has quite a few books about chemical substances and how they can be mixed together. He gave me a story about studying chemistry when I asked ..."

"He could be trying to build a bomb," Kitty mused. Guns and ammunition were plentiful on Avalon, but explosives weren't so easy to obtain. "Does he have any hope of success?"

"I don't know," Six said. "He could have obtained the materials or ... he might have been unable to proceed past the design stage. I do think, however, that Wolfbane could have provided him with a real bomb."

"Assuming they *want* him to blow himself up," Kitty pointed out. "What did you make of him?"

"Repressed anger issues," Six said. "He remained calm, but I could tell he was on the verge of exploding every time he was defied, even minimally. I suspect that might have been why he had problems holding down a job before now. I'd recommend primal scream therapy if I was a psychologist."

Kitty ignored her. "Wolfbane might wish they had someone more reliable in place," she said, thinking out loud. Resentful people could be manipulated, but they could also be dangerously unpredictable. "Someone with anger problems might explode at the wrong time."

"I could jerk around with him a bit," Six said. She shook her head. "He's good at being charming and caring; I could have liked him if I hadn't been meeting him ...professionally. My feeling, though, is that he will quickly become a nasty controlling, if not abusive, boyfriend. I think he hasn't had a long-term relationship in the past because he's driven his prior girlfriends away."

"It sounds likely," Kitty agreed.

She sighed. "I'll talk to the colonel, if the message is sent tonight," she continued. "We might have nothing to gain by leaving them both in place, seemingly untouched. I assume there was no attempt by anyone to touch base with him?"

"I saw nothing to suggest it," Six said. "But he wouldn't be stupid enough to tell me just what he was doing ...unless I posed as someone useful."

Kitty nodded. "You gave him your student identity?"

"Yep," Six said. "I could probably get files for him or some shit like that, but I don't think he'd consider it helpful."

"Get some rest," Kitty said, instead. "I'll speak to the colonel in the morning."

CHAPTER
TWENTY-SIX

> The Empire's treatment of POWs was always a sticking point in the later days of the Empire. Unlike many pre-space human powers, the Empire never faced a genuine peer power. There was, therefore, no incentive to treat POWs decently.
> - Professor Leo Caesius. *The Empire and its Prisoners of War.*

Passing Water, **Wolfbane System, Year 5 (PE)**

"Transit complete," Stewart reported. "We have arrived."

Jasmine nodded. It was silly of her to tense up as they dropped out of phase space, but she hadn't been able to help it. The sense of being in enemy territory surrounded her, even though she *knew* the Wolves were light-hours away. There was little chance of being intercepted as they emerged from phase space. Hell, it would be hours before they were even *detected.* But she still felt tense.

"Send the pre-planned signal to System Command," she ordered. "And then take us into the system."

"Bad idea," Frazier said, quickly. "They won't be expecting us to report in so quickly."

Jasmine gave him a sharp look. "You could have mentioned that earlier."

"Civilian freighters like mine resent having to declare themselves to anyone," Frazier said. "Most will not send any IFF until after they are deep within the system - and some won't announce themselves until they are actually challenged. You're going to make yourselves look suspiciously efficient."

"Belay that order," Jasmine told Stewart. "But keep a careful eye on the sensors for any signs of trouble."

She forced herself to sit back in her command chair as the displays started to fill with tactical data. Wolfbane was a *busy* system. Maybe not as busy as Earth, AlphaCent or Washington Prime had been, before the Stalkers had been banished from the Core Worlds, but busy enough to worry her. Countless freighters headed in and out of the system, while IFF signals pulsing through space revealed the location of hundreds of asteroid mining stations and industrial nodes. It was hard to be sure - civilian-grade passive sensors were pathetic - but she suspected that Wolfbane had two or three times the combined economic might of Avalon, Corinthian and Thule.

"Got a trio of warships heading out," Gary said, from the console he'd worked hard to learn how to use. "I think."

Jasmine stood and paced over to his console, peering over his shoulder. "Looks that way," she said. "Three cruisers, at a guess. We got any matches in the files?"

Gary shook his head. "Nothing."

"They could be reengineered," Watson offered. "Not new-build, just changed enough to confuse the files."

"They could be," Jasmine agreed. She rather hoped they were, but she knew better than to count on it. Avalon had achieved miracles by taking technology past the limits the Empire had believed to be unbreakable and there was no reason Wolfbane couldn't do the same, now they knew the impossible was now possible. They'd seen force shields in action at Thule, where they'd been a nasty surprise. "Keep an eye on them and let me know if their power curves change dramatically."

"Aye, Captain," Gary said.

Jasmine rolled her eyes, then turned and walked back to her viewscreen. New icons were springing into view all the time; some clearly identified, others nothing more than a radio source hooked up to something the Wolves considered important. Most of them were centred around Wolfbane itself, but a distressingly high number were orbiting the gas giant and several more seemed to be floating in interplanetary space. Jasmine stroked her chin as more and more data poured into the computers, wishing she had a proper analysis staff with her. It was impossible to escape the feeling that she was missing something, simply through being unable to interpret all the data.

"He was talking about setting up extra cloudscoops," Stubbins said, from where he was sitting against the rear bulkhead. "I think he must have done it."

"There's nine separate structures orbiting the gas giant, if I understand correctly," Jasmine said, slowly. "And it looks as though they're building two more."

"They're going to run out at this rate," Kailee said. She was seated next to Gary, looking alternatively bored and nervous. "We kept being told to conserve natural resources on Earth."

"There's enough gas in a gas giant to keep the entire sector powered for hundreds of thousands of years," Paula snapped. She'd never seemed to like Kailee, for some reason. "Even Earth could have supported itself for millions of years, just drawing fuel from Jupiter or Saturn. They told you that to keep you from wondering why you weren't allowed infinite power supplies."

Jasmine shot her a warning look, then returned her gaze to the viewscreen. The constant inflow of data worried her, even though she knew the Wolves were unlikely to be concerned about civilian-grade sensors. *She* was used to covering her tracks, where possible; to see what looked like a blatant lack of concern for security was alarming. And yet...she knew there was nothing that could *hide* the system from civilian-grade sensors, let alone a spy ship with mil-spec gear. The Wolves might be wise not to try.

"I think that's another warship," Gary offered. "She just crossed the phase limit; she's currently heading into the system."

"Put it on the main display," Jasmine ordered. A new red icon snapped into existence. She sucked in her breath as she saw it, then shook her head. "If that isn't a battleship, I'll eat my hat."

"It's a battleship," Watson confirmed. "Pity, really; I hear they infused flavours into our hats to make them easier to chew, when we ran out of rations."

Jasmine fought down the urge to make a rude gesture and, instead, looked at Stubbins. "I think the system has changed considerably," she said. "How many of your contacts are still in place?"

"I have no way to know," Stubbins said. "I'd need access to their datanet and then see what names I recognised ..."

"We won't get that at this distance," Watson said. He shot Paula a warm glance that made Jasmine smile inwardly. "I'd be surprised if they let us shoot queries into their datanet from an asteroid - or a ship."

"Then we need to get down to the planet," Stubbins said. "I should still have contacts there."

"We'll see," Jasmine said. They were still light-minutes from Wolfbane, but the sheer output of radio signals suggested the system was an order of magnitude more heavily defended - and policed - than Corinthian. Slipping down to the planet might be impossible, even for highly-trained Marines. "But I think we need a base camp in the system first."

A low chime rang. "We just got pinged," Watson snapped. "Fairly standard challenge, doesn't seem to have changed from the pre-independence days. Send us your IFF or else, etc, etc."

"Send them the IFF," Jasmine ordered. "And then keep a sharp eye on them. If they decide they want to inspect the ship, we will have no choice but to hope we can bluff it out."

She sighed, inwardly. The freighter hadn't been *designed* as a q-ship, which would make life easier if the Wolves *did* decide to board, but there was a great deal of equipment on the ship that would, at best, result in them having to answer a number of hard questions. She'd done her best to hide it, then rig up passenger manifests that would account for the entire crew, yet she knew a careful search of the ship would be disastrous. If the searchers proved too thorough to be tolerated, they would have to fight their way out ...and, in a lumbering freighter, that might be impossible.

It was nearly an hour before they received a second challenge. "They want to know where we're going," Watson said. "I take it they wouldn't be happy with Wolfbane?"

"They'd want to search us before we entered orbit," Frazier confirmed. "Send the planned signal, I think."

Watson looked at Jasmine, who nodded. "Signal sent," he said. "Let's see what sort of wankers they are, shall we?"

"There's no choice," Jasmine said. "But let us pray for lazy wankers."

She smiled inwardly, although she knew it wasn't funny. Customs officers, in her experience, were either officious bureaucrats or outright thieves. The former were very good at coming up with legal reasons to levy fines, while the latter tended to take what they liked in exchange for letting the freighter pass through the net. It was something of a marvel that there had been *any* independent freighters at all; the bigger corporations had the clout to remove particularly unpleasant customs officers, while independents were at their mercy. She had a feeling it was why so many independent freighters had made their way out to the Rim, escaping the Fall of Earth.

And the Trade Federation will probably prevent any planet from developing its own problem children, she thought. Professor Caesius had gone on about it at length, the last time Jasmine had joined him and his family for dinner. *Free Trade will do more to ensure economic growth than anything else.*

She sighed, then looked at Paula. "What sort of trade policies did Brown have?"

"He was a corporate rat," Stubbins growled, before Paula could say a word. "I don't think he ever did anything unless it was in the interests of the corporations."

"There's a small tax on everything imported to Wolfbane," Frazier said, unexpectedly. "But there aren't any taxes on anything *exported*. I was never sure why."

"Economics," Paula said. She looked irked. "The Governor wants Wolfbane to be the sole source of everything from starship components to weapons, at least in this sector. By not taxing exports, he provides incentives to export goods ...and keep the prices relatively low, thus making it hard for any other planet to compete. Once he has a monopoly, he can jerk around with the prices at will, keeping people in line without any need for military force."

Jasmine blinked in surprise. "He can't expect that to work!"

"It can and it does," Paula said. "People find it easy to define why military threats should be resisted, but it's a great deal harder to explain to one's population why they shouldn't have access to cheap goods. Wolfbane has a head start on the rest of the sector, allowing it to produce much more far cheaper than anywhere else. Given time, they can flood the market and utterly destroy competition."

"Well," Watson said, into the silence. "I never thought of it like that."

"You were trained to apply naked force in the interests of whatever policy your ultimate superiors believed to be necessary," Paula said. "Governor Brown's sphere, however, is economics. He thinks in terms of applying pressure rather than naked force."

"He was prepared to invade the Commonwealth," Jasmine said.

"I suspect he thought of you as a long-term threat," Paula said. "Besides, grinding you down might make you more willing to dicker with him on his terms."

She opened her mouth, then paused as the console bleeped. "They're telling us that we will be intercepted before we reach our destination," Watson said. "We're going to be searched."

"That tears it," Stewart muttered.

"Not quite," Jasmine said. She glanced at the console, silently calculating the trajectories and the timing in her head. "We planned for this, didn't we? And we have at least three hours before the inspection crew gets here."

She rose to her feet and smiled. "Let's get to work," she added. "I want to be nothing more than a harmless freighter by the time the bastards arrive."

"Better have a bribe ready too," Frazier added. "They may think nothing of ordering us to report for a more thorough search in the shipyard if we don't offer them a fairly substantial bribe."

Jasmine nodded. It all depended on just how paranoid the Wolves were feeling. There should be nothing to connect *their* freighter with the one that had gone to Meridian - *Passing Water* was one of thousands - but if they were paranoid enough to insist on DNA tests, the crew would be in hot water. The Wolves *had* taken DNA readings from the POWs before shipping them to Meridian - she assumed they had records for Stubbins, Paula and Frazier too - and if they had them included in their datafiles ... she sighed inwardly, then put the thought aside. Even if they had had the gear to spoof such devices, it would have taken longer than they had to re-sequence their DNA before arriving at Wolfbane.

"Don't say anything unless asked," she told Gary and Kailee. The official files stated that they were both trainees, who had bribed someone to be allowed on the ship, but their accents were too hard to change. She'd gone to some trouble to devise a cover story for them, yet she knew it wouldn't hold up under close scrutiny. "And then try and stay out of sight."

It was nearly four hours before the customs boat came alongside. Jasmine studied the ship with some interest; it wasn't much bigger than a standard heavy-lift shuttle, but someone had refitted the drive section to give it additional thrust at the expense of comfort. She had a feeling, based on prior experience, that the boat couldn't carry more than thirty crewmen at most; indeed, if they'd automated as much as possible, she might only need one or two crewmen. Indeed, there was no reason why the ship couldn't be largely automatic ...

Unless they run into trouble, she thought. *Or the unions start getting pissy about computers taking jobs from decent hard-working spacers.*

She shook her head. The Empire had tended to use larger ships, but they'd been deliberately designed without a phase drive, ensuring they could never leave their home system under their own power. Wolfbane - and the Commonwealth - considered such designs inefficient. But on the other hand, she had to admit, the reduced drive section gave the ship room for additional weapons and sensor blisters.

And they were cheaper to build, she recalled, as she strolled down to the airlock. *The Empire considered them suitable for system defence as well as customs duties.*

A dull thud echoed through the freighter as the two ships joined docking tubes. The airlock hissed open a moment later, blowing a wave of cool air into the freighter. Jasmine refused to shiver as four men appeared; one clearly old enough to be her father, the others not much older than Carl Watson. Two of them had the pointy noses favoured by the system's aristocracy, if Stubbins was to be believed. Had they requested this duty because they believed it would be safer than serving in the military?

"God," one of the younger ones muttered. "What an ugly bitch."

Jasmine pasted a smile on her face and stepped forward. "Welcome to *Wandering Soul*," she said, holding out a hand. "I'm Captain Magana."

"Pleased to meet you," the old man said. "I'm Lieutenant Roscoe. If you'll show us your manifest, we'll get started."

"Of course," Jasmine said. She pulled the chip from her jacket and held it out to him. He took it and slotted it into his reader, while the younger men glanced around with the air of bored youngsters everywhere. "I think you'll find we have everything you need."

"We'll be the judges of that," one of the younger men sneered.

Jasmine felt a flicker of sympathy for Lieutenant Roscoe. It couldn't be easy riding herd on a trio of brats, particularly well-connected brats who couldn't be disciplined. There was a reason, after all, that any aristocrats who entered Boot Camp were expected to change their names. Roscoe glowered at his nominal subordinates, then glanced back at Jasmine as he released the chip.

"You have prospective immigrants onboard," he said. "You'll have to take them to the planet for decontamination and registry procedures before they can take up any form of employment."

"I understand," Jasmine said. "However, they were intending to seek employment on Prospero."

"Should aim for Wolfbane," Roscoe commented. He didn't sound as if he really cared, or believed what he was saying. Somehow, Jasmine wasn't surprised. People like Roscoe rarely cared about anything beyond their work. "There's lots of jobs here for those willing to work."

He smiled at her, tiredly. "We have to give your ship a brief inspection," he added. "My men can see to that, while we wait here."

Jasmine nodded, hoping that everyone stuck to the plan. If the shit hit the fan …she knew they could capture or kill all four inspectors, but she wasn't sure what they could do next, apart from try to take the customs ship. And then …an idea started to gestate in her head as she waited, silently planning out her next move. It was nearly forty minutes before the three inspectors reappeared, looking amused.

"Nothing to report, sir," one of them said. "Just a pretty girl who refused to come with us."

Jasmine couldn't help another stab of sympathy. She'd been insulted to her face in a more respectful manner.

"What a smart girl," Roscoe said. He didn't seem inclined to care. "Thank you, Captain, for your time."

He led his subordinates back through the airlock, which slid closed and sealed after him with a sharp *bang*. Jasmine shook her head in some amusement - the man hadn't even demanded a bribe - and then headed back to the bridge. Kailee was sitting just outside the hatch, looking torn between amusement and irritation.

"I could have hit him," she said. "He grabbed my butt and I could have hit him."

"Good thing you didn't," Jasmine said. She understood the impulse, but it would have been disastrous. At best, Kailee would have been beaten and she would have had to stand by and watch. "Just think of it as pulling one over on him."

"I know," Kailee said. She grinned, brightly. "I could have been an actress after all!"

CHAPTER TWENTY-SEVEN

Furthermore, the Empire - by its own logic - was not only the dominant human power, but the only one. All independent states had no right to exist. If they wished to assert their independence, they were rebelling against the sole legitimate power and could be legally crushed.
- Professor Leo Caesius. *The Empire and its Prisoners of War.*

Medusa, **Wolfbane System, Year 5 (PE)**

"*That's* an asteroid colony?"

"A mobile one, yes," Frazier said, as the shuttle headed towards the colony. "What were you expecting?"

Gary shrugged. He'd seen a mining camp on Meridian, but that had been on the planet's surface. It had really been nothing more than a hole in the ground, surrounded by a fence and armed guards, while the workers were prisoners paying their debts to society. He'd never really thought about what an asteroid mining station would look like, or how it might function, even though he would have liked to work on one. It would have taken him away from Earth.

Medusa looked rather like a crude spider, metal legs clinging to the asteroid's rocky surface while the main body hung above the asteroid, as if it were preparing to start gnawing on the rock. A pair of men in spacesuits were scrambling over the asteroid, which was larger than the entire freighter, while a small craft orbited above them, beaming lights down to the surface. Pieces of rock were pulled free of the surface and launched up towards the spider, which caught them and sucked them into its maw. Gary couldn't help admiring the precision of their movements, even though the whole station looked alarmingly simplistic.

He looked at Frazier, who was staring at the colony wistfully. "What does it do?"

"The prospectors suck in ores - everything from simple iron and water to rarer elements like gold, palladium and suchlike - and either refine them themselves or forward the stockpiles to centralised reprocessing facilities," Frazier said. "You can make a good living if you find enough platinum group metals, enough to pay off your debts and mine without obligations to anyone. I imagine even the Wolves pay considerably over the odds to get uninterrupted supplies to their shipyards."

"They probably do," Jasmine agreed. "I would have thought the large-scale mining programs would be more efficient, though."

"Depends what you want," Frazier said. "You still need to test prospective asteroids for mining prospects before you start work. An independent can do that far more effectively than a bigger corporation. They can also haggle over the price, which helps competition."

"I bet the Governor loves that," Jasmine observed.

"Probably," Frazier agreed. "Competition also helps efficiency."

Gary sighed inwardly as the shuttle docked with the mining colony. There was a faint hiss as the airlock opened, allowing the colony's atmosphere to flow into the shuttle. He gagged as the stench of too many unwashed humans greeted him, then swallowed hard to keep himself from vomiting. Frazier looked far too amused at his plight for Gary's peace of mind.

"I thought you said these people were *clean*," he protested. But then, the freighter hadn't smelled too good either, when they'd boarded the craft. "Why do they smell?"

"Too much reprocessed air, I fancy," Frazier said. He paused. "I wouldn't say anything about it if I were you. Not only will you get used to the smell if you don't think about it, they will regard it as an insult. It's going to be hard enough to convince them to help without you insulting them to their faces."

He led the way through the airlock and, after a moment, Gary followed him, with Jasmine bringing up the rear. The sound of something flapping in the distance caught his ear as he entered the colony, then he blinked in surprise as he saw a young boy standing in front of him, wearing nothing more than a pair of shorts. He couldn't have been any older than eight.

"Hi," the boy said. "Dad wants me to bring you to him."

"It's been a while, Brian," Frazier said gravely. "You were five when I saw you last, I think."

Brian nodded, then turned and walked towards a solid metal airlock, which hissed open as he approached. The temperature rose rapidly as they stepped through - Gary felt sweat tickling down his back - suggesting one reason why everyone was scantily-clad. They passed two older boys and a girl, the latter wearing nothing more than a pair of shorts herself; Gary had to remind himself not to stare as they walked past. Public nudity had been unknown on Earth, at least without compulsion, while no one in their right mind went naked on Meridian, when it was easy to get scratched or bitten. The idea of casual public nudity was alien to him - and more than a little disturbing.

"It's a different place," Jasmine said, very quietly. "And it is also very safe."

Gary sighed, feeling a stab of bitter envy. Children on Meridian were safe because they were taught to fight, to defend themselves, to use weapons; children on the asteroid were safe because there were no threats in their tiny community. Earth …he shook his head bitterly, understanding - once again - why Kailee wanted them to learn how to defend themselves against all threats. The universe simply wasn't safe.

"I know," he muttered back. He glanced into a side room and saw three children, perched in front of a teaching machine. "What happens when this place is attacked?"

Jasmine shook her head. "You don't want to know."

They stepped into a command centre, where a dark-skinned man was standing next to a lady with blue skin and a single green eye. The other had been replaced with a prosthetic sensor that spun constantly, fixing on something for a long second and then moving to the next shiny thing. Gary couldn't help feeling uncomfortable being near her, even though it was hard to keep his eyes off her bare breasts. There was something about such casual mutilation of the human form that sickened him.

"Jim," the man said. He sounded pleased to see Frazier. "You're back!"

"Pete," Frazier said. He nodded to the girl. "And Andor. It's good to see you both."

"You sound tired," Andor said. Her eye implant froze, studying Frazier's face. "What happened?"

"It's something of a long story," Frazier said. He took a breath. "Last time we spoke, you told me you wanted out of this system. Is that still true?"

"Yes," Pete said. "This is getting to be an awkward place to raise children."

Jasmine took a step forward. "In what way?"

"They're no longer as intrusive as Earth used to be," Andor said. "But we do get regular inspections and …"

She shrugged. Gary understood and he was sure Jasmine did too. The children must be their sons and daughters …and they were running around, nearly-naked, in front of intruding customs officers, one of whom had grabbed Kailee's butt during his inspection. Who knew what atrocities would be committed on a defenceless mining platform? He could see the value of not bothering to get dressed, when there was no reason to wear anything, but he wouldn't do it on Earth. It would leave him utterly defenceless.

"Then we have an offer for you," Frazier said. He leaned forward. "We can take you out of this system, in exchange for a service."

Pete and Andor exchanged glances. "And take us where?" Pete asked. "We have little interest in going somewhere we would be separated. Or regarded as deviant."

"The Commonwealth," Jasmine said. "Or the Trade Federation, if you wish. You would be rewarded with enough money to buy a whole new asteroid miner, or a starship, or even a small fleet of starships. But we will expect you to work for us until we leave."

"We need to talk." Pete said. He pulled his wife into the corner of the room, then looked back at them. "And I may need to run it past the others."

Gary looked up at Jasmine, who looked unconcerned. It had to be an act, he was sure, yet he couldn't see any cracks in it. This was the one moment when they risked total exposure; too deep in the system to escape, too far from the shipyard or anywhere else to do any real damage before they were killed. And yet Jasmine looked completely calm. What did she know he didn't? Or was it merely an act?

"They're not monsters," he muttered. "Why would anyone see them as deviant?"

"They're a group-marriage," Frazier explained. "Pete is married to four other men and five women. The children they have are a mixed group; some of them are biologically Pete's, but he's one of the fathers of *all* of them. Even the Rim has problems accepting such an arrangement, son. It tangles up the normal inheritance and breeding standards something awful."

He sighed. "The Trade Federation would probably be happy to have them," he added, "but there would still be issues. It wouldn't be a pleasant problem to resolve."

Pete stamped back over to face them. "You've put me and my family in awful danger," he snarled. "I assume you have a plan to keep us under control?"

"It will look as though we have occupied your asteroid," Jasmine said. She held up one hand before he could say a word. "I apologise for the necessity of our actions, but ..."

"My family could be slaughtered if this goes wrong," Pete snapped. "And you haven't given us much of a choice, have you? How are you any better than the bastards holding Jim's daughters as hostages?"

Gary saw Jasmine's eyes flicker, just for a second. It wasn't a pleasant thought. He'd learned, at school, that the abusers were often people who had been abused themselves. It had given him some pleasure to think that Barry or Moe might have been beaten by their parents, but he hadn't really believed it. How could he think otherwise? Big strong assholes like them couldn't be beaten to within an inch of their lives by anyone. And yet ...

Jasmine *had* been a prisoner. And she *had* taken hostages herself. Had she crossed the line already, assuming there *was* a line for the marines ... or was she *worried* about crossing the line. He wondered, absently, if there was anything he could do, but he couldn't think of any options. Everything she'd done could be justified far too easily.

And perhaps that's the problem, he thought. *We rationalise everything we do far too easily.*

"Wolfbane has to be stopped," Jasmine said, finally. "You want to leave this system, with enough money to ensure you don't ever have to split up. The Commonwealth will grant you that, if you assist us; even if you want to be treated as prisoners, we will still pay you. But we cannot leave, or go elsewhere. There's no other way to get into the system."

Pete bunched his fists, as if he intended to take a swing at Jasmine. Gary hoped - prayed - he wouldn't do anything of the sort. Jasmine was probably faster than him, perhaps stronger ...and she had armed men within five minutes of the asteroid colony. She didn't want a fight, but she could win one if she had no choice.

That's why she's confident, Gary realised. *She's covered all the bases in advance.*

"You'd better make damn sure we get the family out before the shit hits the fan," Pete growled. "And that you pay us enough to make it worth our while."

"We will," Jasmine promised. "Now, call in your crew and I'll call in my people, then we can sit down and have a long chat."

It took longer than Gary had expected for the asteroid miners to finally come to terms with the unexpected visitors. They were a diverse lot - at least one of them sounded as though she was from Earth - and not all of them liked the idea of taking sides. The more he thought about it, the less Gary blamed them. They'd been dragged into the middle of a war that could easily cost them everything.

"Make sure everything is secured," Jasmine ordered, once the asteroid miners had finally surrendered to the inevitable. "I want all weapons and long-range communications gear rounded up, then stored on the freighter. Once that's done, we can start preparing to take the children out of the system."

"Of course," Stewart said.

Jasmine looked at Kailee, who had accompanied the troops to the asteroid. "Get a list of everyone on the asteroid, but make sure you write it on disposable paper," Jasmine added, firmly. "I don't want anything on the datacores if it can be avoided. Data-miners can dig up just about anything these days."

Pete sneered at them both. "And just how do you intend to account for keeping the freighter here for a couple of days?"

"We will see if they even notice," Jasmine said.

"They saw us arrive," Gary objected. "They *searched* us for contraband."

Jasmine smirked. "You're thinking of government as brutally efficient," she said. "I rather doubt anyone cares about one old freighter staying near an isolated asteroid-mining station. We might well have dropped off their sensors completely."

"You don't know that," Pete said. "They do take security seriously."

"I don't plan to stay long," Jasmine said. "Now ..."

She looked at Gary. "Help Kailee with the list, then go back to the freighter and perform your regular exercises," she ordered. "It may interest you to know that we will be adding another five push-ups tomorrow, so leaving them undone today will come back to haunt you in the very near future."

"I won't let him slack," Kailee promised.

Gary blushed. Every day, after their exercises, Kailee made love to him. It was a fantastic incentive, as far as he could see. If someone had offered him the same, back on Earth, he would have worked out until he had as many muscles as Darrin. Jasmine laughed, then dismissed them both with a wave. Kailee caught his arm and dragged him away before anything else could happen.

"The children are gathered in the playroom," she said, as they walked through the corridor and down towards yet another airlock. The bulkheads were decorated with childish pictures, suggesting that at least some of the children had artistic talents. He'd never seen anything like it on Earth, where displaying one child's work would either be deemed elitist or discriminatory. "They looked a cute bunch."

Gary kept his opinion to himself as they stepped into the playroom. There weren't many toys, merely a handful of teaching machines and a set of stuffed animals. Thankfully, someone had dressed the children ...but they looked almost disconcertingly calm. A kindergarten on Earth would have been the scene of a riot by now, with the bigger children picking on the smaller children and the supervisor crying in the background. The children before him just watched him calmly and waited.

"Hi," Kailee said. The children smiled at her, then snapped back to wary attention. "I need a list of your names, if you don't mind."

The kids obeyed, one by one. Gary rapidly lost track of their forenames, while they all shared the same surname. It was clear there would be issues in the future, unless they all regarded each other as family...but they probably did, he reasoned. The issues that ripped apart families on Earth simply didn't exist here.

"Done," Kailee said, finally. She paused. "Can the children be left here?"

"Of course we can, silly grounder," one of the older children said. He had a light voice that didn't seem to square with his words. *Grounder* wasn't exactly *Dirty Earther* or *Groundhog*, but it wasn't pleasant. "We're not *babies*."

Gary shrugged, then led the way out of the room. "How does that work?"

"I saw kids with small injuries on Meridian," Kailee commented. "They were allowed to keep pushing the limits until they hurt themselves, then they learned from the experiences and went onwards. I guess these children learned the dangers of space pretty quickly."

"I suppose," Gary said. Austin had once pointed out that anything that didn't kill someone made them stronger. "But those who didn't learn the dangers would have ended up dead."

He shook his head in disbelief. On Earth, leaving children unsupervised would be grounds for immediate dismissal, if not criminal charges. Children under sixteen were assumed to be eternally incompetent to look after themselves. But the supervisors weren't allowed to do anything that might damage their children's self-esteem, let alone keep them from playing as they saw fit. The contradiction had led to a great many ruined lives.

"Ah, Kailee," Jasmine called. She was standing by a processor, studying the station's diagrams. "Do you have the list?"

"Yes, I do," Kailee said. "There's nineteen children in all, ranging from three to nine years old. Anyone older seems to be already part of the workforce."

"Probably," Jasmine said. She didn't seem surprised by the discovery, but then she *had* grown up on a farm. Gary had seen children on Meridian working with their parents as soon as they could, even though it was technically against Imperial Law. "They could do *some* things to help by then, I imagine."

She seemed distracted, but smiled at them both. "Go back to the freighter and do your exercises," she added. She turned her attention back to the display, her voice fading slightly as she called up more files. "I should have a plan of attack within a few hours. By then …"

Gary felt his blood run cold. It was easy to forget where they were, but now …now he felt it, all too clearly. They could be discovered at any moment …

…And if they were, there was no hope of escape.

CHAPTER TWENTY-EIGHT

> The Empire could not, openly, accept any other independent state. If it had done so, it would have raised the issue of why other worlds couldn't be independent, worlds that were restless under the Empire's control. Therefore, the Empire could not grant any legitimate status to POWs.
> - Professor Leo Caesius. *The Empire and its Prisoners of War.*

Avalon, Year 5 (PE)

Kitty couldn't help a feeling of ...*concern*, if not nervousness, as she stepped into Colonel Stalker's office. The last week had been spent watching the suspects and silently cataloguing their movements in order to build up a case against them, but Kitty was grimly aware that the case was far from perfect. They had a link between Hannalore, Gaston and Wolfbane, yet she had no idea if others were also involved. There were two staff members at the Governor's Mansion who might well have assisted with bugging the entire building.

But the case was conclusive enough to justify action, she was sure. All that remained was to convince the colonel to agree.

"Colonel," she said, as she closed the door. "I believe we have a suitable case."

Colonel Stalker nodded, curtly. He was studying a starchart showing Wolfbane's advance into the Commonwealth, an advance that might well have been aided and abetted by the information obtained at the Governor's Mansion. Hannalore - or her husband, if he was involved - had focused on the political side of things, but there were some military titbits included in the DataStream. One of them might have made life easier for the advancing forces.

Kitty sat down, then rested her hands in her lap. "Hannalore, the Governor's wife, appears to be the prime spy," she said. "It was her idea to host the parties, which she apparently funded by selling her jewels. I have checked with the markets and confirmed that she only raised a couple of thousand credits, not enough to pay for one party let alone several. Logic suggests she must have found the money elsewhere."

The colonel frowned. "Didn't her husband notice?"

"He would have bought the jewels for a minimum of two *million* imperial credits," Kitty said, flatly. "I don't think he would have realised just how much their value had fallen, after the collapse of the Empire. Few of the richer men on Avalon care to spend their money on adorning their wives. Why spend a million credits when a thousand credits can be almost as good?"

"They might have been purchased by a wealthy *woman*," Colonel Stalker pointed out.

"Same psychology," Kitty said. "A wealthy man who buys jewels for a million credits apiece makes himself look like a fool. A wealthy woman who does the same makes herself look like a spendthrift. There's a difference between conspicuous consumption and being a greedy asshole - or being married to one. In both cases, it weakens their claim to be responsible businesspeople."

She shrugged. "In any case, most of the jewels are currently listed at two to three hundred credits each," she added. "I think the vast majority were actually picked up by the museum for later display. Jewels worn by the last Governor's Wife or something along those lines."

The Colonel held up his hand. "Very well," he said. "Can you prove your case?"

Kitty ticked off points on her fingers. "Hannalore has a source of money we cannot identify," she said. "The mansion is bugged - and bugged in a manner that suggests it was the owner who did it. Said bugs picked up both false information intended to catch a spy and later snatches of false information we used to prove the bugs and the spies were linked."

She paused for effect. "Hannalore goes to visit the same orphanage the day after each party; Gaston visits the same orphanage at the same time.

Gaston uses one of the computers at the datanet cafe to upload a series of files onto the datanet, which are shifted through a network of automated programs until they finally end up in the out-planet datacore and get transmitted to a remote asteroid station. If all of that is a coincidence, Colonel, I would happily resign on the spot and go to work in a brothel."

The Colonel's lips twitched. "You probably won't have to," he said, dryly. "And Gaston himself?"

"Multiple anger issues," Kitty said. "I had a psychologist do a work-up of him, now we have him under constant surveillance. His conclusion is that Gaston will snap, sooner rather than later, and when he does, the results will not be pleasant. The only mercy is that his plan to build homemade bombs seems to have been derailed."

"Wolfbane wouldn't want him blowing up buildings when spying is much more harmful," the Colonel agreed.

"He may restart," Kitty said. "I don't think he has the personality to handle the task indefinitely. Sooner or later, he will grow tired of not seeing any evidence of his success and start plotting something himself."

The Colonel frowned. "Then why would Wolfbane rely on him?"

"Hannalore has a decent motive to visit the orphanage," Kitty admitted. "I checked; she's a known benefactor, even to the point of giving the children clothes and supplies from the Governor's Mansion. She's even been donating money recently. Gaston, too, has a good reason to visit. They may not have been able to set up a better link before we started running more counter-spy operations."

"Or they don't want to risk someone more competent, if Gaston is a disaster waiting to happen," the Colonel said. He sighed. "And what about the Governor himself?"

"I don't think he's involved," Kitty said. "But he's going to be shocked when he finds out."

She shook her head. It wouldn't be the first time that a spy had embedded so thoroughly into an enemy state that he'd married and had children, developing emotional ties that would shatter when - if - the truth came out. But Hannalore hadn't been a spy when she'd married the Governor, or when she'd come to Avalon. Unless she'd always been an embedded spy and her contact information had ended up on Wolfbane ...she sighed, then dismissed the thought. No one in their right mind would consider the Governor's wife a reliable long-term agent.

"Shocked is one word for it," the Colonel said. "And while he has no political power, he does have influence. Those parties gave him a lot of contacts."

"Shit," Kitty said.

She met the Colonel's eyes. "I don't think she's a professional spy, sir," she said. "There would be nothing to gain by leaving her where she is, without interference. We can take advantage of her without leaving her alone, I think."

The Colonel looked back at her. "And your reasoning is?"

Kitty knew she was being tested, but she couldn't help a flicker of irritation. "If we control her, we can slip false information to Wolfbane and determine what other pieces of information are included in the packets," she said, coolly. "But if we leave her alone, *she* will determine what else goes to Wolfbane. One of those pieces of information might be outright disastrous."

She held up a hand. "One piece that went out last week concerned a dispute between Avalon and Taurus," she added. "I expect the Wolves will be very interested to know about fault lines running through the Commonwealth."

"Probably," Colonel Stalker said.

Kitty pressed her advantage. "They must find dealing with us as strange as we find dealing with them," she said. "Hannalore was giving them insights into our developing politics we're not getting from *their* side. There's already rumblings about Avalon hogging too much of the political power to itself ..."

"You've made your point," the Colonel said, flatly.

"It's going to be used against us," Kitty added. "It was *Avalon* that took the decision to send the CEF to Thule ..."

"Most of which comes *from* Avalon," the Colonel reminded her.

"But it is intended as a *Commonwealth* formation," Kitty countered. "Its deployment was solely debated on Avalon, in the midst of a political dispute over the disastrous mission to that godforsaken hellhole."

"Lakshmibai," the Colonel said.

Kitty ran her hand through her long hair. "My very strong advice, sir, is to move ahead and take Hannalore into custody now," she said. "If we do it covertly, we can make sure she continues to work for us, without betraying us further."

"I assume you have a plan," the Colonel said. "You don't want to send a small army of policemen to her door?"

"That would be a little bit revealing," Kitty agreed. "I'd prefer to invite her here, along with her husband, and then take her into custody. I don't know *how* she will react, when she discovers her cover is blown, but we would have the best chance of containing it here."

"And her husband will not react well either," Colonel Stalker said.

"No, sir," Kitty said. "I rather doubt he will."

She looked down at the floor, then back up at him. "There are too many different ways she could react, sir," she added. "She could break down and beg for mercy, she could try to hide behind her husband, she could coolly offer to trade her assistance for leniency …I've seen all of them, in my time."

"And we couldn't put her on trial. The jury would want her hung."

"They might be right," Colonel Stalker said. "Does she *deserve* mercy?"

"She's a traitor, someone who betrayed us because she fell off the gravy train," Kitty said, flatly. She understood the Colonel's point, but she wanted to make *use* of the spy. "However, we can also use her to mislead Wolfbane. She can redeem herself through service."

"She will never be trusted again," the Colonel said, flatly.

He leaned forward. "I will need to discuss the matter with the President," he warned. "And then we will decide how to proceed."

"Understood, sir," Kitty said. "But it's only two days until the next party. I would prefer to take her into custody tomorrow."

The Colonel nodded. "I'll get back to you," he said. "Dismissed."

Ed knew that people made bad decisions when their lives changed without notice. He knew just how much crap Professor Caesius's wife had put him through, when he'd lost his job for daring to question the establishment, and he knew just how many exiles had committed suicide after leaving Earth for good. In that sense, Hannalore was no different ...but instead of either climbing into the bottle or working to adapt to the new order, she had set out to betray it. And succeeded magnificently.

The hell of it was that the parties *were* useful. Deliberately or otherwise, the Governor and his wife *had* put together an institution that had helped the Commonwealth grow into a powerful state. Ed had read the puff piece in the *Avalon Central* and he had to admit the Governor had found a niche. But none of it counted against the sheer scale of his wife's betrayal. Kitty was right. Hannalore could be used to mislead Wolfbane ...and yet, there was the abiding sense that she should be punished, perhaps executed or sent into permanent exile. The public would demand the maximum sentence for her crimes.

He cursed under his breath, then called Gaby and requested an immediate meeting. The plan he'd been putting together to give Wolfbane a bloody nose was workable, he was sure, but it would be easier to make it work if they could mislead the enemy beforehand. Kitty was right, again. Hannalore would be able to mislead the enemy, if she was used properly. And yet, could they trust her not to slip a single warning message into the datapack? One mistake and the data conduit would be lost forever ...

Shaking his head, he rose to his feet and walked up to the President's office. Gaby hadn't wanted more than a single large room, one where she could host a small gathering or do her paperwork, rather than the giant apartments enjoyed by the Grand Senators on Earth. Ed wondered, absently, if future Presidents would feel the same way too, then pushed the thought aside as he walked through the door. The guard scanned him quickly, then nodded curtly. Ed had given several previous guards chewing outs for not realising that orders to search everyone meant search everyone.

"Ed," Gaby said, as he walked through the inner door. "I rarely see you here in working hours."

Ed smiled. Their relationship was the worst-kept secret on Avalon - they'd been lovers for over three years - but they had to try to keep it professional. They both had political enemies watching them closely for any signs their relationship was colouring their judgement. He kissed her forehead, then sat down facing her.

"We have a situation," he said. "The Governor's wife is a spy."

He outlined the bare bones of the story, then waited for Gaby to finish considering the implications. She had a more twisted mind than he had, as well as a better appreciation of the political realities. *And* she'd been the leader of the Crackers before the Battle of Camelot and the political settlement that had ended the war.

"Shit," Gaby said, finally. "The Governor is quite well liked, Ed."

"Now he's powerless," Ed pointed out. "Was he so well-liked when he was the Empire's representative on Avalon?"

"He was always largely powerless," Gaby said. "The Old Council saw to that, I think. He was just the figurehead for a loathed system that eventually abandoned us."

She sighed. "We can't let this continue," she added. "The war alone is placing a great deal of stress on our political system. If this gets out ...all hell will break loose."

"I know," Ed said. He frowned as a nasty thought occurred to him. That damned reporter would have to be silenced, particularly if Hannalore agreed to cooperate in exchange for not being executed for her crimes. "Colonel Stevenson would like to covertly take her into custody, then make a deal."

"It sticks in my craw to let a spy go unpunished," Gaby said. "But ... hell, we have precedent. There was a general amnesty for just about everyone after the war, wasn't there? And we gave the same offer to Admiral Singh's lower-ranking personnel."

"That was then," Ed said. "This is now."

"The old crowd will understand," Gaby said. "We all did things we're not proud of during the war. Some people ...just found themselves caught between the devil and the deep blue sea. We liked willing cooperation, but we were quite willing to threaten people when we couldn't count on their patriotism. A threat to a person's family can ensure cooperation."

"Hannalore wasn't threatened," Ed said. "She *chose* to betray us."

"We don't know that," Gaby said. "You *assume* she merely wanted a return to power and status, but you could be wrong. She could have been threatened, or blackmailed, into cooperating with the enemy. It sets a very bad precedent if you allow someone to be backed into an inescapable corner."

Ed winced. "If she's being blackmailed," he offered, "it has to be bad."

"Or merely silly," Gaby said. "There's nothing illegal in *our* relationship, but I wouldn't be very happy if someone released recordings of us in bed together onto the datanet. She could be having an affair, one that would rip her marriage apart if it ever became public …she might not be *arrested* for it, but she would certainly be embarrassed."

She took a long breath. "Have your officer take her into covert custody," she ordered, "and interrogated thoroughly. If she is willing to cooperate, we can deal with her afterwards; she won't have a chance to return to power, but she will be alive. If not …"

"Kill her," Ed said, flatly.

"Yeah," Gaby said.

She looked past him for a long moment, her eyes haunted. Ed understood; he'd been a Marine, fighting in the open, while Gaby had been a freedom fighter against a dangerous and powerful enemy. She would have been called a terrorist, he knew, if she'd lost the war; the Crackers might have tried to fight decently, but they'd done their fair share of terrorising people who weren't openly inclined to support them. And Gaby and her people had to live with what they'd done.

"I have two years left as President," she said, slowly. "Do you think I could retire afterwards? Would you come with me?"

"I don't know," Ed admitted. Part of him liked the idea of a rest, part of him knew he was being stupid - and selfish. He had a comfortable office, a comfortable bed and all the food he could eat, while some of his subordinates squatted in foxholes or stood guard in the freezing cold. Had he reached the point where he could move people around as easily as icons on a display? "There's still work to do."

"Knitting the remains of the Empire back together will be the work of generations," Gaby said. "God alone knows how much is left of the Core Worlds …let alone the worlds on the other side of Earth. Our grandchildren might be the ones who put the finishing touches on the next empire."

She smiled. "Do you want children?"

"One day," Ed said. Children had always seemed like hostages to fortune for him; it had been rare to see a serving Marine with children, not when a serving Marine could find himself shipped halfway across the galaxy at a moment's notice. But now ...if he wanted children, he could have them. "But after the war, I think."

"The war may not end soon," Gaby warned. "Life goes on."

"I know," Ed said.

He sat back in his chair and smiled. "But I do have an idea to put in front of you," he added, seriously. "One that could shorten the war."

CHAPTER TWENTY-NINE

That isn't to say that the Empire mistreated them. Most foot soldiers were simply rounded up, then dispatched to a penal world. The Empire calculated they would be unable to affect the struggle on their homeworlds - and, in addition, they might manage to make the penal world habitable.
- Professor Leo Caesius. *The Empire and its Prisoners of War.*

Medusa, **Wolfbane System, Year 5 (PE)**

"Now," Jasmine mused. "*This* is interesting."

"Is it?" Stewart asked. "I would have thought it was awful timing."

Jasmine smirked. Stubbins hadn't exaggerated when he'd described Governor Brown's plans to expand the shipyards at Wolfbane. There were over fifty slips capable of handling heavy cruiser-sized starships, two that might be capable of building battleships and over three hundred industrial, fabrication and habitation nodes. Indeed, there was more industrial power concentrated in the giant shipyard than there was in the entire Commonwealth.

"Our old friend Admiral Singh has returned from the front," Jasmine said. Pete, after some muttering, had given her access to his private communications links to other independent miners. They might not have much political power, but they had their ways to keep an eye on those who did. "Apparently, she's going to be ...*consulting* with Governor Brown."

"It will keep them busy, I suppose," Stewart said, slowly. "Are they coming to the shipyard?"

"Eventually," Jasmine said. "But can we stay here long enough to arrange a proper greeting?"

"We need a diversion," Watson offered. "An attempt on the Governor's life would suffice, I think."

"Getting down to Wolfbane would be tricky," Jasmine pointed out, sharply. "He's not due up here for another two weeks, assuming he sticks to his schedule."

"It should be possible to get down without being caught," Watson countered. "There are smugglers who get people down to Wolfbane, if they're paid well. I could go down with Paula and see what opportunities present themselves."

Stewart snorted. "*You're* volunteering for this? Don't you know you should *never* volunteer?"

"I'm the best choice," Watson said. "Jasmine shouldn't be risking herself; she's the CO. You're needed to serve as her backup. None of the soldiers have the right training to get into hostile territory and remain unnoticed until the crunch comes. I did start the Pathfinder module ..."

"You failed," Stewart snapped.

"I'm still the best qualified," Watson said, flatly. "I go down with Paula. We make contact with some of her contacts, assuming they're still in place. Assuming all goes well, we launch an attack on Governor Brown's residence in hopes of taking him out - if nothing else, it should provide a fantastic diversion."

Jasmine frowned. She couldn't argue with the logic - Watson *was* the best qualified - but she disliked the idea of sending him away. The odds weren't in favour of him making a clean escape, even assuming he carried out the mission successfully. And if he were caught, making his way down to Wolfbane, it would be all too revealing. If nothing else, the Governor's security officers would start looking for any other discrepancies within the system. They would *certainly* tighten security around the shipyard.

But at the same time, it *would* make one hell of a diversion.

"You're talking about taking Paula with you," she said, delaying the final decision. "Do you trust her not to fuck up?"

"I think she's strong enough to handle it," Watson said.

"That's because you're sleeping with her," Stewart sneered.

Jasmine had her doubts. Paula had impressed her, even though she couldn't understand the older woman's career choice. There was a strength in Paula that had enabled her to survive five years of imprisonment, even as her superior started to crack under the strain. She *would* have made a good Marine.

"I don't think fucking her is the same as losing my ability to *judge* her," Watson snapped at Stewart. "I ..."

"Of course it is," Stewart said. "All your blood has run down to your cock, starving your brain of oxygen. You are talking about taking a civilian on an incredibly dangerous mission."

"She's the closest thing we have to a native guide," Watson said, coldly. "I think she would be able to operate within the system better than anyone else."

"But would she pass muster when the security forces sweep past her?" Stewart asked. "One hint of nervousness and you're screwed, perhaps literally."

"I was unaware that being a Marine was *safe*," Watson snapped. "There are times when you just have to gamble."

"True," Jasmine said, holding up a hand to keep the two men from arguing. "Ask her if she wishes to undertake the mission, knowing the odds against escape are poor. If she agrees, you can plan out how to get to Wolfbane without being intercepted."

"There are smugglers who visit the asteroids from time to time," Watson said. "We could depart this afternoon, if we put out a call."

"Go ask her," Jasmine ordered. "And then see if we can get you down to the surface."

She watched Watson leave the office, then looked back at the diagrams of the shipyard complex. The real problem was getting through the outer defences; the designers had ringed the complex with automated weapons platforms and dozens of remote sensor pickets. Even a dedicated stealth ship would have problems sneaking through the defences, although once it was through the barrier it would have become a great deal easier. Jasmine had a feeling, judging by the reports, that there were so many different people working on the shipyard that no one knew *everyone* who happened to be there.

"Risky," Stewart observed, breaking into her thoughts. "We could lose him."

"I know," Jasmine said.

"And there are political implications in trying to assassinate the enemy head of state," Stewart added. "They may seek to retaliate."

Jasmine scowled. Stewart was effectively her XO; it was his *duty* to remind her of potential issues with her planning. But, now she'd made the decision, she really didn't want to be questioned. Watson was right. They needed a diversion and an attack on Governor Brown was perhaps the best idea they could muster. States that were ruled by a single person tended to be very sensitive to threats to their leader. If nothing else, there would be one hell of a succession crisis.

"They attacked Avalon itself," she reminded him. She'd caught up on the news from the front on Saltine. "They made a determined effort to kill Colonel Stalker and the President. I don't think they can complain if we return the favour."

And we might spark off a civil war, she added, silently. Everything she'd heard from Stubbins and Paula - and Pete - suggested that Governor Brown was presiding over a patchwork state. Without him holding the whole edifice together, it might collapse into chaos. *The Commonwealth would have a chance to build up its might while Wolfbane turned on itself.*

She wondered, absently, if Colonel Stalker would approve. He'd always had an idea of war as honourable, something that Jasmine didn't understand. There was a difference between clinging to one's ideals and allowing them to hamper operations. But, in the end, the decision rested with her. Governor Brown's removal might help the Commonwealth win the war and that was all there was to it.

And if Admiral Singh dies too, we might well win quicker, she thought. Admiral Singh might have lost Corinthian, but she was no idiot. And she had a burning lust to prove herself by stamping her will on the universe. *Who knows who will replace her if she dies?*

"Then we should ensure he has the best possible chance to succeed," Stewart said. "Do you have a way to get into the shipyard?"

"I think we have only one option," Jasmine said. The old trick of shutting down all emissions and just *drifting* through the defences was not going to work here. "We need to get them to take us inside."

Stewart lifted an eyebrow. "You plan to bribe our way inside?"

Jasmine shook her head. "There's an ore freighter docking here tomorrow," she said. "We're going to take it, then load it with ore and set course for the shipyard. Their procedures insist on any incoming ships being searched thoroughly before they enter the shipyard ..."

"Which will make it impossible for us to sneak through," Stewart pointed out.

"It will," Jasmine said. "They will board us, like they did earlier. At that point, we take their ship and use it to pass through the defences."

Stewart smiled. "And then?"

"We bail out once we're in the shipyard, then trigger a core breech in the ship's drives," Jasmine said. "That should cause enough confusion for us to get to the habitation nodes without being detected, as we're already be inside their defences. From there, we go to the armoury and take control of the missile pods, then turn them on the shipyards. And then we slip out and sneak back to the freighter."

"I see," Stewart said, after a long moment. "It sounds remarkably complex."

"It is," Jasmine said. "However, I don't see any alternative. I don't know if there's a self-destruct system on the shipyard, but if there is I doubt they would let us get hold of it. Any other damage we can do would be wholly minor, given the sheer scale of the installation."

"There is another possibility," Stewart offered. He tapped the shipyard diagram with some force. "We could deliberately set out to butcher the workforce."

Jasmine blanched. It was easy enough to consider assassinating Governor Brown, but she didn't want to think about slaughtering hundreds of thousands of innocent workers. And yet, didn't Stewart have a point? The workers would be hard to replace, thanks to literally centuries of damage to the Empire's educational system. Hell, even the workers who could train newer workers would be killed. Wolfbane might not recover for centuries.

But she didn't want to cross that line. It would be a step too far.

She frowned as a thought occurred to her. "You think we could *kidnap* them instead?"

"I don't see how," Stewart said. "There aren't any freighters within the shipyard, as far as I can see, and they wouldn't have any difficulty catching up with us if they did. I think we have a choice between killing them all, or at least as many as we can catch, and letting them live."

"We're not going to become murderers," Jasmine said. There were people she would gladly kill - Governor Brown, Admiral Singh - but she wasn't going to slaughter far too many innocents, even if their deaths *were* a tactical advantage. "Leave them in place."

"I hope you can live with yourself later," Stewart said. "And what about our friends?"

"Good question," Jasmine said. Gary and Kailee might come in handy for something, but right now she couldn't think what. "Maybe they should go with the freighter when it heads to the out-system."

"Gary *has* been learning to hack," Stewart reminded her. He looked at the terminal, thoughtfully. "Carl actually managed to have a long chat with him …"

There was a tap on the hatch, which opened. "Speak of the devil," Stewart added, as Watson stepped into the compartment. "We were just talking about you."

"Ah," Watson said. He grinned, openly. "And to think I was going to ask the doctor for something to keep my ears from burning."

Jasmine gave him a sharp look. "What were you and Gary chatting about?"

"Games," Watson said. "Gary played a *lot* of games on Earth. It seems he even had quite a reputation online at one point. He even hacked some of those shitty terminals they hand out to children - you know, the ones with cameras that monitor what you do when you use them."

Stewart shuddered. "They were being used to spy on kids," he said. His face twisted in disgust. "Hardly anyone gave a damn …or dared to protest. It was Earth."

Jasmine winced. What did it say about Earth that someone could put a spy camera into a child's room and hardly anyone dared protest? But Earth had had literally trillions of spy cameras scattered through the CityBlocks …and even then, the crime rate had been astronomically high. She rather doubted that hacking the devices had been hard, even though Earth's students learned very little about how computers actually worked. And Gary had probably escaped detection because there were just so *many* of the devices.

Maybe they just didn't care, she thought. *Or told themselves that they were fighting crime by scattering cameras everywhere. But they are useless without someone monitoring the take ...*

She pushed the thought aside and leaned forward. "Can he crack a mil-spec system?"

"Perhaps, with a hacker kit," Watson said. "He was very cagey about just how far he'd gone on Earth. I think he might have a chance, but he'd have to try to be sure."

Jasmine winced. The Empire might have tried to give each planet a united datanet, but military and political datacores were rarely tied to the network. There had always been nightmares about hackers breaking in and triggering all sorts of disasters, no matter how many precautions were put in place. But then, there had been so few qualified WebHeads when the Empire's time finally ran out that there might have been a very valid threat. A security officer might know nothing more about how a computer actually worked, let alone how to fix it, than the average civilian.

But they do work all kinds of protections into the computers, she thought, sourly. *It might not be possible to break into the system.*

"I'll talk to him about it," she said. It would be useful to have a human in the loop, rather than rely on a hacker kit. "But I don't know if we could trust him on a mission."

Watson frowned. "You don't trust him?"

"I would prefer not to have to count on him being brave at the right time," she said. Gary had had an opportunity to shoot someone, to save Kailee from being raped, and he'd muffed it completely. "A panic attack could screw the entire mission."

She sighed, inwardly. She hated the idea of taking Gary on a mission that required bravery; he might have been training - Kailee was very good at providing incentive - but he simply wasn't very *brave*. It might be years before he overcame his mental blocks, if he ever did, and became an effective fighter. She couldn't recall ever encountering a marine recruit who'd been unwilling to actually *hit* someone.

"Then set up a laser link," Watson suggested. "Have him do his work from a distance, if possible. It should be workable."

"I'll think about it," Jasmine promised. It did seem like a good idea, although the freighter couldn't be *that* far from the shipyard or time-delay problems would start to crop up. The speed of light only seemed fast when compared to a planet's surface. "It will need to be planned carefully."

She looked up at him. "What did Paula say?"

"She said she would be happy to accompany me," Watson said. "I explained the dangers and she accepted them."

"How brave of her," Jasmine said. "I expect you to keep an eye on her, understand? And not just in bed."

"Of course," Watson said, offended.

He passed her a datachip, which she slotted into the terminal. "A free trader can be here in five hours, if we put in a request for them to visit within the next hour," he continued. "Paula and I will board, then bribe our way down to the planet. It will mean riding in a transit crate, but that will get us past the customs monitors without having to register our entry and having our DNA checked against the register. Pete says the system is almost foolproof."

"Really?" Stewart asked. "Some fools are actually quite smart."

Watson didn't rise to the bait. "I can take a handful of weapons with me," he added, "or try to obtain more on the surface."

"Take them with you," Jasmine said. It was a risk, but if Watson were caught the entire mission would be blown anyway. "What do you plan to do after striking at Brown?"

"I plan to go underground, then start looking for other targets of opportunity," Watson said. "It's quite likely there is an underground movement by now; Paula says there were several budding independence movements when Earth fell and Brown took over. I can join them and offer my support. We'll be there when the Commonwealth eventually invests this system."

Unless civil war breaks out, Jasmine thought. It was hard to judge for sure. Neither Paula nor Stubbins could be expected to know the current state of affairs. *The underground might have an opportunity once Brown's subordinates have finished killing each other.*

"Workable," Stewart growled. He didn't seem pleased by the development. "I suppose it is workable. But very dangerous."

"There's no alternative," Watson said. "You need a diversion ...and this is our chance to take a shot at Governor Brown himself. I didn't sign up to be *safe*."

"There's a difference between being brave and being reckless," Jasmine said. "But you're right. And good luck."

She rose to her feet and held out her hand. Watson took it; they shook hands, firmly. Stewart hesitated, then shook hands with Watson too. Jasmine felt an odd pang in her chest, then pushed it aside, sharply. Watson was right. The risk had to be taken ...but so much could easily go wrong.

"The ore freighter is due here tomorrow," Jasmine said. She glanced from one to the other, willing them to understand. One way or the other, they would give Wolfbane a very bloody nose. "We have only a handful of hours to get everything ready, then catch up on our sleep. Tomorrow is going to be a very busy day."

CHAPTER THIRTY

The senior leadership, however, tended to be treated differently. If they were willing to bow the head to the Empire, they would be treated as quislings, rather than outright enemies. They would be ideally placed to exploit their homeworld on the Empire's behalf - and they would know everyone who was likely to pose a threat in the future. Indeed, it says something grim about human nature that many leaders were quite willing to sell out their subordinates, if only to protect their own lives.
- Professor Leo Caesius. *The Empire and its Prisoners of War.*

Wolfbane System, Year 5 (PE)
Admiral Rani Singh knew, without any reasonable doubt, that patience was one of her strong suits. It had kept her going when her commanding officer - her *former* commanding officer - had blocked her career, after she'd refused to sleep with him. Indeed, Admiral Bainbridge had *suffered* when she'd launched her coup and taken control of the fleet base he'd regarded as punishment duty. Patience had given her a chance to stick a knife in his back and take power for herself.

But she also knew the value of acting fast, when opportunity presented itself.

She felt a flicker of cold frustration as she walked down the corridor towards the Governor's office, escorted by a pair of heavily-armed guards. Wolfbane looked like more of an armed camp than ever before; she'd seen hundreds of soldiers patrolling the streets, while the bodyguards on duty had searched her thoroughly and scanned her body down to the atomic level before allowing her to proceed. Governor Brown, it seemed, was feeling paranoid ...and she had to admit he had good reason. The war was threatening to stalemate, something that would encourage his enemies to consider removing him from power.

And yet that might well cost Wolfbane the war.

It was a bitter thought. Rani had been military dictator on Corinthian, the empress of a tiny empire that should have grown to rival Wolfbane. Now, after she'd lost Corinthian, she was just another subordinate of a greater man, although she had to admit that Governor Brown was far more decent and capable than Admiral Bainbridge. But she was under his command, serving his will ...and, whatever his skills, they didn't include making war. Priceless opportunities to strike deep into the heart of the Commonwealth had been wasted because the Governor was unwilling to commit himself. The Battle of Thule had been a victory - of that, Rani had no doubt - but it had also showcased the Commonwealth's technical superiority. And now the Governor was nervous, concerned that his overwhelming superiority in numbers could be negated by a single technical silver bullet.

Rani's lips twisted in disdain as the door opened, allowing her to walk into the Governor's office. If the Commonwealth was so advanced that one of their new-build cruisers was more than a match for a full-sized battleship, the war was already lost. The Commonwealth would advance from star to star, systematically destroying any enemy force that refused to surrender, until they took Wolfbane itself. But they hadn't. And that told Rani, who was far too used to seeing inflated estimates of enemy firepower, that their technical advances were much overrated. Dangerous, yes; decisive, no.

"Governor," she said, as the door closed behind her. "You wanted to see me?"

"I did, Admiral," Governor Brown said. He rose to his feet behind his desk, his calm eyes fixed on her face. "Please, be seated. I will have coffee brought to us."

Rani sat, keeping her face expressionless. The Governor was an odd duck; power-hungry, like so many others, but less interested in military force than she had expected. But then, he *wasn't* a military officer; he'd served as a corporate liaison officer before politics had thrust him into the Sector Governorship. His decision not to focus on the military struck her as foolish - the ties that had bound the Empire together were gone - but it might serve a useful purpose. There was no way he could serve as a military leader.

Certainly not the type of leader we need today, she thought, vindictively. *No proven competence, no track record of looking after his subordinates, nothing to keep men serving him when the source of all power and authority is gone.*

A maid, wearing a long flowing dress, poured them both cups of coffee, then retreated, as silently as she had come. Rani sipped her coffee and smiled, inwardly; the Governor might not be inclined to wrap himself in luxury, unlike some politicians and officers she had met, but he did like his coffee. Governor Brown sat back down and sipped his own coffee, clearly intent on taking a break before speaking. Rani felt another flicker of irritation, but forced it down into the back of her mind. The Governor could still have her executed if he felt like it.

Which is another problem, she thought. *The military is shot through with commissioners, spies and assassins. He's got us so paranoid that we don't know who we can trust to watch our backs, when the shit hits the fan.*

She allowed herself a moment to glance around the office. It was large, easily twice the size of a battleship's bridge, but surprisingly empty. The desk sat in front of a giant window that stared out over the city below; the walls were lined with bookcases and datacores, yet most of the space was wasted. She wasn't sure, despite herself, if the office was a statement of power - a large room in a mansion suggested wealth as well as power - or a warning that Governor Brown had no interests apart from power. There were certainly no pieces of artwork, photographs of his family or anything remotely decadent anywhere within sight.

"Admiral," the Governor said, placing his cup on the desk. "I suppose you're wondering why I called you here."

"I am," Rani said, simply.

She wanted to point out that she'd had to travel all the way back from the war front - God alone knew what would happen in her absence - but there was no point. Instead, she put her cup of coffee down and leaned back in her chair, schooling her face to remain expressionless, betraying nothing of her innermost thoughts. One day, she would make Governor Brown rue the day he'd ever spited her - just like Admiral Bainbridge - but until then, she would be as obedient and loyal as he could reasonably expect.

"I have the reports from my spies," the Governor continued, "but I have no real understanding of the military situation. Their reports are frequently contradictory. I need you to tell me precisely what's happening."

Rani felt a hot flash of rage she ruthlessly suppressed. It was typical that the spies - she knew there were at least ten on her flagship - could keep an eye on her even in her quarters, but not provide a decent explanation of just what was going on to their ultimate superior. Or did Governor Brown *expect* them to always be pessimistic about Rani's intentions? Few spies were considered excellent unless they uncovered proof of treachery ...and what were they to do, if there was no evidence to find?

But they did find nothing, Rani thought, coldly. It had taken months to start building her own network, but she'd succeeded. *If they had found something, I'd be dead by now.*

"The war is threatening to stalemate," she said. "And that will give the Commonwealth a dangerous advantage."

She took a breath and pressed on. "So far, we have been concentrating on securing the border worlds. However, with the exception of Thule, few of those worlds are actually worth the effort involved in taking them. We are tying up our ships and men occupying worlds that offer nothing to us or to the enemy. This has given the Commonwealth a chance to recover from their early missteps and take the war back to us. Their political system, which was dangerously unstable, may have solidified under the weight of our offensive."

"I see," Brown said. "Some of my other commanders insist that we must secure territory before we advance further."

Rani shook her head. "There's too great a risk of them counterattacking in force," she said, warningly. "We're not actually impeding their ability to build new ships, train new soldiers, produce new guns and missiles ...it looks impressive, on a star chart, but it's really light years upon light years of wasted space."

"There's also the danger of encountering new weapons," Governor Brown pointed out. "Some of the estimates are quite scary."

"I know," Rani said. "But they are also unrealistic."

She fought down the urge to roll her eyes like a teenager. Weapons design had stalled under the Empire, which hadn't really been interested in developing something that might badly upset the balance of power. Why bother working to come up with something new when it might be ruthlessly suppressed? But some of the ideas the Governor's cronies had come up with were straight out of a science-fantasy flick. Starships the size of entire planets? Guns that shot beams of energy faster than light? Missiles that moved at just below the speed of light? Nanotech clouds that disassembled entire starships?

"The Commonwealth has already started to deploy force shields," Governor Brown said. "I believed that to be impossible before I read the first reports."

"So did I," Rani admitted.

"So," the Governor said. "Why are the other ideas so unrealistic?"

"Because if they had them, they would have won the war," Rani said, feeling her patience begin to fray. "They would have waltzed up to the high orbitals, blasting their way through any ship that dared to stand in their path, and dictated terms to us. But they haven't."

She took a breath. "And if we are so afraid of what they will discover," she added, "we should take our superior numbers and hammer them flat, now. The war could be won within months if we stabbed deep at their heart."

"And if we lost," Governor Brown said, "we would lose everything."

Rani ground her teeth in frustration, then braced herself for a long argument.

"Was this really a good idea?"

Carl Watson shrugged. "You should try flying in a Raptor through heavy fire," he said, remembering some of the deployments on Han. "It's much - much - worse than this, really."

Paula didn't look convinced. The shipping container was large enough for them to sit comfortably, but it was alarmingly claustrophobic. Carl had endured worse - he'd been born on an asteroid colony - yet Paula didn't seem to be handling it very well. If she'd been alone, he had a feeling she would have been screaming for mercy by now. Hopefully, no one would have heard.

He took her hand as the container shook again. The smugglers had told him that they would be shipped down to the planet, then moved to a warehouse where they would be released, but they hadn't been able to provide a timetable. If Wolfbane followed the same procedures as most other worlds, there would be a delay while the containers were passed through security scanners ...unless the bribes had actually worked. Carl had braced himself, as best as he could, for discovery, but he knew the odds of actually fighting his way out were very low, even without Paula. Paula was nice - and great in bed - yet she didn't have any combat experience.

The container rattled, ominously. He reached for his pistol and checked it automatically, half-expecting to see the metal walls opening outwards and armed men peering in. There was a long pause, then the container shook one final time. Paula yelped and covered her mouth; Carl allowed himself a flicker of amusement, knowing the metal was thick enough to prevent any sound escaping. Some illegal immigrants had starved to death, trapped inside containers they couldn't open from the inside ... he hoped the thought of being trapped for days, rather than hours, hadn't occurred to Paula. It would definitely cause her to panic.

He braced himself as he heard a dull *click* echoing through the container, then hefted his pistol as the lid was lifted off, allowing bright light to stream down from high above. Paula covered her eyes; Carl forced himself to stand upright as the side fell away, revealing a large warehouse and a pair of beaming men grinning at them. He put his pistol back in his belt, then stood up and helped Paula to her feet. The men kept smirking at him, but showed no real sign of being unfriendly.

"Thank you," he said, as Paula leaned against him. "Where do we go now?"

"Straight out the door," the smuggler said. He pressed a credit chip into Carl's hand, then a pair of ID cards. Carl picked up his bag and slung it over his shoulder, before sticking the cards and chip in his pocket. "These were cut specially for you and should pass muster, unless you do something very stupid. Please don't as you could wind up in prison ..."

"And not in an incredibly hot women's prison either," his friend added. "It won't be a pleasant place to go."

"I'm sure," Carl muttered.

He held Paula gently as they walked away from the crate, through a set of metal doors and out into the bright sunlight. In the distance, he could see a set of glittering towers reaching up towards the sky, each one large enough to hold thousands of people. But Wolfbane wasn't Earth, he reminded himself, and there was no shortage of living space. It was far more likely the buildings were office blocks, rather than accommodation ...he pushed the thought aside as they walked past another huge warehouse, then another. The sun seemed to grow hotter as they finally reached the edge of the complex, then hailed a cab as it drove past the entrance.

"Hey," the driver said. Carl couldn't help noticing he wore a black uniform. "Where to, sir?"

"The nearest Haven," Carl ordered, as he climbed into the cab. "And step on it."

The driver nodded, then guided the cab back onto the road and drove towards the city. Carl sat back in his chair and watched the population, thoughtfully; a surprising number of cars were firmly bound to the ground, despite a handful of aircars flying overhead. It suggested a lack of concern for the environment ...or a lack of trust in the automated traffic control system. Carl contemplated the prospect for a long moment, then dismissed the thought as he turned his attention to the population. Almost everyone, from young schoolchildren to old men and women, wore a uniform of some kind.

They must want people who don't wear uniforms to stick out like sore thumbs, he thought, as his eyes followed a pair of teenage girls. They both wore unflattering orange uniforms that made them look like escapees from the POW camps on Meridian. *Maybe they go to boarding school...*

He pushed the thought aside as the cab pulled up in front of the Haven. Carl had used the hotel chain before, knowing them to be discrete and friendly, but his first impressions were spoiled by the receptionist. She asked so many questions that, if Carl hadn't known they desperately needed somewhere to stay, he would have taken his business elsewhere. As it was, he was grateful beyond words they'd spent so long going over their cover stories. By the time they reached their suite, he was half-convinced they'd blown the whole thing and given themselves away.

This is the worst sort of police state, he thought. *Everyone has a place and woe betide them if they go elsewhere.*

"The uniforms are new," Paula commented, as she walked over to the window and peered down at the street far below. Hundreds of people, looking no larger than insects, were walking past the hotel. "I ..."

Carl tapped his lips, then carried out a quick search for bugs. A visual pickup was hidden within the toilet mirror - he couldn't help noticing that it would allow watchers to spy on someone in the shower - while a pair of audio pick-ups were concealed within the main bedroom. He made a show of dropping his bags in front of one of the bugs, then accidentally rendering the other one largely useless by turning on the radio. If there was a second, undiscovered visual bug, it would be tricky for it to do more than watch them, as long as they were careful.

"Keep your voice low," he ordered. It was unlikely they were being spied on constantly, but there was no point in taking chances. "This room is bugged."

Paula frowned. "What should we do?"

"You? Get some rest," Carl said, flatly. He was used to being watched - there were no secrets within a barracks, although sometimes he wished there were - and it didn't bother him, but Paula was a different story. "I'll need to go out soon, just to check out the target."

"You'll need a uniform," Paula pointed out. She nodded towards the window. "What can you wear?"

Carl briefly considered Marine BDUs, then dismissed the thought. He didn't have a set with him ...and even if he had, it would be a dangerous mistake. His ID card marked him as an immigrant worker - Wolfbane was as welcoming as Avalon - but his presence would still raise questions, if he were caught in the right place.

"I'll get one," he said. There were so many people with uniforms around that mugging one of them for his clothes wouldn't be too hard. He'd just need some alcohol to give the victim a chance to explain himself when he was found. "Don't worry about me."

"I won't, then," Paula said. "Good luck."

Carl nodded, then left the room.

CHAPTER
THIRTY-ONE

If they were not willing to surrender and serve the Empire, however, their fates were quite different. The Empire's occupation forces would do whatever it took to break them, including mass round-ups and purges; at worst, they would even use brain-ripping technologies to break the leadership's minds.
- Professor Leo Caesius. *The Empire and its Prisoners of War.*

Avalon, Year 5 (PE)

"Colonel," Governor Brent Roeder said. "I was surprised when you invited us."

"It was a surprise to me too," Ed said, grimly. The door closed behind Hannalore and locked, firmly. "Please could you stay where you are?"

The Governor blinked. "Colonel?"

"Stay where you are," Ed ordered, as the security officers appeared. "I'm afraid we are dealing with a very serious matter."

The officers grabbed Hannalore and yanked her hands behind her back, cuffing them with brutal efficiency. Hannalore yelped in pain, then kicked out at one of the officers. His companions forced her to the floor and shackled her legs, then searched her roughly. The Governor turned, overcoming his shock, but Ed caught his arm before he could do something stupid. Moments later, Hannalore was hustled out of the room between three burly men.

"Colonel," the Governor said. He sounded badly shocked. "What is *happening*?"

Ed felt a pang of sympathy. The Governor wasn't a bad man, merely someone utterly unsuited to the post he'd once held. His new life as elder statesman must have seemed a dream come true. But now it had been ruined ...and it wasn't his fault.

"Come with me," Ed said. The Governor would need to be interrogated, but it could be done gently. "I'll explain in private."

Imperial Intelligence had learned a great deal about interrogating prisoners - and in determining precisely which method of interrogation was best suited for which type of prisoner. Kitty had learned, when she'd been a new trainee, that there were some people who panicked at the mere thought of physical pain and some people who were just too stubborn to talk, even when their teeth were being extracted without benefit of anaesthetic. And then there were suspects who were resistant to truth drugs, smart enough to mislead interrogators despite facing everything from torture to mind-rippers ...it was never easy to be *sure* how someone would react to interrogation.

She watched dispassionately as Hannalore was stripped naked and her body examined carefully, before she was cuffed to a chair in the middle of a darkened cell. It wouldn't be pleasant for her - it wasn't pleasant to watch either - but it would utterly shatter her sense of how the world worked. The sudden shift from mistress of all she surveyed to helpless naked prisoner would leave her uncertain and vulnerable, underlying just how much danger she was in. Kitty recalled being stripped herself, as a new recruit, and shuddered inwardly. There had been some big strong men in the training class who'd blubbered like children when the interrogators had gone to work, without any overt torture. Merely being naked and at someone's mercy, cold hands prodding sensitive parts of the body, had been enough.

Her wristcom buzzed. "We scanned her body down to the atomic level," one of the officers said. "There's nothing apart from faint traces of spliced modifications to help cope with alcohol. They weren't listed in her medical records."

"Understood," Kitty said. She hadn't taken her gaze off Hannalore, who was now pulling at her cuffs as if she couldn't quite believe she was a prisoner. "Was she drinking before she came?"

"Blood tests show nothing," the interrogator said. "Right now, she's shocked and disorientated."

"Get the lie detector online," Kitty ordered. She picked up a communications earpiece and slotted it into her ear. "And then I will go into the room."

She smiled, inwardly. The cuffs Hannalore was wearing were more than just solid metal and plastic; they concealed the sensors the computers could use to monitor Hannalore's responses. A few testing questions and a lie should be instantly noticeable, although Kitty knew better than to take that for granted. There were ways to spoof a lie detector and it was just possible Hannalore had been trained to do it.

"The detector is online and linked to the cuffs," the interrogator said. "We're clearing out now."

"Good," Kitty said. She peered through the one-way glass and nodded to herself. Hannalore was looking broken, even though she was now alone. It was time to see what she thought she was doing. "I'm going in."

The interrogation chamber felt cold as she stepped through the door. Hannalore looked up at her, but didn't seem to recognise Kitty's face. Kitty wasn't too surprised; she hadn't worn a uniform when she'd attended the party, after all. And her hair was tied up and hidden under her cap.

"I didn't do it," Hannalore said. Her eyes were wide and staring. "I didn't do it."

Kitty was tempted to ask what *it* happened to be, but there was a procedure to follow.

"I have some questions to ask you," she said, shortly. "Answer them as quickly and concisely as you can. Do not attempt to lie."

"I have rights," Hannalore said. Her voice was threatening to break. "I demand a lawyer ..."

"Answer my questions," Kitty ordered. "What is your name?"

"Hannalore," Hannalore said. "Why do you want to know?"

Kitty ignored her question. "Where were you born?"

"Earth," Hannalore said. "I ..."

Kitty kept hammering her with questions, all seemingly insignificant. There was no *point* in trying to lie, not when the answers were a matter of public record, and Hannalore would know it. Nor were the questions particularly intrusive. But they *would* allow the computers to get a baseline for the lie detector, when they started asking harder questions, the questions no one could easily verify.

And to dissuade her from trying to tell us what she thinks we want to hear, Kitty added, mentally. *Torture rarely works well because the victim will eventually start lying to us, just to get the pain to stop.*

Her earpiece buzzed. "We should have enough for a baseline now," William Ross said. He was not only a skilled interrogator himself, Kitty recalled; he was an expert in how human beings reacted to stress. "She's currently trying very hard to keep herself from panicking."

"Continue to record her reactions," Kitty subvocalised. She peered down at Hannalore for a long moment, pushing any guilt she might have felt out of her mind. Hannalore might look young, innocent and the victim, but she had betrayed the Commonwealth. "I will move on to more serious issues."

She reached down and lifted Hannalore's chin until the older woman was staring up into her eyes. "You have outfitted your mansion with bugs, in order to record what your guests say or do and forward the information to Wolfbane," she said. "Is this true?"

"No," Hannalore said. "I want a lawyer!"

"She's lying," Ross said, through the earpiece. "I got a very strong ping there, Colonel."

"I know you're lying," Kitty said, aiming to sound saddened rather than angry. "There is really no point in trying to lie to me."

"I'm *not* lying," Hannalore screamed. "Get me a goddamned lawyer!"

"Still lying," Ross said. "She isn't even sure she wants a lawyer."

Hannalore glared up at Kitty, who met her stare evenly. "I want my husband," she snapped. "He'll see to it that you're the next one in this damned chair …"

"I rather doubt it," Kitty said. She knelt down until her head was level with Hannalore's skull. "Let me be blunt.

"We have gathered enough evidence to convince a judge to authorise your detention," she said. "Now, we have interrogated you under a lie detector and …"

"The lie detector is lying," Hannalore protested.

"She's lying," Ross said.

"Shut up," Kitty subvocalised. She cleared her throat and spoke out loud. "Hannalore, we have the evidence necessary to put you in front of a court on a charge of espionage. There is a war on. Even if there wasn't, do you think the councillors you used as unwitting sources of information would stand up and defend you? They'd be screaming for the maximum penalty."

Hannalore jerked against her cuffs, but said nothing.

"Right now, your only hope is to do enough for us to earn ...a reduction in your sentence," she added. "Do that for us and we can make a deal. Refuse ...and we will have to put you before the court!"

"This is illegal," Hannalore protested. "You can't strip a prisoner naked ..."

"You're a spy and a traitor," Kitty said. She rose to her feet. "I'm going to leave you for the moment. When I come back, you can decide if you want to cooperate or not. If the former, expect to be spending considerable amounts of time answering plenty of questions. If the latter ...well, the cell will be your home for the foreseeable future."

She stepped outside and closed the door behind her firmly, then walked to the observation chamber. Leaving Hannalore alone wasn't a big risk; she was cuffed, barely able to do more than rattle her shackles, and naked. Even so, she was still under constant observation. Two pairs of eyes would be peering at her at all times.

"The baseline seems to be working perfectly," Ross said, as she entered the chamber and sat down. "There's no hint she has any form of training to resist interrogation, Colonel."

Kitty wasn't surprised. Hannalore had been a society queen - or at least she'd tried to be - rather than a soldier or an intelligence agent. It didn't keep her from being dangerous, but it did ensure she had little formal training. Wolfbane would have been happier if she had, Kitty suspected, yet how could they have trained her without sending up red flags?

"That's good to hear," Kitty said. "Although if you could keep the flippancy out of the airwaves in future ..."

"My machines don't lie," Ross protested. "Really."

"I know that," Kitty said, tartly.

She poured herself a cup of coffee and watched Hannalore closely. The woman seemed to have sagged in on herself, her breasts rising and falling in a manner that suggested she was on the verge of crying. Kitty felt a flicker of pity, but knew she couldn't allow it to dictate her actions. Hannalore had betrayed her planet and was responsible for God knew how many deaths.

Bitch, she thought coldly.

Kitty gave it nearly thirty minutes before she rose to her feet and walked back into the interrogation chamber. Hannalore's face was streaked with tears, tears she couldn't wipe away because her hands were cuffed, smearing her makeup and leaving her face looking ghastly. Kitty sighed inwardly, then peered down at her prisoner.

"I assume you've made a choice," she said. "What do you choose?"

Hannalore blinked, trying to get the tears out of her eyes. "What are you offering me if I choose to cooperate?"

Kitty frowned. Clearly, Hannalore had managed to use some of the time she'd been given to gather herself and *think*. It would have been admirable if it hadn't been so serious - and irritating. Still, she made a show of giving the question serious consideration.

"Your life," she said, finally. "You would be transported to a farming world, along with your husband, if he chooses to accompany you. It would not be an easy life, but it would beat being on a penal world or simply having your neck snapped on a gallows."

"It would be impossible," Hannalore sneered. "I can't farm to save my life."

"You could always remain in your cell," Kitty said. "I dare say we could find enough bread and water to feed you for a few years."

She shrugged. "I can throw in a small amount of money too," she offered. "You'd have the best opportunity to launch your farm I could give you."

Hannalore hesitated. "Very well," she said, after a long pause. "What do you want to know?"

Kitty stepped backwards. "You will be asked question after question after question," she said. "You will answer them as comprehensively as possible. Should you fail to answer, or be caught in a lie, the deal is off. There won't be a second chance. Do you understand me?"

"Yes," Hannalore said.

"Good," Kitty said. "Now ..."

She bombarded Hannalore with questions for nearly an hour, then stood and walked out of the chamber. Hannalore had been truthful, as far as Ross could tell, but she didn't actually *know* very much. The person who'd contacted her had never been seen again; Kitty had a suspicion he was either underground or had simply left the planet as soon as he'd completed his mission. And Gaston ...as far as she knew, Gaston was her sole contact, rather than anything else. There didn't seem to be any plans to recover contact if something happened to him.

"She's still talkative, but she's reluctant to tell you everything," Ross informed her. "I'll have an analysis on your desk tomorrow morning."

"Understood," Kitty said. She glanced at Olivier and Rupert, two more intelligence officers who specialised in looking like thugs. "Take her to her cell and search her again, then release her hands and let her sleep until I call her in the morning."

The two men nodded. By the time they had finished, Kitty knew, Hannalore wouldn't have any certainty of anything, apart from the fact her life had turned upside down. Keeping her off-balance was the only way to ensure she didn't try to outthink them ...which she would, eventually.

And we can't keep her for very long either, she thought, darkly. *Not if we want her to keep passing information to the bad guys.*

Rising to her feet, she walked out of the complex and took the elevator to the lounge. It had been cleared, at the Colonel's instructions, so he could talk to the Governor in relative privacy. When she entered, Kitty saw the Colonel sitting in front of a table and the Governor lying on the sofa, fast asleep. An opened bottle stood on the table, looking tantalisingly welcome.

"I assume you told him everything," Kitty said, as she sat down facing Colonel Stalker. "What happened?"

"He took it badly," the Colonel said. He picked up the bottle and poured Kitty a glass. "I eventually resorted to insisting he used a sleeping pill."

"I hope you checked it wasn't one that reacted badly with alcohol," Kitty said. "It wouldn't do to kill him."

The Colonel nodded. "It would just put him out for a few hours," he said. "By the time he awakes, the alcohol should have cleared his body."

Kitty nodded, then lifted her glass and took a sip. She'd never been much of a drinker, not on her salary, but she had to admit the alcohol tasted fine on her tongue. Something smoky, with a hint of fire …she cursed under her breath as she realised her mind was wandering and put the glass down before it affected her more than it already had. The Colonel, like all Marines, wouldn't be able to get more than a mild buzz from it, no matter how much he drank. It was quite possible he hadn't realised how strong it was.

Or maybe you're just too tired to think clearly, her thoughts added. *You need your bed too.*

"We did the preliminary interrogation, sir," she said. "She's guilty. None of her permanent staff are guilty, but they were both hired after confirming they didn't have the knowledge to detect or remove the bugs. The rigged privacy generators themselves came from Wolfbane, along with their control systems. She chose what was forwarded up the chain."

"Weak design," the Colonel observed. "They must have trusted her."

"They knew that beaming information out of a building in the middle of Camelot would be noticed," Kitty said. Given their inherent limitations, and the problems of operating in enemy territory, Wolfbane had done a very good job. She would have been impressed if she hadn't been so irked. Lives had been lost, others had been ruined …because one idiotic social queen hadn't been able to endure the loss of her power and position. "I suspect they weren't too happy with it."

She sighed. She needed bed; no, she needed a man, someone who could make her forget herself for a few hours. Or a woman. She wasn't picky …she considered, briefly, just trying to make a visit to a bar, then pushed the thought aside. She'd be better off with a sleeping pill herself.

Because you could never be honest with anyone, she thought, morbidly. She'd had lovers, in the years since she'd been dumped on Avalon, but none of them had lasted. It had been impossible to be honest with them.

So many spies start fucking other spies because no one else understands what they go though.

"I'll make her the offer tomorrow," she added. "We've got her talking now; tomorrow, we'll try to get her to start sending crap to them. I don't think she has much hope of being extracted by Wolfbane, not when she was such a problematic person. The Governor …I hope he does well, sir. Apparently, he wasn't involved."

"That's good to hear," the Colonel said. "But we do need to keep a sharp eye on them both. It won't be a pleasant time for either of them."

Kitty nodded, shortly. It never was. Betrayal was bad enough, but the Governor would be hurting badly. He'd supported the Commonwealth as much as he could, even after he'd lost his power. To find his wife had been undermining it …

"Poor bastard," she muttered. "I'll have him moved to a proper room?"

"Make sure you take care of him," the Colonel ordered. "He didn't deserve this."

"No," Kitty agreed. "He didn't."

CHAPTER THIRTY-TWO

Worse, perhaps, their reputations would be destroyed. The Empire's propaganda departments would work hard to turn former rebel leaders into monsters, charging them with everything taboo to the societies they'd struggled to defend. Even when such claims were not believed, they raised doubts - and doubts were the last thing a resistance organisation needed.
- Professor Leo Caesius. *The Empire and its Prisoners of War.*

Wolfbane System, Year 5 (PE)

"I think I hate you," Pete said.

"I know," Jasmine said. She'd ordered Pete and his extended family into the *Passing Water*, then secured most of them in one of the holds. It would keep them alive, but it would also keep them firmly under control. "And I am sorry."

"We could help," Pete offered, as she motioned him into the hold. "I could assist you …"

"I can't take the chance," Jasmine said. She waved him inside, then closed the hatch. "I'll see you on the far side."

She locked the hatch, then walked up to the bridge. Four CEF soldiers would remain on the ship to provide security, but the course had already been programmed into the computer. Jasmine would have preferred to leave Stewart - or even Frazier - on the ship, yet she knew it would have been far too risky. She needed Stewart in the shipyard and Frazier couldn't be trusted with the shit too close to hitting the fan. His behaviour might become dangerously unpredictable.

"I have the laser link established," Gary said, as she walked in. "But the systems are very different to the ones I used to crack."

"We'll see what happens," Jasmine said. She glanced over at Kailee, then smiled. "I will expect you to continue your exercises on the way to the phase limit and afterwards, or I will be forced to come back and haunt you."

Kailee looked paler than usual. "You might not come back?"

"There's a possibility," Jasmine said. She wondered, briefly, about Watson. One way or the other, she probably wouldn't see him again until after the war. It was just something else for the Colonel to hold against her, when - if - she returned home. "But whatever happens, I don't expect you to waste your lives. Do you understand me?"

"Yes," Gary muttered. He rubbed his arm gently. "But it hurts."

"It always does," Jasmine said, quietly. Ironically, Gary would probably be safe on Avalon, even if he stopped doing exercises. He had skills the Commonwealth needed and the sort of lawlessness that had pervaded Earth wasn't tolerated there. But being able to defend himself would only improve his confidence in the long run. "You'll be fine. Believe me."

"Yeah," Stewart agreed. "On my first day in Boot Camp, I moaned and groaned so much that my bunkmates threatened to cover me with salt."

Kailee blinked. "Why salt?"

"It's for zombies," Gary said. He shook his head. "I thought they were just a myth."

"Someone released a gas that turned a whole town into zombies once," Jasmine commented, dryly. "Not *real* zombies, in the sense they were supernatural, but it turned them against everyone who hadn't been infected. The whole place was eventually firebombed to contain the outbreak."

"Sounds like a nightmare," Gary said. "Were you there?"

Stewart snickered. Jasmine shot him a glance.

"I'm twenty-five," she said, irked. "The outbreak was over two hundred years ago. I read about it in the files."

She sighed, inwardly. No one had ever uncovered the truth behind the outbreak, as far as she knew; officially, terrorists had been blamed, but the files had wondered if a biological weapon had got loose and then been covered up. It struck her as odd that they hadn't seen more outbreaks, if it *was* a terrorist weapon, yet she could see the logic in keeping it under wraps. The Empire's willingness to just obliterate the infected had to have convinced them that the weapon was only of limited value.

Or maybe the whole town just cracked up one day, she thought. God knew she'd seen strange behaviour before, certainly from people who had been stressed beyond belief. A Civil Guard unit on Han had gone collectively mad, just after the fighting ended, and attacked a small village, looting, raping and killing the inhabitants. *The stress got to them.*

"Good luck," she said, instead. "I'll see you on the other side."

She nodded to them both, then surprised herself by giving Kailee a gentle hug. It had been *nice* to be appreciated, then asked for help; she hadn't realised just how badly she missed Mandy and her family until she'd started trying to teach Kailee. But then, Mandy had built a career of her own and Kailee …had a long way to go. Coming to think of it, Kailee was actually a year *older* than Mandy …

"Good luck," Stewart echoed. "And don't fuck up."

He followed her through the airlock and back into the mining colony, down to where the ore freighter was docked. Taking it had been easy; there were only four crewmen onboard, two of which had been teenagers learning the ropes. Jasmine had dumped them on the *Passing Water*, once she'd been sure she knew how to handle the freighter, knowing the Wolves would take their anger out on them. It wouldn't be easy for the prisoners to have to adapt to the Commonwealth, but better that than being executed, just for being unfortunate enough to lose their ship to the wrong people.

"Brigadier," Lieutenant Walter Cheney said. "The freighter is ready to depart."

Jasmine nodded. She had twenty-five men, counting herself and Stewart, to deploy against the shipyard. It didn't seem like much, but she was sure she could use the five strike teams that gave her to cause no end of havoc. Maybe she wouldn't be trying to slaughter the workers …it would still disrupt their work.

She keyed her wristcom. "Launch the *Passing Water*," she ordered, as she stepped through the airlock and into the ore freighter. The air smelt of too many men in close proximity, even though the crew had been tiny. "And then prepare to take us to the shipyard."

Stewart walked with her to the bridge, then sat down in front of the helm console. Jasmine took the other chair and glanced around the compartment, wondering how the vessel's captain managed to get anything done. The bridge was cramped, stuffed with so many jury-rigged systems that there was barely enough room for two or three crewmen. It looked as though the designers had intended the ship to be operated by children. Maybe the original owners had redesigned their bodies to make themselves smaller and lighter - a common RockRat technique - and not bothered to fix the ship when they'd sold it to its next set of owners.

"Engines online," Stewart said. "Airlock detached. Course laid in."

"Take us out," Jasmine ordered. She looked down at the display, watching as *Medusa* fell behind. The asteroid mining station looked normal ... but they'd rigged a series of charges to blow the entire complex, once the shit hit the fan. All evidence of their visit would be destroyed. "And signal for a customs ship."

"Understood," Stewart said. "There's one only an hour away."

Jasmine nodded, then worked on the laser link to *Passing Water* until the customs ship finally approached. She was identical to the previous ship, apart from carrying a missile pod underneath her hull that would give her some additional firepower. Jasmine puzzled over it for a long moment - adding extra mass would only make the ship less mobile - then reasoned that the missiles were probably intended to destroy any threat to the shipyard.

Pity we don't have any ourselves, she thought, as she eyed the ship and issued orders for the boarding party to prepare to move. *But we couldn't pack enough missiles to get through the shipyard's defences.*

"Here she comes," Stewart said. "She's ordering us to cut engines and prepare to be boarded."

"Good," Jasmine said. "You have the bridge."

She walked into the next compartment, where the airlock was already opening to admit the boarding party. They didn't look particularly suspicious, just bored, although she had to admit they looked more competent than the last one. Their leader, a grim-faced woman with a pinched expression, eyed Jasmine in some surprise. The light spacesuit she was wearing had to be unexpected.

"Captain," she said. Her accent reminded Jasmine of Stubbins. "Why are you wearing a suit?"

"There was a hull leak four days ago," Jasmine said, as the hatch cycled closed behind the team. "I ordered spacesuits to be worn at all times."

"Good," the woman said. "Papers?"

Jasmine reached for her belt, then drew her stunner and pulled the trigger, aiming at their faces in hopes of ensuring they all fell before one of them could trigger an alert. It was a risk, but one she had to embrace. They stumbled and collapsed to the deck; Jasmine checked them quickly, then signalled her boarding party. God alone knew if anyone on the ship was monitoring the away team, but if someone was the entire mission was about to fail. She motioned them into the tube as she removed the keycard from the team's commander, then followed them into the customs ship.

"Shoot to stun, if possible," she ordered quietly. "But they mustn't get a chance to scream for help."

She opened the hatch, then led the way into the customs ship. The crew clearly weren't expecting trouble; the soldiers ran through the corridors, stunning everyone they encountered, and made their way towards the bridge. Jasmine forced herself to run faster than she'd ever run in her life, then threw a stun grenade into the bridge as the hatch opened. The crew were knocked out by blue-white flashes of light.

"The ship is secure," Cheney said, through her wristcom. "I get nineteen crewmen, all stunned."

"There's four more here," Jasmine said. "Thomas, bring everyone else onto the customs ship and then reprogram the ore freighter."

"Understood," Stewart said. "We're on our way."

Jasmine rapidly secured the bridge crew, then dumped everyone but the captain out into the corridor. The customs ship was larger on the inside than she'd expected - she made a mental note to try to copy any engineering files before they left - but the bridge wasn't particularly large. Stewart arrived and took control of the helm, then steered the ship back towards the shipyard. Jasmine watched, then took an injector from her belt and pressed it against the captain's neck. Moments later, he jerked awake and glanced around blearily.

"I need the codes that will get us into the shipyard," Jasmine growled, producing a sharp knife from her belt and holding it against his throat. One advantage of using stun grenades was that the victims tended to be badly disorientated for some time, even after they recovered. However, she didn't dare rely on it for long. "Give us the codes or I'll slit your fucking throat."

The captain shuddered, then gasped out a series of numbers. Jasmine nodded to Stewart, who fed them into the navigational system. If the Wolves had copied the Empire's procedures, the first set of codes should get them into the shipyard, but not allow them to dock anywhere without special permission. It was quite possible that they would be expected to dock at the security complex, once they passed through the defences. Pete had made it clear that the custom ships often took bribes, then hurried back to share them with their superiors.

Fucking idiots, Jasmine thought. She knew precisely what Colonel Stalker would have done to someone who had accepted a bribe and it wouldn't have been pretty. On the other hand, guard duty was always boring ...unless the shit hit the fan. *They're probably so used to being away from danger that their reflexes have faded.*

"I've told them that the ore freighter has been ordered to go to the refinery facility instead," Stewart said. "She won't be coming into the shipyard."

"Good," Jasmine said. She hadn't been able to come up with a workable plan to get the ore freighter into the shipyard without raising red flags. "If we can keep them from realising there's a connection between the ore freighter and us, it might work in our favour."

She smirked in memory as the customs ship drew nearer to the outer layer of defences covering the shipyard. Once, during her first tour, her platoon had been ordered to slip through the defences surrounding an Imperial Army base and take the commanding general hostage. It had been surprisingly easy, even though the defenders had *known* the attack was on the way. There had just been too many people in the area for excellent security. One hand hadn't even known what the other hand was doing.

And so we just posed as one of them, she thought. The after-action debriefs had been hilarious, although the Imperial Army hadn't appreciated the joke. *Here we can do the same.*

"We're being pinged," Stewart snapped. "They want more codes."

Jasmine clutched the captain tighter. "Give us the codes to get through the next layer of defences," she said, pressing the knife against his throat. "Now!"

The captain gabbled out a second set of codes. Stewart keyed them in and waited, his face grim. Marines were tough, but a single missile would vaporise the customs ship as well as her entire crew. There was a long pause, then the acknowledgement arrived. Jasmine allowed herself a moment of relief as they slid through the defences, knowing they were committed now. They were deep in the heart of enemy territory.

She glanced at the timer on her wristcom - by her estimate, Watson should be preparing to move by now - and then fought down the butterflies in her chest. Why was she nervous when she'd been a Marine for over six years? The moments before combat were always the worst, yet ...she shook her head in bitter understanding. She'd been forced to risk everything on a plan that had far too many moving parts, without any solid way to keep one part of the plan interacting with the other. A single error in timing could be disastrous.

The complex seemed to grow larger as they approached, a nightmarish mixture of industrial production nodes, giant habitation modules and starship construction slips. Thousands of suited workers and dozens of shuttles drifted everywhere, while the airwaves were full of radio chatter. She took control of the sensors and peered down at a battleship, her rear end wide open and hundreds of workers swarming over her like flies on honey. It looked as though she dated back to the days when Wolfbane was a member of the Empire, but it was impossible to be sure. The Commonwealth had not only started to produce new starships, it had developed ways of speeding up the whole process. Wolfbane might have done the same.

She glanced at Stewart. "How long does it take to build a battleship?"

"The Empire could do it in ten years," Stewart said. "They *were* bloody great ships. Now ..."

He shook his head. Jasmine understood. The Empire had never *needed* to speed up the process, not like either of the two successor states. Could a battleship be built in less than a year? If a new cruiser could be turned out every two months in a Commonwealth yard, it seemed quite likely.

"I've got the armoury located," Stewart said. "It's right at the far end of the shipyard."

"Good," Jasmine said. She keyed her wristcom. "Is everyone ready?"

She waited long enough for everyone to check in, then smiled to herself.

"Get ready to jump," she ordered. "Thomas?"

"Everything is programmed in," Stewart said. "The crew?"

Jasmine winced, then placed the captain on the deck. "I'm sorry," she said, as she injected him with a sedative. His crew would have no time to wake up before the end came. "But I don't have a choice any longer."

She glanced at the body, then hastened towards the airlock. If the timing was right, they would be away from the customs ship before it declared an emergency, then exploded. There would be no trace left of their presence, while - if the Empire's policies were any guide - there would be so much confusion that they would have no difficulty slipping into one of the installations. Like the military base she'd infiltrated on Han, no one could hope to know *everyone* assigned to the shipyard.

"Alright, everyone," she said, as she secured her helmet. "Let's go."

"Opening the airlock now," Stewart said. The team of suited soldiers followed him, with Jasmine waiting to bring up the rear. "Ready to move."

Jasmine nodded, then took a glance at the handful of stunned figures in sight. They would die, die without ever knowing what had hit them ... she had no choice, but it didn't make it any easier.

I'm getting too old for this shit, she thought, as she walked through the airlock and out onto the hull. Her suit's HUD was already tracking dozens of suited workers as they made their way over the complex. *I'm really getting too old for it.*

She shook her head, cursing herself. What she needed was a long holiday, but she knew she was too stubborn to get one. The Colonel would practically have to order her to go on vacation ...and even then, she was damned if she would be *relaxing*. There were quite a few extreme sports she wanted to try.

But would they be anything like as extreme as being a Marine? She asked herself dryly. *A parachute drop from low-level or plunging from high orbit down to a planetary surface ...?*

"Go," Stewart ordered.

Jasmine braced herself and jumped, once again, into the inky darkness of space.

CHAPTER
THIRTY-THREE

Unsurprisingly, this provoked hatred and resentment on a towering scale. The insurgencies might have been shattered, but the hatreds that fuelled them remained - and, if anything, were sharpened by watching helplessly as the Empire subverted and eventually destroyed the whole pre-war order.
- Professor Leo Caesius. *The Empire and its Prisoners of War.*

Wolfbane City, Wolfbane, Year 5 (PE)

Carl Watson hadn't been sure if he should be impressed by Wolfbane City or not. On one hand, it was clearly prosperous; on the other, it lacked the charm and elegance of Camelot, to say nothing of the thriving economic scene. Avalon had countless small businesses opening and closing, all of the time, while all of the businesses he saw on Wolfbane were subsidies of bigger corporations. Indeed, he had a feeling that some of the interplanetary corporations that had played such a vast role in the fall of the Empire were still open for business on Wolfbane.

Getting around hadn't been too difficult either, once he'd mugged a couple of men for their uniforms. The security forces seemed more concerned with potential riots and rioters than spies; indeed, the more he looked around, the more he became aware of a vast sullen underclass that only needed a spark to explode into fire. If there had been more time, he would have made contact with the underground and recruited their assistance, but time had not been on his side. He walked around the city, making a mental note of everything from the location of the Governor's Mansion to a handful of military and security bases within the city, then started the walk back to the hotel. Night was starting to fall - a glance at his watch told him that H-Hour was only three hours away - and hundreds of workers were starting to make their way home.

They didn't look happy, Carl thought, as he blended in with them. Most of them wore uniforms - the entire planet seemed to have a mania for uniforms - and almost all looked downtrodden. He couldn't help being reminded of Gary, who had flinched every time Carl had even looked at him; they were too battered down to be able to stand up for themselves in the future. A regular job had been one of his worst nightmares, before he'd decided to join the Marines, and looking at the workers was enough to tell him why. The sullen mass, so quiet even as it made its way home, lacked any spark of humanity.

They're a mass, he thought, as he cast his eye over a trio of young teenagers who seemed to be starting their first jobs. The boy would have been handsome, if his hair hadn't been cut close to his scalp, while both of the girls wore shapeless uniforms that obscured the curves of their bodies. Their hair, too, was cut into a regulation bowl cut, while their faces had been scrubbed clean of make-up. *They're a mass of zombies, without individuality of their own.*

It wasn't a pleasant thought. Boot Camp was all about breaking down the recruits and then building them up again, in the shape of Marines. By the time the second or third week was done, the recruits - having shed half of their number - looked practically identical, wearing the same outfits and with the same haircuts. But he'd agreed to go to Boot Camp willingly, knowing it would be hell. He didn't think that any of the Wolves before him had made any such agreement. Their planet was almost as closely regulated as Earth.

Maybe more so, Carl thought, as he reached the hotel and stepped inside. *Earth's government never had the power to police the CityBlocks as much as it wanted, no matter how many laws and regulations it made. Here …the government might be able to police the entire world.*

Stubbins - and Paula - had called Governor Brown a corporate rat. Carl hadn't understood, until now, just what that *meant*. Governor Brown had built the ideal corporate state, where everyone had a role in society and God help them if they stepped away from it. Even the underclass had its role to play, both as a warning of how far someone could fall and as a threat, to justify endless police measures. Maybe they were even allowed to commit a certain number of crimes a year, just to keep the population scared. A scared population would cling to their government and its promise of protection.

He narrowed his eyes in disgust as he opened the door to the hotel room ...and stopped, dead. There was no sign of Paula. Alarm bells ringing in his mind, he slipped forward and checked every last inch of the suite. She wasn't in the bed, hiding under it or in the shower, washing herself clean. The whole suite was empty ...he slipped a hand into his bag, checking that the weapons and tools were still there, then took one final look around the room. She'd known not to leave, nor were there any signs of a struggle. It was all too easy to realise she'd left of her own free will.

Get out, you idiot, his thoughts snapped at him.

Carl scooped up his bag, slung it over his shoulder and headed for the door, out onto the corridor. It was as silent as the grave, illuminated only by a flickering light hanging from the white ceiling. He paused, listening, then hurried down to the staff staircase. It was locked, but a quick fiddle with a multitool opened it up, allowing him to hurry down to the rear exit and out into the back alley. It smelled of rotting food and spilled drink, but there was no sign of any guards or soldiers waiting in ambush. Checking that his pistol was still within easy reach, Carl set off, moving through a disorienting stream of dark alleys until he reached a main road. It was darker now, but a stream of cars were still making their way out of the city.

Think, he told himself, sharply. *What happened?*

He didn't want to admit it, but he had a pretty shrewd idea. Paula hadn't been taken, she'd left of her own free will ...and she intended to betray them. She'd volunteered for the mission simply because it would give her a chance to escape and make contact with the enemy. Five years in a POW camp with Stubbins was enough to drive anyone to desperation ...and she might well have believed that she would be paid well for her services. Which she would, Carl was sure. Scum like Governor Brown understood the value of rewarding traitors.

Common sense told him that the mission was blown. Paula didn't know everything Jasmine had planned - *Carl* didn't know everything Jasmine had planned - but she did know *his* intended target. Did she know about the shipyard? If she did, Governor Brown would be moved to an underground bunker, where he would be safe, while the shipyard would be secured against all threats. Indeed, if she had vanished twenty minutes after Carl had gone out onto the streets, she'd had ample time to get to someone in power and make a deal. The mission was blown.

And yet, he didn't dare *not* carry out the mission. Jasmine needed the diversion ...and it had to be big, big enough to keep the Wolves firmly fixed on him. Up in space, Jasmine would already be putting *her* part of the plan into operation, while he had no way to warn her to stop and flee the system. Paula's betrayal had come at the worst possible moment.

Damn you, he thought. He briefly entertained the thought of trying to track her down, then dismissed it as impossible. It would require an improbable amount of luck to find her again, not with his limited knowledge of the city. And that meant the mission had just become suicidal. *Damn you to hell.*

Gritting his teeth, he forced himself to slow down. He had a plan, after all, and he could still use it. Paula didn't know the precise details, after all, just the target. And if he gave up all hope of making it out, he could go nuts. Governor Brown wouldn't know what had hit him.

"Admiral?"

Rani looked up from her desk. Somehow, no matter what she did, there was never a shortage of paperwork that required her personal attention. She had a feeling that it was yet another string Governor Brown used to keep his people in order, although she had enough experience of dealing with bureaucracy to know that the more paperwork was involved, the less efficiency. But then, how would a bureaucrat - or a corporate rat - measure efficiency in the first place?

"Yes," she said, tartly. "What is it?"

Sonja, her current aide, looked nervous. Rani had picked her at random and poked away at her enough to be fairly sure she was nothing more than what she seemed, a young officer intent on using her current posting as a way to boost her promotion prospects. She would really need combat experience to get much further, but that could be arranged.

And she won't have to sleep with anyone to be promoted, Rani added, in the privacy of her own mind. Sonja was pretty, too pretty. If she'd joined up ten years ago, she would have been scooped up by some commanding officer in the Imperial Navy and taken to bed. *Just earn her promotions the hard way instead.*

"Admiral, there's someone at the door who demands to see you," Sonja said. "She claims to be Paula Bartholomew."

Rani shrugged. "The name means nothing to me," she said. "Who is she?"

Sonja looked hesitant. "I checked her against the files," she said. She *meant* the guards had checked the new arrival against the files. "The DNA patterns match. She really is Paula Bartholomew."

"And who," Rani demanded, "is Paula Bartholomew?"

"She was the aide to General Stubbins, who was exiled five years ago," Sonja said. "The files say she was sent to a prison camp and …and there isn't anything else. But she says she needs to talk to you urgently."

Rani frowned. Normally, she would have told the newcomer to go away …but her instincts were telling her this was important.

"Have her scanned by the guards, then brought in here," she ordered. "And then leave us alone."

She looked back at her paperwork as Sonja hurried out the room, then tapped her terminal and called up the file. Twenty minutes later, she returned with two guards and a thin woman with long brown hair. Rani studied her carefully, thinking hard. Paula didn't look like a military officer, but there was a stubborn determination in her that was almost impressive. And there was the simple fact that she'd escaped from a POW camp …

If that's true, Rani thought, slowly. *The files might be wrong and she was simply never sent there in the first place. Or someone could have written a lie into the files. It wouldn't be the first time.*

"You're Paula Bartholomew," Rani said, shortly. There *were* ways to resequence a person's DNA to fool the readers, but they were long and painful and she honestly couldn't imagine why someone would want to pretend to be a mere aide. It would make more sense to have someone pretend to be *her*. "How did you get here and *why* are you here?"

"There's a threat to the system," Paula said. "I came to bring warning."

Rani sighed, inwardly. "And what do you want in exchange for the warning?"

"Money and security," Paula said. "I want a guarantee of both or there will be no warning."

"As clichéd as it sounds," Rani said, "we *do* have ways to make you talk."

"I've been treated," Paula countered. "You wouldn't be able to drug me, or rape my mind, or even hurt me until I talk. And you really don't have the time to waste, if you want to try."

Rani met Paula's eyes and saw nothing but grim determination. If she'd been a general's aide, chances were she *had* been given treatment, if only to ensure she couldn't be forced to divulge information without his permission. Lie detectors would probably still work, yet she would have to be forced to talk in the first place. The mere act of trying to break her would probably kill her, depending on precisely what had been done to her.

"Very well," she said, after a moment's contemplation. "You tell us what you know. If it pans out, you will get both money and security."

"I want the Governor's word on that," Paula said.

"Then you will be disappointed," Rani said. "The Governor is currently hosting a party for his economic movers and shakers. I will not be calling him here just to grant you his word, not when I have no idea of just what you might be offering. Accept *my* word or you can spend the rest of the night in the cells and talk to the Governor tomorrow."

Paula glowered at her. "Very well," she said, finally. "I went to Meridian with General Stubbins, after Governor Brown outmanoeuvred him. Five years of sitting in a steaming hot jungle …we were joined, eventually, by a number of prisoners. Three of them in particular led a breakout. They managed to take a shuttle, then the orbital station and finally a starship."

Rani's eyes narrowed. Meridian. She might have been denied permission to simply execute some of the POWs out of hand, particularly the bitch she knew from Corinthian, but she'd kept an eye on their final disposition. Meridian, a stage-one colony, should have made an acceptable dumping ground. The prisoners might be able to flee the POW camps, yet they wouldn't be able to escape the planet.

Except it seems that some have, she thought, as Paula went on and on. Everything made a horrific kind of sense. *And they came here.*

"So they're planning to assassinate the Governor," she said, when Paula had finished. She didn't see how one man *could* assassinate the Governor, but she knew better than to take anything for granted. A relative handful of men had taken Corinthian from her. "And hopefully trigger off a civil war."

"Yes, Admiral," Paula said. "And they're going to move tonight."

Rani barely heard her. She was too busy considering all the possibilities. If she informed Governor Brown of the plot, he would be grateful …but he wouldn't give her any more power or respect. The war would continue to stalemate until the Commonwealth actually *did* find a viable silver bullet. On the other hand, if she allowed the plot to go ahead …the Governor's spies wouldn't pick up anything, because it wasn't *her* plot, but she might just be able to take advantage of it. A dead governor would leave the reins of power lying on the ground, waiting for someone to pick them up.

"I see," she said, smoothly. It would take some doing to make sure that only *her* people knew about Paula, at least until the attack began, but it could be done. "I will inform the Governor of the threat at once. You will be held here until he has been informed and made safe."

"Thank you," Paula said.

Rani met her eyes. "Why did you come here?"

"Everyone else I knew disliked General Stubbins," Paula admitted. "They would have grabbed me as an escaped prisoner rather than trying to listen to me. You didn't have any history with him."

"I suppose not," Rani said. She kept the smile off her face with the ease of long practice. Paula hadn't told anyone else, then. Brilliant. "The Governor will choose to reward you, I am sure. You will never need to whore for a fat overweight bastard again."

Paula looked relieved. Rani called for her guards, both of whom she thought were loyal to her. "Take Paula to a holding cell and make sure she's comfortable," she ordered. There was no point in trying to panic Paula before it was too late. Once the pieces had stopped flying around, she would know how to thank the turncoat properly. "I'll handle the matter personally."

She waited until they were gone, then started sending a message to the handful of people she trusted. They would hold themselves in readiness, preparing to jump if something happened, but they would do nothing without her signal. If Paula was wrong, or if the attack was called off, the Governor would have no reason to suspect her loyalty.

And if the Governor dies, she thought, *an opportunity opens up before me.*

The garage was precisely where Carl had spotted it on his earlier circuit of the city. Then, it had been open, servicing a number of aircars; now, it was closed, protected only by a simple alarm circuit. Carl cracked it with ease - it was less complex than some of the systems he'd worked on during training - and slipped into the building. Twelve aircars, all in working order, gleamed in the semi-darkness.

He slipped through the building, checking to make sure he was alone. Two men slept in the rear room, too poor to afford an apartment or simply reluctant to leave their property alone overnight. Carl knocked them both on the head before they could wake, then tied their hands and feet with duct tape. They'd probably get some of the blame, when the Wolves worked out what had happened, but there was nothing he could do about it. He checked the rest of the complex, then returned to the garage. The aircars were waiting for him ...

"Well," he muttered to himself, as he removed his multitool from his belt. It had been far too long since he'd done any basic maintenance on aircars, let alone more complex programming, but he still remembered the fundamentals. "Time to get to work."

CHAPTER THIRTY-FOUR

Nor were they inclined to take prisoners themselves. The Empire's official position on negotiations with terrorists/insurgents/freedom fighters was to formally ban them from taking place. Accordingly, any imperial serviceman who fell into enemy hands could expect very rough treatment indeed, both through a natural desire for revenge and an awareness that the serviceman was useless as a bargaining chip.
- Professor Leo Caesius. *The Empire and its Prisoners of War.*

Wolfbane System, Year 5 (PE)

"Sir, I'm picking up an emergency alert!"

Commander Drew Malochy swore, then rose to his feet. Being Traffic Controller for the shipyard was supposed to be a boost to his career, but it was starting to look like a major headache. In theory, he was meant to track and authorise every starship, spacecraft and shuttle flying through the shipyard; in practice, he'd been told to raise as few barriers as possible. The workers didn't appreciate having to file flight plans for every single deployment and his superiors had made it clear.

"Show me," he snapped, as he glowered down at the young ensign. "What's happening?"

"Customs Boat #42 has just transmitted an emergency alert," the ensign said. She looked uncomfortable under his scrutiny, but pressed ahead anyway. "She's suffering a major core overload."

Drew glanced at the display, then cursed under his breath. The flashing red icon was far too close to a major industrial node for him to be happy, even if lives hadn't been at stake. It was all the fault of his superiors …he'd *wanted* to set up flight paths through the shipyard, with strict penalties for anyone who defied them.

"Tell her to get away from the platform," he ordered. A core overload almost certainly meant an imminent explosion, unless the crew managed to dampen the reaction in time. In theory, the design prevented a runaway core, but bitter experience had taught engineers that there were limits to what they could do to their designs without crippling them. "Get the emergency teams scrambled and …"

"Too late," the ensign said. The red icon winked once and vanished, replaced with an expanding sphere representing a hail of debris. "She's gone."

"Send an emergency alert to everyone in the vicinity," Drew snapped. There would be hard questions for everyone, including him, once the chaos had died down to a dull roar. And if he didn't handle the crisis well, his career would be redirected to an asteroid-mining station in the middle of nowhere. "I want them all inside, now."

"Aye, sir," the ensign said. "The emergency teams are still getting ready to move."

"General signal to all shuttles and worker bees," Drew said. "They are to move into position to intercept any pieces of debris that might threaten the facilities. If they have to overload their systems to do it, that's fine. I authorise the risks."

He stalked back to his command chair, cursing the commander of the customs boat under his breath. His record wasn't perfect, but it had been a damn sight better before the fool had brought his ship into the shipyard. No matter what happened, Drew's career had just taken a kick in the pants. All he could do was hope that his recovery was good enough to save him from a lifetime trapped in an asteroid mine.

"And send a signal to Wolfbane," he added. "Inform them of the crisis and request they prepare emergency support, if necessary."

"Aye, sir," the ensign said.

Drew puzzled it over as the emergency craft were *finally* scrambled from their hanger bays and started to make their way towards the scene. A core overload should have been noticeable from the start, even if the captain was a complete incompetent. Unless …he knew enough about design work to know that a great many corners had been cut when the patrol boats had been designed, just to ensure several hundred of them could be put together as quickly as possible. Maybe a warning system had failed, allowing the trouble to build up until it was impossible to contain. Or perhaps the captain had hoped to pass the buck to someone else and ignored it instead of getting help. Or …

He sighed. One way or another, thirty good men were dead, chunks of debris were spinning through the most sensitive complex this side of Wolfbane itself and his career was in the toilet, just waiting for some asshole to flush.

Shaking his head, he forced himself to wait. He'd learn what had happened soon enough.

Jasmine allowed herself a moment of amusement as her team blended with hundreds of other men in spacesuits as they raced towards the emergency shelters, mounted on the side of the giant industrial node. There were so many teams, each one with its own spacesuit markings, that her team just faded into the crowd. Her HUD kept flashing up emergency alerts - she was amused to note that the procedures hadn't changed from the days of the Empire - but there didn't seem to be any security alerts. It seemed, very much so, as though no one suspected that the core overload had been deliberate.

She gathered her team at one side of the shelter and waited, patiently, for the all-clear. It hadn't been certain just how long they would have to wait, but the sheer tempo of the industrial system had convinced her they wouldn't have to wait very long. The workers cowering in the shelters wouldn't be able to do any actual *work* if they were staying in the section. She pushed the thought aside and waited, eavesdropping on a handful of public communications channels. Most of the remarks seemed to be sarcastic observations on the need to do basic maintenance.

"The debris has been handled," a voice said, finally. "You may return to work."

Jasmine nodded, then led her team towards the nearest access hatch. They'd handled the debris quicker than she'd expected, but she had been careful to ensure that the ship would shatter into a cloud of fragments, rather than a handful of pieces of junk. It wasn't certain - nothing was *certain* - but she was fairly sure they wouldn't have been able to track the spacesuits, without more sensors than they seemed to have. The debris would just make it harder for them if she was wrong.

Stewart opened the hatch, then dropped inside; Jasmine followed him, into a small observation tube. If she was right, if Wolfbane had stuck with the Empire's designs, there should be an access port further down the corridor. The remainder of the group brought up the rear as they advanced, trying to look like a team of workers. Thankfully, most workers would still be wearing their emergency suits until it was *definitely* clear. They passed two other groups of workers, one wearing complete spacesuits, as they slipped into the access port. A small terminal sat there, with a single operative. Stewart knocked her out before she could even turn and see the men filing into her compartment.

"Get the hacker pack set up," she ordered. The Trade Federation representatives had told her it should crack most non-military computers, but there was no way to know what advancements Wolfbane had made. "See what we can get out of the computers."

Stewart nodded, slotted the hacker pack into the computer and then went to work. Jasmine waited, forcing herself to remain calm, until he looked up. "I can't get much out of the system," he said, "but the armoury is right where we thought it was. It shouldn't be hard to upload a manifest into the system."

Jasmine looked at him. "Do it," she ordered. She frowned as the diagram popped up in front of them. It looked as though it was better defended than she'd expected. "Teams One, Two and Three will go there. Teams Four and Five will carry out their planned orders."

She waited for Stewart to finish, then led the way out of the compartment. There was a shuttlebay just down the bottom of the compartment, crammed with worker bees. Stealing them would be easy, she was sure. And then ...

Get into the armoury, she thought. *And then see how much damage we can do.*

"They're not part of the main computer network," Stewart reported, as they inspected the worker bees. "But I can link them into the laser beam."

Jasmine smiled. "See what Gary can make of them," she ordered. She led Team One into one of the worker bees, then started the engines. "And hope the shit doesn't hit the fan."

"You know, you can sit down and wait," Lieutenant Julian Chan pointed out. "You won't be at risk, whatever happens."

Gary shook his head. He'd been pacing up and down the freighter's bridge until he'd practically worn lines in the deck plating, simply because he'd been unable to force himself to wait calmly. Back on Earth, he would have eaten something to distract himself from the butterflies in his stomach, but here he didn't dare. Even the thought of kissing Kailee was *too* distracting. All he could do was wait and hope he didn't fuck up when the time came.

There was a beep from his console. "The link is up and running," he said, practically throwing himself into the chair. "And I have a message."

He blinked as he read it, quickly. Jasmine wanted him to try to hack the deeper levels of the shipyard's network, but she also wanted him to prepare to take control of the worker bees and direct them at enemy targets. Gary flinched - how was he supposed to handle two separate tasks at once - and then got to work. The worker bees themselves were easy to subvert; they were designed to be operated remotely, if necessary, and there was almost no protection on their computers at all. Indeed, the only real problem was handling so many at once.

But it was the computer network that posed the real problem. Gary had hacked networks before, on Earth, but he'd never explored a military-grade system. He'd always been too afraid of meeting people even more violent than Barry or Moe. Now, he had no choice, but to try to break the system. Some of his hacking tools worked; others, it seemed, were next to useless. The system was actively designed to make hacking almost impossible.

"I can't get in without a password," he said, finally. In his experience, there was always one idiot who used 'PASSWORD' as his password, but linking the idiot to his ID within the system would be the real pain. A school computer would allow unlimited attempts to enter a password - he smirked at how easy it had been to crack some of the systems - yet some of the gaming companies had been smart enough to break the link after three failed tries. "And they would probably notice if I tried to guess."

Kailee frowned. "How does that work?"

"They have a locked compartment inside their house," Gary admitted. "I need to know where it is to find it and I need the key to get inside. Right now, I can see the firewall blocking access, but I need both an ID and a password to get in."

He cursed under his breath. There were ways to force entry, but he had a feeling they would merely trigger alerts. The system he was touching, however lightly, felt more alert than anything he'd previously encountered. One wrong move would be disastrous.

A message blinked up in front of him. "Keep in touch with the bees, but do nothing else," Jasmine sent. "Deploy them when the time comes."

"We wait," Gary said. "Again."

Jasmine held her breath as they slipped closer to the armoury, a single brooding structure near the centre of the shipyard. Weapons pods surrounded it, ready for installation; it didn't take much imagination to see them pouring fire towards Commonwealth targets. She frowned inwardly as she saw the missiles themselves - it always astonished her just how large they actually were - then pushed the thought aside. The warheads on the tips were the truly important points.

"Docking in five minutes," Stewart said. "They've accepted our manifest - our manifesto."

"A weak joke," Jasmine said, dryly. "But liveable."

She smiled, thinly. They were inside the security wall now; anyone who saw their manifest would assume that someone else had already cleared them to enter the shipyard. But there were places on military bases, even Castle Rock, where access was denied without a proper ID card and clearance from one's superiors. Surely, the armoury would be one of those places.

"They seem to have cleared the wreckage of the boat nicely," Stewart commented. "You wouldn't know that *anything* had happened over there."

"No," Jasmine agreed. She glanced at her watch. Night-time on Wolfbane …Watson, assuming that everything had gone to plan, would be moving into position now. She needed to be in place on the armoury before it was too late. Diversion or no diversion, she was sure alert levels would be raised all over the system once the shit hit the fan. "Check the link with Gary, then take us in."

"Link solid," Stewart said. There was a dull thud as the worker bee connected to the armoury's airlock. "We're in."

Jasmine nodded and rose to her feet as the airlock hissed open. She stepped through the hatch, followed by Stewart, as the inner airlock opened too. Inside, a bemused-looking functionary was staring at his datapad, clearly wondering where the newcomers had actually come from. Clearly, they might have had a valid flight manifest, but not any actual work authorisation codes.

"We're here to check the records," Jasmine said, as she opened her helmet. "I need access to your terminals."

The functionary blinked. "I don't have a record of you in the files," he said. "I …"

He broke off as Jasmine grabbed him by the throat. The spacesuit had no enhancements to give her the strength of ten men, but it felt thoroughly unpleasant. Jasmine smelled urine as she hefted him up in the air, then held him in front of her face.

"I need your ID card and your passwords," she said, sharply. "Now!"

The man stared at her. "I …"

Jasmine nodded to Stewart, who produced a sharp knife from his suit. "Cut him," she ordered. "Make it painful …"

"My card is in my pocket," the man whimpered. "My code is C-O-C-K-S-S-U-C-K-S!"

"Really?" Jasmine asked, doubtfully. "*That's* your access code?"

"Yes," the man said, desperately. "I wanted something no one would ever guess!"

"I dare say you succeeded," Jasmine said. The advice she'd been given in the Marine Corps had been to use random letters and numbers, but she'd also been told never to rely on any system that was connected to the planetary datanet. Gary would hardly be the first young man to hack for fun and games; hell, he probably wasn't even in the top 100. "If this doesn't work, we will hurt you."

She keyed the code into the hacker pack, then turned it over to Gary. "Now, some more questions," she said. "How many people are on this platform?"

"The code works," Gary said, as he dipped into the platform's computer. The laser link wasn't perfect, but better than some of the systems he'd seen on Earth. "I can't get into all of the sections ...hang on."

He smirked as he went to work. Most systems had an inherent flaw, one they never quite seemed to be able to lose. They assumed that someone with access, even limited access, *had* at least *some* right to access the entire system, simply because they were already on the interior of the firewall. It was actually easier to start with a low-ranking peon's code and then work one's way up to the most secure parts of the network.

"Ok," he said. "I've downloaded most of the codes, but I can't find any actual trigger codes."

"Shit," Jasmine said. "They're not stored on the network?"

"Not as far as I can tell," Gary said. "You can launch the missiles, but you can't arm them."

"Understood," Jasmine said.

She cursed under her breath. She'd been expecting something to go wrong, but she hadn't quite expected *this*. In hindsight, perhaps she *should* have expected it; the missiles could be launched, in the event of a disaster, but not actually armed. A nuke that slammed into something without being armed wouldn't make anything like as big a bang.

"We'll target the missiles on the facilities," she said, as her people spread through the installation. "Even unarmed, they will do a great deal of damage."

She led the way into the command core and stunned everyone, including the CO. It was unlikely his codes would be any help. Instead, she sat down in front of the console and accessed the emergency launch system. For once, the Empire's insistence on standardising everything would actually come in handy. The missile pods waiting outside, prepped for being installed into starships, were identical to the ones that could be bolted to hulls or left in orbit for additional firepower. And they could flush their missiles if necessary.

"The other teams are in place," Stewart said. "And Gary has the worker bees ready to go."

Jasmine took a breath, then programmed in the firing sequence. The missiles refused to lock on to anything without the arming codes, so she merely pointed them on courses that would intersect their targets. If nothing else, the combination of immobile targets and imprecise targeting would make it harder for any countermeasures to do their work. And then she hesitated ...

"Carl should be in place," she said. She glanced at her wristcom, then frowned. "But there's no way to know."

"I think they're supposed to check in every hour," Stewart countered. "The last thing we want is a security alert here, now ..."

Jasmine nodded, then smiled in relief as an alert popped up on front of her. "He's done it," she said. She tapped a switch, then smirked. "Firing missiles ...now!"

CHAPTER
THIRTY-FIVE

The Empire didn't care. The people making the decisions, the Grand Senate, were completely disconnected from the situation on the ground. They simply didn't care about either the risk to their servants - or the misery they were inflicting on countless occupied worlds.
- Professor Leo Caesius. *The Empire and its Prisoners of War.*

Wolfbane City, Wolfbane, Year 5 (PE)
Private Jonathan Williams couldn't help feeling uncomfortable as he stood at his post, just outside the Governor's Mansion. It was a cold night and he was grimly aware that it wouldn't be over for hours. He was stuck outside, watching the deserted streets, while his superiors partied inside the mansion, enjoying themselves while he froze halfway to death. It wasn't something he wanted to think about, but he had no choice. He could hear the tinkling of the music from his guardpost on the edge of the complex, making it hard to keep his ears open for problems. It was a persistent distraction.

"Betty should be free when we get off this weekend," Private Hobbes offered. "We can go have some fun with her after this."

Jonathan shook his head. The only advantage to being on the Governor's personal security detail was a brothel, right next to the barracks, and he wasn't sure it made up for the difficulties of the job. Hundreds of high-ranking men and women - and the ass-kissers attached to their bodies who could only be removed through surgical intervention - passed him every day, each and every one of them grumbling over the inconvenience of having to be scanned, searched and then cleared against the master list of permitted guests. It was his duty to check them before they entered, yet he knew a single word from one of them could end his career. The guards wore no nametags merely to make identification difficult, if not impossible. It was the only way to do their job.

"I prefer Sharon myself," he said. "She's kinder."

He ignored Hobbes's rude sound of disbelief. Sharon might be fatter than Betty, but she was far more welcoming - or at least better at faking it. Betty might be hot enough to pass for a porn star, yet it was clear she hated men with a white-hot passion. Jonathan had no idea why a woman who hated men would work in a brothel, but it was hard to blame her for her feelings. None of the troops were very considerate lovers. Besides, there was always a shorter line outside Sharon's door.

"I think you're mad," Hobbes said. "I ..."

He broke off as a fancy car came into view, gleaming black under the streetlights as it slowed to a halt outside the guardpost. The windows were tinted, but he had the impression there was only one man in the car; a moment later, the door opened, revealing a stocky man wearing a very ill-fitting suit. He must be important, Jonathan reasoned, as the man stumbled towards him. The mixture of awful dressing and drinking while driving - he could smell whiskey splashed on the man's suit - meant a very important person indeed. No one else would *dare* show up to the Governor's party in such a state.

Must be one of his senior officers, he thought, as he walked closer. *Someone important enough not to give a damn.*

"I need your ID," he said. "And your name ..."

"Don't have it," the man slurred. He sounded drunk enough to wind up on the ground any second, probably wondering just what had hit him. It was a minor miracle he'd managed to drive without crashing or hitting anyone, although the onboard computer had probably handled most of the driving for him. "Need to go see the Governor ..."

Jonathan winced. A man who could not be allowed admittance, but also a man important enough to have both of them sent to an asteroid mining station or a garrison on a rebellious world ...if they weren't summarily exiled to a penal colony. The man's suit alone cost more than

Jonathan could expect to make in his entire career, yet he could not allow him to pass through the guardpost. He was damned whatever he did ...

There was a whine cutting through the air. Jonathan looked up, just in time to see an aircar flashing overhead and heading right towards the mansion. A brilliant flash of light blasted the aircar out of the air as the plasma cannons engaged automatically, then swung around, searching for new targets, as a whole *line* of aircars appeared out of nowhere. One by one, they died, sending pieces of white-hot-metal flying everywhere. Jonathan cursed, then grabbed the newcomer and dragged him bodily into the guardhouse. With a little bit of luck, he could spin it into a heroic rescue that would save both of their careers. Another aircar exploded, almost directly overhead, as they plunged into the armoured post. He heard the sound of debris bouncing off the roof as he closed the door, firmly.

"The complex is being sealed," Hobbes said. "Our friend will have to stay with us ..."

The newcomer moved like greased lightning. Hobbes bent over, then collapsed to the floor, hitting the ground like a sack of potatoes. Jonathan had barely a second to realise that the newcomer had killed his friend before a second fist slammed right into his throat. There was a moment of absolute pain, then nothing at all.

Carl Watson allowed himself a moment of pleasure as the two guards died, then pushed it aside as he stripped the first man's uniform and pulled it over the expensive suit he'd stolen from a nearby store. It had served its purpose, getting him close enough to the guards to take them all out when the diversion began; now, he needed another disguise to get close to the Governor. The aircars would, he suspected, provide enough inducement to keep the Governor inside, protected by the emplaced defences. They wouldn't be expecting a single man on the ground to be the real threat. Besides, even if they did, the helmet he'd stolen would make it impossible for them to separate him from the remainder of the soldiers.

Scooping up the weapons and ID cards, he ran through the rear door and across to the mansion. The plasma cannons were still firing, bolts of brilliant white fire burning through the darkness, although he wasn't sure what they thought they were engaging. He'd only launched nineteen aircars, after all, and by his count they'd all been destroyed. Their computers wouldn't have been able to handle the evasive manoeuvres required to keep them intact long enough to slam into the mansion.

Not that it would have worked in any case, he thought, as he reached the rear door. *The entire building is laced with hullmetal. A nuke couldn't have done more than wreck the centre of the city.*

He tapped on the door once, hoping someone would be fool enough to open it. It clicked open seconds later, revealing a young girl in a classical maid's outfit. Behind her, there were a handful of others, male and female, all wearing extremely revealing clothes. Carl concealed his amusement with an effort, then nodded to them and walked into the mansion itself. The lower floors didn't look particularly luxurious, but that wasn't too much of a surprise. It was quite possible the Governor and his guests never ventured into the servants quarters.

Can't waste good money on keeping servants in luxury, he thought, as he raced up the stairwell and through a door into a long corridor. *They'd never appreciate the effort.*

"Attention," a voice said, from overhead. "This is a security alert. All guests are advised to remain inside, well away from the windows. I say again, all guests are advised to remain inside, well away from the windows."

Carl smirked - *they must not have found the bodies yet* - and then ran onwards. There was no point in trying to deduce how long it would take them to realise that one of the guardposts wasn't answering. A Marine CO would have called them all at once, then dispatched the QRF to investigate if there was no reply from one or more of the guards. But who knew how Wolfbane would deal with an intruder? They might have drilled endlessly, like the Marines, or they might have allowed themselves to go slack. There was no way to know until it was far too late.

"I say, old chap," a voice called. Carl slowed, then turned to see a middle-aged man carrying a bottle of blood-coloured liquid in one hand. "Do you know where the emergency shelters are?"

"Out the door and on the lawn," Carl said. He had no particular dislike for the man - and he had no idea who he was - but he could serve as a diversion. Maybe he'd wind up being shot by his own people. "Go now."

He ran on, leaving the man spluttering behind him. A large pair of doors loomed in front of him, leading - if the diagrams he'd seen were accurate - to the master ballroom. He pulled a HE grenade from his belt, then opened the doors. Inside, a number of men and women clustered together, drinking fancy wine and chatting about nothing in particular. None of them seemed to care that a security alert had been sounded, although he did have to admit they would have been safe in the inner room, if he hadn't been running through the corridors.

Unhooking the pin from the grenade, he hurled it into the room and slammed the doors closed, counting to three under his breath. The doors shook violently, but held; he pulled them open again to reveal a scene from hell. Dead and wounded bodies lay everywhere, some clearly well beyond salvation, others who might survive, if they got medical treatment before it was too late. Carl felt an odd flicker of guilt - the men and women he'd killed had been defenceless, even though their mere existence was a threat to the Commonwealth - which he ruthlessly pushed aside. There was no sign of the Governor.

"Security alert," his stolen radio proclaimed. "Intruder alert; I say again, intruder alert!"

Carl nodded, then ran into the next room and hastily removed the guard's uniform. They must have found the bodies by now and it wouldn't be hard to deduce what he'd done, not when one of them had been left in his underwear. He briefly considered using the radio to try to sow confusion, then dismissed the thought and dropped the radio on the floor, crushing it below his boot heel. Given time, the security forces could have used it to trace him.

He glanced around, then hastened up the next set of stairs towards the business floors. If the Governor's security team were on the ball, they would have taken him to a panic room ...and the best place to find it would be near his office. Carl would have preferred to get his principal, the person he was trying to protect, out of the building completely, but the aircars would discourage anyone leaving until the entire district was secure. Given how much chaos Carl had tried to sow, it would be hours before anyone felt confident of anything. He reached into his pocket and produced a detonator, then held it in his hand as he reached the top of the stairs. The two guards standing in front of the Governor's office glared at him, nastily.

"You can't hide here," one sneered. He wore a different uniform to the outer set of guards, probably indicating that he worked directly for the Governor. "This place isn't safe."

"Indeed," the other said. They both held their guns at the ready, but the way they held them told Carl that they weren't taking him seriously. "Go downstairs to the shelters and ..."

Carl drew the pistol from his pocket and shot the first one through the head, then ducked to the side as the second one returned fire. He fell a moment later as Carl shot him in the throat. They hadn't expected him to be *dangerous* ...he sighed, then clicked the detonator. A second later, the building shook violently as the explosives he'd left in the stolen car detonated. Whatever the enemy commander thought about the situation - probably that it was getting back under control - he wouldn't be thinking for much longer. Carl smirked - it was so much easier when one had given up all hope of getting out alive - then took one of the uniforms and quickly pulled it over his head. The helmet was a poor fit - it was just short of battlesuit-class - but it would suffice. He pulled the visor down, checked to make sure there was no visible sign of blood, then stepped through the door and into the Governor's office.

It was empty. Carl took a moment to admire the window that made up one of the walls, then glanced around, looking for the panic room. It took him several seconds to find the entrance, hidden behind a giant painting of a dark-skinned woman wearing old-style robes. Carl pulled it open, then stopped. Inside, there was a second armoured door and a camera, watching his every move.

He cursed inwardly, then stepped back into the office and hunted for paper. A panic room *couldn't* be opened from the outside, not when it would defeat the whole objective of the exercise. And, unless he missed his guess, nothing short of a nuke would burn through the hullmetal shielding the occupants from the outside world. The only way to get in would be to make them open the door, somehow. It wouldn't be easy. They'd have an entire life support system to make sure they stayed alive, no matter what happened outside, until help came.

Gritting his teeth, he took a sheet of paper and wrote out a note. BUILDING COMPROMISED - HAVE 2 GET OUT. It was the only way he'd been taught to try to get the occupants out, back when he'd been trying out for the Pathfinders. Stepping back into the antechamber, he held up the note in front of the camera. The Governor would be inside, but who else would be with him? There was a long pause, then the hatch slowly clicked open, revealing a surprisingly comfortable bunker. Carl rolled his eyes, inwardly, then stepped inside. Governor Brown was already rising to his feet.

He looked harmless, nothing like the Old Council or the Grand Senators he'd met - briefly - on Earth. Paula, the treacherous bitch, had described him as a corporate rat; Carl had to admit, reluctantly, that she'd been right. He was no soldier or spacer, no pirate or bandit, merely a corporate rat using the resources around him to leverage himself into a position of power. Behind him, a pair of secretaries - both clearly old enough to be Carl's mother - looked at him, nervously.

Not a military officer, Carl thought. *And not a security expert either.*

Carl couldn't resist. "Greetings from Avalon," he said. "Goodbye."

He shot the Governor through the head, twice. It was unlikely in the extreme the Governor could recover from a single headshot, but modern medicine could work miracles if given half a chance. The two secretaries started screaming; Carl hesitated, torn between shooting them and letting them go, then turned and walked out of the panic room, leaving them behind. It didn't really surprise him that they didn't try to close the hatch, now he was gone. He glanced at the Governor's terminal, then slotted a rigged datachip into the system. If it worked as advertised, a nasty virus would destroy all the data on the terminal before the firewalls managed to keep it from spreading.

The sound of running footsteps outside told him that he'd been discovered. One of the secretaries must have hit an alarm, he guessed, or the panic room's opening had sounded an alert. He shrugged, then hurried through a side door into the Governor's bedroom, which was larger but no more elegant than the hotel room. Carl was almost disappointed in the dead Governor; if *he'd* had access to the resources of an entire star system, *he* would have used it to ensure he had a harem and all the pleasures money could buy.

But you'd get bored, he thought, snidely. He hadn't joined the Marines because he wanted to spend all day in bed, even if it *was* surrounded by hot chicks. *And the Colonel would be disappointed in you.*

Someone crashed into the office behind him, then let off a couple of shots. Carl had no idea what they thought they were shooting at - maybe they'd shot the secretaries - but he hurried to open the window anyway. There was no other way out, save for breaking through the security team and he had no idea how many men he was facing. Cold air slapped at his face as the window opened, allowing him to start scrambling out into the open air. Compared to climbing sheer rock faces at the Slaughterhouse, climbing down the mansion's walls would be a piece of cake.

And then a bullet slammed into his chest. Carl stumbled, feeling a dull pain spreading through his body, and somehow managed to unhook a second grenade from his belt. The newcomers yelled at him to stop, but it was too late; he tossed it towards them, then kept moving through the window. He realised his mistake a second too late. There was a brilliant flash of light, then a kick that hurled him out into the open air …and down towards the ground, far below.

He had barely a moment to trigger the third grenade, priming it to destroy his body, before the ground came up and hit him.

And then there was nothing, nothing at all.

CHAPTER THIRTY-SIX

From the point of view of the Grand Senate, concessions - however made - would only weaken the Empire's bargaining position. It was simpler to round up enemy combatants and imprison them, then deal with their successors - if, indeed, there were successors.
- Professor Leo Caesius. *The Empire and its Prisoners of War.*

Wolfbane System, Year 5 (PE)
Commander Drew Malochy scowled down at the datapad in front of him, wondering if there was ever a rank so high that he could tell the bean-counters to go away or he would personally stuff their beans down their throats, one at a time. It was bad enough that a particularly stupid commanding officer had ignored basic maintenance to the point his ship had suffered a core overload, but somehow *he* had to account for every one of his actions following the explosion. He would have liked to see the bean-counters do better if they were trapped in the command seat ...

"Commander," Ensign Pittman called. "The armoury!"

Drew looked up, just in time to see the first missile streaking away from the missile pods towards one of the industrial nodes. For a moment, his mind refused to accept what he was seeing; the missiles had been locked in place, unable to be armed and fired without the correct command codes! And yet, the missiles were already being launched at targets within the shipyard. They would start hitting home before anyone could do anything to stop them.

"Signal an alert," he snapped, knowing it would be already far too late. More missiles were spewing free of the pods now, aimed at everything from the industrial nodes to the automated weapons platforms. They weren't prepped to deal with threats originating *inside* the shipyard! No one had ever considered the possibility. "Get everyone back into suits and ..."

The first missile slammed into its target. Drew winced, expecting an explosion, but instead the missile punched through the thin layer of material separating the industrial production node from outer space. Atmosphere started to flow out of the gash - he refused to focus his sensors enough to tell if the wriggling shapes were actually *people* - as the missile smashed through several billion credits worth of equipment before finally being wrecked itself by a final impact. The warhead hadn't been armed, part of his mind noted; the rest of him couldn't help focusing on the end of his career ...

"Order everyone into suits and then into space," he ordered, as other missiles sought out their targets. Defensive countermeasures were already deploying, but the missiles didn't seem inclined to be distracted from their targets. Their seeker heads were inactive too, he realised numbly; they were merely flying ballistic trajectories that merely happened to intersect their targets. "And order the weapons platforms to take out the armoury!"

Pittman looked up at him. "Sir?"

"Order the weapons platforms to take out the armoury," Drew ordered. His career was definitely at an end, so he might as well go out with a bang. Besides, whoever had launched those missiles had to be on the armoury itself. "Now!"

"The missiles are away," Jasmine snapped. The first missiles had already begun to strike their targets. "We need to move."

She rose to her feet, then ran through the corridor towards where the worker bees were waiting. Most of her team had moved as soon as the missiles had started to fire, knowing it wouldn't be long before the Wolves targeted the armoury directly. Stewart followed her through the network, one hand tapping his radio to recall the remaining teams. They plunged into the worker bees and hastily disengaged from the armoury, just as the final set of countermeasures began to go active. Anyone trying to use active sensors in the midst of the shipyard was in for a very unpleasant experience.

"Shit," Stewart said. The worker bee rocked violently as the pilot struggled to avoid chunks of debris. "They just struck the armoury!"

"That was quick," Jasmine muttered, as she strapped herself in. "And our drones?"

"Gary has them," Stewart said. "God help us."

Jasmine nodded, then turned her attention to the radio net. Judging from the increasingly frantic pleading, her missiles had done a great deal of damage. The Wolves would take months, if not years, to repair their facilities ...she caught sight of an explosion blossoming into life on one of the large shipbuilding slips and smiled in cold amusement as a half-built cruiser was enveloped in fire. Something big must have exploded ... she puzzled over it for a long moment, then pushed the thought aside. It hardly mattered, not now. There would be time for an after-action review when - if - they survived.

All that mattered was getting out before it was too late.

Gary had plenty of experience in multitasking, from the games he'd played on Earth, but that had been five *years* ago. There were just under a hundred worker bees under his direct control and handling them all at the same time was just impossible. All he could do was take brief control of each worker bee, direct it into a place where it could serve as a weapon and then move to the next one before it ran into something and exploded. Worker bees were fast little craft, but they sure as hell weren't armed or armoured.

Cold hatred burned through him as he directed one worker bee to slam straight into an emergency shuttle, than another one into a thin-skinned habitation module. The Wolves had taken Kailee from him, turned him into a collaborator and then forced him to hide in the spaceport, fearing death as a collaborator. Earth had been bad enough, but the Wolves could have been something different, something better. Everything Paula had told him about their system had convinced him that, in many ways, they were *worse* than Earth.

They were dying. Gary watched, through a sensor, as an emergency bubble was ripped open, casting dozens of people into the icy cold vacuum of space. He felt nothing, not when they were exposed to his drones or when they died, even though part of him knew it was no computer game. They had all been part of a system that had oppressed him, oppressed Kailee, oppressed Meridian ...a planet he might never have liked, but he could have come to love, in time. He didn't want to think about how many people had suffered because of the Wolves, from people like Paula and her General to Jasmine and her men. Watching the Wolves suffer and die - *making* the Wolves suffer and die - felt noble and right. Even the ones who hadn't hurt him directly had enabled the ones who had.

A worker bee popped out of existence. Gary barely noticed, shifting his attention to several other worker bees. Five of them were burning towards weapons platforms, which were rapidly trying to reorientate themselves so they could fire into the shipyard. It struck Gary as a curious oversight, but he had to admit that Jasmine had proved that someone could fire missiles within the shipyard, even without the arming codes. He watched two platforms die as the bees slammed home, then sighed bitterly as three died before they got any closer to their targets. A sixth died seconds later as it flew too close to an armed shuttle. He wondered, nastily, just how many legitimate worker bees, crewed by live personnel, were about to die. The Wolves seemed to be shooting at everything and everyone.

He grabbed control of three more and pointed them towards a habitation node. Emergency craft were already deploying, but it looked like they wouldn't be in time. Gary felt his lips pull back into a sneer, then pushed the worker bees forward. The impact would wipe out hundreds of the bastards ...

Joshua Abram had been sitting in his cabin, cursing the customs crew under his breath, when the alarms started to sound for the second time.

He'd been woken up barely an hour before he was supposed to get up, which meant there hadn't been any real hope of getting back to sleep before he had to get out of bed for good. The CO would have been pissed if he'd been late and docked his pay ...and when he was the only one in the family earning a living wage, he couldn't afford to lose anything. His parents were engaged in make-work, while his sister was too young to do anything beyond schooling. He couldn't risk a reduced pay packet ...

The alarms sounded, again. Joshua rolled his eyes, then reached for his helmet and placed it on his lap. There was no point in actually putting it on until there was a real emergency, not when he hadn't had a chance to verify his shipsuit's inbuilt oxygen supply. In hindsight, putting that off until he had a weekend to spare had been foolish. If the CO found out, he would have torn Joshua a new asshole - not out of concern, but out of the prospect of having to do the paperwork if Joshua died on his watch. Joshua sighed, then smiled in honest relief as he realised the alarms actually helped him. The CO could bitch about anything, as long as it was his subordinates' fault. He wasn't allowed to dock their pay if they were late because of an emergency alert.

He'd probably try, Joshua thought, darkly. Complaining was dangerous, even on the shipyard. A complainer could be given shit duty for weeks ...or simply kicked out and sent back to Wolfbane with a black mark on his record. *I think ...*

Another alarm sounded, a second before a dull *thud* echoed through the habitation node. Joshua hastily donned his helmet, then took a deep breath, praying the life support system was in good condition. The air tasted faintly stale, but it was breathable; he sucked in his breath with relief, then shuddered as a *third* alarm, harsh and uncompromising, echoed through the air. *Hull breach.*

Joshua hurried forward and through the hatch as dull quivers started to shudder through the entire complex. He'd never felt anything like them before, not in real life, but he knew what they portended. The complex had been badly damaged, air was leaking out of one or more gashes in the hull ...and the shockwaves were on the verge of ripping the entire structure apart. Outside, the quivering was louder; he could hear metal screaming in agony as it was bent and broken by forces beyond his ability to grasp. And he could hear, in the distance, the faint hiss of air escaping from the hull.

He stumbled forward as the gravity flickered, then stopped in front of a hatch leading into another cabin. Someone was banging on the hatch, her muffled voice screaming for help; Joshua hit the switch, but the hatch remained firmly closed. The entire hull was being warped, he realised, as he hunted for something - anything - that could be used to open the jammed door. There was nothing in view ....

A great tearing sound echoed through the compartment. Joshua heard something splintering, in the distance, then he was yanked off his feet by a sudden outrush of air. He tried to grab hold of a piece of bulkhead, only to have it come loose in his hand. Helplessly, he plummeted through the ever-widening gash in the hull and out into space. The shipsuit warmed automatically, protecting him from hard vacuum, as he tumbled helplessly away from the structure. He saw a piece of debris, larger than his entire compartment, spinning past him and out into the void. In the distance, he could see flashes of light ...was the entire shipyard under attack?

His suit should be signalling automatically, he knew, screaming for help. Normally, there was always a worker bee or a shuttle in easy range, ready to pick up someone who had found themselves dumped into space unexpectedly. But now ...even if his transmitter was working, and if someone picked it up, he had no idea when he would be recovered. If he ever was recovered ...

Something twinkled with light, in the distance. Joshua sighed, then took a breath and forced himself to relax. There was nothing else he could do, but wait.

"The worker bees have gone mad," Lieutenant N'Banga reported. "They're killing people!"

"They've been *hacked*," Drew said. There were so many problems, one after the other, that his attempts to deal with one issue only made the next one worse. "They're designed for remote control and someone has managed to hijack the link."

He gritted his teeth. Hundreds of people were dying and they *needed* the worker bees, but he couldn't take the risk of leaving the hijacked ones to fly around at will.

"General signal to all worker bees," he ordered. "They are to cut all drives and come to a complete halt, relatively speaking. Any bee that refuses to do so is to be taken out."

N'Banga stared. "Sir?"

"Do as I tell you," Drew snapped. For the first time in his life, he would have been grateful for a more senior officer reporting in and telling him what to do. But there was no one; indeed, judging from the handful of reports over the network, all hell had broken loose on Wolfbane too. "Then pass the word to the security patrols. *Nothing* is to be allowed to operate on remote control until our systems have been secured."

He looked up at the main display and swore under his breath. Thirty-seven installations lost or damaged beyond easy repair, forty-two in need of some repairs before they could go back to work …and thousands of people dead or seriously wounded. It would be months, at best, before the facility could be repaired. By any standards, he had to admit the intruders had managed to cripple the entire shipyard.

He looked over at Ensign Pittman. "Did the troops find any trace of the enemy?"

"Not at the armoury, but it was vaporised," Ensign Pittman said. "There are reports of enemy soldiers attacking an industrial complex …"

"Reroute the troops over there," Drew ordered. If nothing else, catching or killing the rest of the enemy force would feel good. "And try to raise help from Wolfbane. We need more troops out here."

"They're barely responding," Ensign Pittman said. "Something bad happened on the surface."

Drew ground his teeth. "Something bad is happening *here*!"

"They're signalling all worker bees to cut their drives," Stewart reported. "I think they've worked out what we're doing."

"Cut our drives, but keep us gliding out," Jasmine ordered. There was so much sensor distortion around that she would have been impressed if the Wolves had been able to track them; hell, the bees were so small that tracking them was difficult even without it. "We have to make it out before they start slamming the door closed."

She leaned back in her chair, then waited. It would be hours before they reached the *Passing Water*, assuming they made it out, but there was nothing else she could do. One way or another, she'd given Wolfbane a very bloody nose. It would take them months to repair the shipyard, not to mention replace all the supplies she'd smashed. Even a comparatively minor loss would seem disastrous when the system was so tightly wound.

"They missed us," Stewart said, after nearly an hour. "They didn't see us leave."

Jasmine shrugged. "Keep us covert," she ordered. The Wolves had too many other problems to deal with right now, including swarms of debris blasting free from shattered habitats and thousands of people trapped in interplanetary space, running out of air. "We're not clear yet."

She closed her eyes. The remainder of the team had volunteered to strike further into the shipyard, knowing the odds were not in their favour. And, unlike Carl Watson, they didn't have a hope of blending into the civilian population, not once the guards started looking in earnest. She knew it was unlikely any of them would even be taken alive.

I'm sorry, she thought. She would have given anything to accompany them, to take their place, yet she'd known it was impossible. *But your deaths will mean something. I promise you that.*

"They blew themselves up rather than be taken alive," Ensign Pittman reported. "But they did a great deal of damage."

"I know that," Drew snapped. It had been two hours since the attack had begun and the damage totals had only mounted upwards. Even the desperate attempts to save as many lives as possible had only saved a bare handful of workers. The sudden end of his career was starting to look like a quick trial, followed by an even quicker walk out an airlock. "Can you not get any link to Wolfbane?"

"No," Ensign Pittman reported. "The link is open, sir; they're just not replying."

"Then we must make do with our own resources," Drew ordered. He would have *killed* for a battleship's complement of small craft, to say nothing of a fleet repair ship's crews. "The remaining enemy soldiers are dead" - he doubted any of them had actually managed to escape - "so get the security teams working on picking up stranded workers. We'll convert the battlestations to emergency accommodation until we can see just how safe the habitation nodes are ..."

He sighed, inwardly, as he kept rattling off orders. There were emergency procedures no one had ever expected to use, not until now. He put them into play, hoping they lived up to their promise, then forced himself to keep going. It kept him from thinking about the future, what little there was of it. He knew he'd done badly ...

...And that the enemy, whoever they were, had given Wolfbane a very bloody nose.

CHAPTER
THIRTY-SEVEN

In addition, various colony development corporations actually benefited from this state of affairs. Hundreds of thousands of unwilling settlers could be dumped on marginal worlds and forced to work to turn them into profitable concerns, which allowed the development corporations to colonise the worlds on the cheap. They naturally supported the Empire's hard line on POWs.
- Professor Leo Caesius. *The Empire and its Prisoners of War.*

Wolfbane City, Wolfbane, Year 5 (PE)
"You didn't say a word, did you?"

Rani didn't bother to disagree as Paula Bartholomew was shown into her temporary office space, overlooking the scorched and broken Governor's Mansion. She *hadn't* passed on the warning, after all, and it had played out for her. Governor Brown was dead, some of his highest-ranking subordinates were dead …and she was in control. It wouldn't be long, she was sure, before someone decided to challenge her, but for the moment she held the power in her dark hands and she planned to keep it.

"You practically killed him yourself," Paula added. "Didn't you?"

Rani looked up at her and smirked. "Do you *care*?"

"I made a deal," Paula said.

"With me, not with the Governor," Rani said, dryly. "I just saw fit not to pass the message on."

She leaned forward, studying Paula. Her record had made interesting reading; she'd served almost as a political advisor as well as aide to General Stubbins. Clearly, Stubbins hadn't been a particularly competent general, but she'd certainly helped keep him afloat until Governor Brown had outmanoeuvred him. And yet, the cynic in her told her that was no great feat.

"You proved yourself treacherous," she said, softly. "And yet, I cannot find it in myself to blame you for your treachery. It would be hypocritical to blame you for doing something I did myself, for similar reasons. You may, if you wish, take your reward and go."

Paula frowned, but said nothing. Rani understood. Governor Brown would have kept his word, even if he found it something of an embarrassment. His career as a corporate rat had depended on a reputation for honesty; laws could be pushed to the limits, loopholes could be exploited mercilessly, but he could never outright break his word. Rani, on the other hand, might have no hesitation in ending Paula's life, now that she was seemingly no longer useful. A quick accident and the last person who knew that Rani had allowed the assassination attempt to go ahead would be gone.

"However, I require someone to assist me with the politics on Wolfbane," she added. "You may serve as *my* aide, if you wish. I have no interest in you beyond your formidable political skills."

She paused. "Should you betray me, of course, you won't have a second chance."

Paula blinked. "You're serious?"

"You have skills I need," Rani said. "And if anyone else was to find out what you did, I imagine they would be very unhappy. Governor Brown wasn't very popular around here, I fear, but he was respected. Many of his former servants feel a military officer will be a less comfortable head of state."

She met Paula's eyes, recognising a kindred spirit. "If you want to go, I will let you go," she added. It was a lie and she suspected Paula would recognise it as such. There was no way she could leave the only living witness in a position to do any damage. "There will be wealth, safety and a chance to build a whole new life, away from the maddening crowds."

"I will work for you," Paula said, slowly. "If you really want me ..."

"I do," Rani said. And she did. Talent like that shouldn't be wasted; besides, she had enough leverage to keep Paula loyal for the rest of her life. The absence of sexual harassment would probably help too. "Now, answer me one question. Did you know they were planning to attack the shipyard?"

Paula shook her head. "I knew they had something in mind, but I thought it was just the attack on the Governor," she said. "Did …did he make it out alive?"

"We found a body," Rani said. Even dying, the assassin had managed to take out a number of security guards; the final explosion had killed several guards who had been far too close for comfort. "DNA testing confirmed it to be one of the prisoners who escaped Meridian."

She smiled at the relief on Paula's face. "I have a set of quarters for you here," she added. "Go wash, get yourself changed into something more presentable, then report back to me in two hours. We have a lot of work to do."

Paula nodded, then left the room. Rani looked back down at her datapad, then keyed a switch. Moments later, a different door opened and Commander Drew Malochy was escorted into the room. He looked pale; defiant, but pale. Rani had no difficulty recognising an officer wondering why his superior hadn't ordered an immediate execution. Given just how badly he'd screwed up, a quick execution would be almost too good for him …

…And yet he'd done well, coping with the aftermath of the disaster.

"Commander," she said, as he snapped to attention and saluted. "I want a full account of what happened to the shipyard."

She listened, feeling cold ice crawling down the back of her spine, as Commander Malochy outlined the entire story. It was clear, with the benefit of hindsight, that the exploding customs ship had been hijacked, then used to get a team of sabotage experts through the defences and into the shipyard. And then they'd just taken advantage of everything they'd found within to wreak havoc.

"Very well," she said, when he had finished. "How long until we get the shipyard back to a viable level of production?"

Malochy hesitated, noticeably. "I can't give you a straight answer, Admiral," he said. "There are too many variables …"

"Then give me as detailed an answer as necessary," Rani snarled. If nothing else, she was going to make it clear that she wanted simple answers, not five hundred pages of technobabble and jargon when one would suffice. Governor Brown had practically *encouraged* a cult of imprecise answers. "How long until we can start churning out more starships?"

"The damage to the industrial nodes was quite severe," Malochy said. "We can repair some of the damaged units within two to three months, but the remainder cannot be replaced easily; I think we'd be looking at two to three *years* before the shipyard was back up to capacity. In addition, the damage to both construction slips and stockpiles of components will add additional months to the problem. Our system-wide industrial base will need to be re-jiggered to cope with the sudden shortages."

He took a breath. Clearly, he expected her to shoot him out of hand for his next report.

"The real losses, however, come in trained personnel," he continued. "We lost over nine *thousand* technical experts, all of whom will take years to replace. One missile took out the training school and killed several hundred students, along with taking out the teaching machines we had reconfigured for them and the personnel who were serving as teachers. It will take years to restart the program, as teachers working in other places will need to be brought to the shipyard to work there."

"I see," Rani said. "You have the situation under control?"

"The remaining personnel have been secured," Malochy said. "I've ordered the debris to be pushed out of the shipyard, for the moment; we will need to sift through it at a later date to see if anything can be salvaged, but …"

Rani cut him off. "Go back there and resume command," she ordered. "I will expect a fuller report by the end of the month. I'll make my decision about your future then."

She watched him go, then glared down at the datapad. The shipyard had been efficient, all right, at the cost of being a point failure source for the entire Wolfbane Consortium. It hadn't concentrated *all* the Consortium's industrial might in one place, but it had certainly concentrated all the military-grade systems. And now, Wolfbane was paying the price for the Governor's efficiency drive. An industrial base that should have steamrollered the Commonwealth into the ground had been crippled.

But she was in charge now.

Rani smiled, then reached for another datachip. The plan she had tried to sell to the Governor was still workable, after all, and now *she* was in command. It could be used ...

...And once the Commonwealth had been crushed, there would be plenty of time to repair the damage they'd done.

Jasmine didn't relax, not completely, until *Passing Water* had made it over the Phase Limit and vanished into FTL. She'd wondered if the enemy had been toying with them, she'd wondered if they'd just been biding their time before going after the freighter ...but it seemed they genuinely believed the team had been obliterated on the shipyard. It would require a crazy amount of luck to track them through FTL ...and besides, they were heading right for Avalon. They'd be able to report in soon enough.

"We made it," Stewart said.

"Yeah," Jasmine said. "We did."

But it had come at a cost. Carl Watson ...there was no way to know what had happened to him, although some radio chatter had confirmed the Governor's death. Paula ...might be alive or dead. And the others, who had died ...she knew their names and faces, but she didn't know them very well. It galled her, in a way, that she hadn't known them, even though they'd died at her command.

She rose to her feet. "Alert me if anything happens," she said, although it was vanishingly unlikely that anything would. "I'll go see to Gary and Kailee."

"Have fun," Stewart said. "And don't fail to tell Gary he did well."

Jasmine nodded, then walked through the hatch and down into the makeshift cabin. Kailee was sitting on the bench, her arms wrapped around her legs, her dark eyes staring at nothing in particular. Jasmine frowned, then gave her a quick once-over, searching for signs of physical abuse. But there were none.

"Gary started to cry after the link broke," Kailee said. She nodded towards the door, which was locked. "He told me to get away from him, screamed he wasn't worthy ...and just locked himself in there."

"Oh," Jasmine said. It sounded like a breakdown, if internalised rather than externalised, although she would have to check him to be sure. "What did he say?"

"He just said he wasn't worthy," Kailee said. "He ...he always had doubts, but ...I don't understand him."

"I'll talk to him," Jasmine promised. "You go up to the bridge and stay with Thomas for a while, ok?"

Kailee nodded. Jasmine tapped her wristcom, informing Stewart of the situation, then tapped the door. It didn't open. She sighed, waited for Kailee to leave the room, then pulled her multitool from her belt and pressed it against the lock. It clicked open, allowing her to step into the compartment. She wrinkled her nose at the smell - Gary had been drinking, it seemed - and clicked on the light. Gary was curled into a ball, blinking miserably at her. A gun lay beside him on the bed, as if he'd planned to shoot whoever stepped through the door - or himself.

"You're in a mess," she said. How long had it been since she'd encountered Mandy in a similar state? But Mandy had been in very real danger, while Gary was more dangerous to himself than anyone else. "What do you think you're doing?"

Gary flinched, but did nothing. Jasmine kept her relief off her face - if he'd reached for the gun, things would have become very dangerous for both of them - and strode over to the bed, then picked up the gun herself. The safety was off; it struck her, suddenly, that Gary had been contemplating suicide. It wasn't uncommon for recruits to consider suicide, under the pressure of Boot Camp, but the Drill Instructors were usually good at spotting them before they went too far. She couldn't recall a genuine suicide at the Slaughterhouse at all.

"Couldn't do it," Gary said. His voice sounded bleary. "I couldn't pull the trigger. Should have done. Should have ended my life."

Jasmine frowned, then pulled him to his feet and half-carried, half-dragged him into the shower. The suicide rate on Earth had been terrifyingly high - she'd once heard that one in fifty Earthers would kill themselves - but she couldn't understand why Gary would try to kill himself *now*. He had Kailee, he had prospects, he'd proved himself ...he would go to Avalon and get a decent job. Why had he tried to kill himself now?

She turned on the water, then watched as Gary spluttered under the flow of cold liquid. He twisted and turned, but she didn't let go until he was thoroughly drenched. She dragged him back out, helped him to undress and then threw a towel at him. If the water wasn't enough to clear his mind, she would need to tie him down until he sobered up. She didn't know if the medical kit on the ship had any sober-up, or if she wanted to use it if it did.

"All right," she said. Naked, Gary was a mess. It was clear from the way he held himself that he had no pride in his body at all, even though she'd seen worse. "What happened and why?"

Gary picked up a gown, then dressed slowly. "I don't deserve to live," he said, as he pulled the gown over his head. "You should kill me."

Jasmine lifted her eyebrows. "Did you rape Kailee? Did you betray us? Did you put salt in my coffee yesterday?"

"This isn't funny," Gary shouted at her.

"No, it isn't," Jasmine agreed. Gary had always been scared of her, despite his best attempts to hide it. If he was shouting at her, the fear had to have been replaced by something else - bitter self-loathing, perhaps. "Why do you feel you deserve to die?"

"I killed them all," Gary said. "I controlled the bees, I threw them around like they were nothing, I killed hundreds of thousands of people ..."

"I doubt it," Jasmine said. She doubted there had been more than twenty thousand people on the shipyard, in total. "And you had no choice."

"I *gloried* in it," Gary snapped. "I *enjoyed* killing them because they were the bastards who'd wrecked my life. I wanted to make them hurt!"

Jasmine winced. She'd heard stories about people on Earth, people who just snapped and tried to kill as many others as they could before they were brought down. Gary might have been a prime candidate for snapping, given his life before Meridian; he'd grown up in a world where every man's hand was turned against him. And then, given the ability to make them hurt, as he put it, he'd gloried in his newfound power.

You never see that outside the Core Worlds, she thought, morbidly. *Is it because we don't allow the seeds of hatred and madness to take root and grow?*

But Gary had a conscience, she realised, turning her attention back to him. Afterwards, when he'd had a moment to relax and *think*, he'd recognised what he'd done. The others had never been given the chance to consider their actions in the cold light of day. Gary ...had seen the monster within him and recoiled.

"You should kill me," Gary said, bitterly. He reached for a bottle of rotgut. Jasmine snatched it up and shoved it behind her. She would have to pour it down the toilet later, then have a few words with Frazier. If there were any other bottles on the ship, they would have to be locked away or discarded. "Look what I did!"

"You didn't have a choice," Jasmine said, slowly.

She sighed, inwardly. What could she say to convince him he'd done the right thing? His morality, such as it was, rebelled against his actions. *She* had been raised on a world where it was openly acknowledged that some people would never reform and just needed killing. Gary had been taught never to seek his opponent's death. And it *was* quite likely that a great many innocents had been killed in the crossfire.

"I could have said no," Gary said. "I could have accepted what I was doing. But I saw it as nothing more than a game."

"I know," Jasmine said.

He stared at her. "What was it like for you? What happened the first time you killed a man?"

Jasmine met his eyes, unflinchingly. "It was on Han," she said. She'd shot at everything from stationary targets to robots and holographic simulations, but she'd only shot a real man on Han, during her first deployment. In truth, it hadn't been until afterwards that it had gotten to her. Even then, she'd known that one of them would have died. "He was going to hurl a bottle of gas at me, with the flame already lit. I shot him."

And the flames burned him, she thought. She'd had nightmares for weeks afterwards, even after she'd killed countless other insurgents. *He died in agony ...but he would have done it to me, if I'd given him the chance.*

She patted Gary's shoulder, awkwardly. "You're going to be supervised for the rest of the voyage," she said. "Kailee cares about you, a lot. Leaving her alone is no way to thank her."

Gary looked down at the deck. "I'm not a child," he protested. "She doesn't want me."

"She loves you," Jasmine said, flatly. "And instead of complaining, and plotting to end your own life, you might as well come to terms with it. You are not on Earth any longer, Gary, and you can shape a life of your own."

She sighed. "Or you can die," she added. "But it would be something of a waste."

CHAPTER
THIRTY-EIGHT

> And yet, the Fall of Earth left the Empire's successor states struggling with the questions that had bedevilled humanity since the concept of taking prisoners on a large scale had first been developed.
> - Professor Leo Caesius. *The Empire and its Prisoners of War.*

Avalon, Year 5 (PE)

"You don't have to treat me like this," Hannalore protested, as Kitty stepped into the interrogation chamber. "I'm not going anywhere."

Kitty shrugged. Hannalore had not had a very pleasant night. She'd slept on a hard bunk without a cover, then woken at seven in the morning and fed a very basic meal. The guards had collected her an hour later, searched her thoroughly once again, then marched her down, her hands in cuffs, into the interrogation chamber. It would help keep her off-balance ...and remind her that her life was no longer her own.

"Procedure," Kitty said.

She sat down, facing the older woman. "You agreed to cooperate," she said. "I should warn you, here and now, that if you refuse to cooperate at any time in the future, the original charges will be proffered against you and you will stand trial for treason."

Hannalore scowled at her, but said nothing. Kitty studied the older woman for a long moment, trying to decide if Hannalore could be relied upon to keep her word. Was she smart enough to realise, to understand, that she had nowhere to go? Or was she so convinced that *she* was the good guy that she thought she could get out from under Kitty's thumb at a later date? She *looked* beaten, willing to give up and cooperate in exchange for not being executed, but Hannalore had grown up on Earth. Kitty would have been surprised if she hadn't been a skilled dissembler before her coming-out party, when she'd been fifteen.

"There won't be a second chance," Kitty added. "Your every move will be supervised and you will be asked to account for anything that seems suspicious. However, once the war is over, you and your husband will have a chance to live together, far from the maddening crowds."

Hannalore winced. "What happened to my husband?"

"He's still sleeping it off," Kitty said. "I think he drank a little too much last night."

She sighed, openly. In truth, she wasn't sure *what* would happen to the former Governor. Having him hospitalised for something minor might be wise, if only to keep him apart from his treacherous wife. Marriages had been broken for far less than one party committing outright treason. Hell, High Society on Earth hadn't given a damn about adultery. But treason? *That* would put a crimp into any marriage.

Hannalore's eyes narrowed. "He was never much of a drinker."

"It seemed the best way to help him cope with his feelings," Kitty said, dispassionately. "He didn't know, did he, that you were selling us out."

"No," Hannalore said. Her eyes flashed, suddenly. "Why would I trust him for anything?"

Kitty met her eyes. "You married him because you thought he had good prospects," she said, "and would probably go far. And he did; he went all the way to Avalon and took you with him. He saved you from certain death on Earth. And yet you're bitching because you no longer have unearned power and influence? If you'd used those damn parties for what you *said* they were for, you would have had plenty of power and influence ..."

"You don't understand," Hannalore said. "I ..."

"I understand that you were born with a silver spoon in your mouth," Kitty pointed out, fighting to keep her voice calm. "I also understand that, when the spoon was removed, you were unable to cope. Poverty was never an issue for you on Earth, was it? You never had to worry about where the next meal was coming from. I dare say it must have been a terrible shock to have to actually fend for yourself."

She sighed. "Avalon has countless opportunities for young people," she added. "And you could have made something of yourself without resorting to treason."

"Fuck you," Hannalore said. "Being born into High Society comes with a price tag ..."

"I dare say it does," Kitty agreed. "But I think you could have parleyed it into a position of power and influence if you'd wanted. All you *really* wanted to do was hang on to your husband's coattails and let him do the work, while you reaped the reward."

She shrugged. "You are due to hold the next party tomorrow," she added. "I expect you to be ready for duty."

Hannalore blinked, then rattled her cuffs. "Like this?"

"No," Kitty said, dryly. "You'll be expected to wear clothes. Unless you have a habit of walking around naked at your parties."

"Not *these* parties," Hannalore said.

Kitty smiled, then reached into her pocket and produced an injector tube. Hannalore opened her mouth to protest, but Kitty pressed the tube against the side of her neck before she could say a word. The older woman grunted as Kitty pushed the trigger, then glowered at her, one hand reaching up to rub where the tube had touched her bare skin. Kitty returned the tube to her pocket, then smirked.

"You have been injected with a standard tracking implant, coded to you and you alone," she said. "It remains silent, most of the time, but it will activate upon picking up a particular signal. You literally *cannot* run and hide without me tracking you down. And, as these implants are given to prisoners, even a standard security sweep when you pass through a starship's barriers will sound an alarm. You cannot hope to leave the planet without my permission."

Hannalore stared at her. "Get it out!"

"I don't think so," Kitty said. "It won't be removed until you've completed your work with us."

She released Hannalore from the chair, then led her through the door and into a washroom complex. Hannalore looked around her, surprised, as Kitty removed the cuffs and dropped them in a pocket, then nodded towards the shower and a set of drawers, positioned neatly against one wall.

"Shower thoroughly, then get dressed," Kitty ordered. "We took the liberty of ordering you some new clothes from your favourite store. Once you're dressed, we will go back to your mansion and start work."

Hannalore nodded. "But what about Brent?"

"Your husband?" Kitty shrugged. She rather doubted Hannalore cared for her husband, certainly not after he'd lost his power and position. "I think we'll put it about that he was taken ill, suddenly, and has to remain in the hospital. That would probably for the best, wouldn't it?"

She watched Hannalore step into the shower, then walked out of the compartment. It was thoroughly monitored; Hannalore couldn't hope to do anything without being spotted, although Kitty had no idea what she *could* do. The entire chamber had been carefully designed to exclude anything that could be used as a weapon, or used to commit suicide. It wasn't something Kitty cared to think about, but she had to keep reminding herself that Hannalore had no rights. She was a known traitor, after all.

"She's washing herself," Lieutenant Piper reported. "And looking around for trouble."

Kitty shrugged, then swiftly discarded her uniform and donned a simple green tunic. They'd been fashionable, once upon a time, but now they were commonplace, even on Avalon. Kitty had never understood fashion - people like Hannalore had determined what was in and out every season - yet she certainly knew the value of blending in with her surroundings. The tunic would be completely unremarkable and that was all that mattered.

She let her hair down, completing the civilian appearance, then walked back into the washroom. Hannalore had finished her shower and was dressing slowly, donning each item of clothing as though it were a piece of armour. Kitty understood - Hannalore was regaining a little amount of control for herself - but she couldn't be allowed to get too comfortable. It wouldn't matter, Kitty told herself. The Governor's wife was no longer in control of her life.

"Come with me," she said, once Hannalore was dressed. "There's a car waiting for you."

She led the way back through a maze of corridors and out into the garage. The car was nicely anonymous, one of hundreds that had been produced in the wake of the Cracker War; it was unlikely anyone would connect it with Commonwealth Intelligence. She motioned for Hannalore to get into the passenger seat, then climbed into the driver's seat and started the engine. It had been odd, once upon a time, to sit in a car that *didn't* drive itself, but now she was used to it. Hannalore eyed her oddly as she steered the car up the ramp and out onto the main street. Hardly anyone paid any attention as she drove towards the Governor's Mansion.

"You will have to hire new servants," Kitty said, as they pulled up outside the gates. The guard saw Hannalore, then opened the gate to allow them to drive into the grounds. "Some of them will be there to keep an eye on you."

"I can choose my own servants," Hannalore protested.

Kitty gave her a sharp look. "Not any longer," she said. She smirked as a thought occurred to her. "Besides, servants have *eyes*. I think you might find they know more of your secrets than you think."

Hannalore blanched.

Kitty parked the car, then motioned for Hannalore to get out as she looked around. The mansion seemed quieter somehow, now there weren't hundreds of guests clogging up the grounds or swarming in and out of the house. A single gardener was mowing the lawn, but there was no one else in sight. Hannalore sighed, slumping in on herself, then pulled herself together and strode towards the main doors. Kitty followed her, glancing around from side to side as they walked. If Hannalore was plotting treachery, she would never have a better chance.

"Two cups of tea," Hannalore ordered, as they entered the doors and walked past a tired-looking maid. "Bring them both to my office."

The maid nodded and hurried off. Kitty smiled inwardly - clearly, the maid was desperate for work - and then followed Hannalore into her private office. It was a bigger room than she'd expected, surprisingly bland for such a society butterfly. The only real decoration was a large painting of the Childe Roland, the age he'd been when his father had shuffled off the mortal coil. Kitty studied it, wondering why Hannalore had even bothered to buy, let alone keep, the painting. By now, even if the Childe Roland had survived the Fall of Earth, he would be at least twenty-three.

I wonder if he did survive, Kitty thought. *But if he had, would it matter?*

She shook her head, morbidly. Child Emperors rarely lived very long; the Childe Roland had only survived, she suspected, because he had no real power or influence of his own. She knew enough about him, from rumours passed through Imperial Intelligence before she'd been sent to Avalon, to fear what the Empire would become, if he *had* had real power. He'd been a spoilt brat ...

"Hannalore," she said, slowly. "Why did you keep this painting?"

"A reminder," Hannalore said, as the maid entered. "That what you look like isn't as important as what you actually *are*."

Kitty shrugged, then watched as the maid carefully placed a tray on the desk and poured them both a cup of tea. The young girl smiled shyly at Kitty, then curtseyed and withdrew, as silently as she had come. Hannalore sipped her tea, using it to calm herself, while Kitty studied the painting for the second time. The Childe Roland had had no real power ...and neither had the Governor, once he'd left his post. Had Hannalore wanted to remind herself that there was a difference between pretensions of power and *actual* power?

"Very good," she said, flatly. "Show me the bugging system."

Hannalore looked alarmed, but put down her cup of tea and swung the terminal around to face Kitty. Oddly, a wire ran from it to the wall, a dead giveaway that *something* was fishy; it was rare to see any form of hard connection when wireless was far more convenient. But it made sense, Kitty was sure. The great advantage of hard connections was that they were almost impossible to tap without physical access.

"The bugs are linked into the household network," Hannalore said, slowly. "I have the signals forwarded to this system, whereupon the computer scans the recordings for keywords and displays the results to me. I compile reports based upon the recordings and send them onwards."

"To Gaston," Kitty said. She wasn't sure what she wanted to do with that connection, given Gaston's clear instability. Perhaps they could arrange an accident ...no, that would break the chain between Hannalore and Wolfbane. They'd have to monitor Gaston and prepare themselves to intervene, if he snapped completely. "How do you decide what to send?"

"I just send anything that looks interesting," Hannalore said. "Much of the recordings are simply nonsense. Or useless."

She tapped a switch. A deep male voice echoed through the room.

"I want to fuck you," he breathed. There was a hint that someone else was there, the sound of light female breathing. "I want to fuck you so bad."

Kitty had to bite her lip to keep from laughing. "He sounds like a bad actor from a porno flick," she said.

"Councillor Thompson," Hannalore said, darkly. "He's having an affair with one of my regular maids. I think he learned to make love from porno flicks."

"I feel sorry for the maid," Kitty said, honestly. Councillor Thompson didn't sound loving; he sounded rather more than just a little creepy. "I hope you pay her through the nose."

Hannalore nodded. "They are all paid very well," she said. "But I still have quite a high turnover."

"I'm not surprised," Kitty muttered. She cleared her throat. "Why do you encourage it?"

"People need somewhere to relax," Hannalore said. "And they need to relax in different ways."

Kitty frowned. "Maybe," she said, doubtfully. "What other recordings do you have?"

"Thousands," Hannalore said.

She looked down at the terminal, then tapped a switch. Another voice echoed through the room, talking about the importance of bidding collectively for the latest set of government contracts. Kitty listened, silently tagging names to voices, as the recording slowly came to an end. The Governor hadn't been exaggerating when he said his parties helped boost the economy, despite the expense. A collective bid for the latest set of contracts would help ensure that more and more money was flushed into the local economy.

"I see," Kitty said, finally. She glanced at her watch. "My team will be here in an hour, I think. You can give your servants the rest of the day off, as you are going to be having the building cleaned from top to bottom."

Hannalore blinked. "I am?"

"That's the excuse you're going to give," Kitty said, feeling an odd flicker of irritation. "The team will inspect the house, examine the bugs, and then arrange for them to be closely monitored. Tomorrow evening, after your party, you will be told what to send to Wolfbane, through your contacts. I don't think I need to tell you what will happen if you try to trick us."

Hannalore shifted, uncomfortably. "No," she said, clearly. "You don't."

Kitty rose to her feet. "You're sure the bugs don't transmit anything outside your network?"

"I don't think so," Hannalore said. She eyed the terminal for a long moment. "They would have set off all kinds of alerts if they had, wouldn't they?"

"Probably," Kitty said. She smiled, coldly. It had struck her that Hannalore, for all her political savvy, wasn't very confident with technology. There had always been someone there to do it for her. "Show me the rest of the mansion."

She had never really understood, even after her first visit, just how much was crammed into the mansion. The lower floors were for the staff, the middle floors were for entertainment and hosting guests; the upper floors were intended to serve as the centre of colonial government. Now, most of the offices were dark and empty, while the Governor's office was gathering dust. There was literally nothing for him to do, now that power had passed to the planetary council. And yet, there was something odd about the offices ...

"You never stripped them bare," she said, slowly. The offices still *looked* ready for use, even if they hadn't been touched for years. Everything from computer terminals to fancy chairs had been left untouched. There had to be thousands of credits worth of junk in the office. "Why didn't you try to sell the furnishings?"

"Brent used to say they weren't *our* furnishings," Hannalore said. "They belonged to the Empire, not to us personally. Besides, I always had a feeling we would be using the mansion for its original purpose, one day."

"You planned to rule from here," Kitty said. She quirked an eyebrow as they walked back down to the lower levels. Hannalore could have sold the terminals to fund the first few parties and no one would have raised an eyebrow. "You do realise Wolfbane probably wouldn't have kept their word?"

Hannalore sighed. "I did what I considered necessary," she said. "And they would have needed me in the future ..."

"I doubt it," Kitty said. There were businesspeople and military officers who might be useful to Wolfbane, if the Commonwealth surrendered, but Hannalore wouldn't be worth so much to them. "They would simply have killed both of you and dumped your bodies in the gutter."

She shrugged. "But it doesn't matter," she added. "You will do as you're told, or die. I don't mind which, really."

Hannalore swallowed. "I understand," she said. "I won't let you down."

CHAPTER
THIRTY-NINE

Were they to echo the Empire's ruthless treatment of POWs - or work to come up with a more stable system? Unfortunately, perhaps, Wolfbane chose the former - and Avalon chose the latter.
- Professor Leo Caesius. *The Empire and its Prisoners of War.*

Avalon, Year 5 (PE)
"Jasmine Yamane, as I live and breathe," Command Sergeant Gwendolyn Patterson said, as Jasmine and Stewart were shown into her office. "What kept you?"

Jasmine smiled. She'd looked up to Gwendolyn Patterson ever since she'd joined the company; hell, if Gary found *her* intimidating he would have hated to meet the Command Sergeant. No one in their right mind would ever have talked back to her, let alone started a fight. Rumour had it she'd once walked into a bar and flattened every man inside, along with a small army of Shore Patrolmen.

"We ran into some small problems on our way home," Jasmine said. "But we overcame them all and made it back safely. The others?"

"They got back two months ago," Gwendolyn said. "The Colonel was delighted to hear the news."

Jasmine winced. She wasn't looking forward to *that* interview. Indeed, she was surprised the Colonel hadn't ordered her to report to his office so he could rip her head off personally. But then, everyone on the *Passing Water* was being held until they could be inserted back into normal society - or go onwards to the Trade Federation, in some cases. She had a feeling Gary and Kailee would probably go that way too.

"I'm sure he was," she said. "I was expecting to see him ..."

"The Colonel is currently occupied with plans for a future offensive," Gwendolyn said. "Or at least that's the official story. In reality, he's giving you a day or two to decompress before he meets you, formally. I suggest you take advantage of it."

Jasmine winced. It was tradition - and tradition was *important* to the Marine Corps - to have a returning officer met by his or her superior officer. For Colonel Stalker, a man who practically embodied the traditions, to choose to put one aside ...it didn't bode well for her future. He probably wanted to give her a day or two before he unceremoniously informed her she was sacked.

"You need the downtime," Gwendolyn added. She had little tolerance for bullshit. "I read your report, while you were flying here. You did very well."

"Thank you," Jasmine said. "But ..."

She shook her head. "I need to see to Gary and Kailee," she said, instead. "And then I can find a place to rest."

"I took the liberty of arranging a room at the inn for you," Gwendolyn said. "You'll have at least two days, I think, before you meet the Colonel. Make use of them."

Jasmine nodded. The inn wasn't her ideal shore leave, but it was a good place for Marines - and Avalon Knights - to decompress between deployments and returning to civilian life. She could relax there and feel lazy, if only for an hour or two. And then she would probably start champing at the bit to do something - anything - with her time.

"I'll see to Gary and Kailee, then go there," Jasmine said. "Where are they going to stay?"

"They will need to be debriefed," Gwendolyn said. "I believe Colonel Stevenson will take them in hand, but you may as well escort them there. I've already assigned an aircar to you."

She passed Jasmine the keycard, then paused. "And Jasmine?"

Jasmine met her eyes. "Sergeant?"

"You did well out there," Gwendolyn said. "Don't worry about a thing."

Jasmine shrugged, then saluted and walked out of the office. She had a feeling Gwendolyn found the building no more comfortable than she would, but there was a real shortage of trained marines. If nothing else, the Colonel was likely to be angry at her for sacrificing Carl Watson, even if he *had* survived the battle on Wolfbane. One more marine dead or missing in action …how many were left, of the eighty-seven that had landed on Avalon? Fifty?

Outside, Gary and Kailee were sitting on a bench, waiting for her. They both looked tired and worn; Gary had taken weeks to get over his funk, then plunged back into exercise with a new grim determination. Beside him, Kailee looked pretty …but there was a hard edge to her face that told Jasmine she was growing up. She would probably not make it as a combat medic, Jasmine suspected, yet she had potential. A civilian nursing job might be just what she needed.

"You're both going to be debriefed," she said, as they rose to their feet. She wondered, absently, if they knew how rare it was for civilians to set foot on Castle Rock, then reminded herself it probably wouldn't mean anything to either of them. "After that …where do you want to go?"

"I wish I knew," Gary said. He looked stronger now, after weeks of hard exercise, but his face still seemed brittle. "Do you think the Trade Federation would welcome us?"

"I think so," Jasmine said. She led them towards the landing pad, where the aircar was waiting. A glance at the keycard told her it was the right one. "But then, Avalon would welcome you too."

She sucked in her breath as she opened the vehicle, then sat down in the driver's seat and waited for them to sit down behind her. The autopilot had been removed, she noted, but she didn't really mind. She could fly the craft herself, if necessary, and use it as a distraction from her own thoughts. Inserting the keycard into the slot, she powered up the drive and lifted the aircar into the sky. Castle Rock lay below her, home of the remaining marines and training ground for the Knights. How long had it been, she asked herself, since she'd thought of anywhere else as *home*?

"Wow," Gary said, as Camelot came into view. "It's better than Sabre."

"But still far smaller than a single CityBlock," Jasmine commented. Camelot seemed to have grown yet again, in the months she'd been away.

There were new apartment blocks on the edge of the city, while the industrial estates had grown larger. "They're trying to spread out the city as much as possible."

"I see," Gary said.

Kailee leaned forward. "Is it safe here?"

"It's the safest place on Avalon, outside a military base," Jasmine said. "The bandits were driven out years ago. I'd advise getting a firearm anyway, just to be sure. Everyone owns a gun here too."

"Oh," Kailee said. "Why …?"

"Because sometimes they need to defend themselves," Jasmine said. "And sometimes, just being able to defend yourself has a deterrent effect in its own right."

She sighed inwardly, feeling an unaccustomed pit in her stomach, as she steered the aircar towards the landing facility at the edge of the city. It didn't really *look* like a military base, not from overhead, but it served as both an intelligence centre and a place for newcomers to recover, once they arrived on Avalon. Gary and Kailee would be well cared for, she knew, and she would see them as often as possible. She made a mental note to call Emmanuel and see if he could give them both a tour of Camelot. They'd probably find him less intimidating than a military officer.

The aircar touched down neatly, just outside the building. A red-haired officer - it took Jasmine a moment to recognise her as Kitty Stevenson - strode out of the door and waved at them, then waited for Jasmine to climb out of the aircar. Behind her, Gary and Kailee hesitated before joining them. Jasmine gave them both a concerned look, then exchanged salutes with Kitty. In hindsight, maybe she should have asked the intelligence officer not to wear her uniform.

"Gary, Kailee, this is Kitty," she said. She carefully didn't mention any ranks. "She will take care of you, then arrange your debriefing. And then she will organise your passage to wherever you want to go."

"Thank you," Kitty said. She gave Jasmine a wink. "I have someone with me, just inside, who you might want to meet."

Jasmine frowned - she disliked surprises - but allowed Kitty to lead the way into the building and through a pair of security doors. Inside, Emmanuel was sitting on a sofa, reading a datapad. He glanced up when he saw them, stared in surprise and then jumped to his feet and ran to her. Jasmine held out her arms and embraced him tightly.

"Boyfriend," Kailee muttered to Gary. "He must be."

Jasmine laughed. She hadn't realised just how much she'd missed Emmanuel until she'd met him again, after months apart. Kitty politely averted her eyes as they kissed - part of her mind noted that both Gary and Kailee stared - and then cleared her throat.

"You have a room at the inn," she said, gently. "I suggest you both go there."

"We will," Jasmine said. She kissed Emmanuel again, feeling almost like a giddy schoolgirl, then caught herself. "Take care of them both, all right?"

"I will," Kitty promised. "And I'll see you in a couple of days."

"So," Kailee said, that evening. "What do you make of Avalon?"

Gary smiled. "It's better than Meridian," he said. "And much better than Earth."

Kailee nodded. The room they'd been given was surprisingly luxurious, by Meridian's standards; there was a shower, a large bath, a window and - best of all - a large and comfortable bed. A small computer terminal sat in the far corner, linked - they'd been told - to the planetary datanet. Kitty had shown them the room personally, dropped a handful of papers on the bed, then told them to get some rest.

"But we've only seen a little of it," he added, after a moment. "And …"

He shuddered. No matter what Jasmine said, no matter how tightly Kailee held him, he could never wash the blood off his hands. He'd given in to nightmarish impulses and hundreds of people had paid the price. There were times when he still wanted to kill himself - he'd known it was possible, even though Jasmine had kept a close eye on him - and times when he tried to convince himself it didn't matter, that everyone he'd killed had deserved to die. He honestly didn't understand how Jasmine managed to keep herself sane, not when she'd killed far more people. Did it make a difference when it was up close and personal?

Kailee walked over and sat next to him, then picked up one of the pieces of paper. "You could work here," she said. "They're offering computer apprenticeships ..."

Gary snorted, rudely. He'd looked into them on Earth, but the Computer Guilds kept everyone out unless they had very good connections or absolutely brilliant skills. It wasn't something he could do, not unless he got very lucky. Life on Earth was designed to prevent newcomers from entering a long-established field, just to keep jobs for those with family histories of such work.

"You don't need connections," Kailee added, after a moment. "You'd just go in and prove yourself."

"I doubt it," Gary said. He took the piece of paper and skimmed it, carefully. Kailee was right; there were tests, unsurprisingly, but no demands for formal qualifications. Maybe it *was* something he could do. "We could try."

Kailee beamed at him. "And I could try to actually study nursing," she said. "Gary, we could *live* here."

"I hope you're right," Gary said.

Kailee elbowed him, sharply. "I think I *am* right," she said. "And we could be safe here, as safe as we could be anywhere. And isn't that the important thing?"

Gary shrugged. Kailee elbowed him again, then rose to her feet. "They do room service here," she said, checking the instruction booklet they'd found on the desk. "You want to eat something?"

"I could eat you," Gary said. He regretted it almost at once. After what he'd done, part of him no longer felt as if he *deserved* to touch Kailee. He knew she was not innocent, he knew she'd killed Barry after he'd raped her, but he still thought of her as untouched. Why would she want a monster like him? "I ..."

"Idiot," Kailee said, affectionately. "I could eat you too."

She paused. "But I need energy to eat," she added. She glanced at the menu as he spluttered in a mixture of horror and amusement. "You fancy a burger and fries? Or pizza? Or ...something I can't actually pronounce, but is marked as being very spicy."

Gary shook his head. He'd never eaten anything that wasn't bland on Earth and his stomach hadn't adapted very well to Meridian's food. Real meat had given him a bellyache on more than one occasion. Spicy food had *never* agreed with him. It was the height of unfairness, he thought sometimes, that Kailee could eat absolutely anything.

"Pizza will do," he said, quickly. Kailee had tried to get him to broaden his diet, before she'd been taken into the camp, but it hadn't worked very well. "And something nice to drink?"

"No alcohol," Kailee said, after a moment. Her reading skills had always been poor; Gary had a feeling he was one of the few people in their school who could actually read words on a page at a reasonable rate. "But there's juice and stuff."

"Juice, please," Gary said. He'd developed a taste for juice on Meridian, even though by Earth's standards they were sharp and utterly unprocessed. "And then ..."

He sighed, inwardly. Maybe she was right. Maybe he could build a new life on Avalon, even though it was the third world he'd been to in his life. But would he ever be able to get the blood off his hands? He honestly didn't know.

But for the moment, he was safe.

And that, he told himself firmly, *would have to be enough.*

"It's been a long time," Jasmine said.

"I know," Emmanuel said. "I was so worried ..."

Jasmine had to smile. The thought of anyone being worried for her ... apart from her family, there weren't many people who *would* be worried for her. Other Marines looked at her Rifleman's Tab and knew she could handle life, no matter what it threw at her. They might like her, or they might hate her, but they wouldn't *worry* about her. Why should they?

But Emmanuel was the closest thing she had to a partner. He *would* worry about her.

They lay together, the sheets sodden with sweat from their lovemaking, holding each other tightly. Jasmine sighed in simple contentment as his fingers traced patterns on her bare flesh, stroking her small breasts and sliding down to the place between her legs. She'd never had body issues - she hadn't been able to understand Kailee's medical reports until she'd realised that Kailee had been dieting to try to stay thin - but it was nice to be worshipped and admired by a man.

"You shouldn't have been," she said. "I never doubted I would get out of the camp."

She sighed, then gasped as his fingers found a sensitive spot. "What were you doing while I was gone?"

"Some reporting work," Emmanuel said, evasively. "And something I'm not allowed to talk about yet, sadly."

Jasmine gave him a sharp look. "Even to me?"

"I think you'll probably be briefed on it later," Emmanuel said, reluctantly. "It's classified."

"Oh," Jasmine said. It wasn't something she'd ever thought about, but Blake Coleman had dated a girl from Imperial Intelligence once and he'd complained loudly that she hadn't been able to tell him anything. The relationship hadn't lasted. "Don't worry about it, really."

She sat upright, looking down at him. "I don't know how long I will have here," she confessed. "Would you like to go hill walking? Or extreme kayaking?"

"If it's with you, I wouldn't mind in the slightest," Emmanuel said. "I have a week of leave, in any case. We could even go to space, if you liked. There's supposed to be some great tours of the cloudscoops these days."

Jasmine shrugged, then rose and paced over to the window. It was night, but a fire was burning on the beach and a handful of men and women were sitting around it. Some of them, she knew, would be survivors from the CEF, the people she'd brought home. Others ...would be trained to help veterans to decompress before they returned to their civilian families. Colonel Stalker, at least, knew better than to leave such matters in civilian hands, not when they always made matters worse. Veterans needed special help, not hectoring from ignorant civilians.

"I don't know what I'd like," she said. She would have liked to go home, to see if her family was still alive, but she knew it was impossible. "Right now, I'm not sure how to relax."

She heard him stand up, then walk over to her. "You do it by forgetting everything," Emmanuel said. His hands started to trace patterns on her back, his fingertips brushing lightly against the scars Admiral Singh's men had left there. "You do it by leaving tomorrow to tomorrow."

"I have to face the Colonel soon," Jasmine said. She shifted slightly as his fingers moved over her buttocks. "Tomorrow."

Emmanuel tensed. "Why so soon?"

"Get it over with," Jasmine said. She hated uncertainty more than anything else. Life had been much easier when she'd been a simple rifleman. "And then I'd know where I stood."

"Then relax now," Emmanuel said. His fingers moved inside her, then pushed gently at her hips. She sighed, then spread her legs as he moved behind her. His hard cock pressed against her, then into her. "Forget the morning, my love. It will come soon enough."

CHAPTER FORTY

But perhaps that was not surprising. Wolfbane was based on corporate principles, after all, while Avalon was based on honour, personal liberty - and common sense.
- Professor Leo Caesius. *The Empire and its Prisoners of War.*

Avalon, Year 5 (PE)

Ed looked up as Jasmine Yamane was shown into his office, wearing Marine BDUs instead of the CEF uniform she was technically entitled to wear. She looked as he remembered, physically, but there was a weariness around her that concerned him. Marines were tough - two years of training saw to that - yet even they could burn out, given the right set of circumstances. Jasmine had been a FNG on Han, then Platoon Commander on Avalon and Corinthian, then a Brigadier on Lakshmibai and Thule. She hadn't even known the stability of a platoon of her fellow marines.

"Jasmine," he said, as he rose to his feet. She came to a halt in front of him and saluted, perfectly. "Would you like coffee?"

"No thank you, sir," Jasmine said.

Ed sat, feeling perturbed. Offering coffee was a subtle sign that no one was in any real trouble, a sign Jasmine would have had no difficulty in understanding. Had she declined coffee because she thought she was in trouble, or because she didn't feel worthy to share with him? He'd faced both problems in the past.

Jasmine reached into her jacket and produced a simple envelope, which she placed on the table. "My resignation," she said. "If you want it."

Ed allowed his eyebrows to climb upwards. "I would have asked for it," he said, "if I had wanted it."

Or done worse, he added, silently. Marines were rarely busted out of the service, but it did happen. If someone had fucked up that badly, or allowed themselves to become warped, he wouldn't have had any choice, but to give them a dishonourable discharge. And, perhaps, ensure they never posed a threat to anyone else ever again. But Jasmine hadn't done either, had she? She was merely suffering a crisis of confidence.

"I screwed up," Jasmine said, flatly. She made no move to pick up the envelope. "I lost the battle on Thule."

"I checked the records," Ed said. He had; he'd reviewed them obsessively in the weeks and months following the start of the war. "Yes, you made mistakes; no, I don't think you could actually have won."

"My mistakes got people killed," Jasmine hissed. It was rare for her to speak rudely to anyone, particularly her commanding officer. It was easy to recognise that she was at the end of her tether. "Sir ..."

"So have mine," Ed said, sharply. He spoke over her before she could say another word. "I have lost people in the past, Jasmine. All I could do from it was learn and move onwards."

Jasmine met his eyes. "I was happier running a small team," she said, softly. "I shouldn't have accepted the CEF post."

"I might not have considered you for another post," Ed pointed out. He watched her closely as he spoke. Someone refusing a promotion, any promotion, could lose any chance of further promotion. "In any case, the CEF is being reformed and another CO will take your place."

"Thank you, sir," Jasmine said.

She would have done it, Ed knew, if he'd ordered her to return to her post. But it wouldn't have made her happy. She'd been on the edge for so long that having to return to a post she believed she didn't deserve might have broken her. Risking her life was one thing - Ed couldn't help shaking his head in admiration at the mess she'd made of Wolfbane - but being responsible for so many others? He knew, all too well, just what she was feeling ...and *he* had nearly a decade more experience than her.

"Your work in Wolfbane may have given us a fighting chance," he added, changing the subject slightly. "Our best guess is that it will take them at least a year to rebuild most of the shipyard, assuming they have the trained manpower on hand. If they don't, it may take them considerably longer."

"Yes, sir," Jasmine said.

"They will probably try to finish the war, assuming whoever takes over manages to secure complete control over Wolfbane," Ed continued. "I imagine they will launch a major offensive in less than four months, in hopes of destroying us before it's too late."

Jasmine nodded, curtly. "Is there any word on just who has taken over?"

"No," Ed said. He'd thought about the question obsessively, but there were too many question marks hanging over Wolfbane for anyone to answer with any certainty. If nothing else, Stubbins might be able to give them some insight into just how their enemy thought and worked. "It could be anyone - or they could collapse into civil war."

"Let us hope so," Jasmine said, shortly. There was a bitter tone to her voice, a tinge of survivor's guilt. "Carl *died* for this, sir."

Ed met her eyes. "Do you really believe he died?"

"I don't know," Jasmine said. She would have been happier, Ed suspected, with knowing for certain, one way or the other. "But he was launching an attack aimed at one of the most heavily-guarded people on the planet. I don't know if either he or Paula survived."

"We will hope," Ed said. There was nothing else they could do, although he had to admit the odds were against survival. Carl Watson *had* tried out for the Pathfinders, after all. "We have all been in tight spots before."

He cleared his throat. "We have been engaged in an operation to lure the enemy into a battle of our choosing," he said. "There is, as yet, no sign that we have actually been successful, but we do have high hopes. Combined with your operation, they may well take the bait."

He smiled to himself. Telling the Wolves, through Hannalore, that one particular world wasn't going to be heavily defended was one thing; giving them an incentive to finish the war as quickly as possible was another. Governor Brown had moved carefully - Ed had no difficulty in recognising the signs of a conservative player - but now, whoever took over would have to either seek peace or gamble everything on beating the Commonwealth before it was too late. Hopefully, they *would* take the bait.

"Yes, sir," Jasmine said.

"I will be taking personal command of the operation," Ed continued. Given what was at stake, he was damned if he was leaving someone else to handle it. "Your friend Mandy will be in command of the space-side, but I'd like you to serve directly under me on the ground. You'll have 1st Platoon and whatever other SF elements I can scrape up."

Jasmine nodded, slowly. "Thank you, sir."

"It will be several months before we know if the enemy will take the bait," Ed said. "Until then, I want you to take a week's leave and do something - anything - that isn't concerned with your duty. I don't want to hear a *peep* from you until the end of that week. After that, you'll be working in the planning cell, drawing up contingency plans."

"Sir," Jasmine said, slowly. "With the greatest of respect …"

"You're taking a week's leave," Ed said, flatly. He held up a hand to make it clear that arguing would be useless. "It isn't a sign of weakness to need a rest from time to time. Trust me on this; my screw-ups are far worse than yours."

Jasmine eyed him, doubtfully. "Sir?"

Ed hesitated, then decided to be open. "There was the time I managed to sleep through departure time on some godforsaken rock," he said. "I spent two months in disgrace before I was transferred to another company."

"They tossed you out of the company?" Jasmine asked, astonished. "Really?"

"Not willingly," Ed said. He understood her surprise. It was rare for a Marine to leave their company unless they were promoted upwards. "The ship left on schedule, leaving me behind. I wound up serving as an advisor to local fighters until another company was landed and accepted me to fill a hole in their roster. The CO was *not* pleased."

"You didn't get anyone killed," Jasmine said.

"I could have done," Ed said. "It certainly wasn't my proudest moment."

He shrugged. "I would have preferred to send you to OCS, Jasmine," he admitted. "But we don't *have* a real OCS, not any longer. You'll have to learn as best as you can."

"I know, sir," Jasmine said.

"And now, go start your week's leave," Ed ordered. He picked up the envelope, tore it into little pieces and dropped them in the bin. "Go."

Jasmine rose, saluted and left the compartment.

Ed watched her go, his expression shadowed. He didn't blame her for coming close to collapse, not after everything she'd been through. Indeed, her career had been compressed, and then warped, because of the demands of their service. Marines were tough, very tough, but they were still human. They could be broken. Time would tell, he suspected, if Jasmine would survive and grow stronger, or give up and collapse.

And she enjoyed being the CO of 1st Platoon, he thought. That was obvious; she'd commanded in action and done a remarkable job. *She will enjoy doing it again.*

He sighed, then picked up his datapad and returned to the war.

The End

Colonel Stalker's Early Life Will Be Covered in:

FIRST TO FIGHT

Coming Soon!

AFTERWORD

The laws of war, such as they are, are based primarily on a pragmatic understanding that deterring one side from doing pretty much whatever it pleases is not an easy task. Imposing one's will on an entire nation requires a great deal of effort - sanctions, limited military action, outright invasion - and can be costly, if possible. The atrocities committed against their own populations by countries such as Saudi Arabia, China, Iran and Cuba are unstoppable by the civilized world, simply because the civilised world has neither the power nor the will to convince them to behave themselves.

This creates an odd problem that is simply not evident outside the military sphere. A country, one that believes it is fighting for its life, will not give up an option merely because the rest of the world thinks it is an *evil* option. All attempts to civilise war have floundered on the simple fact that, pressed against the wall, countries prefer not to leave any option untouched when the alternative is extinction. Nor are they inclined to allow others to take liberties while they are not allowed to do so themselves.

For example, a civilian insurgent can blend into the civilian population - indeed, he can often be unrecognisable before he strikes - and occupying armies find his existence somewhat unnerving. They therefore have a tendency, like the Germans in 1870-70, to retaliate against the civilian population as a whole, seeing them as sharing the blame for the existence of the insurgent. Such understandings do not judge the rightness or wrongness of the occupying force - or the insurgents, for that matter - but merely seek to prevent acts that spark atrocities.

The principle difference between the laws of war and civilian laws is that the former applies to soldiers, while the latter applies to individuals.

A civilian caught engaged in criminal activity, even as part of a criminal organisation like the Mafia, can be charged, tried and sentenced as an individual. A legitimate combatant *cannot* be tried for simply being part of an army, no matter how hated or detested the army may be. The attack on Pearl Harbour that brought America into the Second World War was treacherous (although the Japanese messed up the timing that would have made it slightly less treacherous) but the Japanese pilots who launched the attack could not be legally executed; they fitted the definition of legitimate combatants, so they should have been taken prisoner rather than simply killed out of hand.

A further difference between the laws of war and civilian criminal law is that the laws are based on *reprisal*. Put crudely, if one side breaks the laws of war - say by gunning down surrendering men - the other side is legally permitted to retaliate against its own POWs. This serves the pragmatic requirement of urging both sets of soldiers to stick to the rules; if one side refuses to take prisoners, the other will do the same. Nor are those who try to take advantage of the rules to gain a brief tactical advantage allowed to prosper. If someone tries to pull an 'I surrender, suckers' bid, that person can be legitimately killed ...and the victims are therefore absolved of any requirement to take prisoners for a certain period of time. They are only obliged to make it clear that this is *why* they are refusing to take prisoners.

Some people will argue that this smacks of *victim-blaming*. They might have a point, but if one side chooses to stand outside the laws of war, they cannot complain if their enemies choose not to follow the rules either.

However, the laws of war were designed to cover wars between different nations. A nation, by definition, could not only make war, it could be collectively held accountable for its actions *during* that war. Furthermore, each nation was accountable for controlling its own territory; failing to do so, either deliberately or through simple inability, constitutes a legitimate cause for war. (Thus Operation Enduring Freedom was justified because the Taliban was either unwilling or unable to hand over Osama Bin Laden and his subordinates.) They were simply not intended to cope with transnational terrorist groups that turned failed states into base camps, or spread themselves across many different nations. Could such terrorists be treated as legitimate combatants under the laws of war?

The short answer is no. The Geneva Conventions established a set of qualifications for POWs and expected states to treat such POWs with human decency. Legitimate combatants had to be under responsible command, have a fixed sign representing themselves (i.e. a uniform), carry arms openly and conduct their operations in line with the laws and customs of war. These conventions deliberately *excluded* both soldiers operating *out* of uniform (spies, for example) and civilian insurgents. Both categories were deemed as illegal combatants and could be legally shot out of hand, after being given a very quick hearing in front of a military court. This could be very perfunctory, because the idea was to deter such acts in the only way that was believed to work.

But the treatment of POWs has become a contentious issue over recent years, because the war we are fighting now is a war unlike no other.

Had we gone to war against the Soviet Union, during the Cold War, the laws of war would have been honoured. Individual Russian soldiers would be held as POWs, then largely returned home once the war was over. There would not, as a general rule, be any thought of charging random Russians with war crimes. However, the terrorist factions we fight today have no inclination to follow the laws of war. Quite apart from striking at civilian targets - New York, London, Paris - with the deliberate intention of causing as much death and suffering as possible, they wear no uniforms and blend in with the civilian population. How, then, can they be treated as regular prisoners of war?

This was the problem that President Bush and his team couldn't begin to solve. Were the terrorists legitimate combatants? No; they wore no uniforms, they were not answerable to any realistic chain of command and they showed no respect for the laws of war. But should they be treated as criminals instead? Should they be given the due protections of American law, including lawyers, then put on the stand with all the 'innocent until proven guilty' preconceptions of American courtrooms?

Such a process would rapidly become absurd. First, the terrorists had planned to turn the nature of American justice against its owners. They were primed to scream abuse whenever they saw a reporter/lawyer/judge.

(While there were cases of abuse at prisoner holding facilities, they were vastly exaggerated by the 'neutral' media.) Putting them in front of a judge would simply give them an opportunity to turn the courtroom into a circus. Second, gathering the high level of evidence required by law would be immensely difficult; a terrorist captured in the middle of a fire-fight would be hard to prosecute, in a civilian court. Third, most simply of all, most terrorists were captured in places that were, quite frankly, incriminating.

Put simply, the terrorists fell into the category of illegitimate combatants. They could be simply given a hearing, then shot out of hand.

However, and understandably, the prospect of shooting prisoners horrified many well-meaning people. To kill someone in the midst of a fight was acceptable; to murder someone in cold blood, and they thought of it as murder, was horrific. And yes, there was also the risk of snatching and executing someone who merely happened to be in the wrong place at the wrong time.

But should they therefore be kept prisoner for years, until the end of the war? And if we did, what should happen to them afterwards?

A POW from Soviet Russia could be released, once the war was over, and repatriated back home. But could one do the same with terrorists? Some have discovered that life as a terrorist isn't quite what the recruiters claimed it would be, but others have grown stronger in their perverted faith and their lust for vengeance. Nor would their home countries be inclined to take them home. Saudi Arabia wouldn't want the seventeen 9/11 hijackers back, even if they could be provided. Indeed, the Taliban and AQ included hundreds of fanatics who had gone to Afghanistan to fight, then discovered they were no longer welcome back home.

The terrorists have, deliberately, created a situation where there are no good choices. If we compromise our values, they can call us hypocrites; if we follow the better angels of our natures, we leave ourselves vulnerable to further attacks. And we are held to far higher standards than any of the terrorists. It's almost as if they're *allowed* to be barbarians.

Of course, the terrorists live to spread terror. They don't give a damn if they're called out for slaughtering children, while the West's leaders bend over backwards to avoid giving offense and scrabble to find a scapegoat when/if the shit hits the fan. The idea that many of our problems come from watching as one side ignores the laws of war, while the other slavishly adheres to them even when they have every legal right not to do so, is beyond our political lords and masters. But then, it seems to beyond the chattering classes too.

In the end, we will have to make some hard choices. Is it wrong of me to want *all* of the terrorists dead? I cannot help, but feel that people who choose to stand outside the laws of civilised society have no call on its protections. But, at the same time, defining one particular category of people as permanently excluded from such protections *weakens* the protections - permanently.

For the moment, all we can really do is keep the captured terrorists locked up indefinitely - and hope we can win the war without becoming the barbarians we hate and fear. I have no other solution.

Christopher G. Nuttall
Edinburgh, 2015

If you enjoyed *Never Surrender*, you might like:
Fenris Unchained - Jake Spriggs

The Wolf is Loose.

Ten years ago, after her parents were killed in a terrorist attack, Melanie Armstrong walked away from a military officer's career to raise her orphaned brother.

Since then she's been captaining a tramp freighter – shuffling from world to world, scraping to barely get by, but content that she's made the right decision.

But when her ship crashes, authorities make her an offer: take a fifteen-year sentence on a prison world where the average lifespan is a third of that.

Or take part in a mission to stop an ancient, and until-now forgotten, robotic warship, the *Fenris*, from completing its hundred-year-old task of destroying a planet, killing millions.

CHAPTER ONE

Time: 0815 Local, 01 June 291 G.D.
Location: Dakota, Dakota System

A yellow light began to flash on the control board.

That was nothing new, not aboard the *Kip Thorne*. Warning lights lit up half the panel. It was a Christmas display of yellow caution lights, flashing priority lights, and red danger lights that gave the board an aspect of impending doom.

The pilot didn't look over to the panel to see what was wrong. One of the red lights indicated a malfunction in the auto-pilot system. That meant that the tall, blond woman had to bring the *Kip Thorne* down by hand.

Not a difficult a task for an experienced pilot. She enjoyed flying, enjoyed it more than anything else, really. She didn't enjoy thirty six hours of flight time spent awake on stimulants while flying a ship that needed far too many repairs.

She shot a glance at the panel, and then flipped on the intercom. "Rawn, take a look at the starboard thruster." She shook her head. Tried to push thoughts through a mind that seemed turned to mud.

The intercom crackled and hissed, his voice difficult to make out. "Uh, Mel, we might have a problem."

The light ceased flashing. She sighed in relief, "No, it cleared up here, good job whatever you did."

The ship bucked. The alarm light flashed red. A moment later, so did six or seven other warning lights. "What the hell did you just do, Rawn?!"

Mel fought the control yoke, eyes wide, as she swore to herself: "Rawn, was that the starboard pod going out?"

The ship yawed over as she overcompensated and she fought it back under control.

"Rawn, you'd better get that thruster back online."

She heard a squeal from the hatch as it opened. It had always reminded her of a ground vehicle's brakes screeching just before an accident.

She tried not to apply that metaphor as some sort of warning to her current flight. Her brother spoke from behind her: "I'm going to pack the escape pod. Anything you want me to throw in?" he asked.

"What?" Mel craned her neck to look at him.

The ship spun sharply and threw her against her straps and tossed her brother into the wall hard. She bit off a curse and struggled with the controls for a moment. It seemed to take an eternity to fight the ship back under control.

The radio crackled, "Freighter *Kip Thorne*, this is Dakota Landing Control, you broke out of your landing queue, return immediately, over."

"We're going to lose the other thruster. The port thruster is in worse shape. What do you want me to put in the pod?" her brother asked.

His calm voice made her clench her teeth.

"We're not abandoning ship," she told him sharply. "I can land this thing." It would be hard, though, with just one thruster. They couldn't engage their warp drive in atmosphere, not without disengaging safeties that were there to prevent that. *Even if we had time,* she thought, *it would be a stupid thing to do.* The warp drive field would tear the atmosphere around them and if they hit anything in warp, the difference in relative velocity would not only kill them but quite possibly wipe out Dakota's biosphere.

She forced her mind to focus. When she spoke, her voice had the calm tone that she emulated from her father: "Dakota Landing Control this is Freighter *Kip Thorne*, we just lost our starboard thruster and are requesting immediate assistance, over."

"Freighter *Kip Thorne*, is this some kind of joke?" The speaker's nasal, officious tone suggested she wasn't amused.

Rawn snorted. "I know the safe combo, I'll grab our cash and some keepsakes. I'll clear out your desk too." He pushed his way back off the bridge.

"Get back here—" Mel clamped her jaws shut. *One thing at a time.* "Negative Dakota Landing, this is no joke, our starboard thruster—"

Her voice broke off as another yellow light began to flash, the warning light for load limit on the other thruster. "Our starboard thruster is out and we're about to lose our port thruster, requesting assistance, over."

"Negative, *Kip Thorne*, you'll have to break off your descent and return to orbit," the nasal voice answered. "A repair craft can be sent to you there."

"Dakota Landing, this is an emergency. We lose our port thruster, there won't be anything keeping us up here." Mel snapped. "We don't have enough thrust to get back into orbit, and you don't have time to—"

"*Kip Thorne*, break off your descent or you will be intercepted by our customs cutter. Over."

"Dakota, I hope they got a tractor," answered. "Because—" The ship shuddered and the other thruster went dead. "We just lost our other thruster. *Kip Thorne*, out."

She turned off the radio and sat in the chair for a long moment as the small freighter bounced. Soon it would begin to tumble, she knew, without the guidance from the thrusters.

"Six years, six years I kept her goin'. Dad, I did my best."

She wiped her eyes; now was not the time to cry.

The ship fell now, without anything to slow its descent besides atmospheric friction. Superheated air flashed across the hull and cast glowing flames across the cockpit glass.

Mel sighed. She kissed her fingertips and touched the control yoke one last time, then unbuckled and left the bridge. She didn't look back.

Time: 1720 Local, 1 June 291 G.D.
Location: Dakota City Detention Center, Dakota System
Marcus looked over at his companions.

"Don't be so gloomy. They're not nearly so angry with us as they are with whoever crashed that freighter." He ran a hand through his brown hair and gave them a shaky smile.

Brian didn't lift his head out of his hands. "You were carrying ten kilos of rex. Do you know how illegal that is? We'll be lucky if they only confiscate our ship and give us a few years in jail."

Strak spoke from where he sat, cross-legged on the floor. "That's overly optimistic really; rex dealers don't get good treatment in jail. Most of the inmates know someone who's OD'd on it."

Marcus winced, looked away.

"Look, I'm sure I can get us out of this."

Rex was a performance drug, and it was the most illegal and the most common illegal drug in known space. Rex's addiction was both chemical and psychological because it gave a person something that was priceless.

A rex junkie didn't act like any other druggie, because rex didn't distort your senses or give you a euphoric feeling. People on rex were confident, their thoughts were clear, they were able to make quick, well thought-out decisions. The most shy, nervous youth could become the self-assured center of activity with a single dose of rex.

Tertius was the third level, the cheapest. It only affected brain activity. Secundus and Primus Rex chemically modified the body.

Primus was the highest level, the most addictive. Secundus heightened the senses and stimulated the central nervous system, giving a person greater control over their body. Primus did all that and also lent strength, streamlined metabolism, and heightened reaction speeds.

Of course, if Rex's benefits were heaven, its side effects were hell.

They sat in silence for a while and Marcus studied his two companions. He'd signed on as crew aboard their ship, the *Varqua*, six months ago. A crew of five, including these two. The *Varqua* was a tramp freighter, a Stout-class, one of thousands that plied the edges of Guard Space, serving the smaller colonies.

Brian Liu was the owner of the ship. Apparently he had a good head for business or good contacts. The *Varqua* had been a profitable ship, unlike most that plied their runs. A short, stocky man, clearly of Asiatic origins, Brian was a decent enough boss, if overly picky about the law most of the time. Marcus couldn't fault him that, though the man's arrogance grated at times.

Strak was something of an enigma. Calm and collected where Brian was loud and arrogant, overweight and slow where Brian was muscular and bird-quick. He had held a sort of general maintenance job aboard the *Varqua*. In reality, he served as an adviser for Brian, and a watchdog over the rest of the crew. Getting anything past the old man was more than difficult, it was damn near impossible. He seemed remarkably loyal to Brian, and Marcus got the feeling that they shared some kind of history.

Marcus hadn't ever felt unwelcome…just the outsider.

"Everything would have been fine except for those damned pirates," he muttered.

The door at the end of the cell block clanged and then groaned open. Two prisoners led the way, followed by two guards. The first prisoner was in his late teens and he wore a ragged set of coveralls. An unruly mop of blond hair hung above a face covered in dirt and oil.

The other prisoner was a tall, statuesque blonde, with dark brown eyes. She wore an equally ragged cut of clothing. As they came past, Marcus blinked in surprise. "Mel?" He asked as he moved close to the bars.

She turned, hearing his voice. Her eyes went wide in recognition.

Then her fist snapped out, slipping between the bars to strike him full in the face.

Marcus dropped like a stone. She kicked through the bars, hitting what she could, punctuating each word with a kick, "You owe me ten thousand dollars, you free-booting piece of—"

One of the guards cuffed her to the ground and then drew her to her feet and pushed her into the cell opposite the other three prisoners.

Both the guards and the other prisoners laughed.

Marcus sat up, touching his nose and wincing, "You bwoke my mose!"

Mel shook her head, jaw clenched in rage, "Too bad I didn't break your neck."

Strak laughed, "Sounds like she knows you fairly well, Marcus."

Marcus sat on his bunk, holding his nose with one hand. "Well, mow that 'ou've gob ib' ou' of yo', you want to talk?" he asked in a calm tone. He felt hot blood run down his face and the salty copper of it in the back of his throat. Well, he'd tasted worse things before.

Mel shook her hand, flexing it a bit. "Sure. You still owe me ten thousand dollars. You're still a piece of shit." She took a seat on one of the bunks in her cell. "So what more do we have to talk about?"

Marcus stared at her for a long moment. There was something more here besides his theft. Granted, Mel had a tendency to overreact at times. "Five years ain't been enough to cool your anger?" He asked. She didn't answer.

Brian looked up, "This bastard screwed you lot over as well?"

The boy spoke, his voice was calm, but his eyes were cold. "Marcus Keller is not a man to be trusted."

"A little late to tell us that." Brian's voice filled with bitterness. "He had ten kilos of rex stashed in his room."

"Wow, I knew you were a bastard," Mel said, "but dealing rex? That's sick, that's really sick." She smiled sweetly. "I hate to think what they'll do to you in a prison."

Marcus held his nose, feeling the blood run down his face. He didn't say anything. There wasn't anything he could say. He looked away from her angry dark eyes and met those of her brother Rawn. *She has every reason to hate me,* Marcus thought grimly, *and her brother, too.*

"Hey, boss, got a couple possible recruits."

Agent Mueller looked up from his paperwork, "Not interested. I wouldn't even want to pick up the other two to get our man if it weren't for the package deal."

"One of them is a pilot. Her brother is certified engine crew."

"Oh?" Mueller raised an eyebrow, "that could be useful, but this is a recruitment mission—"

"Both of them lost their parents to a GFN terrorist attack."

The Agent picked up the file, he browsed both folders quickly. He began to smile slightly, especially as he read the note from the investigating officer. "Interesting…All right, you've convinced me. Tell the magistrate I want them."

"The accused will step forward."

Mel stepped forward into the courtroom. The only occupants were a pair of guards and a man in Guard Fleet uniform. "Sir, I want to—"

"You will be silent or you will be held in contempt of this tribunal," the uniformed man cut her off. "The tribunal is now in session."

There was a faint hum as recording equipment turned on.

"Certified Pilot and Ship's Owner Melanie Armstrong of the Century System is charged with Criminal Negligence, Reckless Endangerment, and Willful Disobedience of Traffic Control Commands." The tribunal officer sounded bored. "How do you plead?"

"Uh, sir, that is—"

"Accused pleads guilty to all charges. Evidence is amended to tribunal recordings."

"Hey, I didn't say—"

"The tribunal finds the accused guilty of above crimes and also for contempt of the tribunal. Sentence for conviction is fifteen years hard labor. Convicted is remanded to Guard Custody for duration of the sentence."

The officer flipped a switch. The hum cut off.

"Hey, wait, you can't do this!" Mel shouted. "That wasn't even a trial! I demand to see a lawyer—"

One of the guards grabbed her by her collar and dragged her out.

Time: 1100 Zulu, 11 June 291 G.D.
Location: Female Block, *Justicar* Prisoner Transport

The cold, dark ship's sole purpose and design came from the need to transport the maximum number of prisoners with minimal difficulties. Cells were just that, cells of solid steel that ran down the length of the ship, each door secured by a digital lock whose combination changed every time the guards opened it.

They separated Mel from her brother and put her in the female block. There were only three other women in the block. Apparently the Guard didn't get many prisoners on this run.

She didn't talk to them. They didn't talk to her. The silence was almost companionable. Her food arrived via a tray slid under her door, twice a day, delivered by a female guard who never spoke.

On the third day, her door opened.

There were two female guards. One of them gestured. "Come on out."

They took her out of the cells, past the security checkpoint and into a clean, sterile room. "Shower's there," one gestured to a door.

"Clothing's there." She gestured to a neatly folded pile of clothing on a table.

"When you're clean and dressed go through that door." She pointed at a second door.

Then they left.

It was the first moment of privacy Mel had had in days. She wanted to cry. Instead, she went to the shower. It was an experience she wanted to savor, but she also didn't want to be dragged out of it. She suspected that or worse would happen if she lingered too long.

She hurried and then got dressed quickly. It was normal, comfortable civilian clothing; it even fit her fairly well, though it was bland and unremarkable. It felt alien after the prison smock she'd worn for what seemed forever. A part of her mind whispered that it had only been a week. She didn't want to imagine the longer period of imprisonment ahead of her.

The second door opened into another sterile room.

A long mirror covered one wall. A man sat behind a table with a slim folder on it.

"Have a seat," he said without rising.

Mel sat. She knew this was some kind of game, knew she was being manipulated. It should have made her angry, but somehow it only made her feel more helpless. Over his shoulder she saw her reflection. Her face looked pale, blonde hair lank, eyes shadowed.

The man opened up his folder. "Melanie Armstrong, born 266 to Anne Marie and Hans Armstrong on the planet Century, of the same system."

His voice was empty and cold, "Your aunt and uncle were archeologists on Century, they and their youngest child were killed in a pirate attack on Century, leaving only your cousin Jiden Armstrong alive. Your grandmother, Admiral Victoria Armstrong of Century's Planetary Militia is something of a local war hero. You got your pilot's license at fifteen, qualified for entry into the Harlequin Sector Fleet Academy at seventeen, rather than joining

Century's Military Academy. You were in the top five percent of your class for three years. Then your parents died in a Guard Free Now terrorist attack two months before graduation. You resigned and took guardianship of your younger brother. In the six years since, you managed the *Kip Thorne* as captain and owner until a week ago when it broke up above Dakota."

"I suppose you even know my calculus test grades from my plebe year," Mel joked weakly, "So what is this about?"

The man smiled thinly, "You got excellent marks, your teacher put in a recommendation that you be sent to further schooling in higher level mathematics." The man stood "Do you know what your sentence is?"

"Penal colony I'd guess." Mel answered.

"Fifteen years on Thornhell." He stood up and looked down at her. He wasn't tall, probably ten centimeters or more shorter than Mel, but he seemed to loom over her.

Mel gulped, "I heard there was a war on there." What she'd heard of the planet left her feeling faintly sick.

The man shook his head, "Not anymore. Not that it matters much. You'd be working in the mines. Fifteen years is ten years longer than the survival rate on that planet."

"It's not fair!" Mel snapped. "I did the best I could, I didn't even get a fair—"

His voice cut across hers like a knife, "No, it's not fair. The universe isn't fair." He smiled a cold, reptilian smile. "Think on this though. How fair would it be if your freighter had landed on someone, rather than smashing into some wilderness on a backwater planet?"

He smiled wider as she shook her head stubbornly. "No, it didn't. But your next stop was Salvation. Think for a moment what would have happened if your thrusters went out there. Something similar happened on Expo just last year. Over fifteen hundred dead when one battered freighter crashed into a residential block in the middle of the night. No warning; definitely not fair to them, eh?"

Mel looked down at her hands. "If we'd made that run, we could have paid for the repairs we needed."

"No, if you'd made the run, you would have needed to make several more to pay for the repairs you needed. We reviewed your logs and analyzed your cargo versus your maintenance bill. Even with some kind of loan, you weren't going to pay for it all." The man answered.

Mel looked up, anger in her face. "What's this about? I'm going to die on some crappy, worthless world, I failed my brother and I failed myself. Is that what you want to hear?"

She gestured at the mirrored wall, "Is that what they want to see?"

The cold man smiled. "What do you know about the Second Sweep?"

Mel's jaw dropped at the complete change in subject. She shook her head while she tried to get her bearing. Finally, she answered, "Started a hundred years ago. Bigger war than the War of Persecution. We almost lost."

"We very nearly were *exterminated*." The cold man spoke softly. His eyes seemed distant and there was a tone of reverence to his voice. "The Culmor were at the front gate. Fifty million soldiers and sailors died. Over three billion civilians wiped out. The entire Sepaso Sector razed; half of Harlequin sector exterminated."

He caught Mel's gaze with his own cold and calculating eyes.

"That certainly wasn't *fair* to them. That didn't stop it from happening. You wrote a paper about the automatons." He paused. "Tell me about them."

Mel stared at him for a long while, "Uh, the Preserve and Triad ran low on trained personnel. They made fully automated vessels for the fighting." She frowned.

"Most had small crews to run them, some were controlled entirely by computers: Artificial Intelligence, supposedly limited by programming to think only within tactical orientations. They weren't supposed to think outside of the mission parameters."

The unknown man picked up a copy of her paper, she could follow along as he read the instructor's comments scrawled on the top, "A decent paper, excellent research but you didn't touch very much on the reasons the ships were discontinued."

Mel shrugged. It seemed a strange topic of conversation, but… "They behaved erratically in combat. Mission parameters were vague in many cases. They were amazingly effective as rear-area raiders, or serving as suicide attackers against Culmor bases. While in formation with human ships, though, they sometimes targeted friend and foe, went berserk. Some took damage and went haywire."

She was slightly surprised at all she remembered after several years. Then again, it had been an interesting topic in history. The subject had been all the more intriguing for the fact that most people didn't like to talk about it.

"And then the war turned, we didn't need them any more. So the ships were discontinued, most of them were scrapped."

Mel nodded impatiently, "Right, they weren't designed to carry crews, the weapons, plants and engines had little shielding, the ships didn't have life support. It was easier and cheaper to scrap them than to refit them for human use."

"Don't worry, this all has a purpose." The cold man smiled, took his seat. "That history is something of a fascination of mine; also, it's part of my job."

"Which would be?" Mel asked.

The man removed a wallet from within his suit, "Guard Intelligence."

Mel pushed back from the table, as if he'd transformed into a venomous snake.

He grinned broadly, "No need to fear, I'm not hunting you or even here to harm you. As bad as it may sound, I'm actually here to help you."

Despite his words, he clearly enjoyed the effect he'd had on her, Mel saw. The light to his eyes and the smirk on his face marked him as someone who cultivated the persona.

Mel knew that she should stay quiet and shouldn't provoke him. Even so, she couldn't help but snort in derision, "Right. As in 'I'm from the government, I'm here to help you.'"

The spook's smirk vanished and his eyes narrowed in irritation. "Some agents believe that coercion is sufficient to gain service from those they need. I do not believe so. Believe me, I will lie to you, I will use you, but I understand that I must give you some incentive if I want you to assist me."

He stared at her in silence for a long moment, almost as if to suggest that he were reconsidering whether he were going to offer Mel anything at all.

Good job, Mel thought to herself, *piss off the guy who holds your life in his hands.*

Even so, she couldn't help a spurt of irritation with the man. He wanted her to feel this way, wanted her to second-guess herself. He was building towards something and he wanted her off balance and uncertain. She fell back on the fire that had gotten her through the Academy and she felt her back straighten, even as she clenched her teeth on the spike of anger at this continued manipulation.

"What do you know about the Wolf-class battlecruisers?" He demanded.

Back to the games, Mel thought with a sigh. She took a moment to think. Part of the Academy had dealt with ship identification, with a basic overview of every Human military ship made in the past three hundred years.

"The class was designed for heavy combat. Fully automated, some self-repair capabilities. Only ten or twelve of them even begun in construction, I don't think any of them ever saw combat."

It was the sum of all her knowledge. She'd been far more fascinated by the smaller ships while at the Academy. *I wanted to be a fighter pilot,* she remembered. That part of her seemed very distant, in many ways as dead as her parents.

"Three Wolves commissioned, two of them went on missions, the third went to the breakers within a month of completion," the agent stated flatly, all emotion gone from his voice.

"The *Romulus* went against a Culmor dreadnought squadron at Baker in order to delay its attack on Harlequin Station. That mission cut the war short by an appreciable margin. It destroyed three of the squadron's four dreadnoughts, and the fourth was destroyed in a follow-up run."

Mel blinked. A *battlecruiser* destroyed three dreadnoughts?

"The other ship, the *Fenris*, departed on a separate mission three weeks later, in March of 193. It first attacked a troop transport convoy, sighted at Bell, then a captured deep-space station serving the enemy as a raider base. Its final target was to be the center of the Culmor advance in this sector, Vagyr."

Mel frowned, "Wasn't Vagyr captured intact nearly a year later?"

"It was, by 'auxiliaries' that were, and are, little more than pirates," the agent replied.

"The *Fenris* never arrived at Vagyr. It intercepted and destroyed the convoy, scouts confirmed the destruction the raider base, and that was it. Guard Fleet presumed it destroyed in the fight at the raider station. Significant debris clouds suggested a significantly larger raider force at the station than intelligence had suggested." He shrugged. "Logic, therefore, suggested the autonomous ship was destroyed in combat."

"I assume we're having this conversation because it wasn't?" Mel snapped, her patience at a ragged end. The history lesson grated, particularly given the fact that her future seemed tied to this random bit of history.

"Indeed." The agent smiled. "In fact, you are quite right."

"Two weeks ago, a merchant ship suffered a minor warp drive failure. Their FTL warp drive kicked off in what was supposed to be an empty, barren system. While undergoing their repairs, they spotted activity in the inner system. They also detected military transmissions in the system. Like any merchant with something to hide, they quietly got their ship repaired and left. Someone aboard talked and one of my colleagues collected their sensor data as a precaution."

"And it was this missing ship?" Mel asked.

"That took confirmation by a cruiser squadron we sent to investigate. They were extremely fortunate: the *Fenris* queried them for identification and accepted their modern codes."

"So the ship was damaged and hid in some backwater system. What's the problem?" Mel asked. Some part of her whispered that she would be better off trying a more helpful tone…but everything about this Guard Intelligence agent made her back go up.

The agent closed his eyes, sighed slightly. "I've had to tell this story twenty-seven times. Do let me finish at my own pace." He opened his eyes and peered at her somewhat inquisitively, "I don't think you want to make me angry."

His gaze reminded her of a snake that had just eaten, regarding a mouse it might make room for. Mel shivered.

"Guard Fleet dispatched a courier ship with the proper clearance codes and query data to order the ship to power down. Upon receiving the query codes, the vessel replied that repairs were 98% completed, and that the mission would continue. Upon receiving the codes to power down, the ship did something it shouldn't have. It ignored the codes and replied that the mission would be completed. Then it engaged it's strategic warp drive."

"And you have no idea where it went." Mel sat back.

"On the contrary. We know exactly where it is going."

Time: 1500 Zulu, 11 June 291 G.D.
Location: Solitary Confinement, *Justicar* Prisoner Transport
Agent Mueller stepped up near the bars and dropped a chair outside. He settled into it backwards, arms crossed over the back, "Leon, you look like shit."

The prisoner didn't look up from where he sat, huddled in the shadows at the rear of the cell.

"Trying to ignore me? You got pretty good at ignoring many things, Leon, but you never could ignore me." Mueller entwined his fingers and rested his chin on them.

"What do you want?" The voice was only a whisper.

"My friend, my mentor, what do you think I want? I want you, the famous agent, I want you working for us again." Mueller let the sincerity drip through his voice. It was easy enough, after all, because it was the truth. They needed him, and men like him, especially now.

"That will never happen," Leon hissed back.

"Come now, never is an awful long time." Mueller replied. "I know you've still got family back on New Paris. For that matter, I'm sure I can find someone a little closer to…focus your mind."

He hated to use threats, not because they weren't effective but because it seemed so dirty. *Why do people continue to make me threaten them*, he thought, *just to do what needs to be done?*

"What do you want?" The whisper was faint, difficult to hear. It was enough.

"I need you on this one. It's bad, I won't lie. Has the potential to be extremely bad. Entire planet annihilated, not a good thing to have happen on my watch, you understand." Mueller shrugged, as if to say it would be an unavoidable tragedy.

"I get the point, what do you want me to do?"

"Don't cause problems. I've talked your friends into helping us. Go along with it. They'll come through this fine; you'll come through this fine. Maybe I can even get you some treatment—"

"No. I have my own ways for dealing with my demons."

The agent shrugged, "Have it your way. It's a shame you left. Yours are hard boots to fill."

"What, the killing, destroying and murdering boots, or the scheming, plotting, manipulating boots?" The prisoner scoffed. "I'm sure you're doing just fine."

"Thanks, Leon, you always knew just how to cheer a fellow up," Agent Mueller smiled. "I must say though…I did learn from the best."

"Get out of my sight bastard, before I kill you," the voice of his former mentor showed some echo of real anger. That surprised him a bit, he thought it would take more than that to break through the man's shell of self-pity.

"Oh, you wouldn't want that to happen, Leon. If I die, well, let's just say you wouldn't want certain other deaths on your already heavy shoulders." Despite his languid words, the man rose quickly and left. He'd already set the hook, no need to further bait the tiger.

CHAPTER TWO

Time: 0800 Zulu, 12 June 291 G.D.
Location: *SS John Kelly*, Expo System
Mel looked the unfamiliar cockpit over with a critical eye. She'd seen a couple of these ships before, though never from the inside. The Lotus Blossom class were somewhat infamous. A far fancier name than was entirely necessary, she thought. The ungainly and actually rather ugly ship had little in the looks department to compare to most small freighters. It wasn't really a freighter at all, more of a military light cargo transport.

Marcus stepped in the door behind her, "Should have known I'd find you here, already. Studying a bit early aren't you? We still got six hours before departure."

She didn't answer him at first. It took her a few seconds to squash her anger so that she didn't erupt from her chair to attack him. He would expect that, she knew from the overly relaxed tone in his voice. He wanted to provoke her. "You're a manipulative son of a bitch, you know that?"

"Mel, I'm hurt...*really*." His innocent tone didn't fool her. Marcus took a seat in the copilot seat behind her.

"Don't you have something else to do?" Mel asked.

"Why? I'm only familiarizing myself with the systems, just like you," Marcus said. She didn't have to look over her shoulder to see the insolent smile on his face.

She sat there for a long while, concentration broken by anger. She hated this man, hated him with every ounce of her body. "Why'd you do it?" She asked finally.

He didn't answer for a moment. She expected another off-handed joke. Instead, when he finally spoke, his voice was gruff. "You wouldn't understand."

"You're right. I probably couldn't understand how a betrayer thinks." She answered. "I don't think I'd want to anyway."

"Things aren't always what they appear, Mel." His voice was sad, somehow. "Keep that in mind when you work with Agent Mueller. Sometimes things aren't what they appear to be."

"And sometimes things are exactly what they look like," Mel snapped back instantly. She didn't want to think he'd had any motivation besides self-interest. Those thoughts robbed her of her anger, left her only with pain.

His seat creaked as he leaned forward to speak softly in her ear. "Don't trust anyone on this ship."

With that he rose and left.

Time: 1400 Zulu, 12 June 291 G.D.
Location: *SS John Kelly*, Expo System
Mel completed the undocking procedure and drew away from the prison ship. She looked out the canopy distastefully, gazing with distaste at the decrepit vessel. "LMV *John Kelly*, clear of your drive, *Justicar*." She couldn't find it in her to wish them a good journey.

She heard a dark chuckle from behind her. "I'd love to be able to take all the prisoners off and blast that bastard out of the sky."

"I'm sure you would, Marcus, but you won't be doing that." Agent Mueller said from behind them both. Marcus muttered something about who he wished was aboard the prison ship when he did it.

Mel smiled in spite of herself.

Her smile broadened as she looked across the indicator panels and saw only two yellow lights. She took her time as she swung the bow around and inserted the coordinates for the warp engines. There was joy in a ship that responded.. There was happiness to be found at the yoke of any vessel, even if it wasn't home. *I have no home now,* she thought, her joy darkened with sorrow. She had lost the last thing she had left of her parents.

"Warp coordinates uploaded. Strategic drive active in thirty seconds," Marcus acknowledged.

Being reminded of his presence killed the smile. It didn't hurt nearly as much this time, but it certainly didn't feel good.

She watched the countdown timer. Most such maneuvers were routine; the good thing about warp drives was that they worked or they didn't. The drive rings that circled the ship did their job unless they suffered actual physical damage, at which time the ship reverted immediately to normal space. *Though they can function at lower levels of capability,* she thought.

Watching a ship go into warp was a sign of how well a ship worked. A ship in top shape engaged smoothly, because its drive was properly aligned. Most civilian ships were slightly misaligned, not enough to cause damage, but enough to cause slight nausea to those unfamiliar to the experience. Local space warp drives, often called 'tactical' warp drives utilized only one ring so noticing any motion was difficult. The faster than light warp drive, often called strategic drive by the military, utilized both drive rings on a ship and so any issues with alignment were more easily detected.

As she'd expected, the drive was very smooth. "Minimal misalignment."

"She goes down like a drunken—"

"If you finish that statement, you're going to wish we had a doctor aboard." Mel stated flatly. She'd heard the phrase before; the last person she wanted to hear it from now was him. She opened the intercom to the engine room. "Rawn, how are things down there?"

"No problems, sis." She could almost hear his shrug. "Strak's monitoring the power plant, and that Giran guy is keeping an eye on the control panel."

"Thanks, Rawn."

She heard the door slide closed, and flipped on one of the internal cameras to watch the Guard Intelligence agent walk down the corridor, toward the hangar bay.

She felt Marcus looking over her shoulder. "Getting a little suspicious of our good friend and boss?"

"I got less reason to trust you. Shut your trap." She spoke without force, though. Why the Guard needed to rely on seven convicts to do this job she didn't know. But she didn't trust it one bit.

She flipped on the receiver for the hangar bay intercom. Two of the other crew members were there, Brian, the third and last member from the *Varqua*, and Stasia, who seemed to be a hacker of some sort. The hacker seemed to have a large number of boxes to sort through and as Mel watched, the woman opened up a box, drew out some computer components and then checked them off an inventory.

"Everything good down there?" Agent Mueller was asking.

"Da, seems good." Stasia was a short, skinny woman with mousy brown hair. Her face had a pinched look and she seemed to squint at everything nearsightedly. Mel had spoken to her briefly; she'd seemed very distant, as if her mind was elsewhere.

As Stasia returned to sorting through her boxes, Brian gestured toward three black crates. Each was long and narrow, roughly the size and shape of a coffin, banded with metal strips. The security camera didn't have a good angle, but Mel zoomed in and was able to read bright orange numbers written on the top of one of them.

"Three crates arrived for you just before departure." Brian spoke. There was an unspoken consensus by the crew that no one would refer to the agent as 'sir'. He hadn't earned any kind of respect, and he gave them that minor victory. That they followed his orders seemed good enough for him.

"Only three?" the agent asked.

Brian held out the inventory list, but Mueller waved it away. "Have them put outside my cabin."

"That crate is carrying MP-11s," Marcus said from behind her. He pointed at the first crate. As the agent turned, the other two crates were clearly visible. "That one is a case for a MG-144, and that is a—" He cut himself off, looking at her.

Mel stared at him for a long moment, the obvious question unasked. Marcus was a smuggler, a thief, and a general scumbag. There was no reason for him to instantly recognize the coded label on a military weapon crate.

Movement on the screen caught her attention and she saw that the Guard Intelligence agent was headed toward the bridge. She cut the camera feed and brought up data on the warp drive just as the door opened.

"I trust everything is well in hand?" He asked.

Mel didn't trust herself to face him without revealing too much. Marcus saved her by unbuckling. "Everything's good here. We can probably go to autopilot for the rest of the trip. Damned good computers – equipment, too – for a freighter. Where'd Guard Intel come up with it?"

"There will be a briefing in five minutes in the lounge. I trust you'll both be there."

The agent turned and left without saying anything.

"Fishing for information?" Mel asked.

"Trying to distract him. Agent Mueller is a very perceptive man. I thought it best to give him some false lead as to what we were doing in here during his absence."

"His name's Mueller?" Mel asked.

There was a moment of silence. "Yeah, Adam Mueller. I caught his name when he flashed his badge."

That sounded a little weak to Mel, "Sounds to me like you know something about this GI agent."

He snorted, "Sure I do. *I* know *he'll* know we're up to something if we aren't on time for his little briefing."

Mel opened her mouth to retort, but too late. He had slipped through the hatch before she could come up with something suitably acidic.

"I *hate* that bastard," she growled. Even she wasn't sure which bastard she meant.

The eight of them met in the lounge for the first time.

Agent Mueller stood next to a holo-projector. Brian and Strak had taken one couch, Mel and Rawn the other. Marcus, Stasia and Giran were seated at the lounge's lone table.

"As most of you can easily guess after our conversations, we are going after the *Fenris*." The agent smiled. "I believe we can dispense with the pleasantries and get straight down to business."

He had a smirk on his face, as if he expected them all to laugh at his turn of phrase. When none of them responded with so much as a smirk, his face went cold. "First: payment." The agent ticked off his fingers as he addressed each item. "All of you will be pardoned for your crimes. Easy enough for me to arrange, I assure you." He shrugged. "Second: each of you receives a bonus for completion. In addition to your freedom, each of you will receive ten thousand dollars."

The seven ex-prisoners eyed each other. Mel judged from the suspicious looks she received that the others trusted her as little or less than she trusted them.

"Each of you has talents that I may find useful." The agent spoke on, "Stasia is our computer expert. Hopefully she's learned her lesson regarding illicit hacking and will not stray. Melanie and Marcus can serve as pilots, Brian and Strak as general crew, Giran and Rawn as engine crew. All of you have other abilities that may come in handy. And all of you were conveniently present when I needed volunteers." He said the last in a light-hearted tone.

Mel didn't feel any surprise when no-one laughed at his joke.

The holo-projector came to life, where it displayed an external view of a ship. "This is the *Fenris*. You all know what it is. So do some others who didn't make the screening process. We are going to shut the vessel down, before it strikes Vagyr. A task force is preparing to meet it in orbit, should we be unable to stop it."

No one looked at him; they all had good ideas what the price of failure would be: a digital pardon was very easy to 'misplace.' *For that matter,* Mel thought darkly, *he could easily have us all killed or marked as escaped prisoners.*

"What should happen is that we catch up to it at one of its navigational stops, and we shut it down via external command. If that proves ineffective, we have to board it. That will not prove to be an easy task." The projector changed, flashing through a deck-by-deck overview. "The entire ship is covered by a security system, which allows the AI to send in security robots, close out sections of the ship, and do all sorts of nasty things."

"So you're giving us all this, just for playing taxi?" Rawn asked.

There was a long, empty silence. The GI agent was silent, his face impassive.

Strak said, "He's using us because we're a cut-out. If this doesn't work, the Guard won't take the blame." The old man stood slowly and shrugged his shoulders, "Probably lots of evidence will point to a salvage ship, us, having activated the ship in the first place."

Everyone looked from him to the agent, Mueller smiled. "A clever idea, but one that is entirely excessive. The Preserve built the *Fenris*. The AI system was produced on Triad, ten decades ago. The forces we're positioning in Vagyr show that the Guard is doing our best to avert tragedy. We don't need any kind of cover-up."

"So," Mel asked, irritated by the agent's smug attitude, "Why do you need us?"

"Because you are expendable," he shrugged. "No reason to send highly trained professionals to deal with a semi-berserk battlecruiser, not when a handful of criminals can do the job just as well. Also, you were easy enough to recruit, whereas mercenaries or professional agents capable of the job would take longer to gather."

"You said this wouldn't be dangerous." Stasia said. Muscles in her right cheek twitched nervously as she spoke.

"I also said I'd be paying you ten thousand in Guard dollars and giving you your freedom. If you're looking to question the terms, by all means, we can discuss any changes right now." They all rapidly got the impression that changes would include first, removing the payment and second, putting them back in their cells.

He's all by himself, Mel thought. *It should feel like an empty threat, but who knows what resources he can call on?*

"Excellent. The *Fenris* needs to drop its drive field in three locations to make navigational checks on the course we believe it is taking. The ship has an older version of our warp drive, meaning our ship has twice its speed. So we have sufficient time to catch it at its second navigation check."

"What command will we be sending?" Stasia asked.

"I've got the authorization codes and copies of its core programming. There wasn't time to put together a program to do the job before we left. That will be your job, Stasia."

Agent Mueller pointed at Rawn and Giran: "You two will be checking her code and making sure that it has no flaws. Our trip should take twenty six days, including two navigational stops, one at Expo and the other at Salvation. Our rendezvous is located in the Crossroads system, two light years west of the Bell system. We should arrive between twenty and thirty-six hours ahead of the *Fenris*. Data on the ship is in the computer. Disabling that ship is our objective, through any means necessary."

Mel shivered at his words. She wondered if she'd have been safer on Thornhell.

Time: 1900 Zulu, 12 June 291 G.D.
Location: Crossroads System
There were many star systems which could be classed as high value. Harlequin Station was one such, with two life-bearing worlds, three metal rich asteroid belts, and gas giants to provide hydrogen for power generation.

If Harlequin Station was high value, then Crossroads was definitely low value. Its only value was to serve as a way-point for ships on their way to bigger and better places.

A number of small, icy rocks orbited the cold, tiny star…along with one large starship that emerged from warp exactly where the Guard Intelligence Agent had said it would be.

Mel felt a tingling along her spine. Reading about all the firepower that ship had was one thing. Knowing it might be aimed at her was quite another.

"It's *Fenris*," Marcus stated. "Right on time."

"Unidentified craft, transmit identification codes or be fired upon."

Everyone started at the voice. It was the voice of a man, gruff and gravelly. It didn't sound like the soulless machine they'd all expected. The sound was dangerous and slightly sinister, but somehow also carried the overtones of irritation at the interruption and perhaps even a sense of boredom.

Agent Mueller nodded at Mel, "Transmit the codes, prepare the upload."

Mel did so and then waited for what seemed to be an eternity.

"Identification codes accepted, *John Kelly*." Perhaps it was Mel's fears talking, but the voice of the AI sounded slightly disappointed that it couldn't open fire. "Transmit your data upload when ready."

"Do it." Mueller said. He had a smile of triumph on his face.

"Transmitting." Mel said.

She watched as the laser transmitter made connection with the receiver on the other ship. As it began downloading the program, she released a sigh of relief.

"Orders have been updated. Receiving programming update." The voice modulated, changed. There was no boredom in its next transmission, only pure hostility: "Security protocols have been engaged. Primary programming cannot be compromised. This vessel will *not* be hijacked."

"Detecting the warp drive powering up." Marcus yelped. "We're being hit by targeting sensors."

Agent Mueller looked around frantically, "Did the upload go through? What happened?"

Mel brought up the communications system on her screen. Her eyes widened as she realized someone else had also accessed the program from the engine room. The other user began to delete the upload as she watched.

She saved the file to a drive on her console, then opened the intercom to the engine console. "Rawn, someone's trying to delete the program, stop whoever it is!"

"What?" he answered. "What's going on up there?"

"Just stop them, lock the console."

She brought up the security camera for the engine room, caught a sight of Rawn yelling something to Giran, and then Agent Mueller stepped in front of her view. "Was the upload complete?" he demanded.

"It wasn't. I can't tell how complete it was either, because whoever tried deleting the file wiped the record of the transmission from the computer first." Marcus said angrily. "It got the opening packet for certain, but I'm not sure beyond that." He looked up from his console. "The *Fenris* just went into warp."

Mel pushed Agent Mueller out of the way of the screen. She felt her stomach sink and her throat seemed to constrict as she forced the words out of her mouth, "We've got a bigger problem. Does anyone know where Giran got a gun and why he has it aimed at my brother?"

For more, go to http://www.amazon.com/dp/B00TUV6NCE !

Printed in Great Britain
by Amazon